MASSAGE

Bi Feiyu was born in 1964 in Jiangsu province, China. Previously an editor for the literary magazine *Yu Hua* and a journalist at *Nanjing Daily*, he is a two-time winner of the Lu Xun Literary Prize. *Massage* won the Mao Dun Literature Prize in 2011 and was successfully adapted for film in 2014, winning several awards at the Golden Horse Awards and the Asian Film Awards.

‘The drama, humor and overall appeal of Bi’s novel, translated by Howard Goldblatt and Sylvia Li-chun Lin, come from the author's ability to plumb the depths of the very real challenges of blindness and make them seem almost universal. The stories arouse empathy – never pity.’

Asian Review of Books

‘Sensitive yet frank’

South China Morning Post

MASSAGE

BI FEIYU

Translated from the Chinese by
Howard Goldblatt and Sylvia Li-chun Lin

CHINA LIBRARY

PENGUIN BOOKS

UK | USA | Canada | Ireland | Australia
India | New Zealand | South Africa | China

Penguin Books is part of the Penguin Random House group of companies
whose addresses can be found at global.penguinrandomhouse.com.

Penguin
Random House
PENGUIN BOOKS CHINA

This paperback edition published by Penguin Group (Australia)
in association with Penguin (Beijing) Ltd, 2016

1 3 5 7 9 10 8 6 4 2

Translated from the Chinese by Howard Goldblatt and Sylvia Li-chun Lin

Originally published in Chinese as *Tui Na* by People's Literature Publishing House.

Cover design by Di Suo © Penguin Group (Australia)
Text design by Steffan Leyshon-Jones © Penguin Group (Australia)
Printed and bound in China by RR Donnelley Asia Printing Solutions Limited

National Library of Australia
Cataloguing-in-Publication data:

Bi, Feiyu
Massage / Bi Feiyu
9780734399113 (paperback)
Blind, China, Fiction

895.1352

penguin.com.cn

MIX
Paper
FSC FSC™ C101537

A NOTE ON CHINESE USAGE AND NAMES

In Chinese, a person's given name always follows the surname. Therefore, the character Sha Fuming has the surname Sha and the given name Fuming. Pinyin, the standard Romanisation method for Chinese characters, has been used throughout this novel.

MASSAGE

BI FEIYU

PROLOGUE

DEFINING THE TERMS

COMPARED TO REGULARS and VIP cardholders, walk-in clients comprise about one-third of the clientele at a tuina therapy centre, sometimes as much as half on busy days. In general, tuina practitioners treat walk-ins with special care, which they demonstrate mainly through words – so-called *business savvy*. If rapport is established, a walk-in might become a regular, who could then be a VIP after purchasing an annual membership card. VIPs are essential, naturally, but you don't need too many of those; seven or eight VIP clients provide a guaranteed monthly income for a tuina therapist. So their business is vital, but walk-ins remain the most valuable of all clients; though this may sound contradictory, it is a fact. For in the end, VIPs have all been cultivated from walk-ins, with whom the masseuses have a well-formulated repertoire of relationship-building techniques. Take terms of address as an example: the therapists are discriminating in choosing who to call 'leader', who should be addressed as 'boss', and who may be better referred to as 'teacher'. In this they are very particular, basing their choices on the client's vocabulary and tone of voice. They know the moment a client opens his mouth whether he's a 'leader', a 'boss' or a 'teacher.' They are never wrong.

Conversations with clients are relatively complex, but revolve mainly around their health. Flattery is the norm; it's a given that a tuina therapist will comment on the client's good health, a convention from which none will deviate. On the other hand, it is also their job to point out minor health issues, for if they didn't, they would be out of work. 'You have some health issues!' a client can count on hearing, and what follows will be health tips to deal with the problem. Take, for instance, a shoulder. Our shoulders have particularly intricate muscle masses, a major muscle group that includes biceps, triceps and trapezius muscles. With prolonged repetitive shoulder movement, the tendon fibres stretch, and that can produce muscle effusion. By itself, the effusion is nothing to worry about, because it will be reabsorbed into the muscles. But when it cannot be reabsorbed after prolonged muscle activity, a health problem emerges. The muscle fibres begin to stick together, which leads to inflammation – known as frozen shoulder, a painful condition. Without effective control and therapy, over time the fibres calcify, turning a minor health issue into a major problem. Just think: calcified muscles lose their elasticity, which results in a loss of movement, until you can't even raise your arm to wave farewell to a friend. A major nuisance, wouldn't you say? So, be nice to your shoulders. Women, as well as men, must take care of themselves. Exercise is important. But if you really have no time for exercise, no problem; let someone do it for you. Try tuina. It helps to separate areas that are stuck together – a form of health maintenance, with an emphasis on maintenance. These health tips are, of course, common knowledge, but at the same time they are gentle reminders and heartfelt advertisements. None of the information is complicated, and the clients don't usually take it seriously; the point is, the therapist must offer these tips, for they make all the difference in customer relations, which is why they never tire of offering them.

On this particular day a walk-in client appeared at noon. With airs of self-importance, he asked to see the owner, drawing Sha Fuming out of the therapists' lounge.

'You're the owner?' the man asked.

'I'm afraid so,' Sha replied respectfully. 'My name is Sha Fuming.' He smiled broadly.

'A full body massage. And I want you to do it.'

'It will be a great honour. This way please,' said Sha, leading the man into one of the therapy rooms.

Xiao Tang, one of the receptionists, quickly and expertly prepared the massage couch. With a flick of his hand, the client tossed his key on the bed. Though blind, Sha had an unerring ability to judge sound, and his ears told him the direction and distance of the thrown object. With precise accuracy, he picked up the key and appraised it by its size. Clearly, the self-important client was a driver, a truck driver whose body gave off the faint odour of petrol, no, of diesel fuel. With a smile, Sha handed the key to Xiao Tang to hang on the wall, then cleared his throat and felt the back of the client's head, which was cold, some twenty-three or twenty-four degrees Celsius. Obviously, he kept the air-conditioning in his truck so low he'd turned it into a refrigerator.

Kneading the client's nape, Sha raised his head and said with a smile, 'Your neck is a trouble spot, Boss. Be careful with cold air.'

The 'boss' sighed. 'I've got a fuck-your-dear-mother stiff neck. I'm dizzy and I'm groggy. Why else would I come here? I have another two hundred kilometres to go yet.'

From the man's accent, Sha could tell he was from Huaiyin. Like everyone else in the country, people from Huaiyin loved to fuck someone's mother, but those from Huaiyin had a higher standard and a stricter requirement – they only fucked dear mothers. They wouldn't fuck anything less.

Sha Fuming began by relaxing the man's trapezius muscles, using a method called stripping. Then he used the heels of his palms to rub the driver's nape at a rapid speed, like sawing something or cutting off a head with a dull knife. Soon the back of the driver's head began to warm up, which made him feel so good it was 'fuck your dear mother' over and over.

'Your neck's all right. The main problem is the cold air in your truck. When you're on a long distance run, be sure to turn up the temperature, Boss,' Sha advised.

Just like a boss, the man stopped talking, and he was soon snoring away.

'Get on with your work,' Fuming told Xiao Tang softly. 'Close the door behind you.'

'If he can sleep with all that loud snoring, why lower your voice?'

Fuming smiled. Xiao Tang was right, so he said nothing more and gently finished the hour-long massage. Then he covered the man's neck with a heated salt pack, which woke the driver into a pain-free healthy state, like a clear blue sky. The 'boss' sat up, blinked, and 'wrote' a Chinese character in the air with his head.

'I feel good! Fuck your dear mother. I feel great.'

'You feel good, then that's great,' Fuming echoed.

But the boss wasn't done; he 'wrote' another pattern in the air, drawing out the last stroke carefully with his chin twisted all the way to one side, like a calligrapher who is expert in the style and aesthetic feel of his writing. Finally he drew his 'brush' in and happily moved his chin back to where it belonged.

'I went to a bathhouse two days ago. The girl touched my head here and there, and it felt great, but did no good. Fuck your dear mother, it was as effective as a fart, and I had to pay for a private room. Now I know that you blind folks give the best massages.'

Fuming turned to face the boss. 'We don't do massage here. We do tuina, it's not the same. Come back any time you want, Boss.'

CHAPTER ONE
WANG DAIFU

THE FIRST POT of gold for Wang Daifu – blind tuina therapists are called *daifu*, or doctor – came in Shenzhen. He plied his trade near the Shenzhen train station at the waning years of the twentieth century, a golden age for blind therapists. Golden age may sound more like something a student would say, but for Wang Daifu there was a crazed quality to money, which frantically found the gaps between his eight fingers.

Why was it so easy to make money at the time? The most immediate cause was the handover of Hong Kong to China. Hong Kong residents are devoted fans of Chinese tuina therapy; it is a deeply ingrained component of their personal and cultural traditions. But the cost can be prohibitive. Tuina is manual labour, pure and simple, and the average resident of Hong Kong, given the high standard of living there, could not afford it. The return of Hong Kong to China changed everything. People swarmed across the border to Shenzhen. Making the trip was as easy as a man and a woman sharing an embrace. Return to the mainland – isn't that a form of embrace? The passion for that embrace flowed from the workers – gold-collar, white-collar and blue-collar – all of whom wriggled into the bosom of the motherland. The residents of Shenzhen immediately grasped this business opportunity, and in no time, tuina therapy began to take off. When you think about it, no matter what sort of business you're dealing with, once manual labour is involved the residents of mainland China will corner the market so fast it could make ghosts and demons weep. And don't forget that Shenzhen is a special economic zone. What does that mean? It means cheap labour.

There was yet another reason why tuina therapy flourished: a century had come to an end, and on the eve of the millennial change people experienced a powerful sense of dread; coming out of nowhere, this anxiety had no basis in reality, and was not a true dread in the normal sense of the word. It was more like a fire deficiency as described in Chinese medicine, something that had an aggressive impact on people and made their muscles twitch. Bright lights shot from their eyes. Go for the money! Go now, or you'll miss out! It was as if the people had gone crazy. And when they went, money followed, which intensified the craze among the people. Madness can wear you out. Then what? Chinese-style tuina therapy is one of the better remedies.

Set against that background, tuina by blind therapists thrived in Shenzhen. It took hold with incredible speed, a phenomenon like surging clouds in a strong wind or a raging firestorm. China's blind population quickly got wind of this exciting good news, telling them that a new epoch was at hand for the sightless in Shenzhen, where the streets were paved with gold and money bounced and hopped around like fish out of water. Outsiders were treated to the grand sight of a flood of blind people arriving at the Shenzhen train station, a new city that was not only a window into China's reform and liberalisation policies, but also a home as well as a paradise for the blind, who were exuberant behind their dark glasses as they negotiated the left side of roadsides and bridge paths with their canes, half of them heading from west to east, half from east to west, or half from south to north and half from north to south. They walked in single file, this way or that, on each other's heels, an army on the move. So happy! So busy! When the lights dimmed, another contingent of people passed by. Dog-tired Hong Kong residents, dog-tired Japanese residents of Hong Kong, dog-tired European residents of Hong Kong, dog-tired American residents of Hong Kong, and, of course, all the dog-tired mainland Chinese – the new breed of capitalists and parvenus, who never counted their money in public by first licking their fingers – descended like a swarm of bees. They were tired, oh so tired, worn down by fin-de-siècle exhaustion. They were tired, so tired their muscles cramped up. When they showed up at a tuina clinic they lay down on the massage couch and fell asleep before saying how long a session they wanted. Choruses of snores, foreign and domestic, rose and fell. The therapists loosened up their clients, and many of the rushed clients simply spent the night in the clinics, not getting up from the tables till daybreak. Once they woke up they tipped the therapist and went out into the world to make more money. Money was their constant companion, swirling around them like snowflakes and never more than a sword's length away. They needed only to reach out, take a step forward, and their sword tips pierced the heart of money without spilling a drop of blood.

Wang Daifu also began earning money, a small sum, to be sure, but since poverty had always been his lot, he was amazed by Shenzhen's wealth. How can money be made this way? It's scary. He'd always survived by his own labour, which meant having enough to eat and clothes to wear. But now he was more than just getting by; it was like sleepwalking. Not only did he take in Chinese yuan, he was also given Hong Kong dollars, Japanese yen, even US greenbacks. The first time he'd held US money in his hand had been early one Saturday morning. His client, a delicate, soft-skinned Japanese with small hands and feet, tipped him with a bill that felt smaller, shorter and narrower than the others. A suspicious Wang thought it might be fake. But as the client was a foreign guest, it didn't seem appropriate to say anything. At that pre-dawn hour, he had been on the verge of collapse from fatigue, but concern over the fake bill had him feeling taut as a stretched tendon as he stood there rubbing the bill suspiciously between his fingers. When the Japanese client noticed Wang's hesitation, he assumed he'd given too little and handed him another bill. It too was short and narrow, intensifying Wang Daifu's suspicions. Why had the man handed him a second bill? Does money mean so little to him? He remained motionless, money in hand, as the befuddled client took out a third bill and slapped it into Wang Daifu's palm.

'Good work!' he said, holding one of Wang's thumbs up in front of him. 'You're really this!'

After such effusive praise, Wang was even more reluctant to say anything except thank you. Convinced he'd been cheated, he was quite unhappy, but he remained too embarrassed to mention it. He held on to the three bills till that afternoon, until he could stand it no longer and asked a sighted acquaintance to tell him what he had. It was American money, a total of three hundred US dollars. Wang Daifu's eyebrows arched, and his mouth fell open and stayed that way for a long time. He started walking and didn't stop until he'd drawn three circles around the nation's Southern Sea.

Crazed, that's what money was. Unreasonable. One bill after another, like flying carpets, leaping and gliding through the air. They soared high, they turned and tumbled, then they dove earthward with a whistle to settle right into Wang Daifu's hands. He could almost hear the eerie engine that powered the money. It roared, accompanied by a sharp trill. Each day was more exciting than the one before, an ongoing battle. That's how Wang Daifu became rich.

Then Wang's springtime arrived in the midst of his battle. He fell in love. It was the dawn of the new millennium, a new century was about to begin. On the last night of the old year a blind girl called Xiao Kong, from the town of Bangfu, arrived at Shenzhen train station on the other side of town to visit Wang. Since there were no clients, the clinic had a lonely, desolate feel that seemed at odds with the last night of the millennium. The therapists crowded into the lounge, slumped over from sheer exhaustion. No one spoke, but the room filled with silent grumblings. Why couldn't the boss give us this day off?

'How could I even think of giving you the day off at a time like this?' he said. 'Other people's days are light, yours are dark, and that's the difference. On their days off they wear themselves out having a good time, and here comes your chance to make some money. Who knows whose legs are going to bring in the business? No, we wait! Everyone.'

Well, they waited, but business suffered a broken leg, for no clients showed up. Wang Daifu and Xiao Kong sat in the lounge with time on their hands. After a while, he sighed softly and went upstairs. Xiao Kong heard him leave, and a few minutes later felt her way over to the stairs and followed him up to the therapy rooms.

The therapy rooms were quieter than the lounge, so they sought out the innermost room, opened the door and walked in, each sitting on one of the tuina beds. Most of the time, these rooms were packed; never before had they been so quiet. For that to happen on the eve of the millennium was especially disconcerting. It felt staged, like a carefully constructed backdrop. Like lying in wait. Seemingly in readiness. But ready for what? Wink-wink. Wang Daifu and Xiao Kong smiled. Private smiles mirroring private thoughts. They couldn't see, but they each knew that the other was smiling. That went on for a while before they each asked, 'What are you smiling about?' 'What are *you* smiling about?' One question on top of another, back and forth, until it felt comical and frivolous, playful. But serious as well. They drew closer to a possibility, and could get even closer, but now all they could do was keep smiling. Before long their cheeks showed the strain, began to stiffen. Not at all natural. From then on, smiling took real effort, but to stop would not be easy. Gradually, the atmosphere turned suggestive, moved in a new direction; ripples appeared in a small corner. Then more ripples, quickly evolving into swells. At some point, the swells began to crest, gaining momentum like a stormy sea. A mighty force. Surging to one side, then reversing direction. Signs of approaching danger loomed. To keep from being swamped by the waves, they clutched the sides of the massage bed as tightly as they could, so tight their equilibrium suffered. They stayed like that for a long time, moments caught up in internal struggles. Finally, he said what was on their minds.

He swallowed hard. 'Have you,' he stammered, 'made up your mind?'

Xiao Kong turned to face him. Before she opened her mouth to speak she habitually cocked her head as a sign that she'd made up her mind. Still clutching the edge of the massage bed, she said, 'Yes, I have. Have you?'

He didn't answer right away. He smiled briefly, off and on, his smile here for a moment and then gone, three or four times, until he finally said, 'You know that you're the important one, not me.'

He drew out that simple comment, long and slow, as Xiao Kong waited patiently, scraping the leatherette bedcover with her finger the whole time, making a scratchy sound. She heard every word and savoured his meaning. It sounded so much better than 'I've made up my mind.' Breathing hard, she was almost burning up, and suddenly sensed that her body had undergone a subtle yet profound change, as if it might collapse on its own. She stepped down off the tuina bed and went up to him. He stood up, and they reached out at the same moment to touch one another's face, then their eyes. And when that happened, they both began to cry. There had been no sign that something like that would happen, and neither was prepared for it. They let their gaze flow into the other's fingers. Tears always have the power to move people, and presage what is to follow. They kissed – badly, bumping noses – and quickly pulled back. Xiao Kong cleverly turned her face to the side, but Wang, no one's fool, detected the breath from her nose and sought out her mouth. When their lips actually met it was their first kiss, the first in their lives, and it lacked passion, even carried a measure of fear. It was that fear that pulled their lips apart, while their bodies moved closer and all but came together. The 'kiss' of their bodies pleased them more than the coming together of their lips; it meant more to them because they now had someone to lean on. What a wonderful feeling that was – someone to lean on. Safety, relief, dependability. The key to survival. He pulled her into his arms, almost brutally. She was ready for a second kiss, but Wang Daifu was too excited.

'I'm going back to Nanjing, and I'll take you with me. I'll open a clinic, my clinic! And you'll be the boss's wife, the woman in charge!'

He was nearly incoherent.

'Kiss me!' Xiao Kong stood on her tiptoes. 'Kiss me!'

This kiss lasted much longer, all the way into the next century. Afterwards, Xiao Kong, being an attentive woman, was reminded of something and, taking out her sound-activated watch, she pressed the button.

'The current Beijing time is twenty-three minutes after midnight,' it reported. Placing the watch in his hand, she cried in a loud sobbing voice, 'It's the new year! The new century!'

The new year, a new century, and Wang Daifu was in love. For him, being in love gave him a goal. His life gained instant clarity: work hard, save up, go back home to open a clinic as soon as possible, and let Xiao Kong, his beloved, be the boss's wife, the woman in charge. He was confident that so long as he didn't loaf on the job, one day his goal would be realised. And he had good reason to be confident. He had faith in his own skills. His physical attributes had a lot to do with that. All you needed to do was to feel his hands: large and broad, a pair of capacious, thickset hands. All his clients knew that when he relaxed them it happened not in the neck, but in the buttocks. He would grab hold of both buttocks and give them a powerful jerk, with the immediate effect of loosening the skeleton. Naturally, the bones stayed in place, but it didn't feel that way, and in the best cases it seemed as if an electric current had shot through the body. Wang was born to be a tuina therapist, whether or not he was blind. Needless to say, big, meaty hands are of no use without the requisite strength. Wang was a big, powerful man whose fingers were more than equal to the task. This concept was critical, since it epitomised the qualities of that strength: evenly distributed, gentle and penetrating, without painful pokes. Therapists whose fingers lack the requisite power instead use exertion, which can cause pain and, at its worst, can damage bones and muscles alike. Tuina requires powerful thrusts, so that the result is deep, solid, vigorous penetration into the muscles. It hurts, to be sure, and is accompanied by an aching tingle and distension. But words cannot describe the sense of comfort it brings. And that's the desired effect. Wang had plenty of strength in his thick fingers and meaty palms, and when he applied his hands to a client, he flawlessly pressed on the precise acupuncture points, seemingly without effort; and with that he grabbed you. No matter how much pain this grab produced, you submitted to it willingly. Given Wang Daifu's skills with his hands, his regular and VIP clients were numerous. Most came for hourly treatments, but many stayed for the night, which translated into considerable earnings from tips alone, far more than most. Wang's co-practitioners were the first to admit that he was a tycoon of massage therapists, a man who had enough money to play the stock market; indeed, he invested in both the Shanghai and the Shenzhen indexes.

Wang was in trouble, and it was all because of the stock market. He had a bit of money, but, after some simple calculations, he realised he would have to settle for a less than ideal set-up if he opened a clinic in Nanjing with what he had. To make it respectable, finding a partner was the practical alternative. But he didn't want that. What good was a partnership? And, in a partnership, which boss's wife would Xiao Kong be? She wouldn't be happy being that kind of boss's wife. And he would rather wait than make her unhappy. He was dead set on the issue of 'boss's wife'. Personally he didn't mind not being the boss, but he would not have Xiao Kong settle for second best. It hadn't been easy to give herself to him, and he was insistent upon making her the boss's wife in return for her devotion. If she sat in his clinic drinking water and cracking melon seeds, it would all be worthwhile, even if he had to work himself to death.

Why had he decided to put his money into stocks? Because he was in love. But what, after all, is love? Now that he had experienced it, he understood that it meant to cherish someone. And he cherished her; or to be more precise, he cherished her hands.

They were both working in Shenzhen, but not at the same place. That made it hard to see one another. When they finally had some time together, it was so limited that all they could manage was a few kisses, her favourite activity, although the kisses never lasted long enough for her. As their situation improved they enjoyed a bit of leisure and some idle pleasures beyond kissing. They would, for instance, smooth each other's hair, or study each other's fingers. Her hands were tiny, soft with pointed fingertips, which must be the type referred to as 'spring onions.' But they had a flaw: small fleshy bumps grew on the knuckles of her thumbs and her index and middle fingers. It was a common, virtually unavoidable consequence of prolonged tuina therapy, but Wang quickly sensed that something wasn't quite right with her hands. The bones of her fingers did not form a straight line; instead, they turned sideways at the second knuckle. He could straighten them out by pulling on them, but they returned to their original shape once he let go. Xiao Kong's hands were so seriously malformed they barely resembled human hands. You call those hands? She knew and, embarrassed, wanted to pull them back from his grasp, but he wouldn't let go. As he held her hands, he was lost in thought.

Xiao Kong was petite and slim, not well suited to tuina therapy. There were all kinds of clients; you could tickle and easily cause pain in some by barely touching them. But others seemed born with leather skin, beef-like flesh, and a high threshold for pain, and if you worked on them with a light touch, they felt they weren't getting their money's worth and would snidely remind you, 'Harder. Give it more pressure.' Wang had run into plenty of people like that; a typical case was a strapping young man from Africa who spoke poor Chinese, but had mastered the word for 'harder'. After an hour, even a tough young man like Wang began to sweat from the hard work. Xiao Kong's fingers must have been deformed by repeated work of that nature. With her modest strength and fingers like that, how could she manage fourteen or fifteen hours a day, day after day?

'Harder. Do it harder.'

As he held her wrist and touched her fingers, Wang felt his heart break. Then, without warning, he swung her hand into his face, giving himself a loud slap. Xiao Kong was too stunned to realise what had happened, and when she did, it was too late; he was about to slap himself again as if he enjoyed it. She held his hand and pulled his head to her breast.

'What are you doing? What does this have to do with you?' She was sobbing.

Investing in the stock market had been a gamble. While he'd been hesitant at first, when he was reminded of her hands he felt an insane urge to get rich quick. Money had gone crazy, but he only had two hands. After nearly a year he'd been struck by a thought: invest in the stock market. However crazed money had become, it had been only on a small scale; the true madness wasn't in money, it was in shares of stock, in investment. When stocks went crazy, they didn't just perform handstands and somersaults; no, they rose up high, like onions pulled out of dry soil. He often heard his clients talk about the stock market, and that had left a strange impression in his mind. It felt familiar and yet sinister and demonic, inescapable yet incredulous. An apt description of the market was: 'Money soars in the sky, so don't let it pass you by; money crawls on the ground and demands to be found;

if you grasp it in your hand, it slips away like sand.' Why not give it a try? Why not indeed? If the next day's market was the legendary *flying monkey*, then the morning after that he should be able to fly straight to Nanjing with Xiao Kong. With a twist of his neck, he had arched his eyebrows and turned his face skywards. Then, gathering all his savings, he'd thrust himself into the stock market.

Wang's timing could not have been worse. The market had been performing well for some time, but soured as soon as he got in. He had the opportunity to get out, of course, and if he had, he would not have lost too much. But he refused to do that. He simply could not accept losses, not a penny. It was more than money to him; it meant the pea-sized fleshy knuckle bumps. It meant malformed bones; one all-nighter after another; the client demanding 'harder, harder'; switching to the index fingers when the thumbs got tired; changing to the middle fingers when the index fingers could work no longer; using the elbow when the middle fingers were worn out; going back to using the index fingers when the elbow gave in. It meant his blood and sweat, and he could not bear to suffer any losses. So he sweated it out. No longer hoping to get rich, he needed to hold on to what he'd invested, and that idea eventually dragged him down into a bottomless pit. A bodiless, voiceless madman he would never actually meet grabbed hold of him in his most vulnerable spot.

The stock market did not do a somersault; it lay flat on the ground. It raised hell, it tumbled, it convulsed, it rolled its eyes, it foamed at the mouth – it did everything but stand. You fucking bear. Damn you. How had the stock market gone crazy in that way, and who had made it do that? Wang cocked his head and hugged his radio whenever he had a moment, and that was where he learned about 'the invisible hand'. Looking at it now, the invisible hand had been tricked into madness by someone. There had to be another hand behind that one, equally invisible but bigger, more powerful, and crazier. Wang also had invisible hands, a pair he couldn't see, but his were insignificant and powerless when compared to the other pair of invisible hands. He was an ant. The other two invisible hands were like heaven and earth, and when they clapped together they could send him from Shenzhen all the way to Uruguay. He did not clap; he could only crack his knuckles. The thumb made two loud pops, while the other knuckles made three, altogether twenty-eight times – pop, pop, pop – like a string of firecrackers.

Money had indeed gone crazy. It went wild and he was rich; it went wild again and he was poor.

'I was a worn-out suitcase that came back empty' – this was a line from an old song he had learned to sing as a child. At the end of 2001, Wang returned to Nanjing with that line playing in his ear. He was dejected, but, on a different level, he was also full of joy – Xiao Kong had come with him. Instead of returning to Bangfu, she had come to Nanjing without telling her parents, with unmistakable implications. His mother was beside herself with joy. Her son had done well! Really well! After making her and her husband's bedroom available for the young couple, she took her son into the kitchen, where she whispered to him, 'Sleep with her. You must take her to bed. She will have no place to go after that.' He turned his head in anger, upset and disgusted at his mother's vulgarity, her philistine nature of which she could not rid herself. He raised his brow and pulled a long face. Some matters were like that; you could do them but not talk about them.

He and Xiao Kong stayed with his parents till the Lantern Festival, the fifteenth day of the first lunar month, during which time she was looking better by the day. His mother could not stop praising her, saying, 'Xiao Kong is so pretty. Xiao Kong has wonderful skin. Nanjing's environment is so much better than Shenzhen, and is good for you. Our Xiao Kong looks different each day.' In order to prove that to Xiao Kong, Wang's mother took Xiao Kong's hand and rubbed it against her own face. 'Am I right? Now tell me, am I right?'

She was. Xiao Kong could feel it; her skin had indeed softened.

Her face was now smooth. But she was a woman, after all, and she quickly realised what had caused the change. She was so embarrassed she began to panic, but instead of being visibly agitated, she froze. Her upper body went taut and stiff, while she balled the fist of her free hand, clamping her fingers down hard on her thumb. The visually impaired all suffer from the same predicament; as they cannot see, when they have a secret they suspect that everyone can see through them, that they cannot keep it to themselves. That is what happened to Xiao Kong; she assumed that her thrillingly happy time was in plain view for all to see.

Wang wasted no time at this opportune moment. One day, while his parents were out, he deftly brought up the subject.

'Why don't we stay here? What do you think?'

All she said in response was, 'What about the suitcases we left behind?'

He considered her question. 'We could take a trip back,' he said. Then he added, 'But that way we'd have to buy two more train tickets, wouldn't we?'

She thought for a moment and agreed, but wasn't willing to leave them there. 'I can go by myself.'

He groped for her hands and fell silent for a moment. 'Don't go,' he said as he held her hands.

'I'll just be a few days,' Xiao Kong replied.

Another pause. Then he said, 'I don't want you to be away from me for even a single day. If you're gone, I'll feel as if I'd been blinded again.'

He sounded so heavy-hearted. Wang was someone who knew where he stood in life, so when he told the truth it always sounded heavy-hearted. Xiao Kong did not know what to say, and as she tried to come up with a response, she felt a sense of happiness rise up from somewhere, up into the heavens and then back down to earth, as the blood rushed to her face. She sighed silently. With blood rushing to her face, how could she not look rosy-cheeked? Holding his hands, she thought with a sense of pride of how radiant she must be at that moment. Her pride, however, quickly vanished and was replaced by a profound sense of regret – he couldn't see her rosy cheeks, or her good looks, not ever. How pleased would he be if he could? Yet her regret did not last long. Don't be greedy, she told herself. Everything is going well, so you mustn't be greedy. Whatever way she looked at it, she was a woman in love.

So she stayed. The issue was no sooner resolved than another concern arose for Wang. He had planned to take her back to Nanjing to be the boss's wife, but where was his therapy clinic? Where? Late at night, when he listened to her even breathing, he touched her fingers one by one – the eight crooked spaces between her fingers – and could not go back to sleep. His insomnia too was crooked, as were his dreams.

After a few days of indecision, he finally placed a call to Sha Fuming's mobile phone. Sha and he went way back; they had been classmates from their elementary school days all the way through college, where they had both studied Chinese medicine and tuina therapy. The only diversion in their paths was that after graduation Wang had gone to Shenzhen and Sha to Shanghai. Now they were both back in Nanjing, but with different outcomes. Sha Fuming had a business of his own, while Wang still had to work for others. By now the fleshy bumps on Boss Sha's fingers must have disappeared.

It was a painful phone call to make. When was it, last year or the year before? It must have been the year before when Sha's tuina centre opened. In a hurry to hire good therapists, Sha had called him in Shenzhen, asking him to return to Nanjing. Sha knew that Wang was good at his work and, with him around, he would have his pillar of support, which meant the centre would be a sort of brand, business would be good, and he would build a reputation. In order to bring Wang back, Sha offered impossibly high percentages and plenty of face. Wang could practically keep everything he earned or they could be partners. Sha was clear about his intention, which was to have

Wang lend grandeur to the place. But Wang had turned him down; money was easy in Shenzhen, so why move? Of course Wang was well aware that money was not the real issue. The real problem was emotional. He didn't want to work for an old schoolmate. Two old friends becoming boss and employee would be too awkward.

As the saying goes, when you're given a toast, you should drink – don't wait until you're forced to drink. Wang had declined Sha's earlier invitation, and now he had to go to Sha to ask for work. On the surface he would just be taking a job, but there was a difference. Wang didn't have to ask Sha for work, since Nanjing was overrun with tuina centres. What difference did it make who he worked for? Yet he was determined to work for Sha Fuming, for Xiao Kong's sake.

Xiao Kong was quite a character, and had only one failing. She was not generous with money; she could even be called stingy. Whenever she got hold of some money, she tucked it under her arm and you couldn't take it from her, even with a machine gun. If she'd been just a friend, that would have spoiled the relationship; but now that she would one day be his wife, that character trait was no longer a flaw – she was not stingy, she was family focused. Back in Shenzhen, her tight-fisted nature had created problems in dealing with receptionists. The interaction between a tuina therapist and a receptionist is important and unique, and a poor relationship can have a direct impact on one's livelihood. Only the sighted work at the reception desk, and they have sharp eyes that enable them to tell at a glance if a client is rich or poor. Deciding who gets the wealthy clients and who gets the poor ones is a complex process, and it all comes down to the receptionist. A tuina therapist relies upon tips, which is how the same eight hours of work can produce drastically different results. Of course, a centre has its own rules of rotation, but they mean little, since someone other than the therapist is in charge of the sequence. Take, for instance, toilet breaks. A rich client walks in while you are in the toilet. If the receptionist wants to be helpful, she will offer the client some water and invite him to take a seat. After you've done your business and have breezed back in, the rich client is sent to you. Conversely, you've just gone to the toilet when the receptionist sends the rich client to the next in line. By the time you finish and rush back from whatever you were doing, the rich client is lying on someone else's couch, chatting and laughing. What can you say? Nothing. That's why you have to maintain a good relationship with whoever is up front. When the receptionist's eyes are on you, your world is filled with seeing eyes, and so how can you make a living? How do you smooth it out? Easy. Squeeze. Squeeze what? Money. The clinics have strict rules against this type of transaction, but what therapist would let a piece of paper control his actions? He'd find a way to get the receptionist to accept a little something. Eyes are nothing if not special. Who doesn't fear them? All therapists want the receptionist to turn a blind eye to certain things, and as long as that's being done, they can live happy, normal lives.

Xiao Kong was tight-fisted and refused to hand out any squeeze, even found justification for her miserly behaviour. With a sense of pride, she told Wang that she was a Taurus and that they love money. To them, money was like oxygen, without which she would find it hard to breathe. It was a joke, of course, though they had talked about it. It's not that Xiao Kong was stingy; she simply could not accept the practice. 'I am a blind woman who works hard for her money. Why should I squeeze some of it into their sighted eyes? I won't do it!' Wang understood, but he had to suppress a sigh. What a foolish girl.

He smiled and said, 'You often get the worst of it, you know that.'

'Of course I know that,' she said with a laugh. 'I lose some, but I save money, and in the end I pretty much break even.'

He turned his face skywards. So, that's how she sees it. He wrapped his arms around her. 'You really don't know how to play politics,' he said.

Wang knew that Xiao Kong's personality would always bring her to grief; wherever she went, she was treated badly. She might not admit it, but she had suffered in Shenzhen to a degree no one knew. Being tight-fisted was only one reason; she suffered mostly because she was too proud. Anyone that proud is fated to suffer, which was why, in the end, Wang decided to work for his old schoolmate. No matter how he looked at it, the boss would be his old friend and classmate, and Xiao Kong would not suffer, since no one would make things difficult for her.

He picked up the phone and dialled Sha Fuming's number.

'Boss Sha,' he said.

Sha was ecstatic to hear his voice, his enthusiasm spilling into Wang's ear. But then he said, 'I'm with a client. Call back in twenty minutes.'

Wang flipped his phone shut with a smile, the corners of his mouth turning upwards. How could Sha forget that he, Wang Daifu, was blind too, a level B-1, authentic sightless man? The visually impaired are alike in one important respect; they can't see what's next to them, but they can see things a million miles away, especially over the phone. Sha wasn't working. He was in the reception area, the noise coming through loud and clear over the phone. To Wang, a reception area and a therapy room were two buttocks; they look the same, but are separated by a crack down the middle. Sha was becoming more like a sighted man in the way he talked and dealt with people. He was becoming somebody. No doubt about it.

Though Wang was not pleased, he didn't let his anger spill out. Twenty minutes later he called again.

'Business is good, Boss Sha,' he said.

'Not bad. Good enough to feed myself.'

'I'd like to come to work and get fed myself,' Wang said.

'You're joking,' Sha said. 'After all these years in Shenzhen you must be pretty thick around the waist, not to mention your thighs and arms. And you want to come here to get fed? I'd have to thank my lucky stars if you didn't take over my business.'

Sha had acquired the gift of the gab; he was getting more like people who can see.

Wang had no time to get angry at him. 'I mean it,' he said. 'I'm in Nanjing. If it's not too much trouble, I'd like to come over. If it is, then I'll come up with something else.'

Now Sha could tell that Wang was not joking. Lighting a cigarette, he laid out the situation. 'Here's how it is. You know that what we get here in Nanjing can't compare with what you get in Shenzhen. Sixty yuan an hour, forty-five for a VIP, and you get fifteen. Sixteen if you work over a hundred hours a month, and eighteen for a hundred and fifty. No tips. People in Nanjing aren't used to tipping. But you know that.'

Of course Wang knew. With an embarrassed laugh, he said, 'I'm bringing another mouth with me.'

Sha understood immediately. 'You're quite the man, aren't you?' he said with a laugh. 'What about her eyes?'

'Same as mine, B-1.'

'You're quite the man,' Sha repeated. 'You really are.' Then he raised his voice. 'Married?'

'Not yet.'

'Good. I wouldn't be able to help if you were. You know I supply room and board. If you were married, I'd have to rent a room for the two of you and I can't afford that. But since you're not, that's easy. You'll stay in the men's dorm and she'll be in the women's. What do you say?'

After hanging up, Wang turned to Xiao Kong. 'We'll go there tomorrow. You can take a look and if you like the place we'll start the day after.'

'Sure,' Xiao Kong said.

Wang had not planned to start working again so soon. In Shenzhen they'd agreed to take some time off to rest over the New Year holiday, treating it as a sort of honeymoon. They'd planned on a simple wedding, since a splendid affair was lost on people who could not see the effects – why do it for someone else's eyes? 'I want you to soak in a honey jar for a month this spring,' he'd said. 'I'll do whatever the bridegroom says,' Xiao Kong had responded sweetly.

In the end, their honeymoon lasted fewer than twenty days. Wang Daifu had changed his plans for practical reasons. He couldn't bear to stay with his parents, mainly because of his younger brother, a troublemaker. It was a long story. This brother should, in fact, never have been born, since the national one-child policy was in effect and strictly enforced. He came into this world as a result of Wang Daifu's eyes. At the time, Wang was old enough to know what his parents' happy laughter meant, and, as a child, was happy owing to a deep sense of relief; at the same time he was bitter because he could not put aside his jealousy. There were times when he harboured such hatred for his brother that sinister, evil thoughts sprouted in his mind. But those transient childhood thoughts evolved into an irrepressible fondness for his kid brother after he grew up; Wang would have willingly died for him. His brother had married on 1 May the year before, and, on the eve of the wedding, had called him in Shenzhen, saying jokingly, 'Older brother, I'm getting married first. I can't wait for you.' Wang Daifu was happy for his brother, and so excited he was shaking from anxiety. Then he counted the days. But he couldn't make it back to Nanjing by train. His first thought was to take an aeroplane, but he was reluctant to spend that kind of money. Still, he had been about to say to his brother 'I'll buy a plane ticket' when his suspicious nature had stopped him and come to his aid. Maybe his brother didn't want a blind man sitting at his wedding banquet. So he'd said, 'Aiya! Why didn't you tell me earlier?' 'It's no big deal,' his brother said. 'It's just a wedding. There's no need for you to come all the way home. I just called to let you know.' Now Wang Daifu realised that his brother simply wanted a red envelope – the traditional wedding gift of money – and nothing else. Lucky for him he was the suspicious type, or he might have embarrassed his brother. After offering his best wishes and some additional auspicious words he hung up, feeling as if he'd fallen ill, as if someone had pulled the tendons right out of his body. He went to the bank, and then to the post office, where he wired twenty thousand yuan to his brother. Originally, he had planned to wire five thousand. But owing to a sense of sadness and a loss of self-esteem, he was so angry he felt like slapping himself; he gritted his teeth and quadrupled the amount. The action was partially motivated by childish pique and a wish to sever all ties. The twenty thousand announced that the brothers would have nothing to do with each other from then on. When the postal clerk took his money she asked, 'You made all this?' Feeling hurt and in a bad mood, he felt like saying, 'I didn't steal it', but had been too well brought up to do that; besides, he could tell that she meant it as a compliment so he smiled and said, 'Yes. With eyes like mine, I could only use my left hand to steal from my right hand.' The self-mockery was humorous; the clerk laughed and so did everyone else in the post office. He knew that they were all looking at him. She leaned forward and patted him on the arm. 'Young man, you're terrific. Your mother will be so happy when she gets this.' He was grateful for the laughter and for the touch of her hand; a strong and totally unexpected current of warmth raced through him and down into his heart, putting him on the verge of tears. Little brother, my own flesh and blood. You're not the equal of a total stranger. I won't cause you to lose face, all right?

After returning to Nanjing, Wang had realised that his brother was blameless. It was the woman, Gu Xiaoning, who had turned him. Wang could tell that Gu was a bossy woman who spoke with a south-side accent and had brassy airs. Not a nice person; nor, for that matter, was his brother, who turned into a good-for-nothing after his marriage and let his wife decide everything. You can't do that! It took Wang Daifu only a second to forgive his brother and shift his hatred to Gu Xiaoning, who set a fire burning in him the moment he heard her voice.

Wang began to worry about his brother. Since neither he nor his wife had a job, how would they get by? Fortunately, her father was in the military, with a relatively spacious home; otherwise, they wouldn't even have had a place to live. Yet they managed to live like carefree immortals, taking in a movie one day and going to a teahouse the next, then off to sing karaoke. Gu even walked around reeking of perfume. Why weren't they worried? How could they keep living like that?

Wang Daifu had been away from home for a long time, living in a dormitory from the age of ten, when he went off to school, until he graduated from college, after which he went straight to Shenzhen. From the age of ten he'd had only sporadic dealings with his family, so he knew little about his younger brother, except that he had been a brat as a child. Wang could not understand why he would marry someone like Gu Xiaoning. Listen to how she talked to her husband: 'You're blind as a bat!' 'Can't you see anything?' She had a total absence of tact, and Wang was always upset to hear how she scolded her husband. The blind do not treat the word 'blind' as a taboo, and often use it themselves, sometimes in a jocular manner. But they tend to be more sensitive with outsiders. Gu may not have intended to be insensitive, but her choice of words proved that her brother-in-law meant nothing to her, and that her attitude would surely carry over to Xiao Kong. That was a given. He did not mind if she didn't care about how he felt, but what about her sister-in-law? How could the woman be so inconsiderate? Xiao Kong must have felt that as well, since she was quiet when Gu Xiaoning was around.

None of these presented serious problems; those he sensed at the dinner table. On New Year's Eve, Wang's brother had agreed to come home for dinner. But they still had not arrived by the time the New Year celebration came on TV. The following evening, around sunset, they came to wish their parents happy new year and left after a few inane exchanges with Wang. The real problem began on the seventh day of the new year. His brother and his wife showed up in time for lunch each day and left immediately afterwards. Come dinnertime, the same thing. That went on until the fifteenth day, when Wang finally figured out what was happening. They must have assumed that he and Xiao Kong were getting free meals at home, and if they could eat for free, how could the two of them be left out? So they joined them in what became a public dining hall.

One meal meant nothing, nor did two or three. But it could not go on indefinitely. When would they stop taking advantage of the old folks, who eked out a meagre living? In a way, what they were doing amounted to forcing Wang Daifu and Xiao Kong to leave, a plan they carried out aggressively. It had to be Gu Xiaoning's idea. It had to be. Wang didn't mind leaving, but what about Xiao Kong and her honeymoon? He said nothing. Though filled with deep anger and resentment, he could say nothing.

Yet he had to say something to Xiao Kong, at least. He'd give her a honeymoon later. One night, after sitting with his parents in the living room *watching* the evening news, he and Xiao Kong went to their room. As they sat on the edge of the bed, he took her hands but could not find the words to begin. She, on the other hand, began to act out of character by kissing him, keeping him from saying anything. As she continued to kiss him, she started taking off his clothes; he could not free his mouth until she was pulling off his sweater. But then, when he was about to say something, her lips returned to block his words. He knew she wanted to make love, but he wasn't in the mood. Feeling gloomy, he hesitated, while she was stripped naked, her body warm to the touch. She pulled him down. 'Come on, darling,' she said. He was reluctant, but couldn't reject her, and their bodies quickly merged. She clamped her legs around his waist before blurting out, 'How many are we now?' He arched his back and said, 'One.' She held up his face and said, 'That's right, darling. You must never forget that. We are one. I know what you're thinking and what you want to say. You don't have to say anything. We'll be one just the way we are now. You're in me and we are one.' He heard every word, but just as he was about to say something, he felt something happening. It was too late to speak, as a powerful sensation surged inside him, and he came. It was so sudden that he thrust his body upwards and felt himself freeze. It was like a stampede of horses. Tears gushed from him, down his cheeks to his chin and falling, one by one, onto her face. She opened her mouth to swallow his tears, a spontaneous wish that brought a surprising result – she came too. The brief sex was simply incredible, unrepeatable; though they hadn't had time to work on it, it was seamless, nearly perfect. She let her legs fall back onto the bed and lay there, hips arched, as if dead. But she was floating, weightless, defying gravity. She was flying away. A dangerous moment. At this critical moment, she grabbed him by the ears and held on with all her might, but again she seemed to be flying away. Danger loomed. She pulled him down onto her; she needed his weight; she needed his body to keep her down.

'Hold me tight – press down – don't let me fly away – I'm afraid.'

CHAPTER TWO

SHA FUMING

TEN O'CLOCK IN the morning was the time when Wang Daifu was scheduled to come 'take a look' with 'another mouth', also the time when Sha Fuming's stomach ache began, an increasingly punctual bodily ailment that also occurred at three or four in the afternoon, and in the middle of the night. He had become an expert whenever his stomach acted up – he took out a Xile tablet, popped it into his mouth and chewed on it before swallowing it without water. In a few minutes the pain would be gone. Chinese medicine was good, but could never be as quick acting.

Fuming was chewing his tablet in the front room when Wang Daifu, who was standing in the doorway of the Sha Zongqi tuina centre, called out, 'Boss Sha!' Wang had, after all, been around, so instead of referring to Sha as an old schoolmate, he shouted 'Boss Sha' in a resounding voice, almost like a truck horn. Fuming came to the door and greeted Wang, who introduced Xiao Kong. Adopting a formal tone, he referred to her as Kong Daifu, which immediately told Sha that the two were indeed not yet married.

Boss Sha and Wang Daifu had a controlled greeting that lasted less than two minutes before Fuming led Wang into the lounge. It was deadly quiet, but Wang sensed that it was crowded with people, who stood when they came in. It caught him off guard.

'You must be having a meeting,' he said with a smile.

'We usually hold our meetings on Mondays. Today we're having study sessions,' Fuming said.

'Then I came at the right time, since I could use a bit of study myself,' Wang said.

'You're joking, old friend. You can teach them things when you find the time. Schools aren't as rigorous these days as they once were, and one generation is worse than the one before. There's no comparison, really. It's just not like it was back in our day.'

Wang laughed, as he realised that Sha was giving his experience full play in front of his employees. Even Xiao Kong, who was standing behind him, heaved a soft sigh.

Rather than let the praise go to his head, Wang replied with a smile, 'Boss Sha is being nice to me. He's the one who's a master of theory *and* practice.'

It mattered little to Sha when people commented on his skill, but he cared a great deal about theory; he wanted to be known as someone with 'theories'. Wang's words brought a smile to his face.

For his part, Wang was not being flattering, since Boss Sha was good at what he did. Within a few minutes, Wang could see that Sha had good business sense and that he ran the place well – in an orderly and disciplined way. It put Wang's mind at ease, for, as an employee, he cared about two things – order and discipline.

Wang was spot on about the place. One thing about the Sha Zongqi tuina centre was the fact that clients weren't all they cared about; they were also serious about employee training. It was an ingenious design on Sha's part, because training was actually a pretence for employee management. Ten o'clock in the morning was usually a downtime at tuina centres. Back when Sha was working for someone else, he would use the downtime to take a nap, since sleeping on the job could not have been easier for the blind. When sighted people close their eyes for a nap they can be spotted straight away, but not the blind. All they have to do is to sit down and lean their heads back; no one can tell that they're napping. Yet people will know they're sleeping if they are startled awake, just from the way they speak, for nappers all have something in common: they either sound sluggish or they talk too fast. One way or the other, they react differently, which Sha had noticed years ago. He'd placed a strict demand on himself: if he became a boss one day he would not give his employees the chance to sneak in some sleep in the centre. He would never allow that to happen. If the employees were in the habit of napping, to the clients it looked as if business was bad, not that the employees were loafing. In contrast, holding a meeting during downtime to talk about their trade gave the lounge a different feel; it showed that they were into self-improvement. The atmosphere in a place is critical: it has a rippling effect that can reach from one person to ten, and from ten to a hundred. Sha had begun by working for someone else, and after learning the ropes of being a hired hand, he knew all about employee management. What it boiled down to was simply knowing each employee's weakness; finding that weakness was what personnel management was all about.

Fuming showed Wang Daifu and Xiao Kong around the centre, looking into every room. Wang gained a pretty good idea of the size of Sha's business; with thirteen or fourteen employees and seventeen or eighteen beds, it wasn't especially large, nor was it small. He'd have had a comparable business if his money hadn't fallen into the stock market trap. The thought depressed him so much he started cracking his knuckles.

After they visited the last room, Sha took a step back and shut the sliding door, a sign to Wang that they had reached the critical moment when they would discuss the important matters. Fuming began in an emotional tone, expressing his heartfelt happiness and a sincere welcome to his old friend, who had come to lend a hand; but the essence of their conversation rested on equality. Wang knew what

Fuming was getting at; he would be like all the other employees and would enjoy no special treatment. So he decided to be frank and open.

'Don't worry, Boss,' he said softly. 'This isn't my first time working for someone.'

Now that Wang had opened the door, Fuming rubbed his hands together and said, 'Well, then go buy what you need, daily necessities and so on. I'll phone the dorm and tell them to prepare two beds for you.'

Wang patted Fuming on the shoulder; Fuming responded by patting Wang's shoulder in return and said, raising his voice, 'The Sha Zongqi tuina centre welcomes you.'

Wang cocked his head and wondered out loud why he used the name Sha Zongqi and not Sha Fuming.

'It's like this,' Fuming offered an explanation. 'Zhang Zongqi and I each put up half the capital to open the centre, so naturally it's called Sha Zongqi.'

'Who's Zhang Zongqi?'

'Someone I met in Shanghai.'

'Where is he now?'

'In the employee's lounge.'

'I should go pay him a visit.'

'What's the hurry?' Fuming said. 'There's plenty of time for that. And there's really no need to pay him a visit. Talking to me is the same as talking to him. He's in a meeting.'

Wang looked up, a gesture of 'Ah, I see', but said nothing. Feeling that a load had been lifted off his chest, he touched Xiao Kong's hand briefly. So Sha Fuming had a business partner and owned only half the centre. One thing was certain: Sha had done no better in Shanghai than Wang had done in Shenzhen.

After seeing Wang and Kong off, Sha Fuming stood out in a cold wind, his head raised to *look* at his business facade, which was a source of dissatisfaction. Strictly speaking, the Sha Zongqi tuina centre did not have a prime location, barely managing to be placed among the second tier of Nanjing's business districts. In fact the area had been farmland barely two decades earlier. These days, a city was nothing but a woman dead set on breast enlargement – size mattered, as did placing breasts in places they hadn't been before. The enlargement added value, turning rice paddy land and cotton fields into second-tier business districts. I'll just have to keep at it, Sha told himself. Once the business got going and grew bigger, he'd open his flagship tuina parlour in a first-tier area, no matter how high the rent, how unaffordable. He'd open it in either the Drum Tower or Xinjiekou business district.

From the first day he started working, living by the sweat of his brow was not what he had in mind; he was simply accumulating capital. Living by the sweat of one's brow was an absurd, arrogant and conceited expression created by normal people, which was what the blind called the sighted, who were actually anything but normal. Be they teachers or government officials, they were forever telling the disabled to live by the sweat of their brow, gaining self-satisfaction from the sound of their inculcation. As if only the disabled needed to live by the sweat of their brow, that they themselves never had to; as if they had everything laid out for them and all they had to do was pick up their chopsticks to feed themselves; as if all the disabled had to do was live by the sweat of their brow, and that it would be an incredible feat if they didn't die of hunger or from the cold. Well, fuck living by the sweat of your brow. Those people could never know of the powerful, resilient heart pumping in the chest of a blind person.

But Sha Fuming's capital accumulation process suffered a miserable defeat. Karl Marx said that primitive accumulation is accompanied by evil, but Sha's capital accumulation did not even qualify for that; it was simply out of his reach. What accompanied his accumulation was sacrifice, the deterioration of his health. He was still young, and yet he'd been afflicted with severe neck pain and gastroptosis, a stomach condition. Over the years, he'd worked on countless people with stiff necks, but his own gave him so much trouble that sometimes he'd be nauseous from dizzy spells. Whenever he felt dizzy, the only thing that flashed through his mind was money. What did he need money for? Not to accomplish the damned *living by the sweat of his brow*, but to accumulate capital. He needed capital, he was madly in love with capital. Each time he had a dizzy spell, he felt his eyes brighten; so many spells later he finally *saw* it. He saw the truth about life, which entailed a simple logic; you either worked for someone or someone worked for you. It was that simple.

Sha was convinced that if he hadn't been born blind, he'd have been capable of dealing with the world all by himself. He excelled at schoolwork, which was why he thought so highly of himself. He was a good student. An example: when they were studying the energy channels and acupuncture points in Chinese medicine, his classmates, including Wang Daifu, were still struggling with the various acupoints – heart, lungs, liver, small intestine, bladder and stomach – while he, with help from his teacher, had begun studying anatomy in Western medicine at a medical school. By examining the skeletons, various systems, organs and muscles of cadavers, he quickly gained a structural grasp of the human body. Chinese medicine is good, but it has its flaws, for it starts and ends with philosophy; the human body is frequently associated with the universe, with yin and yang, and with the five elements. Beginning with something simple, it gets increasingly complicated and arcane; the more you learn, the more esoteric it seems. But not Western medicine, which is the other way around. Everything begins with complexity and ends in simplicity; the human body in the view of Western medicine is involved with materiality and empiricism, not fanciful thoughts and arcane meditation. In a word, anatomy is more practical, more effective, more efficient. A future tuina therapist, a blind one, no less, can take good care of a living person if he learns everything a cadaver has to offer.

He had been progressing well with his studies, but with a different style from the other top student in the class, Wang Daifu. Wang also excelled; he knew exactly what he wanted, which, in a word, was to earn a living from his own labour. Which was why he never stopped bodybuilding; he spent just about every waking moment outside of class in the gym. With a goal of having strong arms and powerful fingers, he could bench press a surprising one hundred and twenty-five kilos. His arms were as thick as the thighs of a female classmate, his thumbs so powerful they could seemingly put a dent in wood.

By contrast, Sha Fuming had never worked at any of the basic skills. One thing was clear to him: no matter how skilful, a therapist will always have to live by his hands. However accomplished, a therapist will only be a good soldier. Sha wanted to be a general, so why waste energy in the gym? He'd be better off learning some English and Japanese, far-reaching, unique and strategic foresight that would later be borne out by reality. When he'd started working in Shanghai, the blind therapists would cower to the side each time a client wafting perfume – that is, non-Chinese – walked in; they would be reluctant to speak with the client. That was when Sha showed his edge over the others. Using his limited English or Japanese, he greeted the newcomer, who naturally became his client. No one could complain that Sha had taken a client away from them; on the contrary, his co-workers envied, even admired him. That was like an epiphany to Sha, whose confidence in his language ability began to grow. He even employed his broken English or Japanese in discussing the issue of tips with these foreign friends; he was, in a word, bargaining with the clients. Back in the dorms, he'd repeat what he'd said to his co-workers, who were stunned by his audacity. To them, this was not bargaining; it was international trade, pure and simple. They were so startled their jaws dropped. Sha Fuming was in the big league now, and he had so many clients he wished he could be torn into many selves.

He worked hard, day and night, all but killing himself in the process. His finger techniques were not particularly good, a fact that was not perceived by the non-Chinese clients, who knew only about biceps and triceps, pecs, latts, trapezius and abs, with no knowledge of the many acupoints, let alone the tuina techniques of push, press, knead, rub, pinch, knock and split. Everything his clients felt, Sha Fuming conveyed orally – he was personable, witty, knowledgeable, and a source of unexpected humour due to his half-baked foreign language ability. A case in point: once a client, noticing that Sha wasn't wearing warm clothes, asked if he was cold. He said, no, that he wasn't susceptible to cold. But when rendered in English, it came out as, 'I am a hot man.' A hunk, that is, which tickled the client endlessly. All his clients were delighted to discover a blind therapist who could be expressive and witty in their language. In a word, Sha Fuming's presence changed people's stereotypes of the disabled, even stereotypes of the Chinese held by foreigners. 'Mr Sha' is so eloquent, so upbeat, open and humorous. As a result, his clients needed to make appointments two or three days in advance; they could not just drop in and get him to work on them. In truth, the appointments really did not have to be made so far ahead. Yet Sha was ostentatious and extravagant; he had flair. The harder it was to get an appointment, the more eager the clients would be to wait. He was doing so well he stopped worrying about domestic demand and focused exclusively on international trade. Many foreigners knew of a tuina centre at the intersection of Minfeng and Sixiang Roads where they would find a terrific Dr Sha with *fantastic* massage and conversational skills.

But hidden troubles began to creep in; his business showed signs of slowing down. One day he realised that his foreign clients were bargaining with him. Unknown to him, they had been instructed to do so by Sha's co-workers. 'You can haggle with him,' said one of them to a foreign client, 'cut the price after cutting it in half.' What did it mean to cut the price after cutting it in half? The client cocked his head to ponder the suggestion. Language can present a barrier, but the desire for expression in language can never be blocked. So another of Sha's co-workers, by way of demonstration, touched the client's abdomen with one hand and, using the outstretched palm of the other to form the shape of a knife, chopped down, cutting him in half. Before the frightened man recovered, the hand rose and fell again, this time landing on his knee; now all that remained was a hairy calf. He looked down at his feet and saw that he could still wiggle his hairy toes. He got the picture – he hadn't encountered a modern-day boxer warrior. Their discussion was on international trade, with strong Chinese characteristics – about how to reduce the 'one' number to a quarter, to one-eighth, even to one-sixteenth. What a fascinating way the Chinese had in dealing with numbers, as splendid as their prose from the Han dynasty or poetry of the Tang. 'Yeah, I got it, I really got it now. Fabulous!' he exclaimed, making the word sound like *flabulous*.

Fuming's business took a nosedive. He made a serious error, as an inflated ego interfered with his judgement. Mirroring Wang Daifu's blunder in the stock market, he did not stop when the going was good; in wanting to save his 'international trade', he made the fatal mistake of using Chinese logic. In his mind, he had a solid relationship with these non-Chinese clients; they were old friends. They would be embarrassed to switch to someone else, wouldn't they? Well, he was wrong. They did that with ease; in the end, it was he who wound up being embarrassed. And it got worse; he was mortified whenever he heard English or Japanese being spoken. He felt as if he'd been abandoned – and he wanted to find a place to hide. Why was he mortified? Why did he have to hide? He had no idea, only that he *was* mortified that his business had tanked. And this was the moment bad health raised its sinister head.

Sha Fuming had suffered from poor health even as a student. How had that happened? He'd studied too hard, never realising that it could be detrimental to a blind person's health. A sighted person can study all he wants, day and night, like the proverbial scholar who poked a hole in the wall to read by a neighbour's light, or by burning the midnight oil. But no matter what, there is always the demarcation between day and night. But not for the blind. They live outside the confines of time. A sighted person will feel eye strain after prolonged reading, a problem that does not afflict the blind, since they read tactilely. Which was why Sha could read with no regard for day or night. He read everything – medicine, literature, history, the arts, science and economics; he read what was written over the past five thousand years and what was written all over the world. He had to. He set great store by the lines of the poet Wang Zhihuan that 'One must go up another floor/ To see far into the distance.' Everyone knew those lines. But to Sha Fuming they weren't poetry, they were philosophy, they were an inspiration. A book represented a floor and he, Sha Fuming, would be able to 'see far into the distance' once he reached a certain level. 'One's heart stirs at the roiling clouds/ One's eyes strain at the sight of homeward birds/ Wu and Chu are separated by a vast lake/ Its surface reflects the boundless universe.' Sha Fuming believed he would regain his sight, as implied in the name his parents had given him, *fu* – to recover, and *ming* – brightness. They had hoped he'd be able to see again. He was convinced that everyone had another pair of eyes, in their hearts, and he wanted each book he read to help open those eyes. With limitless ambition, he lived outside the confines of time.

He read. For him, dawn never came; conversely, darkness never descended.

As a student Sha Fuming was simply too young. The blind normally start school later than the sighted, so he was older than those who had gone through the same educational process. But no matter how much older he was, he was still very young. Being young has its advantage; you can abuse your body without suffering the consequences. A bit of abuse today, nothing happens. A little more tomorrow, no problem, and some more the day after that, still no sign of trouble. Tolstoy was right to say that the body is the slave of the mind.

But he had a neck and he had a stomach, both of which he pushed like a slave driver. His ambition led him to abuse them each and every day, and by the time he sensed their suffering, they were no longer his slaves, but had turned him into an aristocratic young lady, the delicate Lin Daiyu of fiction. His neck and his stomach acted up whenever they felt like it, relentlessly.

One always needs reminders regarding health. 'Sir, you don't look so good. Are you not feeling well?' Yet that convenience is not available to the blind. Only the wearer knows if his shoes are too big or too small. Sha's neck and stomach had already begun acting up when his business was flourishing, but he put up with it, not letting on to anyone. The blind are inordinately proud people, contemptuous of complaint, which they regard as whining, no different than begging for food. Sha had more pride than most, which prevented him from telling others about his ailments. Besides, what was accomplished by talking about them? Business was good and he was busy, there was money to be made – more than ten thousand yuan a month. Ten thousand yuan. That was more than he could have dreamed in the past, when he'd forged a long-term plan, which was to be a boss before he turned forty. Then that plan had seemed too long term; he'd likely have to start much earlier. Which was why he'd decided to put up with the pain; just a little longer. Once he opened his own business, he'd become a member of the bourgeoisie, and someone else would produce health, comfort and wealth for him. The neck and the stomach are not vital organs; as a sort of doctor himself, he knew that. After all, it was nothing but a little discomfort.

On the surface, it looked as if his neck and stomach were giving him trouble, while in fact it was his job that was causing problems for his neck and stomach. He had mistreated his stomach for too long. During his school days, night-time reading kept him from eating breakfast, and that had not changed once he started working, because night shifts – therapy time – made sleeping in more attractive than breakfast. Time for lunch wasn't his call either; it was up to the client, and he couldn't up and leave in order to eat, could he? If he was having lunch and a client came in, what should he do? To finish eating, speed was the answer, and speed became his style of eating. Most of the time Sha didn't really eat his food, he *drank* it. Stirring rice and vegetables together, he added soup, turning the dry rice into porridge so he didn't have to chew. All he had to do was slurp everything, and, with a few perfunctory movements of the lips, it was done. He'd sent everything down to his stomach. But speed is no big deal for tuina therapists – they are all fast eaters. The key is speed and quantity. He had to eat enough to make up for the missed breakfast and for the dinner that surely would not come at a normal time, if it happened at all. Lunch, therefore, became the only meal he could count on, so he *drank* diligently and conscientiously. But drinking enough to be full also caused problems. Clients never asked for tuina therapy after lunch, a time when they preferred foot massages, so that they could take a catnap while the therapist pressed, kneaded, dug and rubbed their feet. Giving a foot massage required the therapist to sit, in Sha's case, with a full stomach, so full he felt like throwing up and had to straighten up and stretch out his neck just to belch. A full stomach gave him trouble; an empty stomach was worse. When he thought back, he saw that he'd suffered more from an empty stomach than a full one. He usually ran out of steam after one o'clock in the morning. When young people are exhausted, they commonly develop a voracious appetite, and when that appetite goes unsatisfied, the stomach turns hysterical and vicious, as if it has grown five fingers to pull, tug, push, rub and knead, as skilful as Sha's tuina movements.

And that was how Sha Fuming slowly ruined his stomach. When it began to ache, he shunned all medicines. Zheng Zhihua's lyrics say it best:

He said in the wind and the rain,
The pain was nothing
Wipe away your tears and do not ask
– Why

Also disabled, the Taiwanese singer employed his upbeat, carefree lyrics to be inspirational, imbuing the song with tenderness as well as a sonorous yet fearless quality. Sha Fuming was convinced that this song was written specially for him. Indeed, the pain was nothing. *Wipe away your tears and do not ask – Why.* In fact, Fuming had no tears to wipe away. Shedding tears was beneath him.

The ache stopped and was replaced by pain. How are those different? In terms of language, they aren't, but to his mind there was a difference. An ache occurs over an area; it can grow and spread, but dully, like the knead and rub in tuina. A pain, on the other hand, is concentrated in a single point, and acutely; it can go deeper, and sharper, like pressure in tuina. Later his pain underwent a minor change, it became a tearing sensation. How did it tear? Where had the two hands in his stomach come from?

CHAPTER THREE
XIAO MA

SO WANG DAIFU moved into the men's dorm, which, like most such accommodations, consisted of remodelled apartments with three or four bunk beds in the former master bedroom, the living room and the study to accommodate from six to eight men.

As a newcomer, Wang Daifu could not expect to have a choice and, sure enough, he was assigned an upper bunk, to his disappointment. People in love instinctively desire lower bunks for convenience; but, of course, he did not complain. Grabbing the railing of the upper bunk, he gave it a hard tug; the bed didn't budge, a sign that it was firmly attached to the wall by expansion screws. For some reason, that little detail pleased him enormously. Sha Fuming was all right. That was the advantage of having a blind man as a boss, someone who paid attention to insignificant details often overlooked by the sighted. More importantly, a blind boss knew just where he needed to display his considerate side.

The lower bunk was occupied by Xiao Ma, or Little Horse, a man who, based on his experience, Wang Daifu treated with special courtesy. In a dorm like this, interactions between the bunkmates are usually quite delicate; while outwardly friendly, they can find it hard to get along. Trouble brews if they are not careful, though it seldom escalates into a major problem and is not something one easily brings up, and that can lead to awkwardness. Wang Daifu preferred to avoid awkward situations. Since he was just trying to make a living, not establish control, why get involved in personal intrigues? Peace can be a source of wealth, as they say. So he was cordial to Xiao Ma. But he soon realised that his civility was pointless, for Xiao Ma was an enigma. He reacted the same whether you treated him well or badly, and he treated everyone with indifference, neither good nor bad.

Xiao Ma was young, early twenties. If not for a traffic accident at the age of nine, what would he be doing and what would he be like now? These hypothetical questions may have been pointless, utterly useless, and yet suppositions lingered. In idle moments, he liked to probe the hypotheses, and before long he would be so mired in them he would lose himself in a dreamlike state. On the surface, the accident had left few marks on him – his limbs were intact and he had no horrific scars. It had simply destroyed his optic nerves, leaving him totally blind, bereft of even the basic sense of light.

And yet his eyes looked perfectly fine, no different from those of a sighted person. To be sure, if you tried hard enough you could see a difference – his eyeballs seemed livelier. When he was deep in thought, or angry, his eyeballs habitually moved, shifting from left to right, back and forth. That went unnoticed by most people, which caused him trouble that other blind people did not experience. Take riding the bus, for instance. The blind – Xiao Ma included – can ride for free, but not a single bus driver ever believed he was blind, which often led to embarrassing situations. Once, after boarding a bus, the driver announced repeatedly over the loudspeaker: 'Attention, passengers, please voluntarily pay the fare.' Xiao Ma knew at once that 'voluntarily' had a specific target: him. He stood in the aisle, holding tightly to the handrail, not saying a word. No blind person will ever advertise, 'I'm blind.' That is unthinkable. So he kept quiet and stayed put. The driver, a stubborn sort, picked up his mug and began to sip tea, waiting as if he had all the time in the world. The engine idled, also waiting patiently, until the silence inside the bus seemed unnatural, actually humiliating. Xiao Ma was the first to blink, after about a minute: he could not pay the fare and could not stand the idea of losing face; better to get off the bus. So he did. With a roar of the engine, the bus blasted his feet with warm exhaust, like invisible consolation or unseen mockery. He was outraged by the public humiliation. But he was smiling. That smile seemed embroidered onto his face, stitched there by needle and thread to hold the skin together. *I can't even be a blind man, the public won't let me*. He managed to smile, but never again stepped onto a bus. He had learned the art of rejection. He shunned – feared, actually – anything connected with 'the public'. There was nothing wrong with staying inside; he had no intention of solemnly announcing to the world, 'Ladies and Gentlemen, I am blind. I am really blind.'

But Xiao Ma was handsome. Anyone who saw him shared the view that he was the personification of good looks. At first he reacted with anger, refusing to believe them, convinced that they were being sarcastic. Only after he'd heard the comment from enough people did he finally calm down and accept what they were saying. He had a handsome face. Having lost his sight at the age of nine, he could not recall what his face was like back then. It was like a dream, an impossibly distant dream. In fact, he'd put his face out of his mind. What a shame. But things were fine now, for he knew he was handsome. Hand-some – two unrelated words put together with unbroken intricacy and crispness to form a description that was pleasing to the ear.

But handsome Xiao Ma had a not-so-handsome imperfection – it was on his neck. A surprisingly large scar, not a memento from the accident, but of his own doing. Soon after the accident, he recovered and began to walk, but the light in front of him had gone out. He panicked, so his father promised him that it was not serious and that everything would be fine soon. So he was plunged into waiting, or more precisely, a long, seemingly endless process of treatment. His father took him all over the country, journeying to Beijing, Shanghai, Guangzhou, Xi'an, Harbin, Chengdu, even as far as Lhasa. Shuttling between cities and between hospitals, the young Xiao Ma was on the road all the time, but he never reached his destination. He arrived only at disappointment. But his father remained in high spirits, brimming with undying enthusiasm, promising his beloved son over and over. *Don't worry. You'll be better. Daddy will make you see again*. Taking his father's words as a cue, Xiao Ma raised his hopes again and again, but deep down he was worried. He wanted to see, he needed to see, yet his damned eyes refused to open. But, of course, they were open. He began using his hands, tearing at the void before his eyes. But no matter how hard he tried, his hands were useless in shredding the darkness. Flying into a rage, he grabbed his father and bit down on his hand, not letting go. That happened in Lhasa. Then his father got wonderful news: in Nanjing, the starting point of their long journey, an ophthalmologist who had recently returned from Germany was practising at Nanjing's First People's Hospital. Xiao Ma had heard of Germany, which was a lot farther than the other places. Scooping him up in his arms, his father shouted, 'Son, we're going back to Nanjing, and this time it will work. I promise you, you will get your sight back.'

No longer in a distant place, the doctor from Germany reached out to touch Xiao Ma's face, inducing in the nine-year-old boy a sense of foreboding. He believed in distance, and had no faith in anyone or anything nearby. Since the hand that had returned from Germany could touch his face, it was no longer distant. Subsequent developments proved him right when a shocking incident took place – his father pinned down the doctor on the floor and used his fists on him. It happened at the far end of the hallway, away from Xiao Ma, who should have been out of earshot but wasn't. By some unthinkable miracle, his ears allowed him to hear everything. His father and the doctor had been engaged in secretive whispering before Xiao Ma's father got down on his knees, but still failed to sway the doctor; so he pounced and pinned the doctor to the floor, demanding a promise that his son would regain his sight in a year. The doctor refused. Xiao Ma heard the doctor clearly say, 'That's impossible.' So his father used his fists.

That was when nine-year-old Xiao Ma exploded, though it was altogether different from other kinds of explosions, for his was marked by an astonishing calm; no one could believe that a nine-year-old was capable of that sort of intensity. As he lay in bed, his ears shifted their focus and he heard people eating in the adjoining ward. Someone was using a spoon, someone was using a bowl; he heard the crisp sound of a spoon scraping against a bowl. It was a pleasant sound, so resonant.

Groping his way along the wall, Xiao Ma walked over; holding on to the door frame, he asked with a smile, 'Auntie, could I have some?' Then turning to face her, he added in a soft voice, 'But please don't feed me. I want to eat on my own.'

The woman placed the bowl in his right hand and the spoon in his left. But instead of eating, he smashed the bowl against the doorjamb, leaving only a broken shard in his hand, which he then jabbed into his neck and ripped it across. Who could conceive of a nine-year-old carrying out such a horrifying act? Stunned, the woman tried to scream, but managed only to stretch her mouth wide without making a sound. His blood spattered, like shrapnel, all over the place. This successful explosion elated him, as he felt the hot blood flying around. But Xiao Ma was, after all, a nine-year-old boy, and forgot that he was not out on the street or in a park, but at a hospital, where they quickly came to his aid. He was left with a horrific scar that grew with him; as he got taller, it turned longer and wider.

The scar was not easy to miss, and many of the non-regular clients noticed it the moment they lay down. Curious, they knew they had to ask about it in a roundabout way. Normally taciturn, he rarely talked to his clients, but at moments like this he was direct, knowing that even more would have to be said if he beat around the bush.

'You want to know about my scar,' he'd say.

'Yes.' Curiosity trumped shame.

'Well, I lost my eyesight. I got desperate when I couldn't see,' he'd answer in a singsong voice, 'and all that desperation made me lose the will to live. I did it to myself.'

'Oh – how about now?' the worried client would ask.

'Now? I'm no longer desperate. What good would that do me?' He'd finish with a smile, in a calm, tranquil voice. Then he'd stop talking to the client altogether.

Wang Daifu tried to avoid speaking with his bunkmate at the tuina centre, owing to Xiao Ma's aversion to conversation, but he had to maintain the appearance of civility in the dorm. So, before going to bed, he'd speak with Xiao Ma, but usually only in brief sentences or a few exchanged words. And he always spoke first. Not to be taken lightly, those few words were essential to a harmonious relationship between the upper and lower bunks. By rights there was no need for him to do that, since he was so much older than Xiao Ma, but he insisted upon a cordial dialogue, and he had his reasons. Both men were blind, but Wang had been born that way, while Xiao Ma had been sighted for a few years. That made a difference, a vast difference. Anyone who took no heed of that would not survive in their world.

Take silence for example. The blind are normally silent in public, but there are different kinds of silences. Those who are born blind are naturally quiet, but not those who lose their sight later in life; they experience two worlds that meet at a special place called purgatory. Not all of them manage to pass through it. At the entrance, they undergo the torment of internal chaos and turmoil, a manic process marked by fierce temper, so cruelly overwhelming that only ruins are left. In the deepest crevice of memory, each of them has not lost his world, only his connection with the world, but without which the world has suddenly become deep, hard and distant. Most importantly, it has turned mysterious and unfathomable, and probably impossible to defend against. In order to deal with the change, he must do one thing – commit a homicide. He must kill himself, not with a knife or a gun, but with fire. His body must roil in an engulfing flame until he smells the stench of burning flesh. What does a phoenix rising from the ashes mean? It means you must first immolate yourself.

But it is not enough merely to immolate yourself, for there remains an even greater test – to remould the self, and that requires steely determination and rock-solid patience. He needs time, for he is a sculptor, not a master artist, progressing chaotically, chipping here and hacking there. Facing an unfamiliar sculpture, few know who they will be when the rebirth begins. Often, the completed sculpture turns out to be radically different from what he had wished for. He does not love himself. He turns taciturn.

The silence of these people is authentic, seemingly devoid of content, but in fact it overflows with bitter laments and anguish, a surfeit of stressful struggle. Hence his silence often goes overboard, as do his quietude and his calmness. Yet he must go overboard to such a degree that silence is transformed into a sort of faith, under whose guidance the present 'I' becomes God while the old 'me' can only be the devil. The devil is still inside him, and he must be forever vigilant and alert. The older me is the karmic evil of three thousand years before, a smiling, self-satisfied snake. A snake is such a vivid, alluring creature, one brimming with enchanting power, that if you're not careful it will doom you to a state beyond redemption. Wavering between the two selves, he turns irascible. He must control his irascibility.

Seen from this perspective, one who loses his sight after birth undergoes none of life's stages – childhood, pre-teen, teens, middle age, or old age. After rising from the ashes, he is immediately thrust into the complexities of life. Beneath his childlike expression are the vicissitudes of life, the secrets of being alive. With the ability to see through everything in life, he displays an unfounded sophistication. His body lacks eyes but is itself a pitch-black eye that reflects everyone except himself. This eye can appear hostile at times, tender and loving at others; it knows how to be an indifferent onlooker, keeping a detached, suspicious attitude. A deity three feet above the ground.

Xiao Ma's silence embraced the solemnity of a sculpture; it was not nature or instinct, but a skill he had honed to perfection. Under normal circumstances, he could maintain that solemnity for hours, weeks, months, even years. To him, life was a process of control and a continuation of repetitiveness.

But life cannot be endlessly repetitive, since it is not an assembly line. No one can turn life into a moulding press for soap or slippers, and produce days with equal sides, quality and weight. Life has its own rhythm of addition and subtraction, allotting more to today, less to tomorrow, and more to the day after. As the real facet of life, this process of addition and subtraction is what makes life interesting, enjoyable and unpredictable, all at the same time.

Addition now appeared in Xiao Ma's life, which had been going along just fine until Wang Daifu and Xiao Kong were added.

It was past one o'clock in the morning when Xiao Kong first showed up in Xiao Ma's dorm room.

Tuina therapists normally work till midnight and 'go home' around a quarter of an hour after that. As a rule, they prefer the term 'going home' to 'getting off work'. Relaxing after fourteen or fifteen hours of hard labour, their bodies are not difficult to please; they can lean against almost anything and feel at home. Instead of washing and heading straight to bed, they sit quietly for a while, a genuine pleasure. Of course, there are lively moments, since they lead a communal life. Someone might suddenly decide to eat something. So they eat, and as they eat, they become animated, and chats turn into silly talk. They talk, they laugh, they clown around. Chatting 'at home' feels good. There are no fixed topics: ice cream, no. 1 subway line, Disney, bank interest, their discrete school friends, cars, Chinese football, funny lines from a client, real estate, mutton skewers, movie stars, stocks, problems in the Middle East, daydreams, the Japanese election, Nike sneakers, New Year's Eve TV shows, Shakespeare, taking a mistress, the Olympics, athlete's foot, the difference between toasted buns and toasted bread, the NBA, love, AIDS, charity, and so on. They talk about anything that strikes their fancy, which sometimes leads to arguments and minor fallings-out. But that doesn't matter, for they find ways to make up. Sometimes, when their conversations need a boost, the men and women visit one another, naturally. That can turn chats into minor riots, accompanied by the noise of cracking melon seeds and the sound of a radio broadcasting stock market numbers, book reviews and sports news, or call-ins, psychological counselling and commercials. To be sure, there are rules regarding visits between the sexes – the men go to the women's dorms before the women head to the men's later. The women tend to have complicated rituals before going to sleep, a sort of prologue. Unlike the women, whose bedtime rituals create a degree of inconvenience, the men simply climb into bed and begin to snore without even taking off their smelly socks.

Xiao Kong finally came to Wang Daifu's dorm after one o'clock in the morning. The moment she arrived, Xu Tailai called out, 'Sao-zi', or sister-in-law. It sounded strange, yet wasn't all that unusual. Wang had not been there long, but people were already calling him 'Da-ge', or big brother, an apt nickname for Wang, who impressed everyone as being a simple, honest man. He was certainly honest, kind, strong and hardworking, but inarticulate, the type who doesn't mind taking it on the chin or being pushed around. It took him time to get his head around things, and he was a slow talker, but with a ready smile. All these were the characteristics of a *da-ge*. And since he was now Da-ge, what else could Xiao Kong be if not Sao-zi?

Normally a man who was mindful of his position, Xu Tailai seldom gave in to banter, but precisely because he was so inarticulate, his calling Xiao Kong Sao-zi created a meaningful effect. Referring to an unmarried woman as Sao-zi was intriguing, for it revealed something hidden by tacit agreement. It was amusing, funny actually, and it sent everyone into a raucous chorus of 'Sao-zi'. Caught by surprise, Xiao Kong did not know how to react. She'd just come from freshening up after a shower, and hadn't expected to become a Sao-zi the moment she stepped inside the men's dorm. Now what? she thought to herself.

Amid the cacophony of noise, the twang of a mattress spring told her that Wang Daifu had made room for her, so she walked towards him. Obviously, she could not climb up onto the upper bunk. So she did the next best thing – she sat on the lower bunk, between Wang on her left and another person on her right, who, she figured, must be Xiao Ma. But before she had a chance to greet Xiao Ma, Zhang Yiguang walked up and began his interrogation.

Zhang had come from the Jiawang coal mine, where he'd been a miner for sixteen years. Already the father of two, he was the liveliest individual 'at home'. He was out of place at the tuina therapy centre, owing to his age, for one thing. Most of the therapists were young, with an average age of twenty-five or twenty-six; he was close to forty – an old man. But that was only one of the ways he didn't fit in, for he was not a typical blind man. Before the age of thirty-five, he'd had bright eyes that could even be called fierce. After that, his eyes lost their lustre and intensity; a gas explosion had buried them in the mine forever. What could he do without his eyesight? Switching to a new profession, he took up tuina therapy, an odd choice for a rough-hewn character like him. Luckily, he had a trump card – amazing strength he was not afraid to use. He put his all into his work, huffing and puffing as if he were digging for coal in the client's body. Some liked it that way, which was why Sha Fuming had taken him on, and he brought in plenty of business. But no matter how old he was, no one would have called him Da-ge. He was one of those older men who somehow just did not command respect. He never acted like an elder. What people noticed about him was his tendency to overdo things and an inability to do them the way they were supposed to be done. Take making friends, for instance. If he liked you, he'd be so devoted that he'd buy you a drink, you'd even think he might rip out his heart or liver to go with it. But if something displeased him, he could be ruthless, ready to fight at the slightest provocation. Not surprisingly, he had no real friends.

Holding onto the edge of the bed, Zhang stood there and announced the rules of the family: all newcomers had to undergo an interrogation to become members, and that included Sao-zi. Xiao Kong knew this was all in fun, but was nervous nonetheless. Zhang was, after all, married with two kids, which meant he knew his way around an interrogation. She was right to be worried, for he started by focusing on the relationship between Da-ge and Sao-zi, though he did it in a roundabout way, relying on insinuation. Adopting an innocent manner, yet all the while centring on unique features, he guided his listeners to make associations that would render *anyone* tongue-tied.

'Let's loosen things up and start with an IQ test, a riddle,' Zhang said. 'Can you tell me which idiom is appropriate for describing Da-ge hugging Sao-zi naked?'

Now what could that be? How could an idiom be sufficient to describe all the things a naked man and woman could do together? It would take a lifetime.

'*Xiong duo ji shao*,' Zhang said, 'boding disaster rather than blessings.'

How could that describe Da-ge and Sao-zi hugging naked? His audience quickly got the joke: the four words sounded just like 'big tits and little dick'. They doubled over laughing. He was quite a clown, this Zhang Yiguang, the centre's answer to the well-known comic actors Pan Changjiang and Zhao Benshan. His mouth was a formidable tool.

Now that they were loosened up, Zhang left Xiao Kong alone and zeroed in on Wang Daifu. 'Yesterday afternoon a client commented on Sao-zi's body, saying she had everything that should be there and nothing that shouldn't. Now tell us, what should and shouldn't be on Sao-zi's body?'

Again everyone laughed, including Wang. While his laughter wasn't entirely natural, he was in fact genuinely happy, for it always pleased him to hear people say nice things about Sao-zi. That went without saying. But it was hard on Xiao Kong, who could not make a fuss over what was said, and was reduced to shifting her body, as if she could cut ties with Da-ge by sitting farther and farther away from him. It did no good, for Zhang was relentless. The harder he pushed, the closer she edged to Xiao Ma, until she was practically sitting on him.

The inarticulate Wang was at the end of his rope, which so panicked Xiao Kong that she jumped to her feet and punched Xiao Ma. 'He's picking on me, Xiao Ma. Why don't you do something?'

Xiao Ma had been wool gathering. He never participated in family business; he was far more interested in letting his mind wander. He hadn't said a word from the moment Xiao Kong entered the dorm, and had not expected her to head straight for his bed. He captured her smell right away; or, to be more precise, her smell captured him the moment she arrived. It was her hair. Still wet from being washed, it carried the lingering fragrance of shampoo. That shampoo was no longer just shampoo, and her hair was no longer just hair, as together they produced a fantastic chemical reaction that endowed her with a wonderful smell and, for some reason, made him nervous. The fact is, it had affected him deeply. She smelled absolutely wonderful. As a result, he was oblivious to Zhang Yiguang's torrential interrogation; all he knew for sure was that Sao-zi, little by little, was moving closer to him. Her body shifted, enveloping him in her fragrance, which seemed to grow fingers and arms that could caress, hold and embrace him. Xiao Ma was mesmerised, trapped in that embrace. Flaring his nostrils, he wanted to breathe deeply, but he lacked the nerve, and ended up holding his breath, to the point of nearly suffocating.

Sao-zi had no time to delve into Xiao Ma's secrets; all she wanted was to rescue Wang Daifu from his predicament by shifting the target. She pummelled Xiao Ma softly and complained in a pouty voice, 'You're so mean, Xiao Ma.'

'I'm not mean, Sao-zi,' he replied, raising his head.

This came from the depths of his heart, layered in fear and trepidation, but it could not have come at a worse time. In the current atmosphere, his 'I'm not mean' sounded more like a witticism, which some might have construed as flirtatious, thus making him complicit in Zhang Yiguang's prank. Who could have predicted that Xiao Ma, who rarely spoke, could be so clever the one time he opened his mouth? But that is how language works – it can make a quiet person sound humorous just by speaking.

Convinced by the raucous laughter that Xiao Ma was being mean, Xiao Kong got down off the bed and complained in an exaggerated tone, 'Damn you, Xiao Ma. I thought you were a nice guy. It turns out you're bad on the inside, which is worse than just bad.' Though she was grumbling, she was, in fact, pleased with herself, since her little trick diverted the attention to Xiao Ma. Why not make it even more noticeable? she thought. Self-satisfaction and a taste of flighty pleasure prodded her to take things as far as they would go: she wrapped her hands around his neck, gently, of course, and said, 'Xiao Ma, are you mean or aren't you?'

Here we must speak of another trait of the blind. Since they are unable to see one another, eye contact or communication through facial expressions are impossible. So in those rare moments when they are involved in horseplay, they – men and women both – cannot avoid using their hands and feet. There are no taboos in regard to physical contact; it is expected of good friends when they are talking and joking – a tap here, a tickle or pinch there. Not touching is as serious a breach as the sighted averting their eyes, for it can only signify sinister motives or a lack of trust.

Xiao Ma had no idea why what he'd said was funny, but Sao-zi wrapped her hands around his neck, and, without intending to, he had come into physical contact with her. To show that she really meant to hurt him, strangle him even, she kept her hands firmly around his neck and grunted to add effect. At some point, her body began to sway, sending her wet hair flying, and each time the ends hit him in the face, it felt as if they were lashing deep into his heart.

'Are you mean or aren't you?' she yelled.

'Yes, I'm mean.'

Xiao Ma could not have anticipated that his simple 'I'm mean' could also become a joke. Without knowing it, he had slowly evolved from an inessential outsider into the main character of the drama. Before he had time to analyse his own feelings, he lost control. How his arms got involved, he didn't know, but one of them abruptly brushed against two fleshy mounds, soft and yet firm, with an indescribable stubborn quality. He was immediately transported back to the age of nine. The sensation was surprising and transient, but there was a childlike, exuberant vitality to it. He went rigid, not daring to move, freezing his arms at that moment when he was nine. His late mother. A birthday cake. Bright red candles forming the number nine. Dazzlingly bright. A loud crash, an overturned car. The overpowering smell of hair swirling all around. Breasts. Everything there that should have been. Sao-zi. Restless and eager for action. Suffocation.

With hot tears suddenly brimming in his eyes, he raised his head and covered her hands with his. 'Sao-zi.'

That, of course, resulted in another round of raucous guffaws, what might normally be called lascivious laughter. Taciturn Xiao Ma, a deadpan joker? Who would have known it? Why, he was more of a hellraiser than Zhang.

'I'm not Sao-zi,' Xiao Kong said with feigned seriousness. 'I'm Xiao Kong.'

'No,' he retorted with the same seriousness, 'you're Sao-zi.'

Amid the waves of laughter, Xiao Kong looked angry; but, of course, she was just playacting. Xiao Ma was so mean, she thought, he could make people die laughing and wouldn't care. Now what? There was nothing she could do about him. Luckily, however, she was secretly pleased with the term of address, so she said with a note of resignation, 'All right, I'm Sao-zi.'

But that's not a term of address that an unmarried woman can accept willingly and with ease; it requires progress through the stages of being coy and shy. In her shy phase, she grabbed Xiao Ma's hand and pinched, as a veiled warning that she would not let him off so lightly the next time.

Sensing her warning, he pursed his lips, which made him realise, to his surprise, that he had been smiling. It was an expression that had come out of nowhere, and he knew that his smile was a special opening that let in something unidentifiable. A fuzzy memory of his mother, slightly cool yet slightly warm. Time is a strange artefact that never truly passes; seemingly lost, it hides in the crevices of facial expressions that, when least expected, call it to return.

Sitting at the far end of the bed, a gleeful Wang Daifu was also smiling. He took out his cigarettes and passed them around, without saying a word, something Xiao Kong found somewhat wanting in him. He was a wonderful man in just about every respect, and she was convinced that he would die for her, if necessary. But there was one thing he could not and would never do, and that was to speak up for her; he was simply no good with words.

So what could she say? Nothing. All she could do was take Xiao Ma's hand as the joking came to an end, and lose herself in thoughts of – Wang Daifu, of course. But being lost in thought meant that she was unconscious of her movements. So Xiao Ma's hand remained in hers, as his body began to levitate, like a balloon. She was another balloon, floating up with him. For him, the sky was not limitless, but formed a cone, and no matter how vast and wide, it must come to an end at a pointed tip. The two balloons passively came together in the air at the tapering dome of sky. In fact, they weren't balloons; they were horses, two weightless, celestial horses soaring through the sky. There was only the smell of fresh grass and hair, as they remained together, rubbing against each other amid other weary movements.

Xiao Kong's first visit to the men's dorm was not a success. But viewed differently, it was. She, as well as Wang Daifu, had got closer to and friendlier with their co-workers, marked by the liberties they could take in their bantering and physical contact. That was important, for it created a harmonious work environment; though they had yet to become confidants, they had managed positive interpersonal relationships that were second only to true friendship.

Following her first visit, Xiao Kong got into the habit of going to Wang's dorm before bedtime. After her shower, of course. The visits became a routine, which in itself is a characteristic of the blind. They are especially attentive to developing and following routines in their daily lives, and do not easily make changes. Once something is done in a certain way, they prefer to keep doing it that way from then on. Routine is a lifesaver; they would suffer without it. When negotiating a turn while out walking, for instance, they follow familiar patterns – not one step more or one step less. Otherwise, they could lose their front teeth.

As the new routine formed, the old one between Xiao Kong and Wang Daifu ended, the one they had developed after coming to Nanjing: they made love twice a night. Wang was usually wild the first time, as if the earth were crumbling, that he was fighting for his life, that he was about to devour her. The second time was tame, detail-oriented and tender, filled with magical attachment, exceptionally touching. If the first time was considered lovemaking, then the second was the embodiment of falling in love. She liked them both, but would probably have chosen the second if forced to, for it was simply rapturous. However, within two weeks, that routine came to an end, for now that they were working again, twice a night was out of the question. When they got off work and came home, she'd be in the grip of desire that started out as a thought but quickly spread to her body. A thought was easy to deal with, but it became sheer torture once her body was involved. She was thrown into a daze, her body burning hot all over, as if engulfed in flames of desire.

This made her act in a peculiar way when she went to the men's dorm. The others, of course, would not notice, and even Wang himself was probably oblivious. Dejected, she put on a high-spirited show, but since the conflicting senses of dejection and excitement were so powerful, they created enormous tension. At such moments, she was irritable, prone to sentimentality, and emotional. Given to pouting, she tried to play the coquette, with an affected sweet and pampered air. She longed to throw herself into Wang's arms, and would have been satisfied just to have him put his arms around her and his lips on hers. All she wanted was physical contact and bodily endearment. But could they do that in a dorm? Of course not. Without knowing it, Xiao Kong had taken a detour, piling coquettish behaviour and pouts intended for Wang onto Xiao Ma. She enjoyed fooling around with him, verbally *and* physically.

Xiao Ma's happiness grew by the day. He became possessed by her fragrance; having no way to describe this pervasive smell, he called it Sao-zi. Sao-zi was everywhere, as if holding Xiao Ma's hand and walking on the floor, on suitcases, on chairs, on walls, on windows, on ceilings, even on pillows. The men's dorm ceased to be a men's dorm and was transformed into the street when he was nine years old. An enchanting street, where, outside the shopping arcade and the major hotels, billboards advertised tropical fruits, Nike basketballs, Adidas T-shirts and ice cream. Sao-zi took him along, with a kind and yet tyrannical attitude that watched over his every move. His mother had been strict with him, but he was the rebellious sort who never stopped fighting her. But not with Sao-zi, who wore a smile as she mocked him, sweetly embarrassed him, and gently straightened him out. He accepted it all, heart and soul. There seemed to be a tacit understanding between them; they were in perfect harmony.

On one particular Tuesday night, she did not show up, having come down with a cold. Xiao Ma could hear her cough off in the distance. Sitting on the edge of the bed, wide awake, all he could do was wait. He waited until nearly everyone in both dorms was asleep, and it was clear she wasn't coming. He lay down fully dressed and tried to invent her smell. It was wasted effort, a disappointing failure. Nothing, there was nothing. *Nothing that should have been there and nothing that should not have.* In his despondency he began searching the bedsheet with his hand, hoping to find even a single strand of her hair. But there too he failed. Yet the absurd action reminded him of something: the mysterious contact between his arm and her breasts through the dry, soft knitted top she wore. At that moment, too wonderful for words, the thing between his legs had a spontaneous reaction. It grew bigger, thicker and harder. Wang Daifu took that moment to roll over and cough. Startled, Xiao Ma grew alert, interpreting Wang's cough as a warning. He wanted that damned thing to stop getting hard, but no means of relief came to him; even worse, the desire intensified.

CHAPTER FOUR
DU HONG

DU HONG CAME to the Sha Zongqi tuina centre earlier than Wang Daifu and Xiao Kong, though not by much, just a few months; she'd been recommended by Ji Tingting. As a newcomer, she hung out with Ji all the time during her early days at the centre. Saying they hung out might be overstating the case somewhat, because the therapists held to a rigid daily routine that limited their activities to the centre and their dorm. In fact, over a dozen people hung out together all the time, yet even given the crowded conditions, some drew closer to one another than to others. *She* and *she* might be especially friendly, just as *he* would spend more time with *him* – such pairings were common occurrences. But Du Hong hung out with Ji for only a couple of months before switching to Gao Wei.

Gao, who was sighted, worked the front desk. If Du Hong had been favoured with normal vision, she'd have seen that Gao Wei was a girl given to laughing, with a tiny nose and small eyes that, when she smiled, nearly shut completely, revealing only a twinkle. Big eyes are charming, small eyes are alluring. When Gao smiled, and her eyes nearly shut, she did have an alluring look about her, but that was not what attracted Du Hong, since she could not see. In any case, they grew closer by the day, to the point that Gao Wei rode Du Hong to and from work on her three-wheeler. Blind people have trouble getting around, particularly out on the streets, and Gao Wei's selfless act made Du Hong's life much easier. Before she realised it, she had begun to neglect Ji Tingting. During meals, Du Hong sat shoulder to shoulder with Gao, chewing and swallowing in unison.

When Gao was hired, she hadn't known how to ride a three-wheeler, though she was an expert cyclist. Sha had asked her to learn how to ride a three-wheeler on her first day at the centre.

'Bicycles have two wheels and riding one is child's play. How hard can it be to ride a three-wheeler?'

So Sha told her to go outside and give it a try. Which she did, and ended up making a fool of herself. She kept bumping into the wall and yelling, capturing the attention of the therapists inside with her helpless screams until, with a loud thud, the wall bounced her and her three-wheeler backwards. Hilarious.

After getting to her feet, she studied the contraption and saw what had happened. A bicycle has handlebars, but it uses the rider's centre of gravity to make a turn, aided by the handlebars. A three-wheeler, owing to the additional wheel, always stays glued to the road surface, so when making a turn, shifting the rider's centre of gravity has no effect. You just keep going in the same direction. How about applying the brakes? That won't work, because you have to reach down to pull the brakes, which aren't attached to the handlebars – a tricky manoeuvre that escapes you at a critical moment. You lose control of your vehicle. Gao was actually lucky she'd tried it out by a wall. If it had been by the Yangtze River, her three-wheeler would have simply rolled into the water, no matter how loud she screamed.

The main duties of a service industry receptionist are assigning clients and keeping therapist work charts. But at a tuina centre, there is the additional critical task of delivering towels and sheets. Sanitation department regulations stipulate that fresh towels and sheets are required for each client. The used towels and sheets will naturally have to be sent to a laundry and brought back the following morning, which requires manpower for dropping off and picking up. Sha Fuming, to make maximum use of his resources, gave that task to his receptionists, and would not hire anyone who could not ride a three-wheeler, no matter how charming or alluring her eyes might be.

Fortunately, three-wheelers are not aeroplanes. After a few tries, Gao Wei got the hang of turning the vehicle, and even learned to reach under the seat to apply the brake, with flair. Compared with the tuina therapists and the other staff, the receptionist had a cushy job, mainly because she could take every other day off. But Gao did not take advantage of that system; she came to work every day so she could serve as Du Hong's early-morning and late-night transportation. Because of that ride, Du Hong's relationship with Ji Tingting cooled, until Gao Wei became her best friend. They engaged in whispered conversations, never speaking loudly enough for people to hear them. If she was asked what they talked about, Du Hong would answer, 'We're gossiping about you.'

Ji Tingting *saw* all this and was understandably upset. But Du Hong was a clever girl who knew how to smooth things over; she often brought Tingting things to eat, like three or four orange slices, or half a dozen peanuts, or four or five chestnuts. Every time, just that little bit, but she was so warm, so friendly, it was as if she'd saved a special something specifically for Sister Tingting, turning the gift of a pathetic amount of food into an act of human kindness. Typically among women, the less you have, the better it tastes. Du Hong also brushed Tingting's hair from time to time. Being a few years older than Du Hong and more broad-minded, Tingting didn't let that bother her, especially since she was happy with Du Hong's attitude. The girl did mean to please her, and that was good enough for Tingting. Being blind herself, she was keenly aware of the convenience that a good relationship with the three-wheeler rider provided.

Du Hong had taken up the study of tuina therapy later than most, and not as a major career path, not at first. Most of her time and energy at the Qingdao School for the Blind had been spent on music. If she'd listened to her teachers, she might have had a career on the stage. They all told her she was a talented musician, particularly where committing music to memory was concerned. Most of the time, you don't start out knowing you have talent in a particular area; that knowledge comes when the talent is on display and you realise how easy it was to do.

That's how it was with Du Hong and music. How had she started? That's a long story that must begin when she was in the fifth grade. One day, the school reserved a cinema for the students to *see* a Hollywood movie. It was a film set in the future, and what they heard were all sorts of shrill sounds. The cacophonous music was the worst – vapid and grating on the ears. This must be what 'space' music is like, they thought. A week later, Du Hong's music teacher was in the toilet when she heard someone humming a familiar tune. Not sure what it was, it then dawned on her that it was the space music from the Hollywood movie. After washing her hands, she waited to see who it was. It turned out to be Du Hong.

'How did you manage to remember that noisy, jumbled tune?' the teacher asked.

Du Hong was puzzled by the question. With a smile, she asked why anyone needed to remember music, since it wasn't something in a textbook. That high-flown comment would have been a boast had it come from a sighted person. No blind person can be that self-confident, nor would they express themselves even if they were. So what might have been a boast was, from Du Hong, quite genuine.

The teacher took her to the staff office, where she played some Brahms on the piano in front of all the teachers, then, with her hands on her knees, asked the girl to hum the four bars she'd played. Standing by the piano with her arms at her sides, Du Hong refused to make a sound, which the teacher knew was a sign of shyness. She signalled for the other teachers to leave the office. But still Du Hong remained stubbornly quiet. Finally, their patience exhausted, the teachers, who had remained just beyond the window, left, and Du Hong began humming the right-hand melody, with perfect pitch and precise intervals. But before the teacher could offer praise, the girl astonished her by next humming the left-hand accompaniment. Something like that was so difficult that only the rare genius could manage it. Her surprised music teacher laid her hands on the girl's shoulder and turned her this way and that way to scrutinise her. Was this girl really Du Hong, the student who seldom scored more than forty points on her maths tests?

It was, of course, Du Hong, a girl who was no good at maths, or language, or PE, but had the remarkable talent of being able to repeat a musical offering after hearing it only once. Why had it taken the teacher so long to discover that? But it wasn't too late, since she was only in the fifth grade. The teacher decided on the spot to teach her to play the piano. Du Hong was not interested.

'What does interest you?' the teacher asked.

'Singing,' Duhong said, 'I like to sing.' As she sat on the piano bench, the teacher slapped her thighs anxiously, to the rhythm of a march.

'You don't understand, Du Hong. You really don't. You're blind, so what do you expect to achieve with your voice? You're not deaf or a mute, so what good will it do you to be a singer? Do you know what special education means? You won't understand even if I explain it to you, but, in any case, special education means to go through the trouble of teaching you how to do something beyond you. For example, teaching deaf mutes to sing, the lame to dance, and the mentally challenged to invent something. That's how the magic of special schools and education is manifested. In a word, disabled people must endure tremendous hardships, like climbing a mountain of knives or stepping into a sea of fire, to do – and do well – something they could not have done before. Only then do they have the power to stir people's emotions, to be an inspiration for their age, and to shake up society. What's so great about a blind girl singing? All you need to do is open your mouth and sing, but playing the piano is hard. The most difficult challenge for the blind is to play the piano. Do you understand? You have such an edge, why don't you treasure it? You're just lazy! Go home and tell your parents to come talk to me.'

But Du Hong did not tell her parents to come; she gave in. Like a carpenter, the teacher turned Du Hong into a bench that she placed at the piano. The girl made phenomenal progress. Within three years, she tested at the eighth grade, which was nothing short of miraculous.

The miracle came to a sudden halt when she was in her second year of middle school. She put a stop to playing and, no matter what anyone said, stubbornly refused to return to the piano.

It was all the result of a performance, a large-scale charity concert to 'show love' to the disabled. Many important figures were in attendance, mostly movie and TV stars past their prime, plus some current pop stars. As a special guest performer, Du Hong went to the concert in a floor-length A-line skirt, to play one of Bach's contrapuntal *Three-part Inventions*, whose difficulty lay in the crossing of the left and right hands. She had a better grasp of the *Two-part Inventions*, but the teacher had encouraged her to go all out with the more difficult piece. As it was her first public performance, she was understandably nervous, which showed mostly in her fingers the moment she got on stage. Her fingers, particularly the ring fingers, turned stiff and behaved badly, and, devoid of their usual deft autonomy, ensured that she would fail to put on a good show. A closer examination would have shown that this had been a problem all along – weak ring fingers. She had worked hard to eliminate that imperfection, and thought she'd been successful. But it resurfaced at this special occasion, and she sought to overcome it by calling upon the strength in her wrist to pound her fingers on the keys. That had the unfortunate effect of upsetting the rhythm. She couldn't bear to listen to what she was playing. Bach? How could this be described as Bach?

A perfectionist, all Du Hong wanted to do was stop and start over, but that was not a practice session, it was a public performance. She had to continue, no matter how lifeless it sounded. Her mood abruptly soured. She was not willing to take this without a fight. She felt as if she'd swallowed flies. And the mistakes mounted. This was worse, far worse than any practice session, and she felt an urge to play as badly as she could. An unspeakable dejection came over her.

At several moments Du Hong felt like crying. To her credit, she didn't. How she finished the performance she did not know, but as the ending notes approached, and powerful resentment rose up inside her, Du Hong raised her arms, wrists down, and spread the fingers of both hands. Her mind seemingly settled, she held her breath and banged her fingers down on the keys. She was waiting. Waiting to play the last few notes. She took a deep breath, lifted her hands, bent at the wrist, struck a pose, and it was over. A hideous *Three-part Invention.* Total embarrassment, a complete failure. Now she really felt like crying, but the applause was deafening, absolutely fervent, and seemingly unending. An emotional wreck, Du Hong stood up and bowed and then bowed again. The mistress of ceremonies appeared next to her and praised her performance with half a dozen adjectives, capped by a rash of comparisons. In a word, Du Hong's performance had been nearly flawless. Her need to cry had vanished, replaced by a cooling inside. A sense of desolation. Du Hong knew that she was a blind person, and that she would always be just that, a blind person. Someone like her had been placed on earth for one purpose, to foster tolerance in the sighted, a girl to feel sorry for. For someone like her to even produce sounds from a piano was, by itself, remarkable.

The mistress of ceremonies took Du Hong's hand and dragged her to the front of the stage, where she called out, 'Camera. Over here, camera.'

It only now dawned on Du Hong that she was on TV, and that people throughout the province, even the whole country, were watching her. She didn't know what to do.

'Tell everyone your name.'

'Du Hong.'

'Louder, please.'

'Du – Hong.' She raised her voice.

'Are you happy?'

'Yes,' she said after a moment's thought.

'Louder.'

'Hap – py!' she shouted, stretching her neck out.

'Why are you happy?'

Why? What kind of question was that? Just what kind of question was that? Du Hong was stuck for an answer.

'Let's try something else. What would you like to say at this moment?'

Du Hong moved her lips, as thoughts of various phrases flashed through her mind – 'constantly striving to improve oneself', 'throttling fate's throat' – all clichés and idioms she'd learned, but she could not string them together to form a coherent expression. Lucky for her, the music started up, a violin that gradually came closer and grew louder, so lyrical, so wrenchingly plaintive. Without waiting for Du Hong to find the words, the mistress of ceremonies herself, accompanied by the violin music, began to narrate Du Hong's story. With a tone normally used for a poetry recitation with musical accompaniment, she informed the audience that 'poor Du Hong' could not see a thing from the moment she was born, that 'poor Du Hong' had to find the courage to go on living. That really upset Du Hong, who hated nothing more than hearing people say 'poor Du Hong' and that she couldn't see a thing. She stood there with a long face, but the woman had worked up an emotional whirlwind, and was ready to reap the reward of her own performance. She stopped to ask a leading question in a tender, emotional voice. 'Why did Du Hong play for us today?'

Yes, why? Du Hong herself wanted to hear the answer. The audience was stilled as the mistress of ceremonies provided an answer to her own question, bound to draw tears. 'Poor Du Hong played today to repay the love given to her by society, from every grannie and grandpa, from every uncle and aunt, from every older brother and sister, and from every kid brother and sister.' The violin music, which had served as background, now formed a duet with the woman's voice, echoing in the concert hall and in every corner of society. It was a heart-rending, sad tune, funereal even, boring into the most vulnerable spot in a listener's heart. Suddenly choking on her own words, the mistress of ceremonies seemed about to break down and sob.

It had never occurred to Du Hong to 'repay' anything. She had simply played a piano piece by Bach. She'd wanted to play it well, but hadn't. How did that count as repayment? Repayment to whom? When had she incurred a debt? And to all of society. Blood rushed to her face as she blurted out a few words. She knew she had said something, but that something amounted to nothing, since she did not have a microphone. The violin music reached a crescendo before coming to a sudden stop, coinciding with the end of the woman's narration. With an arm around Du Hong's shoulder, she haltingly, cautiously led her off the stage. Du Hong hated to be led anywhere; that was an extreme vanity on her part. She could walk unaided. Even though she couldn't see a thing, she was sure she could get backstage on her own. All of society was watching. She would have liked to push the mistress of ceremonies' arm away, but the power of her love was irrepressible, and the woman's arm stayed put. So Du Hong let herself be carefully helped down off the stage. Only then did she realise that she had been invited not for the music, but to highlight people's love, to repay a debt, one she could never pay back in full. So the rousing violin music helped to plead her case. People would cry, and their tears would cancel her debt. Be merciful, come, take pity on me. Du

Hong's hands began to shake. The mistress of ceremonies disgusted her, so did music. She raised her head and proudly thrust out her chin. So this is what music is all about. It's despicable.

Her music teacher welcomed her backstage with an embrace, one that incorporated both happiness and sorrow. Du Hong wondered where all that joy and sorrow had come from, and did not know how to respond to it. The girl felt the overheated breath from her teacher's nostrils.

And it looked as if Du Hong *had* been burned by her teacher's breath, for she never stepped into the piano room again. Her teacher went to her dorm to ask why. After sending her roommates out, Du Hong said, 'I am not going to play the piano ever again, Teacher. Please teach me the two-stringed er-hu.'

'Why the er-hu?' The teacher was baffled.

'It's the best instrument to take with me if I need to make a living singing on the streets.'

Her response came out of nowhere and was too barbed for a girl her age; but it was the truth. She was not a child any more and must think about her future. She could not spend the rest of her life mounting a stage to repay a debt, could she? Could it ever be repaid?

To hell with music! Music was a fucking whore! All she'd done was play a tune by Bach, and had ended up incurring a huge debt, one that she could never repay. The performance constituted a humiliation she would carry with her for the rest of her life.

Halting the proverbial horse at the edge of the cliff, she was steadfast in her refusal to continue piano lessons and all opportunities to perform. Finally she had a clear sense of what charity performance and acts of kindness really meant; in the end, they were merely occasions to drag the disabled out to touch the hearts of healthy people. People like to be touched emotionally, society needs to be touched emotionally. Be moved, shed some tears, that makes you feel good, but don't drag me into that, I'm just fine. Don't waste your time crying for me.

After much consideration, she chose tuina, though it wasn't much of a choice, since that was all she could do. With that decision, she stretched her hands out again, not to touch piano keys, but the bodies of her fellow students. Yet life seemed to play a cruel joke on her when it came to tuina. Playing the piano is hard, yet she mastered the skill with little effort. By contrast, tuina is so much easier and yet she had trouble learning it. Take the acupoints for instance: it took her a long time to memorise their locations, but even once she had, she could not locate them accurately on the body. And when she finally did find a point, her fingers couldn't 'nab' it. Playing the piano requires using the fingers gently or forcefully, quickly or slowly, a skill she applied to the bodies of her classmates during practice. They thought her style was so funny they began to mock her, saying 'do' when she pressed, followed by 're', and naturally ending with 'mi-fa-so-la-ti'. She'd pinch them, making them yelp, and everyone had a good laugh, but Du Hong was mired in remorse. After all that wasted valuable time, what was she going to do after graduation?

After a major detour, Du Hong came to Nanjing. Through the friend of a friend of a friend, she met Ji Tingting, who was working in far-off Nanjing. Ji was one of those extremely helpful types, with an expansive personality that said 'I'll take care of everything'. An uncommon trait among the blind, it had its origin in the eyesight edge she had over the others. With correction, her eyesight could reach level B-3. Though Du Hong was only the friend of a friend of a friend, Ji announced into her mobile phone, 'We're all friends, so come on over, Mei-zi, little sister. Nanjing's not bad.'

Ji began calling Du Hong 'Mei-zi' even before they met, so Du Hong had to follow Ji's logic and called her Tingting jie, big sister Tingting. Du Hong would have preferred not to. It sounded provincial, like something an itinerant entertainer might say, and she abhorred that. But people like that tend to be the no-nonsense type. And as soon as she arrived in Nanjing, Ji Tingting took her to see Sha Fuming.

'Boss Sha, here's another money tree for you.'

Sha Fuming said he wanted an interview, which was given. Tingting had been in this line of work long enough to know that it was a required procedure. So she led him into one of the treatment rooms and pushed him down onto the massage bed. Then she took Du Hong's hand and placed it on his neck. That left a very bad impression with Du Hong. Ji was clearly showing off her ability to see things. One touch of Du Hong's fingers was all Sha needed to know. This was not her calling.

As he lay on the bed, asking questions, Du Hong demonstrated her tuina skills. Where was she from? How old was she? All unimportant questions, which he asked in an unpleasant tone, sounding just like a boss. Du Hong answered all his questions. Eventually he got around to asking where she'd gone to school. She answered him. Rather than follow up in that line, he changed the subject to education while Du Hong worked on his neck. With his face resting in the cradle, he had to laugh to himself. This was no tuina; it was like scratching an itch. He heaved a deep sigh.

'Education these days really misleads the younger generation,' he said.

Du Hong wasn't part of the education that Sha was disparaging, but she was a smart girl and stopped what she was doing. After a brief pause, she removed her hands.

Sha said nothing to Tingting about Du Hong coming to work for him. At the door, he took out a fifty yuan note.

'I'll give you the day off,' he said to Tingting. 'Take her to stroll around the eastern suburbs. She's had a long trip, and it is, after all, Nanjing.' His meaning was crystal clear. But Tingting pushed the bill back into his hand and held it there. She was making a silent request. The corners of his mouth curled into a smile. 'You're forcing my hand,' he said. Then he leaned over and whispered to Tingting, 'She's worse than average bad at this.'

With a couple of pats on her shoulder, he walked off. He'd always looked out for Tingting, treating her a bit better than the others. But this was a matter of principle, and he had to stick to his guns. He didn't go back to the lounge, because he knew Du Hong was still there, and he wanted to make sure they didn't accidentally bump into each other. Better to avoid that.

As Ji stood in the doorway, she felt her heart plunge. She blinked rapidly, before taking out her mobile phone to call Zhao da-jie in a distant city. Zhao had asked her to help Du Hong, so now what was she going to say? 'Do your best to help the girl, no matter what it takes,' Zhao had said over the phone. It had sounded like a plea. But a plea at some point can turn into a demand. Tingting hesitated and thought things over before putting her phone away.

Then her phone rang. She was surprised to hear Du Hong's voice on the other end. 'You don't have to say anything, Tingting jie,' she said. 'It's all right.'

'Where are you?'

'In the bathroom.'

'Why don't you come out and talk to me?'

Du Hong paused before saying softly, 'I'd like to stay in the bathroom a while longer.'

At this point, Ji didn't know what to say. Finally she said, 'Did you know there's a Sun Yat-sen Mausoleum in Nanjing?'

Du Hong neither said she knew nor that she didn't. All she said was, 'It's all right, Tingting jie.'

Tingting felt a tightness in her chest. Du Hong's non-answer could mean only one thing – she was feeling lost. Tingting understood what the girl was going through. It was, after all, her first trip away from home. The most difficult task a blind person faces is that first trip away from home, especially if it's on her own. The worries, anxieties, intimidation and sense of low self-esteem all come together in exaggerated form, like a deep, dark and very scary hole. The fear is both real and unreal, right and wrong at the same time. But real or unreal, right or wrong, it depends on what they encounter. Their fear is boundless, as vast as the world they cannot see. What exactly is there to fear? They cannot say. Luck was not with Du Hong, who had started out by missing a step. She had missed a step, not tripped and fallen, which is substantially different. When you trip and fall, you are still on solid ground, even though it hurts. Missing a step is something else altogether, for you have no place to fall to; you just plunge down and down and down. The shock is much more terrifying than falling and breaking bones.

Clutching her phone tightly, Ji Tingting, who had been there herself, did not know what to say.

That night she let Du Hong squeeze into bed with her. It was such a tiny bed they had to lie on their sides, back to back at first. Feeling awkward, Ji turned to face Du Hong's back. She had nothing else to say to the girl, so she just rubbed her shoulder to try to bring her at least a bit of consolation.

Du Hong rolled over with the intent of draping her arm around Tingting's back. In the process, her arm brushed against Tingting's breast. Cupping her hand over it, she said innocently, 'Yours are so nice!'

It sounded odd, but it worked for the two women, who were trying to find something to say to each other.

'Yours are better,' Ji said as she touched Du Hong. 'Mine used to be nice, but not any more. They're growing farther and farther apart.'

'How can that be?' Du asked.

'Why not?'

Du Hong was wondering if the same thing might happen to her one day, when Ji whispered into her ear, 'Has anyone ever touched them?'

'Yes.'

Having found a worthwhile conversation topic, Ji quickly followed up with another question. 'Who?'

'A female sex maniac. A pervert.'

Ji puzzled over that for a while until she figured out what Du Hong was referring to. She reached over and savagely pinched one of Du Hong's nipples, hurting the girl so much she sucked in one breath of air after another. Tingting didn't know what her fingers could do.

After fooling around for a while, Du Hong, whose spirits were still low, shut her eyes and fell asleep. She snuggled into Ji's arms, her shoulders rising and falling.

The blind's sense of insecurity can be very intense. As to how intense, only they can answer that. Ji put her arm around the girl, only to realise that she wasn't sleepy any more. She thought back to her own first interview, in Beijing. It had lasted less than ten minutes before she'd been sent away. She could still recall the feeling of her body falling, down and down, with no end. But she was lucky. Zhao da-jie showed up and lent her a helping hand. Eternally grateful to Zhao, Tingting wanted to repay her. But how? There didn't seem to be any way to do that, other than to help someone else the way Zhao had helped her. You help me, I help someone else. Had she done that? No. And sleep was out of the question.

Ji felt enormous guilt. She'd failed in her attempt to help Du Hong. Now what would happen to the girl? Tingting could only put her arm around Du Hong. Her heart ached for her.

She had to make Du Hong stay for another day, no matter what. If they didn't go to the eastern suburbs, the girl could use a day of rest. Maybe they could stroll around the Confucius Temple and enjoy some snacks. She'd buy her a little gift. In any case, she had to show the girl that Nanjing wasn't a place of failure for her. She must know that there is someone in Nanjing who cares about her; she's just had lousy luck. With this thought, Ji was almost afraid to fall asleep. At least she mustn't sleep so deeply that Du Hong could sneak out with her luggage early the next morning.

Tingting did not fall asleep till late that night, and was fast asleep when morning came. What had worried her that night didn't happen.

When they woke up, Du Hong told her she didn't want to visit the Sun Yat-sen Mausoleum or the Confucius Temple. She was adamant. Instead, she wanted to go with Tingting to the tuina centre, giving Ji the impression that Du Hong didn't want her to lose out on a day's work and cost her money. When they got there, she realised how wrong she was; she had underestimated her little sister.

Having changed into a red blouse, Du Hong followed Ji into the Sha Zongqi tuina centre, where, in front of everyone, she called out to Sha Fuming.

'Boss Sha, I know my skills are not up to your standard, but can you give me a month? I'll even clean the toilets and work as an assistant. All I ask is three meals a day. I'll sleep with Tingting jie. If after a month I'm still no good, I vow in front of everyone here that I will leave on my own. I'll send you money for my meals within a year. I just want Boss Sha to give me a chance.'

She must have rehearsed this beforehand. In a timid tone, she sounded breathless, pausing often. The whole thing seemed memorised, though she could not have predicted that her action would stun everyone who heard her. While seemingly terror-stricken, she managed to show that she was a girl with backbone.

This was the last thing Sha Fuming expected. If Du Hong had been sighted, this would have been a very ordinary speech. But she wasn't, and it was anything but ordinary. The blind have an astonishing sense of pride. In the face of rejection what matters to them is the preservation of their dignity. They display their flair in the manner of: 'If I'm not wanted here, I'll go where I am.' But not Du Hong, and Sha Fuming was flabbergasted. Under similar circumstances, he asked himself, would he have done the same? The answer was no, he wouldn't have. But she had, and rather than finding that inappropriate, he was impressed by her courage. It seemed to him that the greatest obstacle for a blind person is not eyesight, but courage, as well as the frailty caused by excessive pride. Sha experienced a moment of great clarity. Why should the blind need more dignity than the sighted? We force so many things upon ourselves. There is only human dignity, never dignity belonging only to the blind.

'No problem,' he said, still dazed.

Sha was a natural boss, with the corresponding affliction of the need to teach. So he started teaching Du Hong, giving it his all. Du Hong, on her part, was a hard-working student. Say what you will, tuina is easier than playing the piano; there is no profound learning to be gained, nor does it require great intelligence. The problem with Du Hong was simply a lack of understanding. So Fuming told her it was no big deal if she couldn't find the acupoints right away. She just had to be sharp, and pay attention to a client's reaction. Take the *tianzong* point, for instance – it produces pain when pressed. He demonstrated by pressing down on her *tianzong* point with his thumb, drawing a yelp of pain from her.

'See what I mean? You felt that, didn't you? Your clients will do the same; they'll make a noise or move their legs. What do their reactions mean? They mean you found the point. You must pay special attention to these kinds of things.

'Don't worry about hurting your clients. What's there to worry about? You must look at it from their perspective. This is how they would be thinking: they pay you for tuina and it would be a waste of their money if it didn't hurt at all. People are all the same; they're greedy, but that shows up differently on different people. To some clients, it's real tuina only when it hurts; if it doesn't, then it's massage, the other kind. So go ahead, don't be afraid to hurt them, that's what makes them happy. If a client tells you to be a little less rough, do as he says, because then he won't have any doubts about your skill.'

As she listened, Du Hong realised that language has its acupoints also and Sha was no ordinary boss. He could always locate the acupoints of language, effortlessly clarifying things for his listeners. She soon sensed that the cause of her sub-par skills had been her attitude.

Overly concerned about others, too cautious and too hesitant, she'd been afraid to push down hard. How could she have treated a client's body as a piano? A human body could never be anything like a piano. She needed to press down hard when it was called for; it could not cause damage. Hard, that's what was needed, especially by a new therapist. It was a sign of being responsible and hard-working. If a client cried out in pain, Du Hong would say, 'That hurts a little, doesn't it? You must have been overtiring yourself lately.' How nice that would sound! She'd come across as personally warm and professionally competent and authoritative. She'd be guaranteed return clients. The simple fact is, a tuina centre is just that, a tuina centre, not a hospital; people come to relax, not to be cured. If someone is really sick, why come to a tuina centre? Go straight to a hospital.

Sha Fuming had decided he'd teach Du Hong for a while. After that it was up to her. All he wanted was a clear conscience. If she was good, she stayed; if not, he knew she wouldn't stick around for free food. Absolutely not. But then something unexpected happened. Sha returned from a bathroom visit and found that the girl was with a client.

He called Gao Wei to the side. 'Who told you to assign her a client?'

'A client asked for her.' Gao Wei was stung by the criticism. 'I couldn't say no, could I?'

Fuming didn't say a word, but deep down he was beginning to rue his momentary kindness. Sooner or later, Du Hong's lack of skill would ruin his business. The Sha Zongqi tuina centre had only just started to do well, and he could not turn things around if they gained a bad reputation for substandard work.

What was incredulous was not that Du Hong had a client, but that her business grew right under Sha's eyes, all from client requests, some who gradually became return clients. He couldn't stop her from taking clients, who then came back for more. As a boss, it would have been unthinkable to show, from a theoretical point of view, that one of his employees was not a competent therapist. Still, he was worried, so he made a few furtive observations: Du Hong wasn't just popular, she also got along with the clients extremely well. What was going on here?

The answer to her popularity was soon revealed, almost knocking the wind out of Sha Fuming; she turned out to be a real beauty, stunningly beautiful. Sha had a fairly good sense of what his employees looked like, for he heard the clients talk about their appearance all the time. With nothing else to do, the clients gossiped, and sometimes they said something nice about the therapists' looks, their figures or their faces. They used clichéd expressions, such as this therapist (a woman) was pretty or that therapist (a man) was handsome. Sha himself had been called handsome a few times, but it was just idle talk that no one paid attention to. Besides, he couldn't see, so what was the point of paying attention, even if the clients were telling the truth about a particular therapist's good looks? He didn't care who was pretty and who wasn't; all he cared about was the business. Everyone was pretty when the clients were happy.

One day a group of special clients came in; a production team of seven or eight crowded into the hallway, led by a man in his fifties. Addressed by everyone as 'Director', he spoke with a hoarse voice in a perfect Beijing accent. Sha Fuming knew what a film director was. The group was only passing through the city, but he decided to offer them top service. After ascertaining the headcount, he sent them his best therapists, except himself, naturally, though he did include the other owner, Zhang Zongqi. The centre was not spacious to begin with, and now it seemed to overflow, with eight clients crowded in at once. All of a sudden, the Sha Zongqi tuina centre exuded a bustling air, pleasing Sha endlessly. After pairing up therapists with clients, he came into the lounge, rubbed his hands and said, 'TV dramas. He directed *The Great Tang Dynasty* series. You must have heard of it.'

Du Hong had not only heard of the show but had *seen* a portion of it. The music was just all right, she thought, but the theme song,

'The Moon is Brighter than the Sun', wasn't bad. Sitting to the left of a table facing Sha, she kept a smile on her face as she laid her hands on her thighs. She didn't sit like the others, she sat with style. As a former pianist, she always sat with her torso straight, showing off the curve of the small of her back and highlighting her breasts. A ninety-degree angle was formed between her upper body and her thighs, and between her thighs and her calves. Her shoulders were relaxed, evenly spread out, while her knees were gathered together for her hands, one over the other, to rest serenely on her thighs. It was clearly a posture for a piano performance, as she seemed to be preparing herself for what was to come; or perhaps it was a posture after a lovely piece had been played. So there she was, sitting properly to the left of the table, smiling, though in fact she was stewing in anger. She was mad at Boss Sha and mad at herself. Why hadn't he paired her up with one of the clients? Was she really that much worse than the others? That little bit of income wasn't what bothered her; what she cared about was face. Yet she habitually smiled when she was upset, not for the sake of others, but for herself, stemming from a deep-seated demand upon herself to appear elegant and graceful even when she was displeased.

She smiled for about an hour, which meant she was angry for just as long. An hour later, the film director walked out with his entourage; seemingly in high spirits, he wanted to take a look at the centre. He said he'd like to check it out as a possible location for his next show. Sha took them to the lounge, opened the door and said, 'The director is here to see you. Let's welcome him.' The therapists all stood; some even applauded, creating a warm atmosphere even if the applause was a bit anaemic. It felt somewhat awkward, mainly because the therapists were excited; these were, after all, members of a TV production team.

Du Hong continued to smile, nodding but not getting up. The director spotted her right away, a pianist who had just completed a performance. He stopped in his tracks, silent, before softly calling over a woman from his group. Sha heard the muted exclamation from the woman and knew it was a sigh of admiration. But he naturally did not know the true meaning of that sigh; in the woman's eyes, Du Hong was no longer a pianist, but an empress during a coronation. Personable, elegant, gorgeous, motionless, awe-inspiring and regal.

Oblivious, Sha asked politely, 'Would the director like some water?'

Ignoring his question, the director whispered to the woman, 'She's so beautiful.'

'My God!' the woman responded. 'Truly beautiful,' she added with authority, leaving no room for doubt, like presenting the results of scientific research.

Sha Fuming did not know what was going on. He heard the director walk over and ask in a low voice, 'What's your name?'

'Du Hong.' He heard her answer after a seemingly eternal silence.

'Can you see?' the director asked.

'No.'

The director sighed, expressing boundless regret and profound sadness.

'Take down her mobile number, Little Six.'

'Sorry, I don't have a mobile phone,' Du Hong said in an even tone, neither servile nor haughty.

Sha Fuming heard the director pat Du Hong on the shoulder and walk out.

'What a shame,' he was heard to say just past the door. 'Really, truly beautiful.' This was followed by another long sigh from the woman. She sounded sincere and serious, her sigh coming from the bottom of her heart and filled with deep feeling.

The large group swept out of the centre, plunging it back into silence, although it was a different silence than before, borderline anxiety. It had suddenly dawned on all the blind therapists that they now possessed an unnerving secret; there was a shockingly beautiful girl in their midst, pretty as a fairy descended from heaven. It was not a playful comment from an ordinary client; it had come from the director of *The Great Tang Dynasty*, a comment recited with sincerity and thoughtfulness in Putonghua, standard Mandarin, by the director of *The Great Tang Dynasty*; it sounded like a stage line, and had been substantiated by a woman.

That night, the female therapists sent text messages to friends in distant cities, using high-strung phrases, as if stunned. 'Can you believe it? There's a girl here called Du Hong. You have no idea how pretty she is.'

Not a hint of jealousy. How could there be, since it was a TV director who had spotted her? They could not put Du Hong's beauty into words, but so what? They could rely on exaggeration, and if that wasn't enough, there was sentimentality. To them, beauty could be expressed only in astonished tones. This was not mere speech, it was a chant, it was singing.

It was a solemn night for Sha also, who lay in bed, his mind filled with unformed images of Du Hong. A question surfaced and intensified in his mind, a very serious question: exactly what is beauty?

He could feel his mind growing unhinged as he was mired in profound anxiety.

CHAPTER FIVE
XIAO KONG

SEXUAL DESIRE IS a thoroughfare that leads in all directions; on the surface, it looks like a single thread, but deep down it has endless complexities, like the twisted branches of a tree. From the day they came back to work, Xiao Kong felt consumed by sexual desire, and so did Wang Daifu. When desire reaches a certain level, new branches sprout, new leaves appear. Kong and Wang had a fight. People in love have eager lips best suited for kissing; but if that is denied them, quarrelling is the next best thing. That is a basic pattern for people in love.

Did they really have an argument? Not really, and yet it was worse; it was a cold war, unspoken displeasure with one another. But they knew they were having a fight.

Kong came to Wang's dorm late every night, which made him happy. But when it began happening too often over a period of time, he could tell that she was there to see Xiao Ma, not him. That was fine with him, for he thought of himself as open-minded. Yet little by little it began to bother him, for she wasn't there simply to see Ma but to flirt with him. To his credit, Ma was passive, sitting motionless. But just look at Xiao Kong, the way she's throwing herself at him. Wang could not see his own expression, but he knew he wore a long face, on which his lips moved ceaselessly against his front teeth.

With his mouth opening and closing constantly, he felt wretched, and unspeakably sad.

Kong wasn't at all flirtatious; she was actually feeling somewhat glum, a despondence caused by too much pent-up energy and suppressed excitability, which was most noticeable at work. After work, when she came to the men's dorm, that despondence was transformed into exuberance. Boundless energy. Her enthusiasm was clearly directed at Wang, but it took a curious detour by manifesting itself on Ma. This is a common trait among young women in love, who often point to one direction while heading in another. But Wang knew nothing of that. He just felt that his girlfriend was engaged in inappropriate behaviour, acting coquettish around another man. It was a loss of face for him.

All was going well when suddenly Kong and Ma had a fight. It was not Ma's fault; Xiao Kong hit him first. For what? Still for the term of address, Sao-zi, a problem from early in their history. On this night, Kong was more than usually headstrong, snatching Ma's pillow and threatening to hit him if he called her that again. Unaware that weak, seemingly ineffectual people like Ma can be uncommonly stubborn, she held his pillow with both hands and thumped him on the head. It was just a pillow, she knew, it couldn't hurt him.

Her action created an unintended consequence. Instead of being upset, Ma was secretly pleased. Never one to talk back, on this night he did. 'You *are* my Sao-zi.'

That added fuel to the fire. She turned the pillow into a storm that rained down on him; the more she hit him the better she felt, venting suppressed emotions. So she laughed as she hit him; her laughter grew louder, showing signs of reckless delight.

She was happy, but Wang Daifu was not. His face fell and his lips moved, but he said nothing as he quietly climbed up to his bunk. Xiao Kong was too high-spirited to notice. Holding the pillow over her head, she continued to hit Ma until she wore herself out. Panting hard, she turned to find Wang Daifu, but he wasn't there.

'Hey.' She was baffled. 'Where are you?'

He was already in bed.

'I said, where are you?'

'I'm going to sleep,' he mumbled from the bunk, his mouth partially muffled by the pillow as he lay on his side.

The key to lovers' communication is not the language but the tone; it is what is implied in the voice. Xiao Kong's heart skipped a beat as she sensed that he was upset. A sudden quiet descended in the room, one that put a scowl on Xiao Kong's face, the sort of look that accompanies an embarrassing situation. Now she was unhappy that he was unhappy. *Why are you unhappy? Do you have any idea what I'm feeling? What do you have to be unhappy about?* Her shoulders sagged as she threw down the pillow, a dispirited expression frozen on her face.

She turned to Ma and said politely, 'It's late, Xiao Ma. I'm going to bed. I'll see you tomorrow.'

This marked Wang Daifu's first ever sleepless night. After Xiao Kong left, he tossed and turned, making it impossible for Xiao Ma to sleep, who also tossed and turned. They could sense each other tossing and turning. Wang realised that Xiao Kong was not yet his wife, only his girlfriend. He was wrong to assume that she belonged to him just because they'd had a two-week 'honeymoon'. That realisation made him aware of how serious the situation was. He sat up to phone her, but was startled when he heard the phone ring next door as soon as he dialled. I can't call her now. It would be like a live broadcast. With no time to think, he hung up. Afraid she might call back, he turned off his phone. The thought had never occurred to him that distance could become such a hurdle between people in love – too far was a problem; too close was another problem.

It turned out that there had been no need to turn off his phone, because Kong ignored him, and not just that night but the next day as well. He had gone too far the night before, embarrassing her in front of all those people and making her look like a fickle woman, one who blew hot and cold. She could no longer indulge him. She got up and left whenever she heard his footsteps. *The centre has lots of beds, you can go 'sleep' on any one of them.*

None of this went unnoticed by Wang Daifu, but he did not dare go after her. It was their first argument, and he had no idea how she would react if he braced himself and went to her. A proud man, he could not lose face at the tuina centre. That he refused to do.

Time passed slowly, and Wang Daifu was at a loss. Nightfall finally arrived, and he waited in vain for her to show. He was miserable, but that only further stopped him from going to her dorm. Unable to sleep, he tossed and turned again that night. Ma could not sleep either, but he couldn't allow himself to toss and turn, since he didn't want Wang Daifu to know he couldn't sleep. Forcing himself to lie in the same position and pretend he was sound asleep made for a terrible night.

On the third day, Wang realised that the situation had grown more complicated and more troublesome. *She hasn't fallen for Ma, has she? Hard to say.* By this time, he knew how painful it must be for her. This was the sort of pain she had experienced during the first stirrings of love, and she had grown listless. The same lethargy had reappeared; he could sense it in her voice. Her pain made his pain worse than ever, but he simply could not find a way to untangle the mess. The centre was busier than usual that day, and by the time he'd served a long line of clients, Wang Daifu was exhausted. He blamed himself for what had happened, and he was worried. He could not have known that this is what love is all about. By that afternoon, he could barely hold out. He'd been driven to distraction. He had to phone her, he just knew he had to. Just how he'd do that he wasn't sure. Finally, finishing up with a client, he went into the bathroom, locked the door and called her number.

She picked up at once, but there was no warmth in her voice. 'Hello, who's this?'

He was at a loss for words. Where to begin?

'Who's this?' she repeated.

'I miss you,' he blurted out.

She was with a client and was similarly feeling out of sorts, as distracted as he. When his sudden declaration of 'I miss you' sounded in her ear, she was flooded with a myriad of emotions, relief and gratification, as well as a sense of 'salvation'. A burden was lifted; she couldn't have admitted defeat to Wang, but she had been worried – could this mark the end of their relationship? It was the third day of their cold war. It had gone on too long, much too long, and Xiao Kong was exhausted. All she wanted to do was have a good cry in his arms. Was there any greater happiness than having your lover admit defeat?

But she was still at work; her hands had to remain on the client as she spoke on the phone, which was tucked between her ear and her shoulder. Besides, this was no time for lovers' talk; not only was the client still there, but her co-workers were nearby. She must behave herself.

Opting for a polite response, as if speaking to a friend calling long-distance, she said, 'I know. I'm with a client. We'll talk later.' She clicked off, brimming with happiness.

Gripping the phone tightly, Wang heard click and felt a chill rise up inside. He could tell that he'd been dismissed; only a total idiot could not have told that from her tone of voice. Feeling lost and dazed for a long while, he finally was reminded that he was still in the bathroom. He had to get out, he told himself, leave the bathroom. He reached out to pull the door open but the damned thing was stuck, so enraging him that he tried to force it open, until he recalled that he'd bolted it when he came in.

Xiao Kong rushed into the lounge as soon as she was done with her client, but Wang had already left for one of his. A clever girl, she'd heard water dripping during the brief phone call and knew that Wang had called her from the bathroom. If he could do that, why couldn't she? So she went in, smiled as she took out her phone, and played with it for a moment before punching in the number with her thumbs. The phone rang and she returned the confession to the man she loved, adding 'too' to his three words. 'I miss you too.' What a clever addition, implying that things were back to normal and that their lovers' secret remained intact. Even if more time had separated them, it wouldn't matter, since it took only a moment to bring them back together. How wonderful it is to be in love.

Half an hour had passed since he'd said 'I miss you', a period of great internal conflict, characterised by deep sadness. He was prepared to expect the worst. Then came the words 'I miss you too'. He felt like crying, but, of course, Wang Daifu could not do that. He was with a client and surrounded by co-workers. 'I know. Same here. We'll talk later,' he said politely, hating himself for that impassive tone. But hate it or not, he knew that life is fashioned by misunderstandings and that only personal experience can bring true understanding of many things. He'd learned an important lesson; he must remember to put himself in her shoes next time.

They were finally back in the lounge together. Surrounded by people, they had to watch what they did, so they sat quietly, shoulder to shoulder, on an unused massage bed, their silence different from that of a while before; this silence contained the tenderness of a resurrection, something they could treasure for the rest of their lives. He rested his hand on her leg and she grabbed his hand in hers. Everything was truly fine now; all his fingers were telling the spaces between her fingers 'I love you', and hers did the same. Xiao Kong turned to face him, as if this time they were truly falling in love.

Quietly, ten fingers gripped as tightly as they could, stroking back and forth. They had made love in the past, and this rubbing carried deep meaning, a reminder of other touching details. They so wanted to make love, the one thing that would let the other know the depth of their love. But where could they go? There was no way. They could only hold it in. And not just that, but they had to use their fingers to persuade one another of the need to do so. What sort of persuasion was that? Soundlessly, it actually intensified their desire, and as the persuasion persisted, their desire was virtually irrepressible. And what did that lead to? The need to hold it in even longer. Endurance is not mental activity; it is physical labour, it wears you down. In the end, drained of energy, she leaned weakly against his shoulder and opened her mouth. He could smell her breath, so hot it nearly broke his heart. He was panting softly, desperately hoping that the day he became a boss would arrive soon. He needed to be a boss, and quickly. Working for someone else was no way to get through life.

Xiao Kong never dreamed that an argument could lead to such contentment. But there was no denying that they'd had an argument, and it had been hurtful. Arguments were to be avoided. She thought back to the cause of their argument and had to admit to herself that it had resulted from her inappropriate behaviour. Clearly, she was in need of self-reflection. Whatever else might be said, flirting and carrying on with another man in front of her boyfriend was out of line. She told herself she must stop going to the men's dorm. She hadn't intended any of this, but Wang had misinterpreted her actions, and it had turned out badly.

Now that she would no longer visit the men's dorm, all that was left to them were his visits to the women's dorm. He quickly learned that there are visits and there are *visits*. Wang was a serious-minded man, someone women seldom joked with. And with people around, the two of them avoided whispered conversation, making his visits so bland they could not be mentioned in the same breath as hers. They just sat together, almost ceremoniously. Miserable. Ornamental.

Wang Daifu began paying closer attention to Xiao Kong. She was forever in the grip of anxieties. Though he couldn't see her face, he could tell from her voice that she had changed. Truth was, she'd been in low spirits starting when they went back to work, but he'd failed to notice. What had she been like in Shenzhen? She'd spoken in a bright, loud voice, saying whatever popped into her head, even cursing once in a while. She'd seemed happy. She had always given people the impression that she was happy, and an open book.

He knew why she was unhappy. It was because he had yet to make her the boss's wife. It was reasonable to say she'd been 'tricked' into coming to Nanjing with him. He may not have intended to, but it is what he'd done. The idea weighed heavily on him.

He listened to the radio on his bunk when he felt miserable, a popular diversion among the blind, who enjoy variety shows and sports. Wang had always taken pleasure in listening to them, but no more. All he cared about now was the stock market. With this secret in mind, he bought a pair of earphones so others wouldn't know what he was listening to. With one in each ear, he could listen to stock market news, but the market was like a corpse, cold, with no sign of life.

In addition to stocks, the radio also brought him news of the Nanjing real estate market, which, for him, was a double whammy of misfortune. His money was tied up in stocks when the market crashed, but before he had time to feel sorry for himself, the real estate market in Nanjing began to heat up. How did he keep running into madness? The real estate market wasn't mad in the ordinary sense; it was violently mad, like a rabid dog breaking free of its chain and launching itself towards his face. In retrospect, he really had walked into a trap by returning to Nanjing. Real estate prices determined the rent for a street-front space; given his current financial situation, it would be nearly impossible to open a tuina centre even if he were able to recoup his money from stocks. If he hadn't decided to play the market, at worst he could have bought a two-bedroom house. But no, and see what happened? First the stock market went crazy, followed by the housing market, and his money would soon amount to nothing. Those who live by the sweat of their brow are doomed to a lifetime of poverty, he was sure of that now. No matter how much you earn through hard work, even if you spit blood from exhaustion, you face the danger of dire poverty overnight. He began to fret about his future, sensing he wouldn't even have a plot in which to bury his remains.

When would Xiao Kong ever become the boss's wife?

But he was wrong. She was worry-laden but not because of that. She hadn't told her parents that she'd come to Nanjing, nor about her and Wang Daifu. They would never have consented to the relationship, especially her father.

When it came to boyfriends, her parents had only one simple wish, an order, to be more accurate – they were not demanding on anything other than *sight*. No matter what, he must be able to see, at least a little; they would never accept someone who was totally blind. The night before she left for Shenzhen, they'd had a frank talk with her: in general, they said, 'We won't interfere with your relationships or your marriage, but you must remember that you have to lead your life, not grope your way through it. You are totally blind, and we will never permit you to marry someone who has to grope his way through life.'

In fact, Xiao Kong had tried to find someone who could lead a life with her, but regrettably she had nothing to show for that but tears. She learned something in her failed attempts – no matter how smart someone is, or how rational, they turn blind once they become the parents of a blind child, forever leading a life of wishful thinking. Of course, she would have liked to find someone to lead a life with her, but it was hard. The parents of a blind child are forever just that, the parents of a blind child. They are irrationally obstinate, and for a very simple reason: they have invested an extraordinary amount of effort into their child, for whom they have experienced extraordinary concern, on whom they have pinned extraordinary hope, and in whom they have bestowed extraordinary love. Hence, the demands they place upon their child are themselves extraordinary. Their intention was not to interfere in their child's marriage prospects, but they must, because they are worried.

Wang Daifu was totally blind. When they first came together, Xiao Kong made up her mind not to tell her parents. She'd try it out and see what happened – as luck would have it, she'd met someone just like her, and had fallen in love with him pretty quickly, though she'd always been guarded where feelings were concerned. But for a girl in love for the first time, what good is being guarded? Love is like a tiny ant, which can bring down an immense dike with an ant hole. Xiao Kong had made a tiny hole in the dike of her feelings, and when she tried to patch up the hole, it was too late. And so she cried; after crying, she decided to choose love. The way she figured it, when something had reached the point of no return, what people commonly refer to as 'the rice has been cooked', she could always come up with a solution. She just had to be uncommonly patient. But then patience is essential to a blind person. It is the crux of their being, the only asset they have to compensate for their sightless eyes. In other words, the blind must learn to wait; no matter what happens, they must never rush into action, or they can suffer terribly, they can fall and lose teeth.

She could wait, but love could not. To her surprise, their love had rushed along at such a dizzying speed that she had quickly followed him to Nanjing. At the mention of Nanjing, she had felt her heart swell almost like a surging ocean wave. Wang had said he wanted to go with her to Nanjing for the New Year's holiday. The subtext could not have been clearer. No longer a child, she knew what he had in mind, yet did not respond; she'd wanted to but couldn't. Being self-conscious, she knew that her voice would quiver so much that she'd appear undignified. The lack of a response frightened him into shrinking back. It was more than nerves that stopped her; this would be, after all, the most significant step in her life, and once she took it she could not possibly turn back. That would mean the unavoidable betrayal of her parents. The implications of such a betrayal could not be understood by sighted people. She began crying again; that was all she could do. But there was irresistible magic in the phrase 'go with him to Nanjing', an enticing call with beguiling allure. Like threads, the words bound her, encircled her, tied her up, and eventually she was sewn up. She knew she was spinning silk, wrapping herself into a self-enclosing cocoon that would deny her even the ability to struggle. She was infatuated.

But not really. She took action, shocking action that would have stunned anyone who knew her. First she went to a beauty shop to have her hair done, then she went on a shopping spree, starting with the purchase of a pair of heels. High heels are a taboo for the blind, but she was willing to spend the money even if she wore them only once, only for a day, even for two hours. She then bought a set of Triumph lingerie that was breathtakingly thin and lacy. Mustering her strength, actually more like courage, she splurged on a bottle of Chanel No. 5. Why buy that perfume? Well, it involved two young women, one of whom was Xiao Kong's VIP client, who chatted away as they enjoyed their time on the tuina beds, talk that sounded more like dreams; dreams of a decadent, unfeasible life. Their talk took them to a luxuriously appointed, spacious seaside house with a view, and a luscious man who was an unstoppable machine in bed. The topic led Kong's client to repeat Marilyn Monroe's famous response to what she wore in bed: 'Why, Chanel No. 5, of course.' Her friend laughed and said she was being slutty. Xiao Kong did not understand the reference at first, but she was, after all, a woman, and quickly grasped the meaning. She felt a sudden fright, overwhelmed by the intoxicating fantasy of sleeping only in Chanel No. 5.

She shocked herself once everything was ready. Isn't this the same as marrying myself off? Yes, Xiao Kong was going to secretly marry herself off. The year had neared its end once she was all set, but there was nothing from him. He did not bring up Nanjing again, having lost his nerve after the setback. In the end, she called him. 'The year's almost over. Are you still going back to Nanjing?'

'Yes, uh-huh,' he hummed and hawed.

'What does 'yes, uh-huh' mean?' she asked, trying to be patient. What was the blockhead thinking?

'Yes, uh-huh,' he said a second time.

Finally losing her temper, she yelled in frustration, 'Well, think about it and call me when you've made up your mind!' She hung up.

With the tone of finality in her demand, he scratched his head anxiously; when he'd finished scratching his head and found the right words, he lacked the courage to say them. He called back after two minutes to tell her that he just wanted to be with her. It was empty talk, evasive, but he was pleased with himself for being clever. He raised his eyebrows up and down, feeling smug over his own glibness. What a dope, so simple it was endearing. Wasn't this precisely what had attracted Xiao Kong to him?

'Will you be nice to me?' she asked softly, not so insistently, just like a bride. He did not know the height of this 'mountain' called woman, or the depth of this woman called 'water', but at least her question gave him hope. It turned him serious and stopped him from trying to be glib. When he opened his mouth this time, he was perfectly serious.

'Let me walk out and get hit by a bus if I'm not nice,' he proclaimed loudly.

She felt like a newlywed, who needed the vow but not the taboo curse. 'Don't say unlucky things, you dumb fuck! I'm not going to talk to you ever again.'

And that was how she came to Nanjing, after lying to her parents about going to Hong Kong. It was the first time she'd lied to them and she was beset with guilt, but how could she not lie about this? She could not believe how brave she was, like a fiend with no regard for anything but sex. It frightened her to think about it. On the other hand, her parents would never have believed it if someone had told them what was happening, for their daughter had always been prudent and trustworthy as far as *that* was concerned. Yet, their prudent, trustworthy girl had actually gone and done it.

She was bold, she was willing, and she was ready. Given the choice, she would do it again. When it comes to love, parents are there to be deceived. In her eyes, there was only him, the 'bridegroom'. She loved his neck, his chest and his wilful arms. He was as warm as an oven, emitting endless heat. She wanted his body, and his weight. His arms gave her a sense of security; with those arms around her she felt as if she were in a locked box. But that wasn't all. The most important thing was that he loved her. She knew he did; she knew that with absolute certainty. He would never permit danger to touch her, would use his body to block out everything, be it a knife, fire, a nail, broken glass, a utility pole, the corner of a building, a speeding motor scooter, reckless skates, or piping hot *three-delicacies* soup. But in fact she could handle all these things herself and didn't need his protection, though he would happily give it. Love was terrific, better than having eyes all over your body.

What she liked most about him was his personality; he was solid, hard-working and well respected wherever he went. Of course that 'little brother' of his was naughty and insatiable, day and night. She wanted it too, but really preferred what came after. She put on her Chanel No. 5. That was all she wore. They were quiet, her in his arms, touching each other. Nothing mattered to them now, not wind, not rain, not snow, not ice, not even circling tigers and wolves. They were comfortable and warm, and she didn't want to sleep, instead feigning sleep at moments like this. He kissed her and called her darling, softly, thinking she was asleep. How could she spend such relaxed, fulfilling moments asleep? She tried to hold out, giving up only when she could no longer stay awake, falling asleep in his arms after letting out a deep sigh, her shoulders loosening.

She insisted on resting her hand on his chest even when they were asleep; always uneasy, she touched him all over. Sometimes she unintentionally touched his 'little brother', which seemed to be alert at all times, and began to grow at the touch of her fingers. That woke her up and him too, and he would want her then. It might be the middle of the night, and she would be too tired for that, but she'd bought into the notion that she belonged to him and had to give him what he wanted when he wanted it. Little brother was bad, really bad, not well behaved like the older one.

Xiao Kong was contented. But even at the happiest moments, she never let down her guard with her mobile phone, the one from Shenzhen. She'd already got another phone in Nanjing but relied on the one from Shenzhen, with its different number, to help her lie. The lies dampened her happiness, giving it an unclean feel. Whenever she recalled her parents' exhaustive and excessive efforts, she felt that she, not them, was the target of her lies. Lying is like a forced march; you put one foot after another, left, then right, then left again. Yet lies are unreliable and cannot be repeated, for rather than growing in strength, they gradually lose their power, until they are completely exposed.

Her mother grew suspicious during the cold war between her and Wang Daifu.

'Where are you anyway?'

'In Shenzhen, of course.'

'No, you're not,' her mother insisted.

'Where could I be if not Shenzhen?' Xiao Kong had to sound even firmer in her assertion.

Shenzhen or Nanjing, that was a big problem. She could not even say the word Nanjing, for that would give rise to an even more serious problem: Why did you go to Nanjing anyway?

Liars are given to blindly underestimating those they lie to. Her mother could already hear that she was not in Shenzhen, because of the reduced background noise on her mobile phone. Most importantly, her mother no longer heard the drawling Cantonese, which was a sure sign that her precious girl had left Shenzhen.

Her mother was worried, so was her father. What had happened in the girl's life? Where was she anyway?

Xiao Kong had set her Shenzhen phone to vibrate, and her heart skipped a beat each time she felt the vibration, for that meant it was time to lie again. Like a thief, she had to leave the tuina room to become entangled with her parents in an impossible dispute concerning her current location. With others and Wang Daifu present, she could not have found the nerve to say 'I'm in Shenzhen.' Lying was hard enough; doing it in front of others was worse.

She had to guard against something else as well: Wang Daifu could never know of her parents' objection, for that would hurt him deeply. So she had to lie to him as well.

CHAPTER SIX
JIN YAN AND XU TAILAI

XIAO KONG AND Wang Daifu weren't the only lovers in the tuina centre; there was another couple, Jin Yan and Xu Tailai, whose relationship differed from that of Kong and Wang's in how it began. Xiao Kong and Wang Daifu had come to the centre as a couple, while Jin Yan and Tailai became lovers after coming to work. Their styles too were different. Although Xiao Kong and Wang Daifu had been together longer, they were understated, reserved and restrained in their relationship, appearing much the same as ordinary friends. But not Jin Yan and Xu Tailai, who were unusually demonstrative, especially Jin Yan, who was so expressive all she lacked were a gong and a drum to announce her romance to the world.

A romantic relationship normally begins like this: a man has his eye on a woman and finds an appropriate moment to express his feelings in private. To be sure, some women make the first move, but it is usually more direct, not concealed, as with men, and that was exactly what happened, although Jin had a unique approach. A few days after she met him, she acted on her feelings, out in the open, resolute as a bomb-toting soldier. Before Tailai could react, she made it clear at the centre that he was hers, that she was going to have him, and that no one had better get in her way.

It was way over the top. Tailai was no rare treasure, not a man any woman would want to fight over. He could not have been more average, and most people would be hard pressed to find anything special about him. Start with his appearance, which could be summed up in three words: far from handsome. If you swung a club anywhere on the street, you could easily knock down eight or nine men just like him. The blind cannot see faces, but they live in close proximity to sighted people, and from their conversations gain a pretty good idea of what each other looks like. And in that regard, Jin Yan and Tailai were not a good match. Her relentless pursuit of him seemed irrational. Tailai had dumb luck; there was no logic behind the two of them pairing up, even though if you tried hard you might find a couple of reasons for it. Or perhaps there was something wrong with Jin Yan.

In fact, their complicated relationship went way back; it was like a well whose depth was unknown, even to Tailai himself.

Xu Tailai, originally from northern Jiangsu, found his first job in Shanghai. Where was Jin Yan from? She was from Dalian. One from the south, the other from the north, two people who could not possibly have known one another beforehand. Seriously, no matter how unpredictable life might be, they'd never have met.

Tailai had not been happy working in Shanghai, for he was ill-suited to making it on his own. Simply put, he had low self-esteem owing to insufficient talents, and he was not outgoing. Talking can provide a good example. Every blind person who joins the workforce these days has received a good education, the fundamental manifestation of which is the ability to speak Putonghua, standard Mandarin. Tailai's education did not suffer in quality, but the difference was immediately obvious the moment he opened his mouth. He had a thick northern Jiangsu accent. He could speak Putonghua if forced to, but he hunched his shoulders at the thought of speaking it, and goose pimples popped up on his neck. So he refused to speak it. Having an accent was no big deal – who didn't have one, at least a little? But for him, a man with low self-esteem, he was touchy about his accent and in turn became critical of his own speech.

Why? Because there was something peculiar, sort of funny, about the way he spoke. His northern Jiangsu accent had a noticeable trait – there was no distinction between 'h' and 'f', or, to be more precise, it transposed h and f. So 'fare' became 'hare', 'hat' became 'fat'. People parroted him, including the girl at the front desk, who sometimes had fun with his accent. 'Little Xu, you have a hare on bed number nine.'

The mockery angered Tailai; an accent is nothing but a man's identity. Being blind didn't bother him much, since all the therapists were blind; what mattered most was his rural background, an illness without a cure. No matter how hard he worked to better himself, how much he wanted to 'take fate by the throat', he'd still be a heavily accented man from the countryside. By imitating his speech, they might as well be pointing at him and calling him country bumpkin.

He was upset, all right, though he dared not antagonise the girl at the front desk, but she was the only one. With his blind co-workers he displayed a desire for revenge and would, if necessary, let his fists do the talking – not because he was brave, but because he was a coward. His cowardly nature forced him to put up with others' taunts, even when they became unbearable, until he could take it no longer and he fought back. He was oblivious to how unreasonable his behaviour was, that is, making a big deal out of something so trivial. Yet, what can a decent person do other than be unreasonable at times?

His fists took care of the problem, and no one would mock him again. He could finally hold his head high, but seen in retrospect, this victory was premature, for just about everyone began to ignore him. Even that is an understatement, for they virtually shunned him. A proud person, he pretended not to care. *So what if you ignore me? You think I want to be among you?* He began to shut himself in, putting on arrogant airs. But no matter how much he pretended not to care, he had to be frank with himself, for one thing was clear: he could be haughty if he wanted, but he'd have to bear the consequence of gloom alone, which is what he did. That went on day after day; gloom had its price, like interest that kept compounding, plunging him further and further into his glum state.

In his dejected state of mind, he took notice of Xiao Mei, a girl from the Shaanxi countryside, not because she had any special qualities, but because she never shied from speaking in her hometown dialect; she was comfortable and unabashed, showing no sign of wanting to use Putonghua. It quickly became clear to him how nice the Shaanxi dialect sounded. With so many level tones, it seemed flat and plain, but an emphasis was often placed somewhere in a phrase before falling to a final flat note that was then drawn out, like singing. Her accent was thicker than his, but Xiao Mei didn't care, was seemingly unaware of it. She talked in such a natural way that, after a while, a listener might even begin to see problems in Putonghua, and prefer that everyone talked like her, with a thick Shaanxi accent. By comparison, the northern Jiangsu accent was terrible, with too many glottal stops and falling tones on vowels for no particular reason. It was abrupt, heavy, stubborn even, as if disappearing into a void. He was ashamed of his own accent. What had he done to deserve that? He would not have minded his rural background if he'd been speaking the Shaanxi dialect.

Then something unexpected happened. One night Tailai and Xiao Mei showed up in the washroom at the same time. They were standing by the sink, where she was washing a pair of socks, when she asked him a mortal question. 'How come you never talk?' He blinked a couple of times but didn't answer her. She repeated the question, convinced that he hadn't heard it the first time. This time he answered, in an unfriendly tone.

'What do you mean?'

'Nothing. I just want to hear you talk.'

'What do you want to hear?'

'Nothing in particular. I just want to hear you talk.'

'What does that mean?'

'It has a nice sound.'

'What did you say?'

'Your hometown dialect has a really nice sound.'

That came as a shock, and it took him a while to figure out what she meant. Their rice smells better than yours, is what it was. His accent was his sore spot, the cause of his low self-esteem, but it turned into something good in her ear. He didn't believe her, but he had to. She sounded so truthful, not to mention envious and full of admiration.

Tailai's confidence grew in front of Xiao Mei. He began to talk. Self-assurance in speech is intriguing: when you feel confident speaking with a person, something other than confidence can begin to grow, turning it supple, capable of drawing people close to you. Their relationship matured; they talked to one another in their own accents. The more they talked, the more they had to say to one another, until finally they became an item.

The relationship lasted less than ten months. On a Sunday in September, her father called her from Shanghai, asking her to please come home right away to get married. He made it clear that the man had a mental disability. Her father was not an unreasonable man and dealt with her honestly; he didn't dare deceive his own daughter. He didn't dare force her; he talked it over with her, as a request. He told her all about the deal he'd made, concluding with a guarantee that once it was done, everyone in the family would benefit.

'Come home, my girl.'

She left without giving anything away beforehand. After booking a room in a nearby hotel, she called Tailai to sneak in to her room. When he woke up the next morning he learned of her departure from a letter she'd left him. Touching it with the tips of his fingers, he felt every vowel and every consonant as if it were her skin, or her pores. In the letter she told him everything, ending with, 'You must remember one thing, Brother Tailai. I'm yours and you are mine.' He lost count of how many times he read the letter, finally putting it in his lap to stroke it as he broke into song, softly for the first few lines, but then raising his voice and singing so loudly that hotel security escorted him out of the hotel and sent him back to the tuina centre, where he continued to sing for a day and a half, as if possessed. At first his co-workers felt sorry for him; later, to their sympathy was added surprise. Where had he learned all those songs? He'd begun with tunes from the late 1980s and on into the early twenty-first century, with a mixture of styles and singing methods. What really surprised them was that he had such a good voice and was a different person when he sang, unrestrained, capable of cries of bitter anguish. What most amazed them was that when he sang he was able to differentiate all the 'f's and 'h's and 'n's and 'l's as well as z, c and s in Putonghua, which he confused when he was talking. Lying on his bunk, he sang, refusing to eat or drink, no matter how his co-workers tried to talk him around:

I've never been cold
because you're by my side
You're always saying softly
I'm here on dark nights
You always silently bear with
me like this, without complaint
And now for some reason
you no longer look at me
Am I the one you love most?
Why aren't you saying anything?

Days and nights alternate without exchanging places
Unable to imagine what the other's world is like
We still insist on staying where we are and waiting
Turning each other into two worlds
You'll never understand my sorrows
Just as daytime doesn't understand the darkness of the night

Jiumei, Jiumei, pretty little sister
Jiumei, Jiumei, like a bright red flower bud
Jiumei, Jiumei, lovely little sister
Jiumei, Jiumei, the one in my heart

I gave you my true love
If I could be with you for one day
I wouldn't miss anything in this world
For even the ocean's edge and
heaven's end will change

I've never regretted it

Where are you at this moment

How can I get in touch with you
If my love receives no response

I want to tell you something
I've never said before
to be by your side again
what does the world have to do
with me?

In the wind is a cloud made of rain
The cloud is heartbroken
in the wind
I live on the hills of yellow earth
Be they from the northwest
or from the southeast
They are all songs from me
My songs

A cloud made of rain
Who knows where
the wind will send it?
Gusts of wind blow over the hills

I told you I waited for a long time
I want to take your hands
Your hands are trembling
Could you be telling me

I told you my last request
you will leave with me now
your tears are streaming down
you love me for having nothing
at all

You will leave with me now.

He sang until he lost his voice, until only a wheezing sound was audible. Just when everyone thought something terrible was about to happen, instead of taking his own life, he calmly got out of bed and, with no one urging him to eat, he ate, and with no one urging him to drink, he drank; once he'd eaten and drunk his fill, he went to work, as if nothing had happened.

Jin Yan was still in Dalian at the time. How far is that from Shanghai? At least two thousand kilometres, worlds apart. But, really, what are two thousand kilometres in the age of mobile phones? Nothing at all. A hometown friend relayed the news about Tailai to Jin Yan soon after it happened, but one mobile phone exchange after another had introduced changes. The story had been embellished repeatedly and expansively, running wild and surging, endowed with the temperament of each narrator and instilled with the explosive power of a love story. It was complete but splintered, violent yet dreary. Xu Tailai and Xiao Mei's story spread like a massive whirlwind in the closed-off space of the blind. After hearing it, Jin Yan shut her mobile phone and was touched by love before she even had a chance to wipe away her tears. With a metaphorical 'thud', she fell fast, instantly becoming a woman in love. The object of her affection was the male lead in the story she'd just heard, Xu Tailai.

A week later, she quit her job in Dalian and arrived in Shanghai on the frenzied wheels of a train. It was just a job, which meant little to Jin Yan; as a tuina therapist, her fingers were her ticket from one job to the next. But love was different; love occurred only at this moment. And, of course, it occurred at this place. If she failed to grasp it here and now, it was gone forever. Jin Yan was a pessimist, a blind woman whose pessimism was too deep to fathom. She had a clear sense of what her life entailed, and knew that she could not expect much from this world. Calmed by her pessimism, deep down she was carefree; she wanted little and could give up anything. All she really wanted was love, and as long as she did not go hungry, she would be content. When love came along, she would welcome it the way a rose opens its petals and spreads its scent. She was ready to spend the rest of her life preparing for love, for the chance to become a bride; she was betting everything on love, laying it all out there without a qualm.

But she was too late. A week before she arrived in Shanghai, Tailai left without saying goodbye. He disappeared like the heroes of legends who vanish predictably in the last line of the story. He vanished into a distant place, without a trace. She tried his mobile phone but received the expected recording: 'The number you dialled is no longer in service.' She was not upset. No longer in service may not have been the best news, but it wasn't the worst either. The recording signalled that the story she'd heard was true and that Xu Tailai was a real person. He wasn't here, so he must be out there, and his mobile phone was no longer in service. So what? His phone service had been disconnected, but her love was full steam ahead.

From the beginning, Jin Yan's romance existed in halves: half real and half illusory; half earthbound and half up in the sky; half known and half waiting to be known; half here and half there; half assured and half anticipated. A captivating mix. A tortuous reality. But being tortuous merely made it even more captivating, tinged with dream-like, distant qualities.

Where was he? She had no idea.

But then came the bad, all but fatal news. Her mobile phone told her that his phone was not just no longer in service, but that the number she dialled could not be completed.

Instead of sadness, Jin Yan thought she heard singing, all kinds of singing, like falling rain, like whirling snow, tunes from the late 1980s and on into the early twenty-first century, with a mixture of styles and singing methods. It surrounded her like a mist; her heart sang silently but with abandon.

How could he, Tailai, a man who had lost his beloved, a man destined to start a romance with Jin Yan in an imaginary place, know that he could be in love again? Xu Tailai was his name. Jin Yan's heart was expansive, open and vast. A broad sea has room for leaping fish, a high sky can hold soaring birds. But the world was filled with fish unrelated to her and birds with whom she had no connection. Tailai had been mercilessly swallowed up by the vast ocean and the spacious sky. Where was he? Where?

Jin Yan decided to stay in Shanghai, where she languished. It was like a dream. She stayed on at the tuina centre where he had once worked, sad but not despairing. This was, after all, the place where he had lived and worked. She was convinced that this was no blind adventure. She understood the world of the blind; it might appear big, but in practical terms, it is small, very small. And all blind people share a fatal trait – nostalgia. He had friends in Shanghai, and one of these days he'd phone. All she needed to do was wait, like the farmer waiting for another rabbit to run headlong into a stump. No one knew how her heart beat, no one but her. Other people's hearts beat like a rabbit's; hers beat like that of a tortoise. A tortoise would surely be able to wait under a tree for its rabbit to show up. She firmly believed that every heartbeat of a woman in love was precious; every one of those heartbeats brought her closer, a little closer, closer still to the one she loved. Unable to see, yet she had filled her eyes with images of his receding figure, one upon another, like a wild profusion of vegetation. Jin Yan was in love, and that love encompassed only one person. A one-person love is the most poignant love. A one-person love is true love. *I've come, my dear, I'm right here.*

She gave herself a timeline; she was willing to wait about a year. Time can pass fast if you have a goal. Waiting can be torture, but can also be infused with happiness. With the passing of every day and every hour, you are closer to your goal if you make the best of it. Every moment is precious as long as the goal draws nearer.

It turned out she didn't have to wait a year. Fate is unpredictable. After five months in Shanghai, she heard fate's alluring laughter. One evening after their night shift, some of the guys came over to the women's dorm, where they talked and cracked melon seeds, littering the floor with the shells. It was past one o'clock in the morning when the talk turned to Tailai, which plunged the room into momentary silence.

Then a 'rabbit' sitting by the door spoke up evenly. 'He's doing quite well. In Nanjing.'

A hush settled over the room.

'Who are you talking about?' Cocking her head, Jin Yan turned to the speaker. 'Who's doing well?'

'Ai!' the rabbit sighed. 'A funny fellow called Xu Tailai. You don't know him.'

Though she tried to maintain control, Jin Yan's voice quivered as she asked, 'Do you have his mobile number?'

'Sure,' said the rabbit. 'He called me around noon two days ago.'

'Why didn't you tell me?' Her question made little sense.

Putting a melon seed between his teeth, the rabbit spread his lips, but no sound emerged. Jin Yan's question puzzled him. 'But you don't know him.'

'I do.'

'How?'

'I owe him a debt.'

Nanjing. Ah, Nanjing. When she was still in Dalian, Nanjing had been such a faraway place, like a clue hidden within a riddle. Now, it was so much closer, right there next to Shanghai. She was suddenly apprehensive, experiencing a fear similar to the unsettling feeling a traveller gets when he is nearly home. But she had no time for her fears; her heart was like a bullet that, after being aimed at the target for five months, left the barrel when she pulled the imaginary trigger. At three twenty-seven the following afternoon, after a train ride that took more than two hours, plus a little under half an hour in a taxi, she was deposited at the Sha Zongqi tuina centre.

She pushed open the glass door and walked in gracefully. She asked for a tuina massage with Xu Tailai. The girl at the front desk told her that Xu Daifu had a client. How about someone else?

'I'll wait,' she told the girl calmly.

'I'll wait.' She had been waiting for Tailai so long, what difference would it make to wait a little longer? What had the waiting in the past been like? Fruitless, unrealistic and foolish, accompanied only by her one-person love. It had been a torment. But everything was different now. The wait in the past and the wait now were similarly real and actual, but she was in love with this wait. She wanted to focus on this wait and enjoy it.

'May I have a glass of water, please?'

When she looked back later, she could not believe her own calm composure. How could she have been so relaxed and unruffled? How had she done that? It was so unlike her. She was amazed by the evenness in her heart, like a pond of still water, which convinced her that there was a karmic connection between her and Tailai. After a divergent and complex cycle of rebirth, she and he met up once again. That was all.

He finally appeared before her eyes, fuzzy and blurry, just an outline, but she was sure it was a solid object, about five foot six inches tall. Jin Yan was different from other sightless people in that she was not completely blind; she could see but not clearly. Her eyesight had been ruined ten years earlier by maculopathy, a sinister disease that damaged the eyesight little by little, gradually reducing the field of vision till there was nothing left. Her remaining sight was restricted to the area directly before her eyes, with the limited view of a few millimetres. She could see herself in the mirror if she pressed her nose against it. Or, put differently, if she pulled his face all the way up to hers and tried hard, she could see what he looked like. But she didn't care about his appearance; compared to his undying love, his looks meant nothing to her.

His fingers fell on her, at last, first on the neck to help her relax. His bony hands had strength, but the joints felt loose, a perfect match for his weak and passive nature. From the spread and force of his movements, he appeared not to be a confident man, but a cautious, even submissive, one. He would not cut corners. With his gentle hands, he worked on every acupoint; on sensitive areas, he was especially considerate, imagining the experience from a client's perspective. And he was left-handed.

The old man upstairs was smiling down on her. From the moment she'd heard Xu Tailai's story, she knew what kind of man he was; as if guided by an oracle, she knew everything about a man she had never met. And now it seemed so real. He was the kind of man she wanted; he was her type. Jin Yan did not care for domineering men, for they seek to conquer the world, holding women in their arms like timid little birds. That was not what she wanted, not her ideal man. For her, the most important trait in a man was gentleness, and, even better, a bit of sentimentality. Then she could be like an older sister, or perhaps even a mother, to protect and guide him. Jin Yan was fixated on a romance characterised by indulgence; she would indulge and spoil her man to such a dizzying extent that he would be unable to tear himself away from her. She'd had a brief romance before with a young man who could see better than she. In the end his pathetically limited eyesight was his downfall, for he had too high an opinion of himself and acted like an overlord around her. They had kissed, but only once before she firmly refused to see him again. His kiss repelled her; it was self-centred and aggressive, a kiss that would swallow her up. What she longed for was to hold her beloved in her arms and slowly, little by little, gobble *him* up. Jin Yan knew herself well; her kind of love was abstract and yet expansive, sweeping and engulfing. Like a tigress, she preferred a submissive, obedient, even henpecked man, who was tender and clingy. She cared more about loving than being loved; in fact, she cared only about loving someone.

Jin Yan's eye problems had begun when she was ten, and her life between the ages of ten and seventeen were spent seeing doctors. Eight years of doctors' visits boiled down to the fact that her ailment kept getting more serious and her eyesight kept getting worse; nothing would change that. In the end, she managed to convince her parents not to visit any more doctors. Losing one's sight is painful beyond description, but in her case it was different. She had gone through the process of gradual loss, little by little, and was able to prepare herself mentally for the inevitable result. At seventeen, an age of abundance and vitality for a girl, Jin Yan gave up therapy and resolved to pack as much brilliance into her life as time would allow. She began to squander her sight, seizing her last chance to read, to attend plays, to go to movies, to watch TV and to view films on DVD. From reading and viewing, she developed a focus, a theme – romantic love as portrayed in fiction and film. It was wonderful, poignant, complicated and dramatic, devoid of any concern for daily necessities such as food and clothing, firewood, rice, cooking oil, salt, soy sauce, vinegar and tea, and yes, even medicine. It was fascinating; so what if it was someone else's romance. What was so bad about observing it in books and on the screen? Gradually, she found a new thread, realising that love was only the beginning, a foundation for what pleased her the most – weddings. She loved the weddings in novels and movies, especially the movies. She had lost count of the movie weddings she'd seen, ancient and modern, Chinese and foreign. Soon a pattern was revealed to her: all comedies ended in weddings and all tragedies in deaths. Weddings and deaths, these were everything life had to offer. So no talk about politics, economics, military or foreign affairs, personality, fate, culture, the nation, the times, customs, happiness, sadness, food, clothes – retro or trendy. No need to be so arcane. Just watch a wedding and you'll see everything you need.

A girl with a unique mentality, Jin Yan knew she had to concentrate on more important matters, since she would eventually be blind; the old man upstairs would not give her many opportunities. What else could she do but try to keep from dying of hunger or cold? Only find love. Her love had yet to arrive. She told herself she could live without anything but love, and she would embellish her love with the best she had to offer. How would she do that? She'd have a wonderful romance, and follow that with the grandest of all events – a wedding. In a way, once she gave up treatments, she devoted every day of her life to weddings, inserting herself into novels, movies and TV dramas; she kept getting married, sometimes in the northeast, at other times in the southwest, in China or other countries, in ancient times or present day. This was her secret, and she never felt ashamed; instead, weddings were what supported her, gave her proteins, vitamins, wind, rain, sunlight and snow. Of course, along with happiness, she had worries. Her biggest concern was losing her eyesight before her wedding; she must marry herself off before that happened, no matter what. She'd record the ceremony and, if she was lucky, watch the video every day, even if that required her to sprawl atop the TV screen, until she could no longer see a thing. What was the saying people used? *You can wear your eyes out gazing eagerly.*

There was another saying: gaze with eager anticipation. She still remembered what her eyes were like. Before the onset of the disease, her eyes were clear and bright, with a little ripple and a slight wobble. With slightly upturned corners, those eyes were as pretty as autumn waters. Sometimes she even congratulated herself on her poor eyesight, for otherwise, her eyes would really know how to flirt. Who knows what might happen then?

As she lay on the bed and felt Tailai's fingers on her back, she sighed softly. It was like a dream, but she stubbornly told herself it was not a dream. It was real. Over and over she warned herself to keep at it, not let go. This is not a dream. It's real. She longed to turn over and grab his hands, telling him, *We've been in love for a long time, did you know that?*

'Not so hard,' she said.

'Softer,' she said.

'Can't you take a little pressure?' Tailai said. It was the first thing he'd ever said to her. 'Any softer and it won't do any good.'

How could that be? Once tuina softens to a certain point, it's no longer tuina, it's a back rub. Men don't know things like that. With an all but silent snort, she said, 'May I ask your name, Sir?'

'No need to be so formal,' he said. 'My family name is Xu.'

'Ah,' she said. With her face buried in the cradle, her heart came alive. 'If you'll tell me how many siblings you have, I can guess your given name. Believe me?'

He let go of one hand and considered her offer. 'What do you do for a living?'

'I'm a student of fate logic.'

'Like fortune telling?'

'No. Everything has its logic, like the Tao has its logic, as do mathematics and physics.'

'So, tell me, how many siblings do I have?'

'You'll have to tell me your name. Then I'll know how many siblings you have.'

He thought about it and said, 'Why not tell me my name? I have one young sister.'

So he was indeed from northern Jiangsu, with that thick accent. Only people from northern Jiangsu pronounce the word 'sister' as 'thister'. He'd said he had one thister.

It took her a while to say, 'Your surname is Xu, right? And one sister, am I right? Then your name is Xu-Tai-lai. Yes, you are Xu Tailai.'

He stopped working. 'Who are you?'

'I'm a student of fate logic.'

'How did you know my name?'

'As I said, everything has its logic. Your surname is Xu and you have one sister so you can only be Xu Tailai.'

'Why should I believe you?'

'I don't want you to believe me. I just want you to believe that you are Xu Tailai. Do you believe that?'

He paused and said nothing for a long while. 'What else do you know?'

Jin Yan sat up. There was about her the aura of a sorceress, but she was comfortable in the knowledge that her aura was one of cheerfulness. 'Let me see your hands,' she said.

In line with the convention – men to the left, women to the right – he offered his left hand, but she took both his hands in hers. This was her first contact with him and it made her sad, but just for a moment. Driving out that feeling, she felt his palms, then the backs of his hands, before stopping and saying with calm assurance, 'You are destined to have two women in your life.'

'Why two?'

'Because you can't have the first one.'

'Why?'

'It's your fate. You do not belong to her.'

She sensed a spasm run through his body. Either he was trembling or the air was stirring.

'Why can't she be my woman?'

'Because you belong to the second woman.'

'What if I don't love her?'

'That's the problem,' she said as she dropped his hands. 'You do love her.'

He raised his head, his eyes to the sky, the universe above, standing in the middle of the boundless universe as empyrean winds swirled around him.

Jin Yan decided it was time to stop toying with him. 'Would you do me a favour and ask your boss over?'

He froze, wondering what suddenly was happening in his life. Of course, she was not to be believed, but the blind are superstitious, at least to some degree, and are, by nature, fatalists. Fate cannot be seen, and the blind cannot see, so they feel a particular affinity with fate. Xu called Sha Fuming in, naively thinking that the client was going to lodge a complaint. Sha rushed in, but he knew the moment he walked in that she was not going to complain; she wanted a job.

Taking the initiative, turning from client into boss, Jin Yan asked Sha to lie down, transforming the room into a job interview site. She was about to start a demonstration on him but Sha, a seasoned owner, refused to follow her instructions.

'This is a small place,' Sha turned her down. 'We don't need anyone now.'

'Impossible,' she said. 'Every place needs outstanding workers.'

Jin Yan tugged on Sha Fuming's arm to have him lie down, a new experience for him. But since he did not want to start a scuffle, he had no choice but to do as she wanted. It took only two minutes for him to know that she wasn't bad, with plenty of strength in her hands. But she was not as good as she'd claimed, and certainly nowhere near outstanding.

He coughed and sat up, adopting a pleasant tone, and said, 'This is a small place, a little temple, you see. Now if you follow Reform Road and walk four kilometres, you'll reach another tuina centre at the intersection of Reform and Open-up Roads. You can try your luck there.' To soften the tone, he even tried to be funny. 'Apparently, when it comes to reform and opening up, there are only tuina and massage along the way.'

She didn't laugh. Instead she said, 'I'm not going anywhere. I'm staying here.'

How unreasonable was that! Sha had never seen a jobseeker like her, but he laughed. 'What do you mean?'

'I'm not here to work. I'd have gone someplace else if that's what I had in mind.'

Sha laughed again. 'But we don't need a boss here either.'

'I just like your management style. I want to study that here.'

Equally unreasonable, but well said, to Sha's delight. Her comment loosened him up, like a muscle rub. He stopped smiling, his lips twitching a couple of times before he continued, 'Where'd you hear that?'

'Shanghai.' An evasive answer that said nothing; no specific mention of anyone, it brought all of Shanghai into play. That is to say, all of Shanghai was aware of Sha Fuming's management style. This throwaway comment was no longer a muscle rub; rather, it went straight to Sha's metaphorical acupoint, bringing him tremendous satisfaction. The more pleased he was, the less appropriate it was to show it. With the modesty and decorum befitting a successful businessman, he said in an offhanded way, 'We're just learning as we go. It's nothing special.'

'What I want is to study your management style and open my own place some day. If you're worried, I'll promise you here and now that if I open a tuina centre in Nanjing, I'll make sure it's ten kilometres from here. My repayment for your kindness.'

It may have sounded as if she cared about repaying his kindness, but it was more like a challenge, one that he had to accept. People are like that most of the time; their strength is often their weakness. He laughed again and cleared his throat. 'We're all blind here, so let's not talk about that. If you make a living, I do too. The Sha Zongqi tuina centre welcomes you.'

After thanking him, Jin Yan began to feel apprehensive. There had been no news of Xu Tailai for the longest time, during which she had kept faith with this one-sided romance, boldly moving forwards on a tightrope, fearlessly, calmly, bravely and patiently. Now she'd finally walked up to him. A tightrope walker must never look down, but she did, and she was scared witless – every step had been fraught with the danger of falling. A sudden wave of sadness surged almost uncontrollably through her heart, but she didn't cry, for she realised that love means hardship and suffering, but even more it is a soul-stirring experience. This was real love. Jin Yan had fallen in love with her own love.

The problem was, Tailai was completely unaware of all this; he knew nothing about her love for him. Turning a one-sided romance into a relationship of two was not going to be easy. One thing was clear, though: he had yet to recover from his first setback. But so what, even if he had? How could he know what was on her mind? And what could he say if he did?

She had no intention of dragging things out. After much consideration, she decided to start with language. Nanjing may be close to northern Jiangsu, yet his accent was unmistakable. He was too concerned about his accent, which in turn had caused low self-esteem. They would never be able to communicate freely if she didn't help him overcome this linguistic challenge.

An opportunity finally presented itself. At last she had a moment alone with him, in the lounge. She knew it wouldn't last long, five minutes at the most, maybe only two.

There was one sticking point: Tailai was afraid of her. He had been fearful of her since their first encounter, the moment she offered to read his fortune. Fully aware of that, she refrained from chatting him up right away. Instead, she took out her mobile phone and pretended to make a call to her family in Dalian. No one picked up. She sighed and shut the phone.

'Your home isn't far from Nanjing, is it Tailai?'

'Not far at all,' he said, 'just under three hundred kilometres.'

'Is that all?' She sounded puzzled. 'How can that be?' she continued slowly. 'The Nanjing dialect grates on the ear. Your hometown is less than three hundred kilometres from here, and yet it has such a charming sound. It's wonderful.'

Her comment was like a bomb, a depth charge, drifting in the fluids of his heart, settling deeper and deeper. He could feel it sinking but was powerless to do anything about it. Then he heard a muffled sound. The charge had exploded, turning the fluids into a giant column of water that soared and boiled, rising up in a frenzy and then crashing down in similar fashion. No one could possibly describe the surging waves and roiling tides in his heart, but she heard that he had begun to breathe hard.

As he sat there in a daze, she started to walk away.

'I just know there must be plenty of people who love to hear you talk. I couldn't be the only one.'

It had a deflated sound, hinting at an awareness that she didn't measure up. There was also a hint of self-pity, with lingering and profound implications.

CHAPTER SEVEN
SHA FUMING

WHAT IS BEAUTY? What exactly is it? That question troubled Sha Fuming from the moment the director and his film crew left. He racked his brain trying to come up with an answer, only to grow increasingly confused. What is beauty and where is it located?

To be precise, what he wanted to figure out was Du Hong, not beauty per se. But beauty claimed a place on Du Hong the person, which told him that she and beauty were one and the same. *If you can't figure out what beauty is, you'll never really understand Du Hong.* He was restless, stressed. Nothing came of his anxiety, except for more confusion and, of course, more profound darkness, a world he could never reach. *Let your hands roam over her body.* The very thought frightened Sha Fuming. What would his hands tell him anyway? A hand can tell size, length, firmness, temperature, dryness and shape, but it has its limitations, and with that thought he sank into despair. He spent the rest of that day absorbed in his own thoughts, sitting in the lounge. His stomach ached and his face wore a grave expression.

In the book, beauty is described as lofty. What is lofty?

In the book, beauty is described as graceful and refined. What is that?

In the book, beauty is described as harmonious? How so?

What is *noble simplicity*? What is *serene* greatness? What does *imposing* mean? What does *grandeur* signify? What does *vast and boundless* suggest? What is *solemnity*? How about *sparkling* crystal? What is *pure and fresh*? What does *exquisite* mean? Or *mysterious*? What is a rippling water surface? A misty mountain? A raging fire? Verdant greenery? An emerald island with profuse vegetation? White misty fog? Blanketing yellow sand? Vast greenery? What does it mean to be charming? Fetching? Gentle? Coquettish? Alluringly graceful? An enchanting smile? Handsome? Cool? Carefree and expansive? Mannerly? Sonorously unrestrained? Comfortably free? Why does flowing water murmur? Why do misty waves undulate? Why do heavenly roads twist and turn? Why are wavering lights lustrous? Why are soldiers and horses in a hurry? What does it mean to be a smooth operator? Why is emptiness illusory? What does it mean to have an eventful life?

What is red? What is green? What is 'the thoughts are red and the sorrows green'? Or, 'Do you know? Do you know? Red should be plump and green be slim'.

Sha was born with an outstanding memory, which enabled him to recite a great number of poems and idioms even now. In elementary school, his incredible memory had won him the title 'Little PhD'. But did he understand those poems and idiomatic expressions? No. He understood few of them, and simply parroted the words. That understanding came gradually as he grew older. Just what did it mean to *understand*? To him it meant he could use something. In the strictest terms, the blind don't really understand the world, they use it.

The problem was that beauty cannot be used; it must be understood.

Sha Fuming was getting agitated, deeply agitated, on top of the distress he already felt. But that was utterly unhelpful, and he needed to get a grip on himself. As he sat in the lounge he fidgeted with his fingers, like a meditating old monk fingering his prayer beads. But he was not meditating; his heart was quietly churning.

Were he and the world connected in any way? They must be. Yes, they were. He was clearly living in this world, and a girl called Du Hong was nearby. But the notion of beauty erected a solid barrier between them, which eliminated the connection. With this unforeseen thought, his heart skipped a beat. An almost audible thump. In regard to the world, Sha Fuming was only a supposition; if not, then the world itself was.

The problem was, beauty had power, with incomparable cohesive force. Conversely, it bestowed motivation, forcing you, coercing you to react. The significance of this was that, what attracted Sha was not Du Hong's beauty per se, but the director's exclamation over her beauty, which made Sha gasp in admiration. How could beauty make a man do that? What was the source of its magic?

After racking his brain for a week, Sha could stand it no longer. He found a free moment, and furtively called in Du Hong, pretending to check her skill. Once she was in the room, he shut the door, felt around for the light switch and flipped it on. The light snapped on. It was very dark, as dark as Sha Fuming's eyes. So why had he turned it on? He thought about that but had no answer. His assessment completed, he said, 'Very good.' And immediately had a case of nerves. He laughed, a totally incongruous laugh, which provoked a light-hearted, even glib request. 'Du Hong, everyone says you're beautiful. Can you describe your beauty to me?'

'You're being funny, Boss,' she said, as befitted her status. Modesty was the best sign of good upbringing under such circumstances. 'They're just joking.'

'This is not a joke,' Sha said, no longer laughing. He had turned quite serious.

Du Hong was taken aback. Sha's earnest tone gave her a bit of a fright. 'How could I do that?' she asked. 'Like you, I can't see.'

It was not an unexpected reply, but it took Sha Fuming by surprise. More precisely, it caught him completely off guard; he staggered backwards as if stabbed or clubbed. The person in whom beauty was invested could not describe it either, not at all, and that plunged him into indescribable sadness. It was a quiet, fixed sadness, but capable of stirring up a hornet's nest.

Exhausted, Sha decided to give up, abandoning this thing called beauty, which was like a heresy that could deceive people. Yet he underestimated its power, its temptation and its irresistible allure. It was a whirlpool, endlessly swirling, dangerous but beguiling, sucking him in and drawing him down to the very bottom.

Beauty was a calamity that befell him, gently and unhurriedly.

His stomach acted up again, but it shouldn't hurt like that, not now, two hours before it normally did.

As he endured his aching stomach, he inexplicably began to loathe the director and that woman. If it had been run-of-the-mill clients who had said, 'You're really beautiful, young lady,' would he have given it much thought? Of course not. But it had come from an artist, and had been invested with a rich literary flair. It was like a public broadcast. *They should never have come to the Sha Zongqi tuina centre. Artists are always at fault. Plato was right to banish artists from his Republic. They know how to befog people's minds.* To be sure, he was just venting his confusion. In fact, he was grateful to the director and that woman, thankful for their discovery, for they had given him the gift of a dark, bewitching, but warm springtime.

If spring is here can summer be far behind? He detected the scent of winter jasmine in the person of Du Hong.

But it was still a cause for sadness, for he quickly sensed that the blind must rely upon others' judgement, even when love is just around the corner. The blind are no different from anyone else; when people are in love, they care strongly about one thing – their beloved's appearance. But here is where a difference arises: the blind must take to heart other people's views – like in mathematics where one does the arithmetic step by step until arriving at a solution that seems to be theirs, but is in fact in the public domain. Throughout their lives, the blind are surrounded by comments from others; there is no self, only others, only the director, only directors. And it is through these comments that the blind achieve their love at first sight, that they have their fleeting glimpses of, or brief surprising encounters with, beauty.

Sha Fuming had had one of those surprising encounters, a real one, at the age of sixteen. Still a boarding school student, young Sha had not expected to encounter love on the street.

He could still recall that bright, sunny summer afternoon, the sun shining down on his forehead with such a pervasive intensity that its rays danced on his skin, which seemed to catch fire the moment he emerged from a supermarket; as he walked down the steps, a hand grabbed his when he reached the fifth step. Overcome by shyness, he puckered his lips. Being helped when walking down the street is a common occurrence for the blind, but this hand was different – it belonged to a girl. Feeling the sensation of her skin on his, he underwent a brief internal struggle before yielding to the owner of the hand, oblivious to what this action might lead to. When they reached the corner, he removed his hand and said with an uptight politeness, 'Thank you.'

The girl took back his hand.

'Let's go get something to drink.'

Yes, it was a girl, probably sixteen or seventeen. He was sure of that. At that moment, he didn't know whether he should be happy or upset. Some kind people tend to overdo their charity towards the blind; after helping them, they unwittingly treat them as beggars and try to overwhelm them with their benevolence. He abhorred people like that, and detested that kind of behaviour. So he declined politely. 'Thank you, but I'll be late for school.'

'I'm from No. 14 High School,' she said insistently. 'I have classes too, but let's go anyway.'

He was familiar with her school, which was across the way from his.

In the previous semester, the two schools had put on a joint culture and art performance.

'We can be friends, can't we?' the girl asked. She was swinging her arm, making his swing too. His face felt funny, probably what is known as 'turning bright red, ears and all'. He turned his face away.

'I have classes this afternoon, but thanks anyway.'

The girl brought her lips to his ear. 'Let's cut class together, what do you say?'

Over the next few days, he finally managed to find an idiom that described how he had felt at that moment; it was like a thunderclap on a clear day, one powerful enough to shake his core. He had always been a good student, had never been late for school, let alone cut class. But now things were different. A girl extended an invitation, a fetching one at that: . . . cut class, what do you say? . . . cut class together, what do you say? *Let's* cut class together, what do you say?

He was sorely tempted, could not make up his mind. It was clear that something alluring lay hidden behind this thunderclap on a clear day, and that was mainstream society. No one knows how it began, but the blind stubbornly held on to a belief that mainstream society was wherever sight existed. But on this day, what lay behind the thunderclap was not merely mainstream society, but an alternative corner of that society – mainstream but alternative. He was raring to go; from somewhere deep in his heart emerged a sense of curiosity for adventure and the courage to fight.

They went to a bar on Changle Road, where, clearly a regular, the girl ordered a cold soft drink like a professional. As a first-time bar customer, Sha was besieged by a myriad of sensations – he was excited, to be sure, but also somewhat uneasy, and troubled by a sheepish fear. But mostly he did not want to look stupid in front of a girl. Luckily his head was clear, which enabled him to keep assessing the situation and commit everything to memory. It took about ten minutes to loosen up, a change that was manifested in his speech; the more he talked, the more confident he became. Yet in the end, confidence eluded him, and unavoidably that too was manifested in his speech; he began to talk more and more, virtually non-stop. He began talking about the ambient music at the bar, a minor trick of his, for he knew he must direct their conversation to what he was good at. Gradually he was able to dominate the topics and therefore control their conversation. Like most youngsters their age, they relied upon memory, not understanding, so he peppered his speech with many idioms and, of course, axioms. Using idioms and axioms, he was expansive on the connection between music and the soul, and so on and so forth, until he suddenly realised that the girl had been quiet for some time. Maybe she'd lost interest in what he was saying, so he stopped, or, more precisely, came to a screeching halt.

As if sensing something, the girl said, 'I'm listening.'

To show she really was listening, she grabbed his hand and placed both their hands on the table. 'I'm listening,' she repeated.

He had been holding his hands, palms in, between his knees, which were clamped tight. Now, she had pulled his left hand out and laid it on the table, along with hers, his palm down, hers palm up. Then her fingers found the spaces between his and interlocked them. This was a new situation for him, unseen and far beyond anything he'd ever imagined; the possibility that two unrelated hands could form such a simple yet complex relationship had never occurred to him, like an intricate design, with every finger and every space serving a function. Solid, stable. His hand, though, felt weak and began to tremble. Internally, there were choppy seas, as he experienced a strange clash between his low self-esteem and self-confidence, making his mood rise, then fall, up and down, well in place one moment, and off in the distance the next. Slowly he regained his equilibrium, as the talk turned to Tang poetry, his forte. His outstanding memory also came into play, as he could recite lines; he would talk, adding a few lines of poetry, and talk some more, with a few more lines included. They were simply chatting, but he talked with authority, for he could cite his sources; he was, in a word, well grounded. As they say, the display of learning is in one's demeanour. Sha Fuming's talent showed through, and he was affected by his own intellectual attributes. He talked on, with all his references and interpretations. But he was not confident enough to be sure she was listening. She was; she laid her other hand on top of his. Now his hand was sandwiched between her two tiny palms. He didn't dare open his mouth, afraid that his heart might come leaping out.

'What's your name?' the girl asked.

'Sha Fuming.' He stretched his neck and swallowed before telling her what each syllable meant. 'Sha as in *huangsha*, yellow sand, fu as in *guangfu*, to recover, and ming as in *mingliang*, brightness. How about you?'

She decided to find a more creative way to reveal her name than just saying it. She took an ice cube out of the glass, pulled his arm over and wrote three characters.

Sha Fuming felt the ice on his arm. It formed characters, one stroke at a time. It was a singular feeling, utterly refreshing. The temperature of what the girl was using changed the act of writing into one of engraving, as in the idiom, *engrave on the bones and inscribe in the heart*. Sha Fuming's back straightened almost imperceptibly. He felt like shutting his eyes, afraid that his eyes would reveal his confused mind. But he didn't, he kept them open and fixed on the space ahead.

Feeling playful, the girl asked in a loud voice for him to say her name. 'Tell me, who am I?'

Sha Fuming pulled back his arm and sat quietly for a long moment before saying, 'I . . . can't read.'

That was the truth. He spoke and understood Chinese, but his was a special language, more precisely, it was Braille. He had not studied written Chinese for even a day, though he could recite the entire *Three Hundred Tang Poems* from memory.

She laughed, thinking he was joking. 'Yeah, sure. You can't read, you're illiterate.'

No one can afford to joke when he is trying to shore up his confidence. 'I'm not illiterate,' he said soberly, 'but I really can't read.'

His serious look introduced such gravity to their conversation that she scrutinised his face. 'How can that be?' she said, finally believing that he was serious.

'I learned Chinese Braille.' In order to make himself clear and move their conversation forward, he asked the girl her name. Then, picking up an ice cube, wrote her name on the table, using a pattern of dots to spell Xiang Tianzong.

Xiang Tianzong looked down at the seemingly random but somehow orderly dots on the table. That was her. It spelled out her name. She studied the dots from every angle. What a strange language. They had been conversing, but he had been using a foreign language. How intriguing, how interesting, how fun was that! This was a romantic scene she could not have asked for. Covering Sha's face with her hands, Xiang exclaimed, 'You are so cool!'

Sha Fuming understood the implications of tone as well as he understood the connotations of language; he recaptured his self-assurance from her tone, and it certainly didn't hurt to have his face in her hands. He stiffened his neck and coughed. He felt like laughing, but didn't want the girl to see, so he stopped. It was hard, requiring all the self-control he possessed. Laughter can be something good, but it can also be something bad, depending on the situation. There are times when laughter can lead to a loss of dignity. Under no circumstance would Sha Fuming allow himself to suffer a loss of dignity. Regaining his composure, he began to speak, but this would be no ordinary chat; rather, it took on the air of a formal lecture.

'It's a very young language, invented by someone called Huang Nai. You're probably unfamiliar with his name, but not his father, a famous revolutionary in China's recent history, one of the leaders of the 1911 Revolution, Huang Xing. Huang Nai was Huang Xing's youngest son, born after the death of his father.

'In his youth, Huang Nai loved football, a game that cost him the use of his right eye when struck by a kicked ball. Then in 1949, a detached retina in his left eye ended his sighted days altogether.

'Our beloved Premier Zhou Enlai was particularly concerned over Huang Nai's disability. In 1950, our beloved Premier Zhou sent Huang Nai to the Soviet Union, or more accurately, the former Soviet Union. But it was too late; there was nothing they could do for him.

'Total darkness taught Huang Nai the true significance of the light, and the thought occurred to him that the nation's tens of thousands of blind people were in need of an ideal form of writing so they could study culture and exchange ideas. But the two forms of writing for the blind in use in China then both had deep flaws, so Huang Nai vowed to create a completely new form.

'In 1952, after countless trials and errors, and improvements, Huang Nai created a system of writing for the blind based on the Beijing dialect and pinyin spelling, which the Ministry of Education approved the following year and promoted its use throughout the country.

'Now that they had a writing system, all blind people suddenly had eyes. Many became teachers, writers and musicians. After much hard work, a young blind woman in Zhengzhou was tapped as a TV show host.'

Sha Fuming wasn't talking, he was parroting what he had heard countless times in class. With the exception of the *former* Soviet Union, something he added at the last moment, every word was a product of memory. But how could he be content just reciting what he had learned?

He continued, 'China's writing for the blind is actually pinyin, or Latinised spelling. In the wake of the May Fourth period, many scholars called for the Latinisation of the Chinese language. Unfortunately, it never happened. If it had, the time we spent learning the language could have been cut in half. Only the blind have persevered in the use of Latinised Chinese, which is actually quite scientific.'

Having said what he truly wanted to say, Sha Fuming knew it was the right moment to stop. Time to let her say something.

'How do you know so much?' she asked emotionally.

Sensing the admiration in her voice, Sha felt himself expand like a balloon; it made him feel wonderful, like walking on air.

'We just follow our own path and let people say what they want,' sixteen-year-old Fuming said. Sensing he could have given a better answer, he added earnestly, 'I study while other people drink coffee.'

The background music in the bar lingered and coiled like floating gossamer, imbuing a romantic sentiment that refused to disappear, and it was this romantic atmosphere that prompted Xiang to make an inappropriate move. Taking his hands in hers, she pressed them against her cheeks, so that they were cradling her face. He held his hands still, not daring to move, straining to remain still, so she swivelled her neck to allow him to complete the stirring and shocking act of stroking her face.

A very tall high school student with an athletic build was seated in a corner to their left. The centre for the No. 14 High School basketball team, he had a young girl in flashy clothes in his arms, a sight that Sha obviously could not have witnessed. Four days earlier, Xiang Tianzong had been the girl in those arms, but that spot was now taken by a 'shameless girl'. Refusing to admit defeat, even as her heart bled, she had decided to act when she ran into Sha. She had taken him by the hand and dragged him to the bar, determined to have another boy in tow to show the basketball centre.

As she listened to Sha Fuming her eyes were fixed on the spot ahead, watching that dog and his bitch the whole time. The basketball centre looked out the window, while Xiang and the flashy girl waged a staring contest, trying to provoke a reaction. Yet it was an adorable kind of provocation, for their eyes were devoid of aggression; rather, they were filled with contentment and tenderness. They were in competition and this was their Olympics to see who had the gentler, softer, more alluring gaze. In other words, they were vying to see which one of them was happier and merrier. As the victor, that girl had a more graceful charm, something akin to a line of poetry: *'Mist blankets the cold water and the moon looms over the sand.'* Knowing she could not lose the match, Xiang looked away from the little fox to focus on Sha, with eyes that turned increasingly glazed until she appeared to be totally contented, with overwhelming devotion to and infatuation with Sha Fuming. *Don't even think about outfoxing me. You're still wet behind the ears. Get out of here! You think your eyes sparkle, but that's because of your contacts. Don't think you can pull that on me.*

Just because Sha Fuming was blind did not mean he was unaware of people's emotions. He knew; the only thing he didn't know was what was going on to his left. To him, happiness had come out of the blue.

'Was it nice cutting class today?'

'It was.'

'Are you happy?'

He moved his lips, but was unable to find the right words; it was not easy for a sixteen-year-old to describe his feelings of the moment. A jumble of thoughts flooded his head, but his mind was clear enough to recall a line of Tang poetry: *'This feeling creates an eternal memory.'* He breathed deeply, fully satisfied with his answer.

Xiang fell into his arms. 'I want to sit like this forever.'

Sha put an ice cube into his mouth, which began to melt while the ice burned hot.

He had no idea where the love had come from or where it went, but the romance in the bar did not last forever. His pitiful 'little love' died out in less than three hours, and after that, nothing, nothing at all. Less than three hours, so brief, yet long enough to be called a stretch of time. It would not be till much later that he would finally understand how two or three hours could be considered a period of his life. In any case, his love was gone, vanished without a trace. It had indeed become an eternal memory, but only that: a memory, a dream. In his dreamlike memory, there were only two things – hands and ice.

The hands clung to him with an audible murmur, soft and slender, like flowers from the heavens. Then without warning they turned to ice and floated into Sha Fuming's memory, where they remained, refusing to melt for years, despite the temperature in his dream. He could never get over how the ice retained the shape of hands, all five fingers together, no interlocking spaces between them, so no matter how hard he tried, it was no longer possible to hold hands. Floating hands covered the surface of the water, frigid, hard, vast and mighty.

The 'little love' that had lasted less than three hours had an enormous effect on him; he longed for a pair of eyes, eyes that would sparkle and that forced him to make strict demands on love and marriage: his love must come with a pair of eyes, for only with eyes could he become a member of mainstream society.

And that was how he had remained single for all those years. He was sealed up by two terms, eyes and mainstream society. More than demands of love and marriage, they became a matter of faith. That's how people are – once they have faith in something, they gain a determination and a resolve to waste time.

Blind people commonly prefer to fall in love with someone who sees better than they do; it is a matter of practicality and vanity. This is even more pronounced with girls, who are by nature competitive; finding a sighted person is a glorious cause for further celebration.

But not Sha Fuming. He adhered only to his faith. Without eyes he would rather never fall in love, never marry. But his belief was powerless in the face of beauty. Faith can be a chimera, and there are times when its collapse results from a single internal activity.

But more than internal activity, there will be corresponding external behaviour.

One day during the downtime after lunch, he went to the lounge and knocked on the door, 'Du Hong.' Du Hong stood up. 'Come with me, would you?' he said, very businesslike.

Instead of telling her why he wanted her to come with him, he just sat on one of the therapy tables and made no move to do anything. What was she supposed to do? She stood there and, like him, remained motionless. She was on edge. The boss had been in a bad mood recently, and she wondered if that had anything to do with her. She was not yet a regular employee of the Sha Zongqi tuina centre. After going over what she'd said and done over the past few days, she was relieved to find nothing that could be considered a problem. 'What can I do to relax you, Boss?'

Sha did not respond to her question. She could not know that he had raised his arms into the air. They were poised to stroke her face. Their goal was to verify and gain some understanding of that thing called beauty. They wavered in their determination. They lacked the courage. In the end, he took her hand. It was icy cold. But it wasn't ice. It lacked the hardness. It was soft. Like a remembered sentiment. Du Hong's hand felt like a hand. Five fingers. Sha stroked each of them, one at a time, and from those touches he made a stimulating discovery: there were indeed four spaces between Du Hong's fingers, and without thinking, he inserted his fingers into them. The fit was a perfect seal, and at this point he realised that the icy cold hand wasn't hers, it was his. The ice melted. His hand began to melt, drip by drip, about to become a flow and then surge.

In a moment of rashness, Sha tugged on Du Hong's hand, wanting to do something he'd longed to do for a long time before the melting was complete. He laid it against his own cheek. She dared not move. His head turned slightly, causing her to stroke him. Du Hong felt so warm to him.

'This is no good, Boss.'

What a long dream it was, passing through such humiliating times.

'I'd like you to stay,' he said. 'Du Hong, I want you here always.'

She took back her hand, which was coated with sweat. 'Boss Sha,' she said, 'doesn't this make it some sort of transaction?'

CHAPTER EIGHT
XIAO MA

SAO-ZI ABRUPTLY STOPPED coming over to the men's dorm. She hadn't visited in quite some time.

Xiao Ma sensed that she was making a point of avoiding him, both at the dorm and in the therapy centre.

He was in a funk almost from the moment he realised that she was avoiding him. Why was she doing that? A smile flickered over his sad face, faint and fleeting. He could see what lay behind her behaviour, and he felt a stirring down below.

He recalled her smell. The smell of her hair. A moist smell. She had everything she ought to have and nothing she shouldn't.

Xiao Ma turned reticent, as reticent as Sao-zi's smell. No one saw anything different in him, for he was usually silent. But he knew he was different. Whereas he had always been silent, he was now silent within silence.

What exactly is silence? And how does it become silence within silence? Xiao Ma knew.

When he was silent, he normally sat quietly, and in others' eyes, he was simply not making any noise. But that was just a front. In fact, he was playing with his toy, a toy unknown to everyone else. That toy was time itself.

Xiao Ma did not wear a watch or rely upon clocks. When a client came for him, he walked serenely into one of the rooms, where, an hour later, he would say to the client that he was finished, before serenely leaving the room. Not a minute more, not a second less. That was Xiao Ma's special talent, an astonishingly accurate sense of time. To him, time had its own materiality; it was concrete and tangible, with its own circumference and area, its own texture and weight. He was nine years old when he first learned about time, but that was too soon for it to become his toy. During those toyless days, his brows were forever heaving up, constantly arching. He wanted to open his eyes. He held the hope of luck in his heart, wishing for a miracle. Day and night, all he looked forward to was a morning like this when he would wake up, his eyesight shooting out from the sockets like nails, piercing his eyelids and filling the sockets with blood. His longing was accompanied by violence incomprehensible to the average person; it was akin to death.

Four years later, at the age of thirteen, his unsurpassed wisdom saved him. The violence came to an end. He gained peace of mind and turned time into a toy.

He had never forgotten the old-style desk clock at his parents' house. It was round, with hands for hours, minutes and seconds. The tip of the second hand was adorned with a small red triangle. At nine, he'd thought that time was a prisoner behind a piece of round glass. At that age, he had also mistaken time as a red signal, ticking away a tiny fraction every second. For more than a year, he had cradled the clock in his arms the day long, his permanent time-marking companion. Holding the ticking clock in his hands, he invented a game. First a tick, then a tock. But whether it went with a tick or returned with a tock, no matter how intricate and complex the ticking was, it had a rhythm all its own, and that was critical. Tick-tock, tick-tock, tick-tock, tick-tock, tick-tock, tick-tock. Neither too fast nor too slow, it never varied in its speed, the space between ticks constant. Everlasting, patient and interminable.

Tick-tock, tick-tock, tick-tock, tick-tock, tick-tock, tick-tock, tick-tock, tick-tock.

Time was ticking away; it was not time, but tick-tocks. It was not tick-tocks, but time. Delighted by the ticks, he fell in love with time.

Actually, he discarded the old desk clock a year after that. He had no more need of it, as he had learned how to tick within himself. With a body that now possessed the rhythm of ticking, it was never wrong. Time ticked away inside him. Without exerting mental energy or redirecting his attention, he could employ his ticking prowess under any circumstance. He was a new-style desk clock, only livelier, for he could eat, sleep and breathe, and he knew what cold and pain were. He was pleased with this. When he ate, he ticked away the rice kernels; he ticked the air in and out when he breathed. When it was cold, he still could tell how long the tick-tocks lasted; the same was true for pain. Sleep provided the only exception. But his body immediately began to tick on its own as soon as he was awake. He was ticking, ticking away.

It was not enough for him just to tick. This lack of fulfilment brought him new joy. He realised that he was not just part of time, but was capable of playing with it. There were many ways to do that, the simplest of which was assembly.

Each tick was one second. One second could be measured in length or width. That being the case, a tick could be a geometric shape, like a square mosaic tile. So he began to assemble the mosaic tiles, one tick, two ticks, and they came together, an endless, inexhaustible supply of ticks. Two weeks later, Xiao Ma looked up and made the surprising discovery of a profound truth: that crisscrossing ticks, neat and tidy, devoid of a single blade of grass or tree, blanketed the vast earth. No buildings. No utility poles. Even if a blind man were to ride a blind horse, the animal's hooves would gallop as freely as floating snowflakes. Xiao Ma did not move, and yet his ears imagined the sound of whistling wind. His hair flowed behind him.

As time passed, however, he grew tired of the monotony of assembly, the tedium of construction. Since everything was built by men, it required men to take it all apart. An insane thought occurred to him; he sought destruction, the desire to take things apart. But before then, he formed a hypothesis. There are five hours in an average afternoon, which made it easy. He divided his afternoon into five one-hour sections. Dividing each hour into sixty segments gave him sixty minutes, which were then further divided to form the tiniest fractions, the seconds. A tick removed one second; another tick removed another second. After removing the very last tick, an inexhaustible afternoon magically disappeared. A vacant smile appeared on his face. A magnificent afternoon. Where had it gone? Who had taken it apart? Where had it been placed and by whom? This was a secret. A puzzle.

He could play with time by approaching it from different angles or using other methods. He tried to move along with time. Since clocks are round, he knew he must move in a circular pattern, and he did, over and over again, on the outer edge of the circle. After three months had passed that way, he asked himself why time must move in circles. Time could be a triangle. Every hour could be a triangle. Each side would represent twenty minutes, each of which could in turn be a triangle, twenty seconds to each side. That new discovery helped him pass more time before a bolder, even crazier thought emerged. Why must the two ends of time be connected? They didn't have to be. Could he open up time? Who said he couldn't? He tried a new experiment, imagining time as a vertical line. With each tick, he climbed up one fragment, and so on. So the climb began, and facts quickly showed that there was nothing to stop him. Two hours passed, two whole hours, and Xiao Ma had no intention of turning back. Yet he suddenly sensed, with crystal clarity, that he had reached the apex. He was in the clouds. Cold sweat was his physical reaction to the shocking discovery; he was excited yet frightened, mainly because heights terrified him. But Xiao Ma was smart and had a cool head. He clenched his fists to ensure that he would not fall from such a height. Suspended in the air, he was drifting, all by himself. Wow. Wow. Wow! He was up in the sky. This was breathtaking, exhilarating. At such a moment, even a fleeting thought would cause him to disintegrate.

Saved by his cool head and composure, Xiao Ma made an unerringly accurate decision – he would get down the same way he went up. Taking a deep breath, he began his descent, one tick at a time, patiently, tick, tick, tick. After seven hundred and twenty ticks, a mere seven hundred and twenty, a miracle occurred – he landed, triumphantly, on the chair beneath him. It had been an intrepid adventure and an arduous feat to save himself. Drenched in cold sweat, he gripped the chair's arms for support as he stood up. He'd done it, he'd actually done it! Filled with elation and excitement, he experienced a wild abandonment he'd never known, prompting him to shout in the otherwise unoccupied living room, 'I've made a discovery! I've discovered that time is not round. Nor is it a triangle. It's not sealed up.'

Time was not sealed up, so his ticks could not be imprisoned; they never had been. They had endless possibilities. Through an adventure filled with hardship and exploration, Xiao Ma discovered time's most basic truth, one that had been obstructed by his eyes: seeing was not believing. If he had been born blind, or if he had never seen that damned old desk clock, he would never have considered time to be round. The ticks had not been imprisoned, not ever.

Not being able to see is a limitation; so is being able to see. A superior smile appeared on his face.

Time can be hard or soft; time can exist outside an object or within it. There might be a dubious space between the tick and the tock; there might be nothing at all. Time can have a shape; it can be formless. Now he began to see the magical side of time; it was unfathomable. The only way to see it clearly was to penetrate it, from one end to the other.

Humans lie. They believe in their own importance. They put time in a box, thinking they can control it, that they can see it, that they make it tick and tock. Everyone is blind in the presence of time. The only way to see time's true colours is to detach yourself from it.

From that moment on Xiao Ma understood the real meaning of time; to be together with time you had to give up your body, give up people, give up your self. And that can only be accomplished by a blind person. The sighted, controlled by their eyes, can never be on intimate terms with time.

Being together with time and with the tick-tocks marked Xiao Ma's silence.

But silence within silence was different, for it was no longer silence. Abandoned by time, Xiao Ma taught himself to be more observant. He began to pay close attention to Sao-zi, following her every move, even when she turned around. The air stirred when she turned, a slight, nearly imperceptible tremor that could only be detected by him. The lounge ceased to be a lounge, as scenes from his youth appeared in the space before him: there were mountains, and water, and grass, and trees, a blue sky, white clouds, even golden sunshine. Sao-zi was a butterfly, silently flitting in the air. So many butterflies, filling the sky in colourful swarms, and yet she stood out among them. As the only jade butterfly, she would have differed from the others no matter how great their numbers; she was eye-catching, her wings resplendent with gorgeous patterns that gave off fuzzy rays of light. She danced; she fluttered noiselessly, up and down, finally leaving the swarm to land quietly on a long, slender leaf. She appeared as a pair of giant jade wings, parallel, perfectly symmetrical and splendidly lithe.

'Why are you following me, Xiao Ma?' she said. 'You're bad. You're horrible.'

He mustered the courage to land on the same leaf beside her. She was weightless, so was he, but the leaf trembled just enough for her to quickly take flight. This time it was different, though, as she fluttered up into a vast, cloudless blue sky so clear it seemed washed. Only two objects existed in that clear blue sky: Sao-zi and Xiao Ma. He was in a breezy, light-hearted mood as he followed her; there was nothing in the world but two pairs of carefree wings.

She landed again, this time by the water, so he circled her, cautiously, before coming to rest. It was a glorious landing– he alighted on top of her. A breeze jolted them into the air, where they lurched in the turbulence and tumbled in the ripples; though exciting, it left room for an easy conscience. Turning his head, Xiao Ma spotted their reflection in the water, which made it appear as if she were resting on top of him. Her reflection was utterly gorgeous, but what about his? It was of a black butterfly, looking clumsy. Nothing less than a clumsy moth. Ashamed of what he'd seen, he felt his eyes darken as he slid off her body and, irretrievably, fell into the water.

Fish thronged towards him at that moment. A school of fish. A dark mass. Tens of thousands of them. Every one was the same colour, the same length, the same size. Xiao Ma was surprised to see that he was no longer a moth, but a fish. He was just another fish, the same colour, the same size. It was a frightening discovery, for he was unsure which one was him. A vast ocean, filled with fish, one fish among many. Would she still be able to recognise him? Xiao Ma struggled to swim to the surface, used every ounce of strength to leap out of the water. He struggled in vain. His leaps were ineffectual, and each time he fell back in. He made no sound, created not even a spray of water.

For the sake of self-confirmation, he wanted to detach himself from the school, but he lacked the nerve. Away from it, he'd have to face the boundless ocean alone. He could not do that. To be apart from the school meant living with unbearable loneliness. He could not do that. Should he leave or not? He wavered and eventually ended up in despair. He was near death, hanging on for dear life. Sensing that he was losing the last bit of strength, Xiao Ma turned over, exposing his white underbelly. He was fated to end up as a carcass carried by the tides.

A dolphin appeared at that moment, a smooth, silky creature with clean, graceful lines. It swam over, undulating to propel itself forwards and shouting at the school of fish, 'Xiao Ma, it's me, Sao-zi.' This rousing shout energised Xiao Ma, and he swam up to her. 'Sao-zi, it's me, Xiao Ma.' She stopped and looked at him, suspicion hidden in her shiny, round eyes. She did not believe that the creature in front of her was Xiao Ma. If he was, then wouldn't every creature in the ocean be a Xiao Ma? Panicked, he rolled over and said, 'Look, Sao-zi, there's a large scar on my neck.' She saw it, she saw the scar. Xiao Ma would never have been able to prove his identity by his face; it took a hideous scar to reunite them. Such a sad truth. But they were not sad. They were excited, virtually transcended, and they wanted to embrace. But they had no arms and no hands. All they could do was look at each other and cry, sending enormous drops of water down their faces. Their teardrops were air bubbles, popping up towards a distant sky.

'I've never cried like this,' she said. 'You're horrible, Xiao Ma.'

He sat in the lounge, immersed in his endless daydreams. In them, Sao-zi had him in her grasp. Though she was still quiet, she had been a butterfly, a fish, a ray of light, a whiff of fragrance, a dewdrop on a flower petal, a cloud on a mountaintop. Beyond that, she was a snake, slithering at his feet before coiling up his body all the way to the top of his head. He stood up silently, encircled by a snake. Out of nothing, he had become a lounge ornament.

But Sao-zi could not be always seated while in the lounge. She had to get up and walk around, and when she did, he recognised the sound as soon as she took the first step, however tiny, and magnified it to a startling degree. Her footsteps were characterised by one foot always slightly louder than the other. She became a horse. When she appeared as a horse, the lounge livened up, instantly turning into a prairie with lush grass and sweet water, all prepared for her.

Xiao Ma held stubbornly to the belief that she was a chestnut horse. He once overheard clients saying that her hair had been dyed a typical chestnut colour. Now her mane and tail were a chestnut colour. As she galloped along, her long mane rippled like waves in the wind, as did her slender tail. Xiao Ma had seen an actual horse when he was eight years old, and had been deeply impressed by its long eyelashes. The animal's moist eyes were bright and clear, surrounded by lashes to form an irregular ellipsis. Captivating. So filled with emotion they reflected mountains in the distance. Glancing at him with her rounded moist eyes, Sao-zi whinnied indulgently before taking off, with him close behind, but off to the side. Galloping together, they stirred up wind that rushed into his eyes and formed an undetectable arc; it glided over his cornea, so cool, so melodious. Her eyes must have felt the wind also, for her happy hooves nearly lifted her off the ground.

'Xiao Ma,' she said. 'You're a horse, and not just by name.'

It was an extraordinary phrase, seemingly commonplace yet open to interpretation. Pounding the ground with his indulgent hooves, he climbed a hill with her, where a broad golden pasture spread out below when they reached the highest point. The pasture was in fact an enormous basin, emerald green in some places and golden yellow in others, overlaid with the cloud shadows. As the shadows drifted, the pasture began to move and spin on its own, centring on the chestnut mare – Sao-zi. Oblivious, she reared up, whinnied, and snorted. When she did that, her tail flew up to form countless chestnut lines under the setting sun, thousands upon thousands of hair strands spreading in all directions, graceful and alluring. Those transparent strands emitted a burning bright light, like cold flames, burning and defying all logic. He nudged her with his nose, she brushed his face with the flames, their intoxicating fragrance entering his nostrils. Then she turned around, her back to the golden pasture, and rested her neck on his back. She had an unusual neck, warm, smooth and unimaginably soft. Motionless, he focused on experiencing the startling sensation, until finally he turned around and laid his neck across her back. She was drenched in sweat, her muscles twitched. A wind blew over, bringing her body closer to his, until they were pressed together, enmeshed in each other's body heat and breathing together. They gazed at each other with the near eye. She did not know that the golden pasture and his head were reflected in her sparkling eye, his head curved to form an arc parallel with hers.

She blinked. At that moment her lashes combined to make it a beautiful action. Closing, then snapping open. Moved by the snapping sound, he rubbed his neck against her. Maybe as repayment, a reprimand, or a sign of intimacy, she rubbed her neck against him, so enthralling him that he felt he could bathe half of his face in her breath forever, till death.

A herdsman strode up, carrying a saddle over his shoulder. As if he didn't even see Xiao Ma, he walked up to Sao-zi and threw the saddle over her.

'Take that away,' Xiao Ma shouted. 'Don't touch her.'

'Giddy —' the herdsman said, patting her on the neck as he climbed into the saddle – 'up.'

The herdsman rode off, Sao-zi as his mount, his retreating back jolting between heaven and earth. Xiao Ma started to race after them but had barely taken a few steps before sensing that something was wrong. He turned and discovered to his horror that his body had disintegrated, littering the ground with screws, gears, an hour hand, a minute hand and a second hand. He was not a horse; he was an old alarm clock in desperate need of repair. His earlier gallop had caused the disintegration of his body. Now he could hear her hooves hitting the ground – tick-tock, tick-tock, tick-tock. Eyes shut, Xiao Ma continued letting his mind roam the wide open spaces until the quiet in the lobby was shattered by Gao Wei's announcement.

'Wang Daifu, Kong Daifu, Xiao Ma, you're up.'

Xiao Ma stirred. He awoke not from silence, but from the silence within the silence. He stood up. Sao-zi stood up as well. She yawned grandly and stretched lazily. 'Well,' she said, 'time to go back to work. I'm sleepy.'

Three clients came in together, and, as luck would have it, Wang

Daifu, Xiao Kong and Xiao Ma were up at the same time. Xiao Ma did not want to do it, but he had no choice. When you work for someone, you can't do only what you want.

The clients, obviously friends, asked for a room for three. Xiao Ma was on the inside, with Sao-zi in the middle and Wang Daifu by the door, all squeezed into one room. Xiao Ma was not alone in feeling awkward; the others were too, which produced silence. It was noon, which, like night-time, was perfectly suited for sleeping – peaceful, quiet. Within three or four minutes the clients drifted off to sleep. Wang's client slept so deeply he was snoring loudly.

Once the snores rose from one end, Xiao Ma's client, not to be outdone, joined in from the other end, interestingly a half beat behind. First one, then the other, back and forth. They were such good friends they even corresponded when they snored, like performing a vocal round. What started out as 4/4 rhythm turned into something akin to a march. To the trained ear, it sounded hurried, for no apparent reason, as if sleep were busy work. How interesting. 'Isn't that nice?' Xiao Kong said with a laugh. 'I'll be the conductor and you two sing. We'll be a great team.'

She gave little thought to what she was saying, but sometimes that's how it is – speech is always linked to circumstance. You can say something, and if that occurs under a certain set of circumstances, it takes on special significance and must not be overanalysed, for that can cause it to take on additional meaning; the more thought, the more meaningful everything becomes.

What had she meant by 'I'll be the conductor and you two sing'? Wang Daifu wondered. So did Xiao Ma. Wang's mind began to wander. So did Xiao Ma's.

The room was quiet except for the clients' snores, but it did not stay that way for long. Wang Daifu and Xiao Kong struck up a conversation, starting with him. The talk focused on the food they'd been given recently. She said it was getting worse, that was clear, but he didn't pick up the thread, not wanting to let it go too far. If their complaints reached Jin da-jie, the cook, a woman with a sharp tongue, it could present a problem. Wang Daifu changed the subject and began reminiscing about Shenzhen. The food was better in Shenzhen, he said. Xiao Kong agreed. So they looked back on Shenzhen's seafood and soups.

Because the clients were napping, the therapists kept their voices low, a relaxed conversation that avoided any talk dealing with feelings. A simple conversation, back and forth, which took on domestic airs, like a married couple talking in their bedroom or kitchen, as if Xiao Ma were not there. But he *was* there, and he heard every word. From where he stood, he felt they'd moved beyond idle chatting and into flirting. He'd never been to Shenzhen, and even if he had, he'd best keep quiet. All he could do was to enter his silence within a silence. His internal emotional engine went into overdrive; he was somewhat envious and somewhat sad; but mostly he was jealous.

And yet Sao-zi was, after all, Sao-zi, so she found something to say to him every few minutes, which calmed him considerably. Say what you will, Xiao Ma meant something to her. He continued feeling envious, sad and jealous, but now to that was added a bit of consolation.

In any case, it was a long hour for the three of them; uneventful, yet it couldn't end soon enough. Luckily, Xiao Ma's client woke up first, and breathed a long sigh of relief, which woke up the other two and restored a sense of normality to the room, no longer the kitchen or bedroom of a married couple. The still sleepy clients talked among themselves about their nap, agreeing that it had been a terrific noontime experience and that they had made a great, glorious and accurate choice by coming here for tuina.

Gao Wei came in and whispered something to Wang. One of his VIP clients was waiting in room four, where the massage bed was ready. 'Got it,' Wang said, as he massaged his client's thighs before uttering a few polite parting comments and leaving. While the clients were looking for their shoes, Xiao Kong took out her Shenzhen phone so she could call her father after the clients left. Xiao Ma could tell she was in no hurry to leave. Xiao Kong could not know that time and his heart were ticking away.

Finally, the clients left. Xiao Ma walked to the door and listened for sounds in the hallway; all was quiet. He locked the door and called out softly – 'Sao-zi.' Obviously, he had something to say, so she put the phone back in her pocket and turned to face him. He didn't know what he wanted to say, and noticed the smell of her hair, which was right in front of him; the scent was calming yet vigorous. He lowered his head and rashly took a deep, very deep, breath.

'Sao-zi.'

That deep breath had brought him a carefree sense of happiness. Its effect far surpassed any smell he could detect. 'Sao-zi.' He wrapped his arms around her and held her tight, sniffing the air above her head.

Stunned and confused, she felt like shouting, but stopped herself at the last second. She struggled and squirmed and said, her voice soft but her tone incomparably severe, 'Let me go. If you don't, I'll call Wang da-ge.'

CHAPTER NINE
JIN YAN

FINALLY XU TAILAI began to talk, and everything got easier after that. Jin Yan launched her emotional assault, a unique one that started from the outside, levelling everything around him like a mopping-up operation. What did that mean anyway? It meant that by the time he sensed her feelings for him, everyone in the centre already knew that she was pursuing him.

She did two things. One, she sat next to him during mealtime, and two, she held his hand on the way home after work. These were common actions among the blind and generally devoid of any special implications, especially the hand holding. The blind therapists normally left work in threes and fours, hand in hand and led by a sighted individual. But Jin Yan, being Jin Yan, did things her own way.

No one in the centre, it's safe to say, was prepared for Jin Yan and Xu Tailai's romance. For one thing, people usually had a sense of which man would be pursuing which woman and vice versa. Put simply, they must come across as a good match, an abstract concept that's hard to describe and yet, when it comes to an actual couple and becomes a fait accompli, the notion of compatibility becomes concrete and easy to define. No matter how one looks at it, no one would say that Lin Daiyu, the frail girl from *Dream of the Red Chamber*, and Lu Zhishen, the rowdy monk from *The Water Margin*, were a good match. Xu Tailai and Jin Yan were not a good match either, which was why no one had given their romance a thought.

Jin Yan made a flamboyant move one day when Jin da-jie came in at noon, a signal that lunch was ready. A sighted person, da-jie was the centre's full-time cook, a woman known for her punctuality. She arrived at precisely twelve noon, like clockwork. Earnest and polite, she put rice bowls in the hands of the therapists, who immediately began to wolf down the food, a typical trait of youngsters, male or female, who ate like there was no tomorrow. But not Jin Yan on that day. Setting her bowl down, she took a sip of water.

'Dig in, Jin Yan,' da-jie said, 'the food's pretty good today.'

'I'm not in a hurry,' Jin Yan responded calmly. 'I'm waiting for Tailai so we can eat together.'

At that moment Tailai was working on a VIP client who had sprained an ankle and required an additional thirty minutes of therapy. Jin Yan's reply reminded everyone of something from the day before, when she had walked up to Tailai. 'May I sit next to you, Tailai?' she'd asked gracefully, though everyone thought she was just being witty and gave it no more thought. Du Hong had got up and given her seat to Jin Yan. *Tailai is no Beckham, so be my guest and sit there as long as you like.*

But everyone went silent the next day when she said she was waiting for him so they could eat together. So understated, though at heart a clarion call. She's only been here a few days, they were thinking. Isn't she moving a bit too fast? And on Xu Tailai, no less.

It couldn't be. It must be a mistake.

It was no mistake. Jin Yan had her eye set on Tailai; it was not yet clear if she was in love with him, but she'd certainly made it appear so. She was very nice to him, more than nice, and different from how co-workers treated one another. When he finished with his client, she told him to wash his hands. When he'd finished that, they sat down to eat together. She kept urging him, 'Slow down.' She put some of her own food into his bowl. Meanwhile, she chattered away. This was not the way of a co-worker. The lounge felt uncomfortably quiet to Tailai, who tried to refuse her gestures. She laid down her bowl, nudged him, and said, 'Men have to eat more. Understand?' He was so embarrassed all he could do was shovel rice into his mouth, forgetting even to chew; his cheeks puffed up. *Doesn't she know where we are? It's the lounge, everyone is here.* But that sort of expansiveness was typical of Jin Yan; the more people who were around, the more she acted as if no one else mattered.

As she ate and talked, Jin Yan laughed softly once or twice, giving the impression of an intimacy only lovers could share. The others in the lounge found it hard to talk too loudly under these circumstances, and the place quieted down, except for the synchronised sounds of Jin Yan and Tailai eating, like a married couple. Everyone else ate silently, but their inner feelings were anything but simple. *Who is Xu Tailai? Who is he anyway? Why would a new arrival, a pretty girl, fall for him, and no one else? And why is he pretending not to be interested? Who believes that?*

Jin Yan acted boldly and expansively when she and Tailai were eating, but she was a different person on the way back to the dorm late at night. Seemingly helpless and timid, she stuck close to Tailai, insisting on taking his hand, and no one else's.

All was quiet on the late-night streets, where there were no more noisy pedestrians or streams of vehicles, and suddenly the streets seemed deserted. They appeared wider, a carefree world for the blind, though it was also a lonely world; the blind walked in groups but were alone. Jin Yan liked the solitude. Walking down the left side of the street, they whispered and shared laughs; it was an endlessly intoxicating moment for her, when the world seemed to belong to her and Tailai alone. It was like a desert.

I'm a wolf from the north
Loping through boundless wind and rain
The shrill north wind blows over
Drifting yellow sand sweeps by

What could be better than this? Nothing. Just imagine a girl holding the hand of a young man as they walk down a deserted street late at night, or perhaps a desolate wilderness; they walk on, obliged not to turn back. Pleasantly sombre.

Slowly walking with you
Slowly the outcome emerges
. . .
Till the end of the world
Love is forever.

Tailai was afraid to reciprocate, owing partly to his shy nature but also to the traumatic experience of his failed first love. Once bitten, twice shy. But this was precisely the cause of her infatuation with him; she was plagued by the urge to heal his wound. Would she have been so taken by him if he hadn't been hurt? Hard to say. She knew what she was like; a broken heart was what had attracted her, not a stone-cold or impregnable one. No matter how torn his heart was, she would gather all the pieces and hold them in her palm to sew them back together, one careful stitch at a time. She wanted to see his heart begin to stir until it was as good as new, to contract and expand. This was the kind of love Jin Yan wanted.

After eating every lunch together and going home night after night as a pair, Jin Yan and Tailai finally became an item, a basic fact known to everyone at the centre. They were in love. And that was fine. The world has a place for fresh flowers and for manure, so why can't a flower be stuck in manure?

But they were not in love yet. Jin Yan knew they weren't. What makes being in love unique is that it requires a rite, a single word or a gesture, or both. Only with a certain action to lay bare what is on the minds of both parties can they be considered in love.

She had done everything she could, out in the open and with grace, but she maintained a reservation befitting of a girl when it came to that rite. It was out of the question for her to say 'I love you'. He would have to be the one who said it first. This was something on which she would not and could not compromise. She would wait till that day; she had an abundance of patience. Those three words meant a great deal to her, and she must have them. She was entitled to them. She was worthy of getting them. Only with those three words could love be meaningful.

But Tailai withheld the three words from her, something she had anticipated, and now she was torn. On the one hand, the sooner the words came to her the better, but on the other hand, she wanted his confession to come a bit later. He had, after all, loved someone before. Jin Yan didn't care if a man had loved before, had been married, or had children; all she cared about was the way he treated women, particularly the woman before her. Tailai had recently suffered a traumatic loss of love, so if he were to turn right around to show his love for her with those three words, Jin Yan would be disappointed. She was in no hurry. Confessions of love are like good soup: they take time to make.

The days went by. Then a week, and two weeks. He had yet to express himself to her. She was a patient woman, but that didn't mean she wasn't waiting for him to do so. As time passed, her patience wore thin. He remained the same, no matter what she did or how she did it. Eating with her, that was fine; walking with her, no problem there; chatting with her, sure. But he was silence personified at each critical moment; he simply refused to react.

His silence was unnerving, to say the least, and as she looked back, Jin Yan was surprised; they had known each other for quite some time, but it appeared he didn't intend to show his feelings at all. It wasn't that he stammered or that he couldn't let it all out; he was just unresponsive at every critical moment, which nearly destroyed her self-confidence. Maybe he really wasn't in love with her. Could manure reject a fresh flower? Of course it could.

Realising that she wasn't doing as well as expected, Jin Yan was tired, but the situation had reached the point of no return. Tailai's silence was not the prime source of her exhaustion. Everyone at the therapy centre knew about their relationship. She'd started out with grandiose gestures, and now that they were in love, was there anything to keep her from more such gestures? No. She needed to keep up the act of flowers blooming in spring, but that was getting old fast.

Tailai did not come forward; neither did she. She was patient, but his patience was greater than hers. She had thought she could wait forever; she was wrong. Instead of Tailai, she was in fact waiting out time. Time was interminable, and there was always a tomorrow to outwait her. Tomorrow was like a bottomless pit, an unreachable goal. Finally she realised that she could not wait any longer, defeated by her own patience. She had crumbled in the face of Tailai's resilient, long-lasting patience. In a word, his patience was frightening, inhuman even. She had only one thought – she needed to cry. Luckily she knew herself well enough to anticipate how she would shock people by her wails, so she asked for half a day off and went to Ka-le-men, a karaoke joint. Shutting herself inside a room, she turned the music volume all the way up and had a good cry.

Besides crying her heart out, she made some private arrangements. First, she called her mother, telling her that her health wasn't as good as it had been, with full knowledge that her mother would tell her to come home, and she would take the opportunity to say, 'We'll see.' It was a highly loaded response that entailed a decision; she would have a frank talk with Xu. If it worked out, she'd stay in Nanjing; if not, she'd go home right away.

So in the end she blinked first. On that night, Zhang Zongqi, Ji Tingting, Tailai and Jin Yan walked home in a group, led by Xiao Tang, one of the receptionists. When they reached the door, Jin Yan stopped and walked up to Zhang, where she took Tailai's hand from his. 'Why don't you all go up? Boss Zhang,' she said, 'Tailai and I will take a little walk.' Zhang smiled and, taking the receptionist's hand, headed upstairs. Taking hold of Tailai's lapel, Jin Yan led him off to the side of the road, and, once she could tell that the others had all climbed the stairs, came straight to the point.

'We need to talk, Tailai.' His expression turned sombre at that declaration; he lowered his head, not sure if she saw his face. Instinct told him that something was going to happen tonight.

He made up his mind not to say anything, no matter what. Intending to have a heart-to-heart talk with him, Jin Yan was upset when she noticed his attitude, and quickly adopted the approach of stubbornly refusing to speak first. *We'll keep at it like this and see who can hold out longer. If you want to hold out till daybreak, I'll be right there with you.*

But she was wrong again. She was patient, all right, but never as patient as he. Barely a quarter of an hour had passed before she gave up and her temper flared. Struggling to control herself, she laid a hand on his shoulder. 'Everyone in the centre is blind, Tailai, yet they all can see what's going on; they know. Can't you see? Has it escaped you?'

Tailai coughed and dragged the tip of his shoe back and forth across the street surface.

'I guess you're going to force me to come out into the open then,' she said, her voice cracking. 'I'm a woman, after all, Tailai.'

'You're not going to say it, are you? Tailai.'

'You're forcing me to say it first, is that right, Tailai?'

'Are you going to say it or not, Tailai?'

His foot continued to drag across the ground; his lips were moving, but not his tongue.

Now incensed, she put her hands on his shoulders as the anger and unhappiness that had built up over time erupted. 'Will you say it or won't you?' she demanded loudly.

'I will,' Tailai shuddered and blurted out, 'I will.' Fixing his gaze on her, it still took some time for him to open his mouth. 'I'm not a good match for you.' He was heartbroken by the confession and appeared to be crying. He knew he was not good for her. 'I'm really not a good match, Jin Yan,' he repeated himself earnestly, afraid she hadn't heard him the first time.

So that's what it was all about. God! So that's what was bothering him. She'd imagined thousands of scenarios, but never once had she anticipated this. *I'm not a good match for you. I'm really not a good match.* Could there be a better beginning for romance anywhere? No, there could not. Love had humbled her, yet her humbled heart had met an even humbler one. Humility, modesty and self-deprecation are unbearable. But where love is concerned, they can be touching, alluring and heart-warming. So this is what love is like. You can strip naked in order to cover the one you love with feathers. Pulling her hands back, she stared at him. First her shoulders quaked, then her whole body. What more could she say? What *should* she say? Balling up her fists, Jin Yan felt a blankness engulf her. At a moment like this, all she could do was cry. She began to wail.

Her wails came on suddenly and shattered the late night quiet of the residential area. Zhang Zongqi quickly came down with Jin da-jie and Gao Wei to take her inside. But she refused to go with them.

Left with no choice, Zhang tried to talk her round, looking unhappy. 'We're renters, Jin Yan, and the people will complain if you keep this up.' But she was beyond reason. She didn't care; she just wanted to cry. Was there any better time for her to cry?

Da-jie had been asleep when Zhang woke her up. Before she could clear her mind, she heard Jin Yan's loud wails, without knowing the cause. Yet for her, there could be only one reason for Jin Yan to cry like that; it must have been Tailai's fault. A staunch believer that women must always support one another, taking on the role of big sister, she demanded, 'How dare you mistreat Jin Yan, Xu Tailai?'

Tailai didn't know why Jin Yan was carrying on like that. It wasn't his fault.

Zhang dragged Tailai away, while da-jie put her arms around Jin Yan. 'It's all right. Let's stop crying.'

'You go back, da-jie,' Jin Yan said, still choked up. 'Let me cry for another five minutes.'

That didn't sound right. What kind of sorrow lasts another five minutes? With the aid of the streetlight, da-jie took a closer look at Jin Yan, whose expression seemed out of sync with her wailing. Now da-jie knew what was going on; she'd obviously wrongly accused Tailai of mistreating Jin Yan. Well, there was nothing she could do now except to give him a couple of extra pieces of meat at the next meal. And Jin Yan was clearly fine, since Tailai was innocent. 'Be a good girl,' da-jie said in a tender voice, 'and come upstairs with me. Maybe you don't want to sleep, but others do.'

'No.' Jin Yan gently pushed her away. 'I need to cry some more.'

Jin da-jie sighed inwardly. The world had certainly changed. She could not understand young people, the way they talked. Just what did it mean to need to cry some more?

In the end, it was Jin Yan who said 'I love you' first, and in his arms, no less. A man with low self-esteem, Tailai was frightened of love and even more so when it came to expressing his feelings, though she could sense that he adored her. He tiptoed around her, afraid to cause her damage, to do her harm; he was anxious to the point of not knowing what best to do except breathe hard. Even his fingers were stiff. Leaning into his embrace, she brimmed with tender love when she blurted out those three words. *If he refuses to say them, so be it; there's no point in forcing him.* Finally it all became clear: where love was concerned, Tailai was a farmer – timid, clumsy, wooden and stubborn, all of which were personality flaws, but which became something unique when they characterised his love. Jin Yan decided that she would be a snake in the farmer's arms, not venomous, just a small, slinky water snake. Snakes bite, and so would she. Her love must come with teeth. The thought brought a smile to her face.

'Am I nice, Tailai?'

'Yes.'

'Do you love me?'

'Yes.'

'Do you think about me before you fall asleep?'

'Yes.'

'Will you be nice to me for the rest of our lives?'

'Yes.'

She bit him, a real bite, not a playful nibble. Her teeth sank into his neck and didn't let go until he cried out in pain.

'Did that hurt?'

'Yes.'

'Do you know I love you, too?'

'Yes.'

'Do you know you're the kind of man I want to marry?'

'Yes.'

'Bite me back, then,' she said.

'No, I won't.'

'Go ahead.'

'No, I won't.'

'Why not?'

'I don't want to hurt you.'

His reply was touching, so touching that she gave his neck another bite. He was covered in bruises before they had even been together for an hour.

Then suddenly reminded of something, she struggled out of his arms and instead put hers around him, before asking a serious question. 'I'm a pretty girl, a ravishing beauty. Did you know that? Tailai.'

'Yes.'

'Touch my face.' She took his hand. 'Am I pretty?'

'Yes, you are.'

'Keep touching. Am I pretty?'

'Yes, you are.'

'How so?'

That was a tough question. Born blind, Tailai could not have known what a pretty girl looked like. It took a long while before he said, as if taking a vow, 'Prettier than braised pork.'

CHAPTER TEN
WANG DAIFU

WANG DAIFU WENT home alone. He didn't take Xiao Kong with him, because his mother sounded strange over the phone. Instead of trying to get more information, he mentioned the call to Sha Fuming after a treatment session, and then went home. Any talk of home instilled a sense of fright in Wang. He longed to draw close to home, but also wanted to keep his distance. The sticking point was, he didn't know what to say to his parents. It should have made perfect sense for him to go home often after returning to Nanjing. But he didn't. He met his family obligations by phoning daily. Wang was in love, and most of the time a man in love is well served by going home on a regular basis, where so many things are made easier. But not Wang Daifu. He would prefer that his parents lived far from him, for then they would be just a concern, a thought. This was something he'd seemingly got used to.

He sensed that something was wrong the moment he set foot in the house. His parents were quiet, and it seemed they weren't alone. Something bad must have happened; it felt spooky.

Suddenly seized by a minor panic, he wished he'd phoned his younger brother on the way home. After all, his brother was sighted; he was the family's pillar, and everything would surely be fine with him around. Wang managed to keep calm and greeted his mother, then his father. With one hand resting on the sofa, he felt his phone with the other hand and dialled his brother's phone number.

'This must be the older brother,' said a strange but pleasant voice.

'I see we have a guest,' Wang laughed, pretending to be surprised. 'How should I address you?' A voice emerged from the phone in his pocket: *We're sorry. This phone has been turned off.*

'There's no need to tell you that. You could ask your brother, but his phone is off all the time.'

We're sorry. This phone has been turned off, the voice repeated mechanically.

The silence in the living room made the recording sound even louder. Embarrassed, Wang switched off the phone as his fears intensified uncontrollably.

'Why don't you offer our guest some tea, Mother?'

'She already did. Not to worry.'

'Then please go ahead and drink it.'

'Don't you worry about the tea. We have been drinking. We're here for our money.'

Wang's heart skipped a beat. Yes, this was definitely trouble. These were not people to take lightly. Then it occurred to him that they could not possibly be here to rob them. 'Could you tell me who owes you money?' he asked amicably.

'Your younger brother.'

He took a deep breath as everything became clear, and that drove away the fear.

'Can you tell me where you're from?'

'We're from the gang.'

'What does that mean?'

'The gang, like in a street gang, but we're not mobsters. We're from the mahjong gang, we play by the rules.'

Wang began to crack his knuckles, starting with the left hand, then the right. He repeated the process but the knuckles would only crack once. 'Money owed must, of course, be repaid,' he said. 'But my father doesn't owe you anything, nor does my mother, and neither do I.'

'We don't need you to tell us about gang rules. Here's an IOU from him, with an address and a phone number. We go by the IOU, not people. We play by the rules.'

The pleasant voice said that a second time, sending a chill through Wang's heart. His fears returned. What did 'play by the rules' mean? It sounded ambiguous.

'We don't have any money,' he said.

'We don't care,' the pleasant voice replied.

Wang took another breath to puff up his courage. 'And we wouldn't give it to you if we did.'

'That's not an option.'

'What are you going to do?'

'We're not going to do anything,' the voice continued. 'We just want our money. If we can't get it, we'll leave. Someone else will follow up and take care of business. These are our rules, and we play by the rules.'

What a sinister comment. Wang heard a threat in every word.

'How much does he owe you?'

'Twenty-five thousand. A nice figure, wherever you happen to be, Jiangxi or northern Shaanxi.'

'What do you want anyway?'

'Our money.'

'What happened to the law of the land?' Wang said, raising his voice, an act of bravado.

'Not the law of the land,' the pleasant voice replied lightly to deflect Wang's challenge. 'It's laws, not the law of the land. We know all about laws.'

Wang was breathing hard, unable to say more. He jumped to his feet, took out his mobile phone and jabbed at the numbers. *We're sorry. This phone has been turned off.* He raised his hand, ready to fling his phone to the floor, but someone grabbed his arm. He struggled, but his powerful arm was no match for the other man's.

'Don't take it out on your phone,' the voice said, not the owner of the arm. So there was another person.

'You deal with me,' Wang said. 'Don't touch my parents.'

'We can't deal with you.'

As a handicapped individual, Wang knew exactly what the voice meant. It was intended to belittle and humiliate him, which had the opposite effect – it calmed him. 'What do you want anyway?'

'Money.'

'But we don't have it. We really don't have it.'

'We'll give you some time.'

'All right,' he said. 'A year.'

'Five days.'

'Six months.'

'Ten days.'

'Three months,' Wang said.

'All right, two weeks.' The same voice. 'This is the last two weeks. Your brother's no good, he doesn't follow the rules.'

It was past nine in the evening when Wang arrived back at the therapy centre after a ride in a crowded bus, where he had stared straight ahead, his usual posture in public places. But there was no straight ahead in his mind, only money. He did a calculation; he didn't have twenty-five thousand. The only way he could put that much together was to squeeze money out of his stocks. He immediately vetoed that idea. He wouldn't do that even to get married. No, and especially not for this. He hardened his heart. Fuck it, he didn't owe money to anyone.

In reality, hardening his heart was a trick to make him feel better. As the sportscaster Han Qiaosheng said when commenting on Chinese football games, so-and-so made a beautiful feint when no one was guarding him. Right after the feint, his heart softened, like the legs of football players on the Chinese team. Soft-hearted people hate easily. Wang Daifu hated money, hated the gang. Hated the gang members. Hated his brother.

His brother was a scumbag, a pile of stinky rotten flesh, clearly spoiled by their parents, and Wang felt sorry for them. They had worn themselves out, had showered their love for two sons on one, and in the end, this is what they'd wound up with. His younger brother had been born as Wang's replacement. That thought led him to self-loathing. He hated himself and hated his eyes. If not for his bad eyes, his parents would never have had a second child, and they definitely would not have turned him into a prodigal son. No matter how he looked at it, Wang realised that he was the source of all the trouble.

He had to settle the debt himself. It was his fate.

Wang thought about calling the police, but he couldn't. He could not win, not when they held his brother's IOU. Wang knew he'd never learn what was on that piece of paper. The bastards had a tight organisation, and acted properly, because they played by the rules.

But the money. Where could he get the money?

Suddenly it dawned on him that he had yet to speak with his brother. He dialled the number; the phone was still off. Why not talk to his wife, Wang thought. He called his mother to get the number for his brother's wife. It worked. When she answered, ear-pounding sounds of explosions and dive-bombers assailed his ears, a sign that she was at a movie. 'Xiaoning?' Wang Daifu said, consciously lowering his voice.

'Who's this?'

'Elder brother. Is he there?'

'We're watching a movie.'

'I know,' Wang said with an ingratiating laugh. 'Would you hand him the phone?'

Finally he'd found his younger brother, who was in hiding. But at least he'd located him. 'It's your brother,' Wang said. 'Where are you?'

'Anhui, in the countryside.'

Ah, Anhui. The countryside. A pretty place. Well, he could hide there for now, but not forever.

'What's up?' his brother said. 'I'm watching a movie.'

'You owe the gang money, don't you?' Wang asked cautiously, trying to stay calm so his brother wouldn't get angry and hang up.

'Right.'

'They came for it.'

'So they came for it. What's the big deal?'

'What do you mean, so they came for it? You're hiding in Anhui, but where are Ma and Pa going to hide?'

'What do I have to hide from? Xiaoning and I came to climb Huangshan.'

'Then why did you turn off your phone?'

'There's no money in the phone account, so what's the point in keeping it on?'

That effectively shut Wang up. He could tell that his brother was not on the run; he didn't sound like he was hiding out. He was calm and poised, and didn't sound like he was faking it. His younger brother was a great man, with a wide-open mind, who could treat weighty matters lightly. Flustered by this realisation, Wang raised his voice. 'Why aren't you worried? You owe them a lot of money!'

'Why worry? It's me who owes them money, not they who owe me.'

'Aren't you afraid they'll take it out on Ma and Pa?'

'What's the big deal? Why worry? It's not enough for them to resort to violence.'

'How can you not pay what you owe?' Wang demanded.

'Did I say I wouldn't?'

'Then do it.'

'I don't have it.'

'You have to do it, even if you don't have the money.'

'What are you worried about? Why can't you just enjoy life?'

His brother was smiling; Wang could not hear the smile, but he could sense that his younger brother was smiling in Anhui. That smile made Wang feel like a lout, that he was less than human, from head to toe. Stung by a sense of shame, he snapped his phone shut.

Wang Daifu stood alongside the road, looking around with a blank stare.

He was reminded that people in Nanjing had a nickname for people like his brother – living ghost. Wang had never known what it meant, until now. These living ghosts were wondrous creatures; no one knew how they managed to survive in this world. Their existence was a deep, deep secret, hinting at evil magic. Everyone was worried that they were fated to die, yet they not only survived but lived well, better than most people. They lived outside of life, but inside it as well. They were at the bottom of life, as well as at the top. They were neither optimists nor pessimists. A smile was never absent from their faces. They shared one observable trait, or, better yet, trademark: pet phrases that encompassed their philosophy of life – 'Why worry?' and 'What's the big deal?' They dealt with any problem, no matter how serious, with 'What's the big deal?' and 'Why worry?'

The sun sets, what's the big deal? Why worry? It'll rise again. It rises every day, so not to worry. It sets every evening, so what's the big deal?

Xiao Kong was with a client when Wang returned to the therapy centre. Suddenly tired, he sank into an easy chair to rest and do nothing but sit there. All he could think about was money. He decided to make two preparations, no matter what: first he had to put the amount together, that was the right thing to do. It wasn't his fault his brother had been born to replace him. So he decided that he would act as a replacement for his younger brother. He had to laugh: so this is life. It was all about replacing one thing with another. Raze the east wall to repair the west wall, and then raze the west wall to repair the east wall; raze the south wall to repair the north wall and then raze the north wall to repair the south wall; raze an inner wall to repair an outer wall and then raze an outer wall to repair an inner wall; raze a tall wall to repair a low wall and then raze a low wall to repair a tall wall. Raze and repair, and when you finish razing and repairing, life remains the same and yet has taken on a brand new look.

He didn't think he'd have any trouble borrowing the money from Xiao Kong. But then again, she wasn't the easiest person to deal with where money was concerned. He decided to talk it over with her. She finished with her client a little before ten o'clock, so Wang took Sha Fuming outside and whispered to him that he'd like to have an early-off and go back to the dorm with Xiao Kong before the others. The therapists were allowed to get off work early, which was part of the policy of early-on and early-off. In general, the therapy centre had few clients before ten in the morning, so most of the therapists came to work at ten, but some had to be there before ten to keep the place open, which was called early-on. For the sake of fairness, those who came early in the morning were permitted to leave an hour early the previous night. Pressing a button on his talking watch, Sha learned that it was ten o'clock, an hour before the early-off time of eleven.

Sha ran a tight ship and was impartial in regard to work scheduling, of which he was about to remind Wang. But then it dawned on him that Wang and Kong were lovers. This was the first time Wang had made such a request, which Sha appreciated. A manager had to be strict but not lose sight of humane treatment.

'Sure,' Sha said. 'But let me be clear. Only this time and you'll have to pay me back.'

'Of course,' Wang said.

Before Wang turned around, Sha found his shoulder and slapped him once, then a couple more times. The last two slaps were loaded with meaning, which embarrassed Wang tremendously when he understood. 'No, that's not it,' he hastened to say. But what was it? Wang could not explain.

'Go on now,' Sha said cheerfully, which intensified the insinuation and so mortified Wang that he was even more tongue-tied. Wordlessly he went into the lounge.

'Xiao Kong,' he said softly, 'let's go to the dorm now. I've talked to the boss and he said it was all right.' Wang thought he sounded sneaky.

She did not know what he had in mind, but true to her straightforward nature she blurted out, 'It's still early. What are we going to do if we go back now?'

She understood even before she finished. What else could a couple of lovers do when they returned early? She turned red as blood rushed to her face.

A dry cough from Xiao Ma in the corner turned the situation odd, or maybe it was odd only to Xiao Kong's ears. Ever since Xiao Ma's ill-considered move, both he and Xiao Kong had been on edge, which had introduced tension into their relationship. Known only to them, of course. Xiao Ma was concerned that she would tell Wang what he had done, while she was worried that he'd try it again. That tension caused them to desperately avoid bodily contact, which, in effect, made them even more conscious of the other.

He stood up after coughing and moved slowly to the door, banging his knee against something before he got there. Xiao Kong did not turn around, but she sensed an immense void that had opened up behind Xiao Ma.

Xiao Kong's heart ached for him, which surprised even her. Why did she feel that way? It wasn't right. And at that moment, she actually saw herself as his sister-in-law, his Sao-zi. Almost motherly. This role, which had materialised out of the blue, made her feel warm all over. She was, after all, a woman, and she wished the best for Xiao Ma.

To be sure, this was little more than an incidental thought. Mainly she was embarrassed. And when people are embarrassed, they turn slightly obtuse, something that often manifests itself in affected attempts at cleverness. 'Have you brought me something good to eat?' she said, unnecessarily, of course.

Wang Daifu was weighted down by what was on his mind. He stood there dawdling for a moment before replying, 'No.'

A real blockhead, a dope of the first order! Would it have killed him to lie to her?

'Go on,' Zhang Yiguang spoke up, 'go with him and sample the treat.'

It was a funny line that no one in the lounge laughed at. Xiao Kong was mortified. It felt to her as if what she and Wang were up to was out in the open for everyone to see.

No matter how embarrassed she felt, she knew she could not make Wang lose face in front of so many people. So, with her face burning and feeling larger than ever, she took his hand. 'Let's go.' The vigorous sound of her voice belied the confusion she felt. There was a measure of displeasure towards Wang amid that confusion.

What had been anticipated as a talk about money had, through twists and turns, become something quite different. There was nothing he could do now but take her hand and walk to the door. By then he was so flustered he'd no sooner stepped through the door than he stumbled and would have fallen if not for her hand.

'Slow down,' she said, in a strange, slightly tremulous voice. Wang Daifu forced himself to hold back, but that was the wrong thing to do, for now slowing down required even greater control.

It was ten o'clock Beijing time, an hour before the early-off hour of eleven o'clock, which meant they had an hour together, or, to be more precise, forty-three minutes, after the seventeen-minute walk. When their forty-three minutes were up, Zhang Yiguang and Ji Tingting, the early-off therapists, would be back. The situation was dire and urgent, meaning they had to take advantage of every minute and every second. They didn't exchange a word on the way and were drenched in sweat by the time they got home, where they confronted the first question: where do they go, her room or his? They were breathing hard as they hesitated. Time for Wang to be decisive, so he chose his room. He opened the door and stepped in, followed by Xiao Kong after a pause. He shut the door when she was barely in and secured it with the deadbolt. Then they kissed. Xiao Kong let out a sigh of relief and fell limply into his arms.

They quickly separated, knowing they couldn't afford to waste their precious time on kissing. Still kissing, they began to move and stopped when they reached Xiao Ma's bed, where they stripped themselves naked, littering the floor with their clothes. Wang hoisted Xiao Kong up to the upper bunk and she lay down, but then suddenly realised that they had been too rash. They should have taken off their clothes one item at a time and laid each one down carefully. This is a routine the blind invariably follow before bedtime. Everything they take off has to be piled item by item – socks at the bottom, followed by pants, shirts, sweater, and jacket or a coat. Only with this regimen would they be able to get dressed in an orderly fashion after getting out of bed, picking up and putting on each item in its proper order. But they'd been in too great a hurry, and their clothes were strewn all over the floor; worse yet, they were all jumbled together. It had taken no time to undress, but how would they put the clothes back on? They couldn't still be groping for their socks when the early-offs returned. The blind can never be impulsive, not even a little. Xiao Kong was agitated and upset.

'Our clothes, what about our clothes?'

'What about our clothes?' Wang asked as he climbed up to the bunk.

'They're all over the place. How are we going to put them back on? Hurry, would you?'

He finally got up, by then bone-hard. With virtually no foreplay, he entered her and immediately felt her shudder and tighten, something that had never happened before. But he had no time to ask why; all either of them could think of was time. They were fighting for time, which meant fighting for speed. He moved faster and pushed harder, almost aggressively. After a series of violent movements, he let out a sigh and it was over, filling the room with his smell. They were breathing hard, panting together. Before she could calm her breathing, Xiao Kong urged, 'Get off and get dressed. Hurry.'

Swiftly wiping themselves, they climbed out of bed, ruing the fact that they had lacked self-control a moment before. Now, see what happened, they had to grope for and identify each piece of clothing. This is yours, that's mine. But time waits for no one. What if the others returned now? Their hands busy, their hearts fluttering, they couldn't afford to panic; patience and composure were what was needed. After a quarter of an hour, they were finally dressed, but, still worried, they checked themselves in their mind's eyes. By the time they were sitting down their foreheads were bathed in sweat. Not bothering to wipe his forehead, Wang opened the door and picked up his talking watch: ten twenty-four. He was stunned. Still thirty-six minutes left. Take away the time spent on the road and the time for undressing and dressing, and they'd probably spent less than a minute in actual lovemaking. If it could be called lovemaking. He had simply and hurriedly ejaculated inside the woman he loved.

Maybe this was all that a working man like him could do for his woman. Wang Daifu said nothing. Thirty-six minutes. They had fought for the extra twenty-one hundred and sixty seconds, and instead of giving them to his woman, they would now be wasted in meaningless waiting. What were they waiting for? For the early-offs to return so they could prove they hadn't done anything? How absurd. Wang Daifu stood blankly at the door, doing nothing, not knowing what he could do. He took a deep breath and exhaled slowly. It sounded like a sigh, a sweaty sigh. Walking back to her he found her hand and caressed it with extra care, tender and loving. It was only at this moment that he felt boundless, tender love for Kong. What had he just done? *Baby, my woman*. His heart ached for her.

Xiao Kong was also aching, though it was her body. Bending over on her knees, she was in pain, feeling a burning sensation deep in that part of her body, worse than her first time. While similar, the pain this time was different. She'd cried back then, filled with a sense of proof for what the two of them possessed. Unable to put that happiness into words, she had cried. Like an idiot, Wang had felt the tears on her face and had apologised repeatedly, 'I'm sorry.' Only the word *heartbreaking* fit Kong's happiness. The ache that time had been wet. This time? Bone dry. She couldn't cry, she could only despair. What was she doing? Just what was she doing? She felt cheap. No one had defiled her and yet, for the first time, she felt humiliated. She had turned herself into a shameless bitch.

'Let's get married.' She looked up and grabbed his hands.

'What?'

She cocked her head. 'Let's get married.'

He thought for a moment. 'But we haven't made any preparations.'

'For what? What preparations do we need as long as we have each other?' Her hot breath spread across his face.

'But . . . I have no money.'

'I don't want your money. I have my own. We can use my money. All we need is a simple wedding. Won't that work?'

'Your money? How could I do that?'

'Then what would work?'

His lips twitched, but nothing came out.

'What's the hurry?' he said at last.

That hurt. Xiao Kong had just about given up all the proper restraints of a young woman by bringing up the topic of marriage. What did he mean, a *hurry*? It sounded awful, as if she were used goods no one wanted, and she had to force him into marrying her in a hurry. Had it really come to that?

'Of course I'm in a hurry,' she said. 'The way I am now, who would want me? Who would be in a hurry if not me?'

She had gone too far. They'd climbed down off the bed, and she was already talking about 'the way' she was. She might have meant something entirely different, but to him it sounded like a reproach;

she was chiding him – isn't it the case that he was happy to have sex with her, but when it came to talking about marriage, not a word.

But he needed the money. So after a protracted silence, he relented and muttered, 'You want to get married, we'll get married.'

'What's that supposed to mean?' she said, unaware of her tears, as she was reminded of the pressure from her parents and the awkwardness caused by Xiao Ma's unexpected move. *And for what? All because of you! She was overcome with grief. You got your wish when I came to Nanjing, but you can't appreciate the difficult situation I'm in. You don't realise how well I treat you. 'You want to get married, we'll get married.' What a demeaning, cold thing to say!* Choking up, she screamed, 'I came with you all the way to Nanjing and this is what I get? "You want to get married, we'll get married." Does that sound like it came from a human being? You can marry a stool, or a chair, or the sole of your shoe. You can go marry yourself. And you can go fuck yourself!'

There was no way Wang could bring up the subject of a loan now. He was miserable. 'How can you say something like that?' he said softly. 'How am I going to go fuck myself?'

Xiao Kong rubbed her eyes. 'Go fuck yourself.'

CHAPTER ELEVEN

JIN YAN

THEIR CO-WORKERS AT the centre were unaware that Jin Yan and Tailai's romance had begun. She abruptly put an end to her fanatical pursuit of him and turned overnight into a proper, well-behaved lady. Their co-workers were hardly ever again witness to her blatant attacks; she was mostly quiet these days. Now they worried about him, concerned that something terrible was about to happen.

In fact, flamboyant Jin Yan was incapable of breaking the mould of a typical blind couple, which can be summed up in the phrase, 'seeking quiet amid chaos'. And that was pretty much what they did; they found a secluded corner, where they sat quietly, hugging and kissing, and then wordlessly held hands. Normally, when young people are in love, they are on the go all the time, taking in a movie, going to coffee shops, visiting scenic sites. They chase one another, flirt, and fool around, all of which young blind couples would like to do but cannot. Too many obstacles. So what did Jin Yan and Tailai do? They restrained their bodies and passion, and turned themselves into a form of waiting. Holding hands, they engaged in shared waiting. Their wait was endless, their embraces endless, their kisses endless, and they never called attention to themselves. If no clients showed up, they could sit like that all day, not in the least bored. They parted only when they had clients, and, before they left, they touched the other's face and whispered, 'I'll be right back.' Or, they said nothing, letting go reluctantly, as if they could spend the rest of their lives just like that. Even as the distance spread, their index fingers would still be linked.

In the broadest terms, Jin Yan's romance did not really deviate from the norm, though there were differences because she was, after all, unlike other girls. She turned lethargic as she initiated another period of waiting. Waiting for what? For her wedding. She waited and she thought, and whenever she sat next to Tailai, her thoughts invariably drifted to her wedding and stayed there.

Jin Yan's brain functioned like a hard disk, a repository for data on weddings. If not for her disability, she could have been a wedding consultant. Her extensive knowledge provided limitless space for fantasies; strictly speaking, she was not so much in love as imagining her wedding.

A Chinese-style wedding was not her favourite, for its most noticeable trait and flaw is its focus on eating. The guests bring cash gifts, so they must eat back what they've given. It also involves drinking, and that usually brings trouble. Some of the men drink too much and steal the limelight, diverting attention from the point of the banquet; that is the biggest pitfall of a Chinese wedding, since it precludes the possible effect of the moon encircled by stars. Besides, it is vulgar. Even though the Chinese claim their country is a land of courtesy and propriety, one must admit that they know nothing about either. Just see how a Chinese wedding wraps up: tables littered with dishes and glasses, a filthy, jumbled, clattering mess. On the other hand, a Chinese wedding has its own charm, and that is the bridal chamber. Jin Yan coined a catch-all term for the bridal chamber: the man show. Very sexy.

Tailai's father must have talked to the guests beforehand, for as soon as the banquet is over, they walk off in twos and threes, picking their teeth and belching along the way. The master of ceremonies leads Jin Yan and Tailai into their bridal chamber, where they sit side by side on the edge of the bed. His mother, a woman with a face creased with wrinkles and a broad smile, has a few words for her son before she backs out of the room and closes the door from the outside. Through her red veil, Jin Yan can see the flame on the candles flicker before straightening out, sweet and charming, a soft yellow. The pagoda-shaped candles are bright red with gilded patterns for double happiness on the sides.

The candles burn brightly but, when dwarfed by the size of the room, appear dim and light up only half the bride's face, leaving the other half hidden in mysterious darkness. That is why candles are perfect, their unique quality of shrouding one side of everything, like a woman covering half her face with a *pipa* lute. The bright side of the bride's face is unique; it is deep, deep scarlet, lustrous from its redness, red from its lustre. Her blouse and veil are made of red satin, which come alive under the candlelight, but so briefly, that they surge forward like a torrential wave. The scene in the room gives the illusion that the candles ignore everything else in order to light up only the bride or, to be more precise, only one side of her face. All else is in darkness, the candles' mission is to highlight the bride, to make one side of her beautiful. Bright red. Comfortably warm. Sitting primly on the edge of the bed, she looks bashful, alluring, serene and quiet, like the reflection of a flower in water.

Tailai has led her into the chamber with a band of red satin, a red, bowl-sized satin flower in the middle. Another band of red satin is tied to him, like a rope attached to a prisoner in ancient China, and rather comical. Also on his chest is a red, bowl-sized satin flower. After being taken to the wedding bed, she finds the edge, not with her hands but by shifting her buttocks. She sits down. All is quiet except for one thing, and that is her heart, lub-dup, lub-dup, lub-dup. What is she to do? Her heart is not in sync with the silent world; she could die of shame.

Jin Yan is not shy, and never has been. On the contrary, there is something almost manly about her, an expansive, bold, even reckless quality. If not for her eyesight, she might truly have become one of those women who boldly sail the open seas. But this is, after all, a wedding—no, not a wedding, a marital union. She wants to be a blushing bride on this, the day of her marital union, even if she has to learn how.

At last Tailai moves close enough for their shoulders to touch, and hers drop so suddenly that her bracelet slips from forearm to wrist. The bracelet has a natural lustre, sleek and glistening, like congealed fat, or like the special aura given off by a bride. He rubs his fingers over the bracelet for a while before covering the back of her hand with the palm of his. All she can do is squeeze the handkerchief in her hand, refusing to let go.

Now comes the high point of the night. He removes the veil covering her face and head, at which moment, Jin Yan, the bold young woman, is actually bashful. He kisses her, no, not kisses, but touches her lips with his; they touch lips. His lips and mouth are burning hot.

'Am I nice?' she asks, a question she was determined to ask.

'Yes.'

'Do you love me?'

'Yes.'

'Then be gentle.'

Everything is done in a covert, indirect manner, including the odd things they say, all of which display a reticence that only makes the situation exciting and titillating. She blows out the candles, as if angry.

A Chinese wedding may not be her favourite, but she finds the bridal chamber infinitely fascinating; it is unfathomable, bewitching, even rather eerie and intoxicating, and yet quiet and serene, impossible to imagine. Sex, of course, is the most important activity inside a bridal chamber, but sex must be secondary to the special affection between the couple, who are now husband and wife, but could also be brother and sister. Westerners cannot understand how the bridegroom could be the bride's brother or the bride the bridegroom's sister. This is wrong. This is incest. But that is not how the Chinese look at it; for them it's not wrong at all. In fact, it is something entirely Chinese, understood only by Chinese, and appreciated by Chinese alone. Jin Yan is a fan of this Oriental style of sexuality and affection. The ancients referred to the three most important events in a man's life: his wedding night, the moment he passes the imperial exam, and running into an old friend in a strange city. There is a reason why the wedding night is placed first, which is why she finds its attraction impossible to resist. To savour this particular night, she has retained her virginity and has said no to Tailai, no matter how hard he has tried, how often he has begged. No, no. She refused to have sex with him before they were married; she wanted to wait till this night and, as described by the famed writer Eileen Chang, reach a state of ecstasy with him.

To Jin Yan, the greatest defect of a Chinese wedding is not the eating and drinking. No, it is the absence of something that, to her, should make every girl's heart flutter: a white wedding dress.

How could she not wear a white wedding dress? Something that lovely is not just clothing, it is the stuff of a young maiden's dreams, something that lays over her skin. It is a new, special skin that falls away like a cicada's cocoon, totally transforming a girl. It can be simple, it can be elaborate; it can be extravagant and luxurious, providing the girl with a graceful pose and charming walk. Jin Yan has been infatuated with the idea of a white wedding dress for another reason besides its dreamlike quality: she has a wonderful figure, one she would call alluring if you asked her. With such a striking figure, not to drape it in a white wedding dress once would be a waste. She has a typical northeastern Chinese woman's body, with a characteristic slenderness, fully displayed on her arms. They are tall and straight, which she knows is an inaccurate expression for arms, but she insists on thinking of them this way. Just think how lovely it will be when her sleeveless dress with its low-cut neckline shows off her curves and her smooth, slender arms, just born for a wedding. Jin Yan will love the way her arms look, even if the bridegroom cannot see them and she will have only a blurred view. At least she can prove that she has everything a woman ought to have, which to her is of the greatest importance.

There is only one slight imperfection: she has been gaining weight. That is unavoidable for the blind, who cannot exercise, and spend much of their time inactive. She can tell that flab is accumulating on the outside of her upper arms, which were once straight, sleek and soft.

In order to wear a white wedding dress, Jin Yan has secretly learned everything there is to know about the dress, and has found six areas that require her attention:

1. No red accessories for the white dress. So no red shoes, which symbolise walking into a fire pit, bad luck. In addition, no red flowers, red belt or red underwear.
2. The bride does not bow after putting on her white dress; she nods slightly if necessary, not because she is reserved, but to avoid showing too much cleavage.
3. No petticoat for the dress and not too much movement at the hemline.
4. After putting on the dress, the bride should hold her bouquet while walking but remember to pause after each step.
5. The veil must be worn during the ceremony, and only the bridegroom is allowed to remove it.
6. The man stands to the right of the woman, contrary to the Chinese custom.

It won't matter if it is a bright spring or a cool, pleasant autumn day. The most important element is sunlight shining down on everything, a rainbow sprinkling the world with its colourful rays, like a light rain or feathers to brighten every flower petal, every smiling face, even every exposed tooth. The sun will highlight the colour of everything, making the green of the earth greener, the red redder, the purple more purplish, and the yellow even more yellow. A splendid array of colours. That's how plants are unique: whatever their colours, they always match the other vegetation, and no one will consider it gaudy, no matter how splashy or loud. All their friends and family are there, standing on the lush green lawn; everyone is happy and well dressed, the sunshine highlighting their broad foreheads, clean-shaven chins and high, straight noses. Then the 'Wedding March' begins to play. Taking her hand, Tailai opens the door of the hall, and she walks with him to the lawn. The grass underfoot is spongy; they take slow, graceful steps. Everyone moves away; family and friends part to make room for them as if they are walking down a lane. Her train trails across the grass; she is graceful, lovely, bashful but proud, and so happy she is about to faint. They reach the centre of the lawn, surrounded by applause and best wishes.

Tailai's dark-blue suit presents a contrast to her white dress and makes it sparkle under the sun, like ice, like snow. Jin Yan is as pure and clean as jade.

The most attractive parts of a man's suit are the shoulders. Tailai's shoulders, which are not particularly broad, spread out nicely thanks to the tailoring, making him look taller. Leaning against his chest, she shows off her bosom, her breasts in perfect symmetry, with just a hint of cleavage, which, at that moment, is bathed in sunlight, enhancing her bridal glow. And then there are her shoulders, which are unique, the fleshy parts full and round, the bony parts fetchingly slim. A wind blows past her, saddened that it is unable to linger, but that sadness has nothing to do with Jin Yan. She is proud of herself.

'Do you take Jin Yan to be your wife?'

'I do, of course.'

'Do you take Tailai to be your husband?'

'Of course,' Jin Yan says. 'I do.'

Since they both are willing, Tailai places a tiny lock on Jin Yan and she does the same with him, and oh, the tiny lock has a lovely name: it's called a ring. There is a pair of them, from her to him and from him to her. They are a tender warning and reminder: you are mine now. Made of platinum, they will never corrode, sparkling bright as new even after ten thousand years.

Now Jin Yan is locked to Tailai; Tailai is locked to Jin Yan. They will not be apart again. Jin Yan is Tailai's kite, tied to his ring finger, no matter how high the sky or how far the horizon. But he is not her kite. Instead, he is a yo-yo, which quickly reverses itself to hurry back into her hand, no matter how far out she tosses it. Merry laughter erupts on the lawn, touching everyone's heart.

Surrounded by their friends and families, the bride and bridegroom are asked to share their story. He is too shy to say anything, but the bride is eager to tell everyone in a loud voice how she chased after him. But for maximum effect, she opts to describe it as *nabbing him*, and everyone laughs uproariously. People from the northeast of China love to be funny, both men and women; they would not be called northeasterners otherwise. After her witty remark, she decides that she and Tailai will sing. She will choose the best songs, ten altogether, each the most representative song of that year. The significance lies in the number ten, which symbolises a lifetime. They will sing, holding hands, until the sun sets in the west, until the last lingering hint of colour disappears from the sky, when each lamp lets out its finest, most brilliant light.

She will have to take off her wedding dress, but it will still be her wedding dress; hung up, it will be like the beginning of a legendary tale – once upon a time.

Then, as she thinks about her wedding dress, a preposterous idea begins to churn in her head: why not have a Western-style wedding, since she is so fond of that style of dress? And if they are going to have a non-Chinese wedding, why not have the ceremony in a church? She has never been to church, but has seen them in movies; to her, the loveliest part of a church is its interior, not its exterior. A church is heaven on earth, with its many arches holding up the vault, lending it an impressive air that is solemn, solid and sacred, but pure at the same time. The organ begins to play songs of praise and eulogy that swirl atop the stone floor, the lingering strains reverberating between heaven and earth. As her fantasy continues, she sees herself walking into church with him, nearly floating above the floor, while the dazzling colours of the stained-glass windows fill her head. She knows that above her is heaven and below her the earth, and between the two are her wedding and her love, both of which are filled with the sound of organ music.

Why not have a church wedding then? Yes, why not? After hearing an ad on 'Voice of Jinling', Jin Yan placed a call to Romance Wedding Company on a Tuesday afternoon. The pleasant salesgirl patiently listened until Jin Yan was finished before asking her an unexpected question. 'Are you a Christian?' Confused, Jin Yan did not know how to answer, prompting the girl to use the more popular expression. 'Do you believe in God? Only one of you needs to.' It was a serious question, one she had not considered. She snapped her phone shut the moment she understood its significance; she could not say she did, because she didn't. But saying no did not bode well. To make sure the wedding company did not call her back, she turned off her phone. The possibility of even more difficult questions frightened her.

On the other hand, the salesgirl's questions reminded her that either the bride or the bridegroom must believe in something if they expected a formal wedding.

What did she believe in? She mulled the question over for a long time, but still did not know what to believe. She had believed in light, but light had rejected her. She had once believed in her eyes, but they had rejected her. As her eyesight deteriorated, her field of vision shrank and her world grew increasingly dark, increasingly narrow; the world had rejected her. The blue sky rejected her, white clouds rejected her, green mountains rejected her, green water rejected her, even her own face rejected her. What was she expected to believe in? All she could do was probe and speculate. For a woman whose life depends on probing and speculation, it is hard to *believe*. As she played with her mobile phone, Jin Yan said to herself, Not believing in anything is right. No beliefs means fewer disappointments. From now everything will be fine, like facing an open sea or blooming flowers in the warmth of spring.

She believed only in a wedding, that was all she needed. With a wedding you are no longer alone. At the very least there is one person with whom you share a life. That is worth believing. A wedding is a sort of magic. It turns the world into a home. It completes things.

Jin Yan happily discovered that developing a belief in her wedding transformed her into a marriage fanatic. Weddings were everywhere for her, they occupied every moment of her time. Take meals, for instance. In the past, she had always eaten with a spoon, for its obvious convenience. Now she stopped eating with a spoon and began using chopsticks. She notched the thick end of one chopstick and tied it to its mate with a string. Now they were married. She carried out a grand ceremony for them, imagining the sumptuous setting in the Austrian movie *Sissi*, a tale of royalty. The ceremony took place during lunch one day. Grand luxury was the mood of the hour, in which the sound of her chewing was like that of a symphonic orchestra.

Cupping jars can marry too. Cupping is one of the most popular supplemental treatments offered by tuina therapists. 'Qi', or energy, plays an important role in traditional Chinese medicine. The human body has both hot and cold qi. If you have cold qi, it needs to be drawn out of you, and that's where cupping comes in. Jin Yan had a special way of cupping her clients. She did everything in pairs. Sometimes there were four pairs, at other times five or six, thereby turning the client's back into a grand hall, the perfect site for a group wedding.

Group weddings are not desirable, but they can be more fun, since the arrangements are satisfying. They embody the uniqueness of China, for even the most private matters brim with the spirit of collectivism.

Flavours can marry too. The two perfectly paired flavours are sweet and sour, and peppery and spicy. Sweet is a woman, with a manly side; sour is a man, with a feminine aspect. Their marriage is, without doubt, sweet and sour pork. Sour but sweet. Sour *and* sweet. This is a marriage for the poor and lowly born, who understand gratitude and contentment. They most easily embody the flavours of life. It is the poor but honest scholar marrying the pretty daughter of a humble family, the kindergarten teacher marrying a taxi driver. The couple don't need an extravagant wedding to be happy, two hearts beating as one, passing the difficult days in homely familiarity.

The peppery flavour is an unreasonable man, while spicy is a difficult woman. They are ill-suited, rivals from a previous life, and reason dictates that they will not walk the path of life together. No one holds out any hope for them. But here is where the pleasure and richness of life intercede, as peppery and spicy are a predestined pair. They give not an inch to the other from the day their romance begins. *I mock you. You bully me.* They are feared by all, but bickering only draws them closer, fighting makes them stick together. Until one day, they are married. Even at their wedding they find it hard to believe there could ever be such a day. More bickering, mollified only by mediators. The wedding ending on bad terms, they go their own way to make preparations for the divorce. Which, strangely enough, never occurs. They grow old until, my goodness, a golden wedding anniversary. Fifty years of fighting and bickering, upsetting their neighbours, but not each other. The longer it goes on, the more delicious it gets. Though they do not know it, they are like most things in life, like lamb skewers at roadside stands, they stay together even after a lifetime of discontent. Regret sets in as life ebbs, when they realise they did not have a decent wedding. Late at night, when all is quiet, they wonder:

Why could I not have treated you better back then? Have another skewer. What they want is a second chance. It'll turn out the same, for that's life, one lovely scene after another.

The most interesting wedding is that of a bicycle. Two wheels, one just like the other, thrown together. A man is thrown together with a woman, and vice versa. The bride and groom are equal, but only in appearance. One is always in front of the other, or one on the outside and the other inside, and it stays that way, even at the wedding; one moves and the other obediently goes along. They are forever separated by a distance, one leading and the other following, step for step, without protest. But take a closer look, and something's wrong here. The one at the rear is the real motive force. It pushes, while the one in front is a mere puppet. The one in front willingly acknowledges that reality, since the one at the rear is so good to it. This kind of marriage is that most often seen on the streets, which is filled with pairs of bicycle tyres, one in front and one behind, neatly paired. They sometimes separate, and that's when the one at the rear wants to be up front. Bad things happen then. The rear wheel pushes too hard, and disaster follows.

Jin Yan has a fondness for peanuts. Nearly every shell encloses two peanuts. They are close neighbours, quiet, but happy to keep their distance. Yet that will never do. So Jin Yan removes the shell, revealing a *Golden Youth* and *Jade Maiden*. 'How can you stand being apart?' she asks. She brings them together by holding a secret wedding ceremony in the palm of her hand. They are a natural couple, a good match in virtually every way. But they are shy. Jin Yan sends them into the bridal chamber, where she removes their clothes. A brand new couple, naked, sleek, incredibly sexy. And completely in love. A marriage made to be consummated. Jin Yan once invited Xu Tailai to participate by taking his hand and placing this new couple in his palm.

'You eat them,' he said.

Dense! Dense! A fool!

She thought long and hard, of course, and realised that she could not be arranging weddings for others. Mostly she thought about her own wedding. No, she wasn't thinking, she was wavering, comparing, weighing. Which was better, a Chinese or a Western-style wedding? She couldn't make up her mind. But so what? Seized by folly, she wanted them both. Who says a couple can only have one wedding? That's not national policy. She decided she would get married in a white wedding dress first and then Tailai would marry her amid charming, romantic candlelight. What's the big deal with two weddings? All that requires is money. She is willing to part with it; she wants to spend the money. Why do we say 'spend money'? Why 'spend'? That's obvious. You spend money in order to buy a good time, and every penny brings a minute of happiness, like a sudden spring breeze, with blossoms opening on thousands of pear trees.

CHAPTER TWELVE
GAO WEI

DU HONG FOUND it hard to believe that she could so quickly establish herself at the tuina centre. Fortunately, she had enough self-awareness to realise that her skills alone were insufficient to attract many return clients; the key, already revealed, was her looks. As this was her first job, she had yet to accurately comprehend the importance of a woman's looks. But she knew that appearance was linked to productivity.

One fact closely related to her looks was that all her return clients were male, mostly in the age group of thirty-five to forty-five. She was happy and proud of her appearance, and, naturally, found it strange, a new experience for her, one that made her happy, the natural delight for women. If she'd stayed home, she'd never have known how pretty she was. She'd known she was good-looking, but not that she was pretty. They are not the same; they embody different qualities. That is what made her proud. Then another fundamental fact occurred to her; young, single men rarely came to her, and that gave her an indescribable sense of loss until she found a convincing explanation: young men are usually in good health, and so hardly any of them showed up for tuina therapy. It wasn't that they did not find her attractive, but that she never had a chance to encounter them. If they showed up – a big if – who knew what would happen?

It was good to know she was pretty, but there were times when it wasn't. She sensed that she was becoming 'complicated', which is common among girls, whose worries all seem to stem from knowing how they look. Du Hong actually sort of wished she didn't know about her looks.

The busier she was, the more contacts she made with people, which complicated matters. People truly are strange creatures, and there are all kinds. How can the differences be so huge? It is no exaggeration to say that no two people are alike. She could not see them, but their differences were clear to her as she worked on their bodies and talked to them. Some were heavy, some skinny; some strong, some frail; some genteel, some rude; some laughed a lot, some were quiet; some stank of alcohol, some of cigarettes. But no matter how different, they had one thing in common: they all carried mobile phones, which came equipped with the owners' favourite jokes. The first one she heard went like this: When a farmer went out into the field, his wife's lover showed up. But before they could get anything on, the farmer came home for his hoe. The panicked wife had an idea: she told her lover to hide in a hemp sack behind the door. Picking up his hoe, the husband spotted the sack as he was walking out the door. It looked full, so he gave it a kick. 'Hey, what's in there?' he wondered out loud. 'Corn!' the wife's lover yelled out.

Du Hong was in stitches when she first heard the joke, but things got complicated after listening to a few more. Not every joke was as clean as 'corn'. Being a young woman, she did not understand many of the jokes, so, with a bemused look, she'd ask a client what the punchline meant; but she usually got it before she even finished asking. And that was terrible. She felt dirty, sordid and obscene. Blood rushed to her face and she was overwhelmed by dejection, upset that she had become part of a dirty joke. But there were many jokes, and as time went by, she actually got used to them; for one thing, she could not possibly stop her clients from talking, and she early on discovered that men of this type were especially fond of telling jokes to girls, and telling them in such a way as to imply that the joke was really about them. Those men earned Du Hong's secret contempt, and she pretended either that she wasn't listening or did not understand the joke. The problem was, she did understand some of them and it was hard to keep from laughing. She didn't want to laugh at their jokes, but it was hard to hold back, and so she laughed. That always made her feel as if she'd swallowed a fly.

Since Du Hong's clients all carried mobile phones, and each phone arrived with a joke, she came to know that the world was one big mobile phone, and that the true colour of life is a joke.

The jokes all shared one thing in common: *hun*, a term both for meat and things carnal. Du Hong knew all about the dietary use of *hun*, as opposed to *su*, or vegetarian. What lay behind *hun* could only be meat and all things carnal. As a term for the flesh, it frightened her, made her uneasy. After listening to many jokes from her clients, she reached a conclusion that formed her general impression, or appraisal, of the world; that is, she lived in a carnal world. That thing that had carried her away – society – was *hun*; all men were *hun*, and so were all women. Everyone was busily engaged in their bodily affairs: unbridled sexual intercourse, disorder, insanity and infatuation. Unbridled. Du Hong congratulated herself for being blind; it was better not to be able to see. If she could see, where would she look? Everyone was the embodiment of flesh. Flesh with raging desire.

She recalled how terrified she'd been when she first left home, worried that she would not find a place in society. But she had to admit that in addition to fear, she'd also felt a sense of longing. She'd longed for the world; she'd longed to meet strangers and see unusual things; she'd longed for days that were different. Eager for action, she'd hoped to be recognised and accepted by the world and become part of it as soon as possible. Life meant something to her, for it contained all her dreams; but its true face was now revealed through the jokes from all those mobile phones. The world was depraved, lewd, filthy, tiring and vulgar. There was nothing for her to long for. From emperor to beggar, from CEO to secretary, from pilot to flight attendant, and from village chief to village elder, there was no difference at all. She went through daily life feeling as if she were standing on a pile of dog shit, and if she left it, she could not be self-sufficient. Sooner or later she too would be just like them, flesh with raging desire.

Truth was, Sha Fuming had already begun to let his desire rage towards Du Hong by touching her face. And he would surely want to let loose his desire in more secretive ways, closing in on her. Tension gripped her at that thought; she was in danger. At any moment, she could become the corn that was stuffed naked into a hemp sack, and from there be transformed into material for jokes in mobile phones.

Du Hong was guarded, but did not want to offend him. He was, after all, the boss. She would have to leave if he told her to; walking out would be easy, but where could she go? Sure, she could go to another place, but nothing would change; wherever she went, there would be men, women, jokes, mobile phones and hemp sacks filled with corn. In fact, all people were corn stuffed in hemp sacks.

She decided on a strategy of ignorance and keeping a polite distance, acceptably polite to Sha Fuming, not too close but not too distant, neither responding nor rejecting. He could let his desire rage; the key was how to use it to her advantage. Ignorance was her best weapon, a girl's nuclear weapon, invincible. No matter how his desire raged, she would simply feign ignorance. Feigned ignorance is true ignorance, like people pretending to be asleep who will not awaken regardless of how others try to rouse them.

And that was precisely what hurt Sha Fuming the most. His intentions were pure. He had already given up his faith for her, for he had ceased wishing that he could see. No longer did he seek to be part of mainstream society; he would rather live the life allotted to him, through the darkness with the unsighted Du Hong. So he began his pursuit. Du Hong cleverly neither accommodated nor refused him. Feigned ignorance was her weapon of choice. She pretended to be clueless. Nothing he did or said broke through her unenlightened veneer. She never veered from a simple and cheerful tone, like a child consumed by the act of eating a piece of candy. Sha Fuming went at it in a roundabout way, hinted to her, begged her with an increasing sense of urgency and openness. She treated all that with incomprehension. What was he to do? He had to tell her, plead with her, 'I love you, Du Hong.'

Pitiful young Du Hong. 'I'm too young.'

Now what could he say? The more pitiful she sounded, the more besotted he became and the more he longed to be her protector, to watch over her. He was possessed, and could not extricate himself from that state. All right, then, he was not only possessed, he was also stubborn. Too young? Then I'll wait. If not this year, then next year, or the year after that, and on and on. You'll be old enough one day. Sha Fuming was convinced he could wait for that day, as long as he was patient and, more importantly, in love with her.

He kept his vigil confidential, a closely held secret, something that existed only in his heart. He cautioned himself to be prudent, for he was, after all, the boss, and he mustn't let his employees get the dreadful impression that he was guilty of abusing his power. And there was more to it than that: in a word, Sha Fuming's vanity. If he were too open in his intentions, it could easily be misinterpreted as taking advantage of his position to win her over. That would make him appear dishonourable. So, before everything was out in the open, better not to let anyone know what he was up to.

But Sha Fuming was wrong. Someone did know. Who? Gao Wei, the receptionist. She saw through him the moment he fell for Du Hong. One thing the blind tend to forget is their eyes – dead eyes that cannot be the windows to their souls – can truly be the doors through which their hearts are revealed. When something interests them, they don't know what it means to hide what is behind their eyes; they will begin twisting their necks, sometimes even their whole upper bodies. Mired in a depressed mood, Sha Fuming perked up whenever Du Hong was around, and his neck and torso began to twist. In Gao Wei's view, Du Hong was the sun and Sha Fuming was a sunflower. He might appear motionless but there were subtle movements, for he was listening, yet he didn't know that the expression on his face had made him part of Du Hong's movements. His lips twitched in a special way, slight yet hurried, followed by the abrupt hint of a smile that quickly disappeared. He was losing self-control. He was hopelessly immersed in feelings of love.

Gao Wei could stare at her boss without worrying that he would know.

What she had never figured out was how Sha Fuming, whose neck twisted in Du Hong's direction whenever she started to move, knew that it was her. Intrigued, Gao Wei closely observed Du Hong's legs and there was her answer. Both Du Hong and Xiao Kong stepped more heavily with the left foot than with the right, though the difference was subtle. Xiao Kong's heels touched the floor first, while for Du Hong it was the balls of her feet. Du Hong was more timid than Xiao Kong, so each step was a sort of probe. When Gao Wei shut her eyes, she could clearly distinguish Du Hong's footsteps.

Gao Wei and Du Hong became friends that night. When they got off work, Gao took Du Hong's hand and led her over to the three-wheeler. Du Hong hesitated, but Gao helped her up before taking off Du Hong's shoes for her to sit comfortably on the soft mound of bedsheets. It is easy to imagine how that touched Du Hong: *Gao Wei is a good person, so warm-hearted. I have nothing to offer, and yet she treats me with kindness.* Fate had favoured Du Hong by letting her encounter such a good person.

And so they became friends. Close friends. Distance is a constant; as the distance between Du Hong and Gao Wei shrank, that between

Du Hong and Tingting lengthened. She felt somewhat guilty about that; she was, in the end, a bit of an opportunist. That manifested itself not in relation to a three-wheeler, but to sight. Say what you will, Gao Wei was sighted, and Du Hong was in need of a friendly pair of eyes.

The friendship blossomed, and in a very short time they were talking about everything under the sun. And yet Du Hong held back when it came to revealing her most private thoughts. She said nothing about Sha Fuming. That is the last thing she could reveal to Gao Wei. It wasn't that she didn't trust Gao; it was just that, to her, a different pair of eyes came with a different mouth. The blind and the sighted exist on different levels, and maintaining a distance between them can preserve a friendship.

Du Hong was not the only one whom Gao Wei treated with kindness; to be fair, she was nice to all the blind therapists. Her issues were with the centre's sighted employees: two receptionists – herself and Du Li – two staff members, who were also called assistants – Xiao Tang and Xiao Song – and the cook, Jin da-jie. Gao Wei and Du Li did not get along, hadn't from the very beginning. Jin da-jie, a distant relative of Zhang Zongqi, was better connected than the others, and Du Li had got her job because of her. Unaware of that connection at first, Gao Wei came on a bit too strong, because she had completed two years of high school, while Du had not even finished junior high. By the time she had a fallout with Du Li and learned of the connection, she had already seriously offended Jin da-jie. Who was Jin da-jie? She was the one who controlled everyone's meal at the centre; more of one thing, less of another, and the days were not the same. That was why Xiao Tang and Xiao Song tried hard to butter her up, which made things difficult for Gao. Life is hard for an intellectual.

In the broadest terms, there were two groups at the therapy centre, the blind and the sighted, and they managed to get along quite well. If it had to be said which side had the edge, then it would be the blind, who had a profession, were skilled and were paid better. The sighted, on the other hand, played supporting roles, the helpers. Generally speaking, neither side meddled in the affairs of the other. They worked well together, though different, water from the well and water from the river, one safe and secure beneath the surface, the other gushing along on top.

Gao Wei got along fine with the other sighted employees at first, but a meting out of punishment caused a rift between her and Du Li. One night, Du Li was scheduled to be on duty and asked Gao to switch with her so she could take care of some personal business. Gao agreed. Unfortunately, she carelessly forgot to turn off the air-conditioning in room six that night. The following morning, Sha Fuming and Zhang Zongqi determined that Gao Wei was responsible for the air-conditioning running all night and fined her ten yuan, an unjust outcome, in her view. To make matters worse, Du Li never paid back the shift she owed.

Did Du Li never make a mistake? In fact, she made far more mistakes than Gao Wei. The reception desk was the scene of most mistakes. Couldn't there be minor discrepancies in the accounts. Wasn't it inevitable that a client's name might be entered incorrectly? Wasn't it unpreventable that a client would lodge a complaint because of the receptionist's tone of voice? Wasn't it likely that a receptionist might occasionally doze off? Could it happen that a receptionist forgot to turn off the lights or air conditioner before leaving at night? Everyone makes mistakes. Running the reception desk at the Sha Zongqi tuina centre was a high-risk job. At other therapy centres, the receptionist could make a little extra by opportune client assignments, but not at the Sha Zongqi tuina centre, whose bosses had both worked in the trade and knew all the tricks. A wrong move could cost a receptionist her job.

Gao Wei's and Du Li's mistakes were dealt with differently. When Du Li made a mistake, she was punished privately. But not Gao Wei, for whom there would be a meeting every time she did something wrong. Meetings terrified her. There was something special about them. While there were only so many employees, only so many mouths at the centre, everything changed at a meeting. Everyday conversational tone was abandoned, as the people took pains to speak standard Mandarin and to reach a consensus. A meeting was called, agreement was reached, the results were announced. Everyone else was right – Gao Wei was the daughter of a whore and deserved to be taken out and shot. She felt she was always walking on eggshells.

Given how hard things were for her at the centre, Gao Wei had thought of leaving, but it was just a thought, because she found it difficult to admit defeat; she had attended high school, and it would be a huge loss of face if she could not outsmart a junior high student. So she forced herself to stay, a believer in the adage that after thirty years of floating eastwards, the river will turn and flow westwards. One must always take the long view, and as time passes, life can get better. One mustn't hurry things along.

When had Sha Fuming fallen in love with Du Hong? There had been no prior indications. Du Hong was a beauty, Gao Wei knew that. But Sha Fuming could not see, so why would he care what she looked like? Gao gave this plenty of thought, without coming up with an answer. No matter. At least she discovered that the blind also care about appearance. And that made things easy. We'll see what happens the next time Sha Fuming calls a meeting. She was well aware that Sha was a smart man. If a smart man wants to win over a woman, he cannot overlook her confidante. One's appearance is manifested in people's tongues.

Gao Wei treated Du Hong like royalty and was totally selfless. She expected nothing in return. She had only one goal in mind, and that was for everyone to see that she and Du Hong were best friends. Then, when Boss Sha and Du Hong finally got together, she could be his most trusted ally. Meetings? Go ahead, have them. Sometimes they're useful, sometimes not. That's how it goes.

In contrast to Gao Wei's selflessness, Du Hong wanted to repay Gao for her friendship. She went overboard to make known the fact that she and Gao Wei were friends. It was a safety measure to ward off hidden dangers. She didn't know when or from where Sha Fuming's desire would rage towards her. Only one end of sugar cane is sweet. If letting his desire rage was what the boss had in mind, that secured her job; but she had to face the dangers of that desire. Now she had Gao Wei, and she was safe. Gao Wei had eyes that could see. Sha Fuming had to be cognisant of that fact. Gao Wei's eyes were Du Hong's sun in the day and her moon at night. If he dared to make a move, and Gao Wei's eyes were the switch, *bam*, the desire would disperse.

One day at noon, Du Hong and Ji Tingting went to the supermarket and asked Gao Wei to come along as their guide. They held hands, two blind girls and their sighted companion. Gao Wei was on her best behaviour, mainly by not talking too much. Normally, when a blind person is with a sighted one, low self-esteem keeps the blind person quiet; they rarely speak. But things were different now; as the two blind girls kept up a conversation on the way, Gao held her tongue, which was so unusual and commendable that even Ji noticed. She said to Du Hong later that night, 'Gao Wei's okay. She doesn't talk much.' Du Hong thought about it and had to agree. On the following morning, Du Hong got out her key and went to her lounge locker, from which she took out two chocolate wafers before locking it and going to the front desk, where she ate one of the wafers and gave the other one to Gao. Gao Wei knew that the blind therapists rarely exchanged gifts, which added special significance to Du's gesture. Cheerfully putting the wafer into her mouth, Gao began to goof around with Du Hong for the first time. Grabbing her ponytail from behind, she gave it a gentle tug and turned the girl's face upwards. Du smiled at the ceiling. This girl is a real beauty; a smile like that could win many hearts. Boss Sha fell for her, but what does he know? He knows nothing. Her visible charms are wasted. What a shame.

Gao Wei finally got up the nerve to start giving Du Hong special favours with her appointments, so brazenly that the sensitive blind therapists detected the difference almost immediately. When word reached Du Li, who was direct by nature, she had a fit. But, lacking proof, she dodged the issue of favouritism and turned her attention to the three-wheeler issue, bringing it up at the beginning of the next meeting. 'Who does the three-wheeler belong to?' she asked. 'The centre or some individual? Do centre rules mean anything?' she demanded.

What was left unspoken was obvious. A hush fell over the lounge. Not a sound. They were expecting Gao Wei to say something. She didn't. She was waiting. She knew that Boss Sha would speak up. He did, he talked about professional matters, specifically youthful anorexia, focusing on the parents of those children, asking if they are willing to treat the condition pharmaceutically. The answer was no. The best way to deal with anorexia was physiotherapy. Kneading the stomach area relaxed the stomach. It was a new area, one awaiting development.

From there he elevated the tenor of his talk. He spoke of humanism, the most important element of which is compassion. He quickly raised the issue of 'mutual assistance' to the lofty notion of 'spiritual civilisation'. He was quite serious, but maintained a tone of affability. He did not bring up the three-wheeler, but he did offer everyone his conclusion. 'People working together in the same unit should help each other out, and that is worth promoting.' He followed that with a question: 'Should we hold to the old rules?' He answered it himself: 'The good ones, yes. The bad ones need to be changed. Reform is nothing but continuity and change. Even the central government suggests that reform is carried out like groping at the rocks to cross a river. So what reason do we blind people have not to do the same?'

Du Li sneered. She didn't say it, but she inwardly cursed Sha for the crap that had come out of his mouth. Continue what? Change what? You're just flapping your lips. Du Li stole a look at Gao Wei, who was not looking at her. What was there to see on her face? Gao Wei was surprised to hear a connection between her action and the central government, something she could never have imagined. She was unworthy of such a comparison. Still, she could not help but be nervous.

Xiao Kong, who was sitting on the sofa, felt extremely unhappy. She didn't care who rode in the three-wheeler, but she could not tolerate any collusion between a tuina therapist and the front desk. Back in Shenzhen she'd been victimised by people at the reception desk and had no good thoughts for them. But what particularly upset her was any therapist who buttered up a receptionist. *How can they demean themselves like that? It's a huge slap in the face of the disabled. Du Hong is a force to be reckoned with. You've sewn up a solid relationship with a receptionist. No wonder you're doing so well. Gao Wei's helping you out. Now I get it.*

Xiao Kong did not easily hold her tongue. She and Tingting were on the same shift, and Xiao Kong could not keep it in. 'Damn,' she said. 'There are ass-kissers no matter where you go!' It sounded vague, but was suggestive. Xiao Kong was well aware that Ji Tingting and Du Hong were good friends, and she wanted to know what Tingting would say.

But before another word was spoken, Wang Daifu heard the comment as he was walking down the hallway. He coughed. Ji Tingting smiled and coughed back, as a reply both to Wang and to Xiao Kong. Not responding to Xiao Kong's complaint, Tingting teased her instead. 'Wang Daifu is so nice, Xiao Kong, he's too good for you. Can I have him?'

Disappointed at not getting the answer she wanted, Xiao Kong returned with her own teasing. 'No you can't. But if you want, you can be his number two, and I'll treat you nicely.'

Ji's client laughed. He was a return client, and knew her well. 'Congratulations, Ji Daifu,' he said. 'You're a concubine now.'

Without a word, Ji quietly reached under the client's buttock and, with her left thumb, pressed down hard on the *weizhong* acupoint, such a sore spot that the client yelped.

'Concubine, my foot!' Ji said. 'I'm the grand aunt.'

That night Du Li dropped a bombshell in front of everyone. Du Hong wasn't kissing ass. What was gained by kissing Gao Wei's ass? Was it worth the effort? The real ass-kisser was Gao Wei. She wasn't kissing Du Hong's ass; she was kissing the ass of the future boss lady.

Du Li was not making this up. More and more indications showed that Boss Sha had fallen in love. A man who placed such importance on face, he made a fool of himself when Du Hong was around. That was bad enough, but he made a fool of himself around Gao Wei too. He wore a goofy smile when he talked to her. Everyone could hear it. Love is toxic. Anyone in love is a fool. Boss Sha, you're finished. You're done.

CHAPTER THIRTEEN
ZHANG ZONGQI

OUTSIDERS, OR THE NEW arrivals, often mistakenly assumed that Sha Fuming was the sole owner of the tuina centre. That was not the case. There were, from the beginning, two bosses. If only one were to be picked, then it would have to be Zhang Zongqi, not Sha Fuming.

In contrast to Sha, an extrovert and a show-off who was articulate and talkative, Zhang behaved more like a blind man. His blindness was most severe. When he was a year old, he had lost his eyesight during a botched medical procedure. On the surface, he was considered blinded after birth, but where visual memory was concerned, it made more sense to consider him having been born blind. On the other hand, even if he'd had perfect eyesight, he could not easily have changed his introverted and reserved nature, which he seemed to have further magnified. He was extremely reticent, borderline autistic, for he hardly ever spoke. Put differently, he never said anything superfluous; whatever he said had to reflect how things should be, and he would rather not say anything if a word from him could not change or determine the outcome of a matter.

As one of the bosses, Sha Fuming rarely took clients, since his responsibility at the centre was day-to-day management. He walked around checking things, the clients' perfect image of a boss. Zhang was different; he was a boss *and* a tuina therapist, never giving up on working with clients. This meant that he had two incomes, one the year-end bonus, which was the same as Sha's, the other from the therapy work, fifteen yuan an hour, nearly the same as Wang Daifu's. With an aversion to being idle, Zhang always found something to do, even when taking a break in the lounge – reading, for instance. His favourite book was *Dream of the Red Chamber*, with the two characters he liked the most. One was Lin Daiyu, whose brows were described as 'frowning but not quite, as if shrouded in misty smoke', and whose 'eyes, filled with emotion, seemed to be happy but not quite'. Lin was blind to reality; she was smart and she was clever, but she saw nothing, and she could not even control her own destiny, which was a pity. The other person Zhang liked was Jiao Da, a rough-hewn man, totally lacking in literary qualities, but who knew everything. It made no difference which branch of the family, the Rongguo or the Ningguo, nothing escaped his attention. He even spotted his daughter-in-law's frantic footprints in the doorway.

Sha Fuming liked to do things in a big way; he loved the style of being a boss, and since he was fond of acting like one, he *was* the boss, something Zhang was happy to concede. Zhang liked things one way, Sha the other way, and that made everything easy. Since each got what he wanted, they were both happy. Unlike Sha, who was overambitious and unrealistic, Zhang was more practical, with eyes only for actual profits. He would never let his hands go idle simply because of the empty title of a boss; he considered himself to be an employee. Only when he and Sha sat down face to face was he a boss, the boss's boss, that is to say, but never the domineering type. Since Sha made most of the decisions, it would not be unseemly for Zhang to share his views on some matters; besides, they were friends to begin with. His understated style turned out to be more effective, and in any case, he was invariably meticulous when it came to important matters. One thing Zhang was sure of was that, since he was not directly involved in management, he could not easily offend the others; yet his opinions were usually treated as guidelines during votes. He suffered no loss of power and had two sources of income. Not bad. All he wanted was for the centre to run smoothly and stay in operation.

But the centre stopped running smoothly. The disturbance came out of nowhere.

It was lunchtime. Jin da-jie walked into the lounge with a pot of soup. That was her routine: soup first, followed by the rice and other food. The employees ate out of identical lunch boxes, which she filled with food in the dorm, then carried over to the lounge and handed out one by one.

'Lunchtime,' she called out while distributing the boxes. 'Lunch is ready. We're having mutton today.'

Zhang Zongqi knew it was mutton from the smell the moment Jin da-jie had walked in. He loved mutton, mostly because of the unique gamy smell. Many people were given to showing off their hometown by saying that the mutton in their village had no gamy smell. That struck Zhang as utter nonsense. How could they call it mutton if it wasn't gamy? If it's not gamy, could it deserve to be sold at places where they palm off dog meat as mutton? It was one of his favourite dishes, but he didn't eat it as often as he'd have liked. The reason was simple: the tuina centre had rules stipulating that room and board was provided for all employees. If the bosses wanted to bring in more money, the employees' palates would have to suffer. Since bosses and employees ate together, controlling one controlled all. Dining on mutton was a rarity.

Taking the lunch box from Jin da-jie, Zhang opened it and let his nose savour the fragrance. That is how you treat good food. Instead of digging in, you must enjoy the aroma until you can't hold out any longer, and then slowly bring it up to your mouth. That's what whetting the appetite means. The better the food, the greater the need to whet your appetite, and the more you whet your appetite, the better the food tastes in the end.

But without warning, Gao Wei stood up and slammed her lunch box down on the table. It made a loud noise. 'Hold on, everyone. I have something to say.' She sounded hostile.

Clueless, Zhang cocked his head and waited, a piece of mutton suspended in the air between his chopsticks.

'I have three pieces of mutton in my lunch box. Count those in yours, Du Li, and tell us how many there are.'

It was so sudden that Du Li was caught off guard; Gao Wei snatched her box away before she could react, opened it, and set it on the table.

'Du Li, none of the *daifu* can see, but you can. So count them out so everyone can hear.'

Du Li could see, of course, that there were two lunch boxes in front of her and that hers was virtually blanketed by mutton pieces, a staggering sight. She didn't dare make a sound.

'You won't do it?' Gao Wei said. 'Well, then, I'll do it for you.'

'I didn't prepare the lunch boxes,' Du Li blurted out, 'so don't blame me. I haven't touched mine yet. Why should I count the mutton pieces?'

'You're right,' Gao said. 'You had nothing to do with it. I won't blame you, so move over.' Gao took Du's box to Jin da-jie. 'Jin da-jie, Du Li says this has nothing to do with her. You packed the boxes, didn't you? So here, please count them.'

It was not the first time Jin da-jie had done that, and she never worried that anyone would find out. The blind cannot see, of course, and as for the sighted, who would bother to count? Who would do anything like that? But Gao Wei could see, and she didn't think twice about counting. Beads of sweat formed on Jin da-jie's forehead.

'You won't? All right. I'll do it for you.' Gao Wei began to count, taking her time to make sure that none of the numbers she called out escaped the ears of the therapists. The lounge was deadly quiet, but people began to fidget when she reached twelve; it was the sound of indignation, of reproach, and perhaps also the sound of anger. But Gao Wei was not finished. When she reached fifteen, she showed her ability to keep things under control, for instead of saying 'There are fifteen altogether,' she said, 'That's far enough, isn't it?' Her restraint left plenty of room for others' imaginations to take hold.

'Jin da-jie, the mutton money is the centre's, not yours, am I right?' She paused. 'Heaven watches our every move.' Taking the box back to Du Li, Gao continued, 'Please check my count, Du Li, to make sure I'm not lying.'

Du was getting angry from embarrassment, a state that can make people act rashly without considering the consequences. She reached out and knocked over the lunch box. Rice and mutton rained down around the lounge. 'This has nothing to do with me!' she screamed.

'That's not quite true,' Gao Wei replied. 'How does it make Jin da-jie feel when you push everything on to her? Wasn't she feeding a dog?'

'Of course I am,' Jin da-jie raged. 'I'm feeding a dog.'

'I'm glad to hear Jin da-jie tell the truth,' Gao said. 'I'm sorry to have interrupted lunch. Let's eat.'

Sha Fuming had already completed a silent count of the mutton pieces in his lunch box; he hadn't wanted to and detested his own action, but he couldn't help himself. The count from his box was an embarrassment for a boss, but his mind shifted from Du Li to the other boss, Zhang Zongqi, or more precisely, Zhang Zongqi's box. Obviously, he couldn't reach out and count the mutton in Zhang's lunch box, but the results could not be good, would in fact be terrible. It would be an extravagant number, overwhelming. Sha had to admit that Gao Wei was petty and her action mean-spirited, but he could not control his own anger. Picking up his lunch box, he left the lounge and opened the door to a foot massage room, where he tossed it aside and lay down. What was the point? Why get all hot and bothered? What did a few pieces of mutton mean anyway? But why would someone keep doing that? Why was someone allowed to keep doing it? How corrupt! Pure corruption. The centre was going downhill.

Zhang stayed put. He was eating; he had to. At a moment like this, eating was probably the only thing he could do. Everyone at the centre knew that he was the one who had hired Jin da-jie, a woman with a tenuous family connection to him. A distant relative. And everyone knew that too. He had ten thousand reasons to be convinced that Du Li was Gao Wei's target, but who would care about Du Li now?

Who was backing Gao Wei? Who told her to act up like that? The questions raised goose pimples on Zhang's neck, as he became aware of the seriousness of the situation. When had it started? Why had he been in the dark all along? *And you call yourself an old hand?*

Something had to be done when it had got to this point. Jin da-jie had obviously incurred the wrath of the whole place and democracy would not work any more.

Zhang had hired Jin da-jie, who had brought Du Li into the centre, so they were commonly considered his people; so he was the only one who could fix the problems. Common practice demanded that. He began chewing at a frenzied pace as his mind went into overdrive. Eventually he made the decision to fire someone. The centre needed a major clean-up, he decided, and Gao Wei must go. If she stayed, there would be no peace.

Jin da-jie had to stay. No matter what she'd done, he could not let her go. If he kept her on, he'd have to also keep Du Li on, or Jin da-jie would leave. He licked his upper lip and then the lower lip; he swallowed hard, aware of the predicament he faced.

There was only one way to deal with a dilemma, and that was to do nothing. Drag it out to a certain point, and then it becomes easy.

Silently Zhang decided to wait, and, after reaching that decision, he got up and went into a massage room with his Braille copy of *Dream of the Red Chamber*; traditional literature was the best companion during difficult times.

Why couldn't Jin da-jie leave? Well, that was a long story.

One thing always frightened Zhang Zongqi, and that was people. No matter who it was, they frightened him. The fear had been planted in his heart at the age of five, when his father remarried. He hadn't been aware that anything was going on until his father, a construction contractor, came home one day with a woman who reeked of perfume. His unscented mother had left, his scented mother had arrived.

But five-year-old Zongqi didn't think she smelled good. Silently, he called her stinky mum. She had it coming, as she was often beaten at night by his father, who had never beaten Zongqi's birth mother. He heard it all when stinky mum cried and moaned sadly, bleak and constant, louder and louder; he was happy. But strangely, even though his father beat her up like that, she was nice to Zongqi, rubbing his head with her soft hand the morning after. This woman is cheap goods, Zongqi thought, and he didn't want to be touched by cheap goods. He turned his head whenever her fragrance came his way. All the world's fragrances stank.

The situation at home underwent a fundamental change when his baby sister was born. After the baby arrived, the fragrance was gone from stinky mum, and his father stopped beating her late at night. In fact, his father rarely came home now, though he brought back another woman, who was to cook for stinky mum and Zongqi. He didn't like this woman either, for she gossiped with stinky mum; they were forever whispering, back and forth. And she was a snitch, telling stinky mum that Zongqi said she stank.

After a brief whispered exchange, stinky mum dealt the 'little blind kid' his first punishment. Instead of beating or pinching, she twisted his skinny arms behind his back and pulled them upwards; it hurt so much he felt his heart would burst from the pain, but he didn't cry. It was clear to him that the conniving woman wanted him to cry like her, but he refused to make that awful sound. Stinky mum's crying at night had elated him, so he'd make sure not to give her the pleasure of hearing him cry. He would not let her kind of sad cries reach her ears. So it hurt like hell, but he didn't make a sound; he was a bone in pain, flesh that hurt.

Exhausted, stinky mum let go of the pained bone and hurting flesh and admitted defeat. He could still recall the wonderful feeling and sense of relief when he was released from the pain; it was, in a word, bliss. With a smile, he waited for his father's return, when he would tell him everything, and more, with embellishment and exaggeration.

There's a night of howling ahead of you!

Obviously stinky mum knew what was going on in his mind and anticipated his move. His cheek felt the heat from her mouth as she pressed her lips to his ear. 'If you dare say a word, little blind boy,' she whispered, 'I'll kill you with poison. Don't think I won't.'

With a shudder, something lit up inside him, accompanied by a little pop. This marked the only time in his life when he could see the inside of his body – it was empty. A black light burst inside him at the sound of the word poison, and then everything slowly returned to normal. Zhang grew up at the instant the light went out. A grown-up now, he believed her; he knew she could kill him with poison, so could the woman who cooked for them.

He stopped talking to the cook; words were dangerous. No matter how secluded or faraway he was, he must not say anything because his words would spread through other people's mouths and travel far. *Be careful when you talk and be even more careful when you eat.* He might ingest any kind of poison. In his attempt at more effective prevention, his hearing became eerily acute, as if aided by a demonic power to exceed the ability of a normal ear. The hearing power in his ears was tube-shaped, like symmetrical outstretched arms, crazily reaching outwards; his ears were now endowed with such unimaginable flexibility that they could change shape, big or small, short or long, going anywhere he wished and making timely adjustments as necessary, omnipresent and omnipotent. They could detect, without error, any movement in the kitchen and on the dining table: the sounds of pots and bowls, plates and chopsticks, ladles and spatulas, chopsticks banging against bowls, bottles and lids, lids being opened and lids being closed, screws, pulling and plugging, the sound of raw rice and cooked rice, flour and noodles. Hearing was not enough; he learned to tell things apart unerringly. He could determine the totality of a rice pot and identify different bowls of rice from that totality. And, of course, he was ever more cautious with his actions; he would never eat anything, anything at all, before he was sure someone else had put the same thing in their mouth and swallowed it. His life was taken over by one thing and one thing only – waging an airtight defence against being poisoned at home. He was still alive, which could only mean one thing – that is, they had failed. But they were alive, too, leaving open the possibility that one day they would succeed. To him, every day posed a harsh test; he tried not to eat or drink, but he could not skip the three daily meals. Starting with breakfast, then lunch, followed by dinner, only after which he felt liberated. He could finally relax his tense mind and body, for now he was absolutely, completely safe.

To Zhang Zongqi, home life was no longer plain old home life, but was being on guard against poison. The vigilance was an organ that took root on his body. It grew as he grew; it developed along with him. As he got older, he sensed that, due to the extreme tension, his heart began to secrete a poison. He had become a toxic person, with poison in his bones, on his skin and in his blood. This was a good thing. He had to become a toxic person before anything happened; then he could fight poison with poison, conquer it with toxicity.

He was convinced that, in the face of food and water or anything else he could put into his mouth, he now possessed nerves of steel. They were as thick as his neck, as thick as his thigh, as thick, even, as his waist. Zhang believed that there were a thousand ways he might die, but that poison was not one of them, not in this lifetime.

Love finally came to Zhang when he was working in Shanghai. But it was more complicated than it sounds. In simplest terms, he went through hell and back to steal his girlfriend from someone else. At this point, it wasn't just love, but also conquest. It is easy to imagine how he was able to hold his head high. He loved his girlfriend desperately, and it was a high-speed romance. What 'high-speed' means here is that it went from strolls to hand holding to hugging, kissing and making love. What else is there to love? That's about it.

They were already kissing on their second date. She kissed him first. But the moment their lips touched, he stopped short and pulled back. She held his hand without saying anything, and just stood there for the longest time before she began to cry. She told him she had kissed someone before, but only once, just that one time, she would swear to it. Zhang Zongqi touched his fingers to her lips to keep her from saying more. 'I love you,' he said, 'I don't care about that.'

'Honest?'

'Honest. I'd swear to it.'

She kept him from swearing by covering his mouth with her hot lips. Playfully, she stuck the tip of her tongue between his lips and tried to pry open his mouth and then his teeth. He clamped his teeth tight, but a lover's tongue is a magic incantation: *open sesame, open sesame, open sesame*.

Zhang relented long enough for his girlfriend to break through the barrier and enter his mouth. Wow! The tongues touched. It was high excitement. One of those private, shuddering moments for two people. His girlfriend manipulated his tongue with hers. On the verge of fainting, he spat out her tongue, and then, to cover that up, pretended to be nauseous. Pretence immediately led to reality, as he threw up right in front of her. What could she do? Love him even more, as it turned out. She thumped him on the back with her hand and followed that with back rubs.

From the day of his first kiss, Zhang developed a fear of kissing. He'd suffered badly on the way home. He actually enjoyed kissing, and his body told him he wanted and needed to kiss. He hungered for it. But he was afraid. His mouth and his tongue were fearful of anything, even his girlfriend's tongue, violating the space in his mouth.

Could they not kiss? It was a question he couldn't ask.

How could anyone be in love without kissing? Kisses are the air and water, the protein and vitamins of romance, without which love dies.

To kiss or not to kiss, that is the question. To love or not to love, that is another question.

It couldn't be. His girlfriend couldn't be toxic. No. Impossible. He told himself over and over that he must have faith, that his girlfriend could not possibly be toxic. But he wavered again when the moment came to act. He could not do it. He dawdled, not just with kissing but also when she brought him food; he would not touch his food until she began eating. He doubted her. He was suspicious. There is no salvation for a person consumed by suspicion. Even in death, the expression frozen on his face will be one of doubt.

The girl broke up with him in the end, and left him a note that said, 'Zongqi, you don't have to say anything; I understand how you feel. I'm just like you. It was love that gave me courage. You lack the courage, not because you're a coward, but because you don't love me.'

Touching the page with his index figure, he felt the words one by one. He did love her but he had lost her. He now understood what love was by checking the underside of love, like reading braille; only through the underside of the paper can one touch, read and understand. It all seemed predestined.

To his surprise, as he held the letter in his hand, the tear-streaked corners of his mouth slowly curled upwards. After drying the tears, he realised that he was actually smiling. He was liberated.

Internal secrets remain secret forever. When he began running his own business, he was dead set on one thing. He would seek out a cook, he would do the interviews and he would do the hiring. There would be no negotiations.

In fact, when he and Sha Fuming talked about opening a tuina centre together, they had agreed that neither boss would hire his own relatives. Yet in the end, Zhang brought over Jin da-jie. Sha did not pursue the issue, and accepted the arrangement. It was, after all, just for a cook, not a sensitive position, so it didn't really matter. So go ahead.

Who'd have thought that 'not a very sensitive position' would create such a sensitive commotion?

Jin da-jie must go, Sha thought, as he sprawled on the foot massage chair.

Jin da-jie must stay, Zhang Zongqi thought, as he lay on the massage bed.

Unaware of what was on Zhang's mind, Jin da-jie went back to the dorm, her heart in turmoil. The more she thought about the situation, the worse it appeared to her. For someone in her late thirties, a job like this did not open up every day in Nanjing. She had been left alone in the village when her husband and daughter went to work in Dongguan. Living alone was hard to bear, something most people cannot begin to understand. The fourth year after her husband and daughter left, Jin da-jie had struck up with Second Uncle, a villager from the eastern end. Struck up is not really how it deserves to be described – rape is more like it. She could have screamed when it happened, but a fleeting thought had made her change her mind. A man in his late sixties, Second Uncle was a stallion with his pants off, though his wrinkly body with folds of skin and the aged odour of grime made her want to throw up. She even had thoughts of strangling herself. But she could not resist the stallion's movements and actually experienced the feeling of *losing herself* twice, her body floating like a dead fish, something that had never happened to her before. It was frightening yet exciting, and she arched wildly upwards for him; she felt sordid, her mind filled with disgust and an energising smuttiness, all of which drove her crazy. They had only been together once, after which she cried till her eyes were puffy. From then on, the image of him floated around the village day and night like a wandering ghost, and her heart nearly stopped whenever she saw him.

That was why she left home to work, or, to be more precise, fled the village. Now that she had left, one of the hardest decisions in her life, how could she go back? She couldn't. Her demon was in that village, and she'd rather die than return to it.

It was all Du Li's fault. That damned girl was well into her twenties, an age when most girls would be interested in what happened between their legs, but not Du Li. All she thought about was food, glutton-like. If not for her, Jin da-jie would never have been involved in such a scandalous affair. And what did she get in return? *Nothing. Heaven is my witness, nothing at all.* She thanked her lucky stars for the monthly salary of a thousand yuan. She was never guilty of any shenanigans with the meals or reaped even the slightest profit from them.

A naturally kind-hearted person, she could never change her habit of giving more food to people she liked and punishing those she disliked at mealtime. She had recommended Du Li, who never stopped buttering her up. How could she not favour the girl when parcelling out the food? And if Du Li got more, Gao Wei had to take less; it was just her bad luck that she had someone like Gao Wei for an enemy. *That girl is a slut, and sooner or later she'll be selling herself.*

But now that it had reached this point, Jin da-jie pulled herself together. She couldn't sit around waiting for something to happen to her; she couldn't do that.

After crying for a whole afternoon, she cooked dinner and delivered the food with a long face; then she went back to the dorm, where she stripped her bed and quietly packed her things. After that she sat down on the edge of the bed to wait. Sha Fuming returned after midnight; so did Zhang and all the other therapists. She picked up her bundle and quietly knocked on the door of Zhang's private room.

She set down her bundle and came straight to the point, though in a low voice. 'Boss Zhang, are you still the boss? Do you still count here at the centre?'

It may have been a meaningless question, but it was wide of the mark, and it hit Zhang where it hurt. His eye began to twitch.

Sha Fuming slept in the next room, so Zhang kept his voice low as he demanded, 'What kind of rubbish is that?'

He'd lowered his voice, but that's not what she wanted. Instead, she raised her voice, which was loud to begin with.

'I made a mistake, Boss Zhang, and I'm too ashamed to stay. I'm sorry I let Boss Sha and you down. I let everyone down. I was just waiting for you to return so I could apologise to you all. I've packed up my things and will leave for home tonight. I'm going now.' She had begun to sob midway through and was nearly choking by the time she finished. Her crying grated on his ear. She was nearly wailing, an ugly howl leaving the impression that she no longer had any regard for face.

The dormitory was just an apartment with four bedrooms, plus two other rooms that, along with the master bedroom, were further partitioned to create more rooms, big and small. Who wouldn't have heard Jin da-jie's outburst? No one, except those who pretended not to.

Sha Fuming came out, reluctantly. Zhang Zongqi should have taken care of the problem with Jin da-jie, and Sha would only make matters worse if he got involved, but she'd raised such a racket he had to do something. He coughed from where he stood in Zhang's doorway. 'It's almost one o'clock now and everyone is tired. We all need our sleep.'

She heard only that he wanted her to stop making a scene; he said nothing about leaving. His comment was ambiguous. Did he want her to leave or not? Zhang Zongqi also got Sha's drift; Sha was saving face for him but also handing him a hot potato. Sha's stance was clear: he did not want to express his view regarding whether or not Jin da-jie should go. He tossed the responsibility to Zhang Zongqi.

All the others, except Du Hong and Xiao Ma, followed Sha Fuming out, crowding into the narrow hallway outside Zhang's room. It was a good sign. With her face in her hands, Jin da-jie peeked through the spaces between her fingers, saw them out there, and felt pretty good.

Even if she was expected to leave, it wouldn't be easy to squeeze her way through the crowd.

She kept crying and muttering through her tears, mostly to criticise herself and express her remorse, as well as her plan to leave. Then they heard a loud thump on the ceiling. It was very late and they'd been making too much noise, upsetting their upstairs neighbours. As if worried that one thump would not quiet the blind people downstairs, the owner of the foot stomped again, sending the hollow noise echoing in the apartment, in everyone's ears, including Sha's and Zhang's.

Pulling a long face, Zhang said loudly, 'Did you hear that? Enough already! Don't you care at all about social etiquette? Go on, everyone, go back to your rooms.'

Not daring to move, Jin da-jie glanced at Zhang Zongqi and noticed the dark look on his face; she then looked at Sha, who wore the same expression. Then she turned her head, accidentally locking eyes with Gao Wei, who shut her eyes and, after a while, opened them to return the gaze. Among the many who could not see, the two pairs of eyes exchanged looks, confident and highly provocative, though, of course, not cocksure. But at least they reached a tacit agreement on the matter; each standing in front of her own room, they issued challenges before looking away: *Let's wait and see, then.*

CHAPTER FOURTEEN
ZHANG YIGUANG

THE MUTTON COUNT changed the tuina centre, which was now shrouded in a cheerless and forlorn aura, with an undercurrent of apprehension. Everyone sensed that something was about to happen, but in the end nothing did, though, of course, that did not mean that nothing would. On the contrary, it was only a matter of time. And everyone waited with bated breath, watching with their unseeing eyes. The mood had changed, the clearest sign of which was the cordial way the two bosses treated all the employees. The quality of food also improved noticeably. Zhang Zongqi was clearly more talkative, mixing casual chats with hints of managerial intent. This was not a good sign, as it made known an unspoken fact that a major rift had appeared between the two bosses, who were now engaged in a battle for a united front to win public support for their side.

Winning public support was fraught with peril, for at some point, the public could become a bomb that, when exploded, would leave only some standing.

The employees were caught in the middle – everyone needed to choose sides, one camp or the other, Sha or Zhang. There was no third option. Choosing sides is never easy, since one cannot know beforehand which side will remain standing. To be sure, being on the wrong side would not be the end of the world, since you could leave. But no blind person leaves a job willingly. It's too much trouble to pick up and leave. Once your bedding is rolled up, you'll find that countless roads open up before you, and you must walk down one of them, on the road all over again.

Amid this gloomy atmosphere, Zhang Yiguang unexpectedly became friendly with Xiao Ma. Whenever he had a free moment, he groped his way over to Xiao Ma and draped his arm around his shoulders, acting like the younger man's best buddy. Xiao Ma read him wrong. He had never had much to do with Zhang, and wondered what he was up to, especially at a time when everyone was on guard. He was convinced that Zhang had been sent by either Boss Sha or Boss Zhang. He'd made up his mind not to choose sides, refusing to be anyone's man. So when Zhang Yiguang's arm encircled his shoulders, he forced his way free; Ma was put off by Yiguang's arm, especially his hot, complex underarm odour.

Where are you going? Zhang Yiguang was thinking. *I've got something to say to you, and it's for your own good.*

Zhang was a unique case among those who had lost their sight after birth. Most people in this category start out being highly excitable, and by the time they've calmed down, they've probably lost hope, forever giving the impression of total exhaustion. But not him. He had survived a gas explosion that took the lives of one hundred and thirteen of his co-workers, men whose corpses filled a room. He was the only one who'd made it out, a miracle incarnate, though paying the price of his eyes. After the accident, instead of fixating on his eyes, he fixed those 'black' sightless eyes on a heart filled with boundless joy and, naturally, endless fear.

His fear was the kind that came after the fact, a tormenting fear that is worse than losing sight. On a certain level, losing his eyesight had stopped being so important. Since he could no longer detect light, for a long time he believed that he was still in the mine. He would sit on a stool, a club in his hand, and when visited by the fear, he would poke into the air, which would then tell him that the space above him was a ceiling, not the roof of a mine.

Fear was a snake that, instead of biting, simply coiled inside him. It slithered up to his heart at times and, coiling its body, began to squeeze. That is what Zhang feared the most, for it took his breath away, though, of course, it was his own heart that was constricting, and that was the undisputed truth. Seen from this angle, fear was not bad; it was good. Since being alive led to fear, then a sense of fear must mean that he was not dead. *Hey, you're alive, young man. So go burn a few incense sticks. You've got a second chance at life; you came out on top.*

Coming out on top at any given moment makes a person feel good, especially when it means getting out alive. He'd died, and all his responsibilities had ended. But then his wife did not become a widow, his parents did not lose a son and his children still had their father. So what did all this mean? It meant his family had come out on top. What does it mean to be a survivor? What if he hadn't been lucky enough to survive the others? Yet he no longer had anything to do with this world; he was dead, a walking corpse, a drifting, lingering soul of the dead. From that point on, he lived every day for himself only. He was free.

Zhang stayed at home for only six months after the accident before leaving. The freedom he'd enjoyed at home was not real freedom; it was not total, complete. Only thirty-five, he had just passed the midway mark of his life if he was to live to seventy. He still had thirty-five good years, which he had no intention of spending at home. He'd done everything he could for that family, even handing over the compensation for losing his eyesight, so as a living corpse he should not be required to make any more sacrifices for them. Newly reborn, he wanted to grow up strong in the world of darkness.

So he went to Xuzhou to learn tuina, which was not hard, just a bit of physical exertion, easy work for someone who had spent sixteen years labouring in a mine. It was also safe and steady, and he could chat and laugh with his clients. Zhang congratulated himself for choosing this line of work. A year later, he made the successful transformation of his life, turning from a disabled miner to an able-bodied tuina therapist. Of course he'd need a qualifying certificate if he wanted to make a living, but that was not difficult. Was it hard to have one hundred and thirteen buddies die in a mine? Of course it was, it was terrible. So if he'd made it in the mine, what was so hard about a mere certificate? He'd taken care of that with four hundred yuan and a pack of top-quality cigarettes, King Size Sequoia. Certificate in hand, he walked out onto the street, where he discovered there was one cigarette left in the pack. He lit up, and had an immediate coughing fit. Then it dawned on him that he was smoking a fine cigarette, one of those they called 'tribute cigarettes'. *Emperors must have been smokers. Why else would they be called 'tribute'?* He finished the cigarette, feeling like an emperor, though to be honest, it had been a so-so smoke. But no matter how little it impressed him, Zhang Yiguang had had a taste of being an emperor. *Was it really that easy? Yes, I guess so.*

After crumpling the cigarette pack and tossing it into the street, he bought a train ticket to Nanjing, the old capital, where emperors had lived, a land of prosperity and decadence. On the train he was raring to go; even his fingers seemed to sparkle like bright seeing eyes, giving him the feeling that they were hungering for the life he'd longed for.

After receiving his first month's salary in Nanjing, he groped his way into one of those *special hair salons* – a brothel, that is. He wanted to be an emperor, spending his hard-earned cash on a woman, any one who struck his fancy. Almost immediately he was hooked on whoring, but he didn't see it that way. To him he was just doing what an emperor used to do, flipping cards to find the concubine he wanted.

'My beloved consort! My dear, sweet consort!'

The girl would laugh, joined by the others. They never expected a blind man like him to be so entertaining. He was an emperor. Didn't they hear him when he paid up? 'A reward!' he would say.

He went to a hair salon every few days. After several visits, he sensed a major change inside; he was no longer stifled, not a 'man-show' any more; in fact he was livelier and more outgoing than when he'd worked in the mine. He could still recall how stifling it had been for him as a miner; all he could think about back then was going to 'that place', but he'd never made it, not once. It cost money that he could not bear to spend, because his parents no longer worked and he had two school-age children. He'd suppressed his urge till he began to have wet dreams, a shameful act that embarrassed him and turned him into the butt of his co-workers' jokes. When they saw his sticky sheets, they gave him a malicious nickname – land-to-air missile – which was shortened as land-to-air. When he thought back to those days, he had to agree with them; he'd been a pig. To his wife he was a castrated pig. To the owner of the mine, he was not castrated, but was sold, skin and all, when he was done shooting blanks. The compensation was nothing but the final payment for his flesh.

He was lucky to have lost his sight. When he could see, he had noticed nothing, but once he was blind, Zhang Yiguang, a man from the countryside, saw everything. He was not land-to-air; he was an emperor.

What incredible luck! When the gas exploded, the flying rocks took only his sight, not his family jewels. If he'd lost them, would he ever be an emperor? Of course not.

He worked doubly hard at the tuina centre for one reason only; that is, the harder he worked, the more he earned and the more prostitutes he could visit. Likewise, he worked doubly hard at the *hair salon* for the simple reason that he had set a strict goal for himself; he must sleep with eighty-one women. He had once read that an emperor had one woman in each of his three palaces, one in each of his six courts, plus seventy-two consorts, a total of eighty-one. Once Zhang had slept with eighty-one whores, he would be an emperor, an amateur one at least.

'My beloved consort! My dear, sweet consort!'

For the most part, Zhang Yiguang had conquered his fear of the mine. But when he was working, in the dark, a sensation of being in the mine returned. He could never completely free himself of the feeling that he was down there with his buddies. Because of this, his relationships with the other therapists were unique. To him they were all his brothers, at least he wanted them to be. But they did not consider him one of their own. In part that was age-related, but mainly it was due to his background.

He had been able to see for thirty-five years, and when he lost his sight, he retained the mentality and habits of a sighted person. Without a blind man's history, schooling experience and the standard apprenticeship in the trade, he was new to the life, and could never be accepted as one of them. Or to put it differently, he had left 'that world' but had failed to enter 'this world'; he had forced his way in, and was an intruder, destined to be a loner.

Being a loner can be awkward, which was why he was temperamental and moody. By nature, he was outgoing, if a bit on the flighty side, unlike born-blind therapists, who tend to be more grounded, calmer. As they had to interact with each other, his outgoing approach inevitably clashed with their understated reactions; as an older man trying to befriend the younger therapists, he felt underappreciated. When he was down, he lacked the fortitude of someone born blind, making conflicts unavoidable. In the end, he clashed with the others too easily, and then felt bad afterwards. He would try to repair the damage, which required him to condescend to the younger ones. And he felt aggrieved. Back at the mine, he had clashed with other miners, but those conflicts were easy to deal with. Even if they got into a physical fight, a round of drinks and a slap on the shoulder smoothed everything over, for his buddies never bore a grudge. But not the blind therapists; they bore grudges, a deeply rooted character trait, and the source of Zhang's difficulty. It didn't take him long to antagonise everyone at the centre and, lacking a single close friend, he felt lonely and isolated.

Loners don't just feel awkward, they also tend to meddle in other people's affairs. Zhang Yiguang liked to meddle. Meddlers share the characteristic of shifty eyes. Zhang did not have shifty eyes, but his ears learned to turn this way and that. His antennae revealed a problem – Xiao Ma was in love with Xiao Kong.

Enthralled in his one-sided romance, Xiao Ma lived in a mixture of sweet happiness and pain, an unstoppable longing. Zhang saw everything and felt sorry for Ma, who would suffer greatly in the end, even if he did not yet know it. He would be destroyed. Xiao Ma not only imagined himself to be Xiao Kong's love interest, but also considered himself clever, blithely convinced that no one had noticed anything as he fixated on her with his ears and nose, often for as long as half an hour. His mouth hung open. A blind man's ears and nose are his *eyes*. If a sighted man stares at a woman, the secret in his eyes will sooner or later be detected by other eyes; likewise, the secrets of ears and nose will sooner or later be detected by other ears and noses. *How could you fancy her, Xiao Ma? You can't. How would you keep your job at the centre if you were found out? Wang Daifu hasn't said anything, but that doesn't mean he can't tell. Xiao Ma, you'll ruin yourself and take others along with you.* Zhang decided that Xiao Ma's fanciful thoughts were like gas, as if he was enshrouded in odourless gas. Gas you can't smell is the most dangerous of all. One careless action can lead to an explosion, causing a major collapse.

He must save Xiao Ma, his lost little buddy.

Zhang thought long and hard, but could find no good solution, so he decided to take drastic action. For a young 'rooster' like Xiao Ma, the cause of his trouble could be traced to his reservoir of sperm. Like he himself back at the mine. He'd come off work so exhausted he didn't even have the strength to take a shower, but once he lay in bed his body was energised, and he couldn't stop thinking about his wife. It was, in fact, just his sperm gnawing at him. They were tiny, but there were so many of them, tens of millions of unstoppable soldiers that can vanquish a six-foot man, like hordes of ants shaking a tree. The fundamental solution was to coax them out, after which everything would be fine; he'd sigh and fall asleep as soon as he shut his eyes.

In the end, Xiao Ma was tricked into going to the hair salon with Zhang Yiguang. Unsure what it was all about, the younger man went anyway. Zhang had been so meticulous in making the arrangements that it was too late for Ma by the time everything became clear to him. Zhang sent Xiaoman, Zhang's own favourite consort and the consort he'd favoured many times recently, to Ma. She was good in bed, so sweet she could talk a dead man alive. Truth be told, Zhang was reluctant to give her up and had to talk himself into parting with her so that Xiao Ma could have some pleasure and would get hooked on the hair salon. Once he'd expelled his sperm over and over, he would come to his senses and lose interest in Sao-zi.

CHAPTER FIFTEEN

JIN YAN AND XIAO KONG, TAILAI AND WANG DAIFU

HUMAN INTERACTIONS ARE often intriguing. As the atmosphere worsened daily, Xiao Kong and Jin Yan quietly and suddenly became best friends. Wang Daifu had heard privately from Xiao Kong that Jin Yan gave her a negative impression – there was something not quite right about that woman. *Take what she wears, for example. Just look at her, how she makes noise with every step, either a tinkling or a rustling. Like she's forever marrying herself off. You can't get married every day, so what does that mean? That she's a flashy woman.* With that basic judgement, Xiao Kong had never liked the woman, making it clear to all that there could be no friendship between them. All the therapists could tell. She was straightforward when she talked to the others, but with Jin Yan, she put on airs. Wang had brought that up with her once. 'What's the point? We're all therapists working away from home.'

'I don't give a damn,' Xiao Kong had replied in her newly acquired Nanjing dialect.

Jin Yan was aware of Xiao Kong's attitude but did not let it bother her, not because she didn't care, but because she didn't want to sink to Xiao Kong's level. She had her own way of dealing with Xiao Kong – by talking to *her* man. Xiao Kong could not get jealous, since Jin Yan did it in front of everyone, not behind her back. *Can't you take a joke?* Besides, it wasn't as if Jin Yan had no boyfriend of her own. How did Jin Yan talk to Wang Daifu? Here's an example: if they were especially busy, Wang might say to his client, 'I'm sorry, I really can't hold it any longer. I need to use the toilet.'

When Jin Yan heard that, she'd say thoughtfully, 'Go on, Old Wang. It's not a valuable necklace, something you have to keep with you forever.'

Xiao Kong knew she'd never win a battle with Jin Yan, so she adopted a certain attitude when dealing with her. Jin Yan knew that Xiao Kong disliked her for no apparent reason, and nothing she did could change that, so why try? As long as she got along with Wang Daifu she was okay.

And yet, the two became best friends. Women are like that; if they have a problem with each other, once it's solved they can become best friends. They could then be on such intimate terms that they would happily cut off their head to put it on the other person's neck. That's how it was with Xiao Kong and Jin Yan. Once they linked up, they often looked as if they could exchange heads onto each other's shoulders. They poured out their hearts to one another the day long, even ignoring their own men. They spent every free moment whispering back and forth, as if they were the only two people on earth.

The cause of their sudden friendship was a particular work assignment. Du Li had assigned them to a double room for a pair of male clients, a boss and his driver. The boss had been drinking, the driver hadn't. Du Li had called Xiao Kong's name when making the arrangement, so she was saddled with the boss; Jin Yan was given the driver.

Xiao Kong did not like alcohol, especially the smell, so she sighed softly when the clients lay down. Sighing is a bit of an exaggeration. She just breathed a little more heavily than usual. Jin Yan walked up to her and, without a word, took over her client. It was a totally unexpected move, but Xiao Kong was grateful. How did Jin Yan know she did not like the smell of alcohol? She must have heard it from

Wang Daifu. To Xiao Kong, the woman was quite something. Even after the way she had treated her, she continued to chat with Wang Daifu, even sharing a few private thoughts.

The smell of alcohol had bothered Xiao Kong since childhood. In her earliest memories, her father always stank of alcohol. After she was blinded at the age of two, her father, a teacher in the northern Anhui countryside, frequently stumbled his way home after drinking too much, reeking of alcohol. His arrival at home was the beginning of Xiao Kong's misery. He'd put his daughter on his lap and tell her to open her eyes. Her eyes were open, always, but she could not see, which would send him into a drunken rage. 'Open your eyes!' he'd demand, over and over. She tried, but didn't understand what it meant to 'open' her eyes. Intending to open his poor daughter's eyes with his savage fingers, he'd pull at her upper lids so hard it felt more like he was tearing them off. But it did no good. Then he'd begin to beat her. What could the girl's mother do except try to shield her daughter with her own body? What terrified Xiao Kong most was not the beating, but what happened the following morning, when her father sobered up and saw the bruises. He would begin to cry, in the most heart-wrenching, self-abandoned way. Putting his arms around his beloved daughter, he would howl and wail, turning their home into hell on earth. Her mother, not wanting her to grow up fatherless, put up with him until Xiao Kong was six, when she asked for a divorce. He refused. Her mother said she would stay married to him if he accepted her non-negotiable demand that, for their daughter's sake, he would not drink again for the rest of his life. He remained silent all afternoon before he finally agreed. 'All right,' he'd said, and with that, he quit drinking and never again lay a finger on his daughter. To prove his devotion to her, he even went secretly to the hospital for a vasectomy operation.

Once she had grown up, Xiao Kong began to understand her father and his unbearable love for her – intense, extreme, distorted, pathological, filled with self-sacrifice and touchingly tragic. He loved her dearly, and that love, she finally realised, motivated her to keep improving herself. Yet her fear of the smell of alcohol never completely vanished; it was like a branding iron that produced an acrid burning smell in her memory.

Naturally, Jin Yan didn't know any of this. And she didn't ask. What was there to ask about? Maybe she thought any questions were unnecessary, since all blind people have their own taboos and each one is loaded with burns that no one would wish to look at.

In any case, Jin Yan's casual move softened Xiao Kong's attitude. *Maybe this woman isn't so bad, after all. Maybe this is what she's really like.* She was, to Xiao Kong, a 'character', but there was warmth deep down.

One stormy day, when business was slow, Jin Yan and Xiao Kong went into a massage room, shunning the lounge, a place no one wanted to be these days. Sha Fuming and Zhang Zongqi were like opposing magnets, and all anyone could feel was the force each exerted, with nothing in between. They would continue to 'bounce off' each other, unless and until one was willing to back down.

With no paying clients, Jin Yan and Xiao Kong decided to give each other a massage. Not tuina in the strictest sense, it was 'I'll serve you first' and 'you can serve me later'. Sounded interesting, and lots of fun. They settled on belly fat reduction, which, in terms of physics, with powerful rubbing, kneading, pressing, pushing and pinching, raised the temperature of the belly and burned enough fat to reach the grand goal of body sculpting. Belly fat reduction, it must be pointed out, means extreme pain. Just think, there is a concentration of ultra-sensitive meridian points on the belly, which is extra-skeletal to begin with, and the skin on a woman's belly is extraordinarily tender. When a tuina therapist grabs hold and begins to knead and pinch, it feels as if the skin is on fire. Yet the pain did not deter their female clients; in fact, it was a service in high demand. What did that mean? It meant that Chinese women were caring more and more about themselves. Without a nice flat belly, their fancy clothes would be wasted, no matter how fine the fabric quality or how trendy the style. A flat belly has an added charm factor, an ultra-secret value that makes itself known in bed and builds the foundation of great sex. Hence, the belly plays too critical a role to worry about a little pain; being a woman means to endure pain anyway.

Neither Jin Yan nor Xiao Kong was fat, but they were both women in love – and what woman in love is happy with the way her belly looks? None. No, she cannot be happy. The reason is not hard to spot. She is thinking back to what she looked like at sixteen or seventeen. *It wasn't like this before.* All women in love share the basic belief that they looked better when they were younger, a time that their current boyfriends missed. Only through painstaking work can they return to what they were before. They can never forgive their current bellies.

Xiao Kong's hands were small but powerful, and Jin Yan soon found the pressure too much. Xiao Kong was using more force than usual, to be playful. *I had to endure the pain under your fingers, so now it's your turn to have a taste of my strength.* Finally Jin Yan could not take it any longer. 'You little tramp!' she blurted out.

'Little tramp' is a special term suggesting the flighty and intimate nature of friendship between girls, like biting someone you like. Two women can be each other's tramp only when their relationship has reached a certain stage; that is, you cannot become a tramp with just anyone. *You called me a tramp? Very well then*. Without a word, Xiao Kong grabbed a handful of Jin Yan's belly and held it firmly. 'Say it again,' she said happily.

Not used to losing an argument, Jin Yan said it again. 'Little tramp.'

'Again.' Xiao Kong tightened her grip so much that Jin Yan's mouth, already open from the pain, stretched even wider, reaching its limit. She began sucking in air and begging for forgiveness.

'I won't say it again, Miss. Please let go and I'll be your maid.'

Xiao Kong slowly released her grip; it would have caused even greater pain if she'd done that too fast, as she knew from experience; it was a different kind of torture. 'That'll do it.' Finally she let go and laid her hands on Jin Yan's belly, alternating between gentle massaging and light slapping, a necessary step. Jin Yan had a washboard belly, flat and well defined like a tiled floor, much better than her own, and she liked it a great deal.

She began to caress and gently tug at the skin again while pressing her lips against Jin Yan's ear to whisper conspiratorially, 'Such a nice, sexy belly. Tailai must love it. Tell me, have you done you-know-what with him?'

Jin Yan seemed to have anticipated Xiao Kong's question. She had never done it with Tailai. Never. She stretched out her legs and said assertively, 'No. We've been able to hold off.'

The response seemed loaded, fraught with insinuation. Xiao Kong was suddenly abashed, and, with nothing better to say, gripped Jin Yan's belly again.

'Yes or no? Tell me.'

The pain made Jin Yan whip her legs into the air, looking more suggestive than ever.

'You're forcing me into a false confession,' she said, panting from the pain.

'Yes or no? Why did you stick your legs up like that?'

Jin Yan was momentarily puzzled before bursting out laughing. 'How would I know about *that*? You're the one who's shown her card.'

'You really haven't done it?'

'No, honest.'

'Why not?' Xiao Kong demanded unreasonably, as if she were shamed into anger.

'Why not? What kind of question is that?' Jin Yan turned serious. 'I want to save that for my wedding night.'

Now Xiao Kong believed her, and, as she lost herself in her own thoughts, her hands began to roam all over Jin Yan's belly. For women, the topic of 'you-know-what' is always important, and when it comes up in conversation between two women, it causes a major shift in their relationship, elevating it to the level of confidantes who can then talk about anything and everything.

The downpour continued outside, creating a constant pitter-patter on the sliding sash window. The room was plunged into silence as the two young women stopped fooling around; a warm, cosy silence, like the room was lit up by a muted, diffuse overhead light. But in fact it was dark, and because of that the room didn't exactly feel cosy, more like sad. After revealing their most intimate secrets, Xiao Kong and Jin Yan went quiet, perhaps startled into silence by the abrupt mention of 'wedding', each now lost in their own thoughts. Wedding, marriage. No one could know what it felt like before reaching that point. They had both been vexed by the notion of marriage; being in love is sweet, but it can also bring pain. Who knew what would happen the next day? The tuina centre seemed to be in crisis, so who could tell if there might be major changes, and when those happened, no one would know what to do. Even the heavens would not know.

Xiao Kong was distressed after hearing Jin Yan say, 'I want to save that for my wedding night.' Xiao Kong knew she'd never be able to say that. She had gone all the way, and there was nothing to hold off. She felt bad, though not remorseful. She did not regret going all the way with Wang Daifu; what troubled her was how Jin Yan seemed so sure of her marriage to Tailai, which was why she could save the you-know-what for her wedding night. Jin Yan knew it would happen, and that was Xiao Kong's sore spot. She was not particular about her wedding; she didn't mind if it was not well done or was shabby. But her parents must be present, and they had to at least have a meal together, before her father would solemnly give her hand to his son-in-law. Now that her parents would disapprove of the marriage, what would her wedding look like? It was obvious she would have to do it behind their backs, like a thief, sneaking off to get married. What did it all mean? It meant she owed her parents an even greater debt. And there was something else: as a woman, she would have liked the man to be the one pressing for marriage; better yet, she wanted him to beg for her hand in marriage. Love is one thing, and how a woman feels is something else. In Xiao Kong's case, it felt as if she were begging him to marry her and she had ended up with a scold. '*What's the hurry?*' That question had stripped her of her self-esteem, and so, in comparison, Jin Yan was so much happier, so much luckier, which made Xiao Kong's heart ache, and made her jealous. Her hands stopped moving; she felt like crying. She did, she began to cry, sending a teardrop down onto Jin Yan's belly.

In reaction to the sudden drop of water, Jin Yan stretched her hand out, but nothing more came, and that told her that it had been Kong's teardrop. She sat up to take the girl's hands, but Xiao Kong pulled them back.

'When you get married, Yanzi,' Xiao Kong said, 'you must let me know, no matter how far apart we are. I want to attend your wedding.'

Jin Yan had no response. Wedding? she mouthed the word. She had no idea when that would be.

She had always been dominant in her relationship with Tailai, and dominant types share the common trait that when they make plans they tend to base everything on wishful thinking. That is, they usually believe that their ideas mirror those of others and so they do not have to take other people into consideration. Jin Yan had been quietly pondering her wedding for some time and had not discussed it with Tailai. One thing she didn't know was that long before Tailai left home to work, he and his parents had reached an agreement that they would not have a wedding ceremony for him. The reason was simple: Tailai would likely marry another blind person, and it would not look respectful or good to have two sightless people marrying in the village. People might even laugh at them. Tailai's father had been quite blunt: they would spare no expense, give him whatever he wanted, but no ceremony. He did not object, for that was what he wanted all along. Having grown up amid people's mockery and ridicule, Tailai knew he had no friends in the village. Everyone looked down on him, and that included his own little sister. Money was so much better; he would get fifty or sixty thousand at least and possibly seventy or eighty. It would be so much more practical to have money in hand without having to go through a demeaning process. A tangibly profitable transaction.

And this was how he described their wedding to Jin Yan. 'In my mind, our kiss was our wedding. I want to spend every penny on *you*, not throw it away on a wedding for others to see.'

It was a touching and emotional confession, meticulous in its telling, the sort of talk she liked, for it was sincere, straightforward and resolute, showing his total devotion and utmost loyalty to their love. It was, quite simply, romantic. But it was also anti-wedding; she was moved and yet she felt like crying.

'You'll have to wait.'

Jin Yan took Xiao Kong's hand to play with the fingers dolefully, having learned that Xiao Kong wanted to attend her wedding. 'Even I don't know when that will be.'

'What do you mean?'

'Tailai doesn't want a wedding.'

Xiao Kong said nothing. As a blind woman, she knew what was on Tailai's mind and she understood why. 'What about you?'

'Me?' Jin Yan said. 'I'll wait.'

'Till when?'

'I don't know,' she said. 'I'm happy to wait, till I'm thirty, or forty.' Resting her forehead against Xiao Kong's, she continued, 'I'm a woman.' She added in a low voice, 'How can a woman not have a wedding?'

Xiao Kong detected a stubborn edge to Jin Yan's voice, its softness belying the determination that she would not stop until she reached her goal.

As a woman, she understood Jin Yan's thoughts perfectly. Draping her arm over the other woman's shoulders, she said, 'I know.'

'You have it so much better,' Jin Yan said. 'You and Wang Daifu are so happy together. You'll get married before we do. You have to let me know when you're getting married. I want to attend your wedding and sing for you. I'll sing all the songs I know.'

That friendly comment virtually forced Xiao Kong to open up. She could not be a real friend if she kept it to herself. 'I don't know when that will be either.' It was exactly what Jin Yan had said a moment ago and she was now hearing it again.

'Why?' It was Jin Yan's turn to be surprised.

'My parents disapprove of our relationship.'

'Why?'

'They won't let me marry a blind man.'

So that's it. That's what's going on. Ai! Then there's no one worth envying.

'They let me do anything I want except for that,' Xiao Kong continued. 'They're worried about me. They've devoted their whole life to me. I more or less eloped to Nanjing.' She took out her Shenzhen phone. 'I use two phones. I keep telling them I'm in Shenzhen.'

Jin Yan took the phone from her and stroked it. What kind of life was it to lie like that day in and day out? It was her turn to put her arm around her friend's shoulders. 'I understand.'

Now the two women were practically hugging each other, though they hadn't meant to; it was their understanding of the other's situation that drew them together, an accidental embrace. With their left hands, they rubbed and patted the other's back; the rain continued outside, turning the windowpanes into drums and gongs.

'Here's a riddle for you, Yanzi. What is two blind girls hugging each other?'

'A blind embrace.'

'Another one – what is two blind girls rubbing each other?'

'A blind rub.'

'One more – what is two blind girls whispering to each other?'

'Blind talk, prattle.'

'You're a prattler.'

'No, you're a prattler.'

'No, you are.'

'No, you are.'

Back and forth they went, a dozen times at least, as if both were eager to hang a label on the other. Neither was willing to give in before they started laughing, muffled at first, sending their breasts jiggling silently in each other's arms, tickling them so much they held their bodies apart, but kept their foreheads touching. Unable to hold it in any longer, Xiao Kong laughed out loud, prompting Jin Yan to follow suit. Her voice was so much louder than Xiao Kong's, and now it was ear-splitting; a laugh that emerged from her navel, forced out by the power from her abdomen. Xiao Kong in turn was so tickled by Jin Yan's laughter that she let loose as well. They forgot they were still at the centre, completely forgot; they even forgot who they were, completely forgot that too. Full-throttle laughter. It made them happy, euphoric. Their laughter bounced off each other; they egged each other on, like a contest, each louder than the other. They couldn't stop. They were howling. They went wild, totally crazy; they were hysterical, and it felt good.

The other therapists were crowded into the lounge, sitting up prim and proper, including Sha Fuming and Zhang Zongqi, whose magnetic repellent force was a silent ban against noise; even the rain fell with caution. When the stillness was shattered by the women's hysterical laughter in one of the massage rooms, all heads in the lounge turned in that direction. What's making them laugh like that? How could they be happy like that? They sounded as if they could laugh their heads off. It was funny, and it brought a smile to everyone's face.

'No one's going to die laughing, are they?' Zhang Yiguang said to Wang Daifu.

'Two silly girls.' Wang was smiling, but his mind was elsewhere. He had just over two weeks to pay off his brother's debt, and the days were flying by. The deadline was nearly upon him. Taking a cigarette from behind his ear, he walked out of the centre.

An overhang shielding the entrance was where the therapists came out for a smoke. Wang was not a real smoker, but he accepted cigarettes from smoking clients who enjoyed sharing them with the therapists after their treatment. Sometimes, when he had nothing better to do, he would light up just for the hell of it.

Even outside he could hear the frenzied laughter from the two silly girls.

'Crazy,' he said to himself just as he discovered, to his surprise, that he wasn't alone. He mumbled a greeting, and the response from the other person told him it was Tailai.

Wang Daifu and Xu Tailai did not normally fraternise, although they maintained a cordial relationship typical of co-workers, neither interfering in the affairs of the other. Now an interesting situation had developed, with their girlfriends suddenly best friends and making quite a commotion. Momentary embarrassment gave way to an unspoken idea that they too ought to be friends. Putting his cares aside for the moment, Wang took another cigarette from behind his ear – a Zhonghua, a good brand, from a soft case, as the client took pains to remind him.

'Here, Tailai.' He thrust the cigarette towards Tailai's hand.

Tailai touched it and realised it was a cigarette. 'I don't smoke.'

'Neither do I,' Wang said. 'Just for kicks. We don't get a slow day like this very often.'

Wang handed Tailai his lighter before lighting his own. 'Don't inhale. You don't want to get hooked.'

It was Tailai's first cigarette and he lit the filter end. Then when he turned it around to light it and took a puff, he burned his lips. He licked them and finally managed a bit of smoke, a full mouthful.

Closing his mouth lightly, he tried to exhale the smoke through his nose, but he choked so badly he couldn't stop coughing. Finally, when he managed to stop, he said, 'Good cigarette.' Like a connoisseur.

'Of course it's good.'

They began discussing cigarettes, but about all they could come up with was 'good'. With nothing much to say, they fell quiet; they wanted to talk, but had to search for a topic, which made them both uncomfortable. All they could do was keep smoking. So they puffed away, one as fast as the other, like non-smokers. Gao Wei, who was sitting at the receptionist desk, looked out through the French doors and saw the two men smoking, the tips of their cigarettes flickering red.

A naturally serious person, Tailai treated this first cigarette as important. He took every puff carefully, precisely and fully, and finished his cigarette in record time. Reaching into his pocket, he took out an object, also a cigarette, and handed it to Wang.

'Have another, Brother Wang,' he said, like a seasoned man.

The two women had finally stopped laughing and were likely back to whispering. After lighting the new cigarette with the first one, Wang flipped the butt out into the street, where it sizzled briefly in the rain before dying out. Being the older of the two, he eventually found something to say. 'You and Jin Yan have been together for some time, haven't you?'

'No, not really,' Tailai replied.

'When are you getting married?'

Tailai smacked his lips, not knowing what to say. It was some time before he answered with a question of his own. 'How about you?'

'Us?' Wang said. 'We're in no hurry.'

'You must be planning on a big wedding.'

'No, nothing big,' Wang said. 'There's no need for that. Simple is better.' There was more he wanted to say. 'Marriage just means two people living together. A wedding's not important.' He paused before adding, 'Xiao Kong feels the same way.'

Finally finding someone who shared his view, Tailai edged closer, and was about to say something, but stopped. Instead he heaved a sigh. 'Trouble.'

'What kind of trouble?'

'Jin Yan insists on a big wedding,' Tailai whispered. 'Otherwise, she'd rather not get married.'

'Why?'

'She said that the one thing a woman wants in life is the wedding.'

'I doubt that.' Wang smiled. 'How can a wedding be the one thing a woman wants?'

'I'm with you on that.'

'What else does she say?'

'She says that every woman feels that way.'

Wang Daifu reacted to Tailai's remark by slowly exhaling a mouthful of smoke. *If every woman feels that way, why doesn't Xiao Kong?* He realised that he and Xiao Kong hadn't talked much about a wedding, though he knew she wanted to get married soon. She never said a word about the arrangement or scale of their wedding, for she had always gone along with him. Wang realised that this could be a problem, and that he'd have to ask her about it one of these days. He could not take advantage of her reticence.

'Ai!' Tailai grumbled. 'She insists on an impressive wedding, and I can't talk her out of it.'

'That doesn't sound right,' Wang said, more or less to himself.

'Go ask Xiao Kong,' Tailai replied. 'I wouldn't be surprised if Jin Yan has already shared her thoughts with her.'

As they stood under the overhang, the two men were lost in their own thoughts. They did need to have a good talk and share ideas with each other. It would be good for them, and that suddenly made them feel like brothers-in-law, even before they'd finished their second cigarettes.

CHAPTER SIXTEEN
WANG DAIFU

WANG DAIFU KNEW it was bad news the minute he picked up the phone. The voice on the other end sounded pleasant as it asked him to please come home, to return to his parents' house. It was such a nice voice, like a family member calling out to him, but, of course, he knew it was nothing of the sort.

Over the previous two weeks, the twenty-five thousand yuan had been weighing heavily on his mind. He'd told himself not to think about it, that he'd come up with something as the deadline approached, like believing there will always be a path when the cart reaches the mountains. He did find a solution, which was to borrow ten thousand against his wages from Sha, which, when added to his savings, came to twenty-five thousand. He did not tell Sha why he needed the money, and luckily Sha didn't ask.

His problem now, as he fingered the money, was that he could not bear to part with it. He recalled what an older woman, also blind, had once said to him: 'Money is like children. If you keep your distance, no problem. But lay your hands on them and you have to hold them close.' This money meant the world to Wang Daifu, and his heart bled. He could smell the blood. It was so unfair. He'd give whatever he had if his brother was going to buy a house, get married or needed it to save his own life. But it was none of these; it was a gambling debt, a bottomless pit. What if his brother kept gambling? What if he wound up owing another twenty-five thousand? How would Wang manage that *and* live his own life?

For the first time in his life, Wang felt self-loathing. Why did he have to be the older brother? Why was he so fond of being taken advantage of? Why did he have to step up? Really, there was no need for that. Without him the world would continue to turn. He needed to change that. Not this time, of course, but next time. He promised those people he'd pay them back. You can be blind, but you mustn't let yourself be mute. If your tongue remains still, the whole world is blind.

A debt must be repaid. That is, and has always been, an unassailable principle.

After listening to the message, he shut his mobile phone and touched his waistband, where he'd tied the money to the inside. A vital precaution. He took out his dark glasses, put them on and walked to the street. As he stood by the side of the road, which was pitch black to him, the sounds of cars whizzing by filled his ears. They were not so much whizzing as peeling away the road surface, skinning the ground.

This is the last time, the very last time, Wang kept telling himself. From now on, he would stay away no matter what happened to his brother. At that moment, his heart was as hard and cold as stone; this would absolutely be the last time. Twenty-five thousand yuan. It was not just money, it was Wang's own ransom; he would not owe this world anything once he handed over the money. He would be debt free. His only regret, of course, was that the money could not have found a better use than giving it to those bastards. *Go ahead, take the money and choke on it.*

He thrust out his arm, a grand gesture to hail a taxi. *Fuck it! Why worry about the piddling cab fare now that I'm going to throw away twenty-five thousand yuan? Spend it! Spend it any way I want! I'm going to treat myself today and take a taxi. For the first time in my life!*

A taxi rolled up. He heard it stop, but didn't move, since he didn't know how to open the door. The cabbie yelled out impatiently, 'Are you going to get in or not? What's your problem?'

Wang was gripped by a sudden panic. He'd been too rash. How on earth had he got the idea to hail a taxi? He didn't even know how to get in. He calmed down after a moment of self-reproach and embarrassment. He was in a bad mood, a very bad mood indeed. 'What are you yelling about? Get out and open the door for me.'

The driver cocked his head to size him up through the window. Wang Daifu, wearing a grim look, had on a pair of dark glasses, which, like those on all blind people, were oversized and very dark, virtually wrapping around the eyes. So he's blind, the driver said to himself, but maybe not. The more he sized up Wang, the less he appeared to be blind. Wondering what kind of suspicious character he'd run into that day, the driver nevertheless got out to open the door while puzzling over what sort of eyes lay behind those dark glasses.

Wang was focused; overtaken by a sudden surge of vanity, he didn't want to look timorous, nor did he want people to know that he was blind. Judging by the sound of the door opening, he eased in by holding onto the edge.

'Where to, sir?' the driver asked politely, almost humbly, once he was back behind the steering wheel.

When had he become a 'sir'? Wang felt like laughing. Then it dawned on him that he had been rude, which was not like him, but his rudeness was being handsomely repaid by the driver's polite request. *What has the world come to?* He'd need to take stock later.

'The market at Gongyuan Road.'

He was home. His heart was racing as he climbed the stairs, caused by hesitation and timidity. Mainly timidity. The blind are always intimidated when dealing with the sighted, for the simple reason that they are visible, while the sighted are not; that is why the blind try to avoid interactions with the sighted. In their minds, the sighted are a different animal, one of a higher branch, with eyes and omniscience, almost deity-like. They deal with the sighted the same way the sighted deal with spirits and deities: respect at a distance.

He was confronting the people who play by the rules – not all that different from spirits and deities.

A surprise awaited him when he stepped inside; his brother was actually home. The nerve of that asshole, sitting at home like a guest, carefree as can be, just waiting for the sucker to show up. That made Wang's blood boil. There were several people sitting in easy chairs, obviously waiting for him. They were totally self-assured – they were watching TV. A cacophony of noise emerged from the set, clangs and clanks filling the room, the sounds of metal on metal, the sound of combat, to be exact, with knives, spears, swords and halberds. Violent and sharp, even with a pleasantness to it, almost melodious. It was either a martial arts film or a gangster movie. Wang knew all about martial arts films, which worked under a certain premise: fists or bullets are the ultimate defenders of truth. He recalled the cab ride that had brought him here. He had been rude, which had elicited a humble response. He'd become a 'sir'. Wang walked up to the sofa, and the TV volume was turned down. He felt a hand on his shoulder. It was his brother, Wang could tell, and his blood really began to boil, out of control. He could see his own body, infused with light and fully transparent, sending out intermittent rays. With a soft laugh, he extended his right hand to shake his brother's, but, the moment the two brothers' hands came into contact, like a gust of wind, Wang's left hand smacked his brother across the face.

'Get out,' Wang shouted. 'Get the hell out of here. You've got no right to be here.'

'He has to stay,' said the pleasant voice.

'I don't want him here,' Wang said. 'Didn't I tell you it's between you and me?' He laughed. 'I won't go anywhere,' he added. 'I wouldn't want to even if I could.'

'Did you bring the money?'

'Yes.'

'Give us the money and we'll leave.'

'No. He has to go first.'

'He can't.' Again the pleasant voice.

'He leaves and you get the money. He stays, no money. You talk it out.'

With that, he left the room and walked into the kitchen.

He went straight to the refrigerator, where he turned over his waistband, took out the money, and tossed it into the freezer. He took out two ice cubes and put them in his mouth. When he heard his brother go out the door, he began to chomp on the ice cubes, making a loud crunching noise. Feeling himself no longer human, he stripped off his shirt and returned to the living room with a kitchen knife.

It was deathly quiet, so quiet he could sense the wall, the chairs, and the cups and dishes on the tea table, as well as the knife, of course; it made a loud, crisp sound.

'So you've thought it through. You're the one who wants to do it this way, not us, but we can do it that way too. We're just people who play by the rules.'

'I didn't ask you to do this.' He raised the knife and sliced his chest. As if shy, the blood waited to emerge, but when it did, no more shyness; it spread its legs and ran down Wang Daifu's chest, then his abdomen, and finally, with unerring accuracy, into his pants. It was hot as it stroked him like a loved one.

Wang Daifu said, 'Do you know what we blind people like most?'

Wang Daifu said, 'Money.'

Wang Daifu said, 'Our money is different from yours.'

Wang Daifu said, 'Your money is called money while ours is called life.'

Wang Daifu said, 'With no money we have no lives. No one knows where we blind people will die.'

Wang Daifu said, 'Have you seen blind beggars on the street? Of course you have.'

Wang Daifu said, 'I know how to beg too. Believe it or not.'

Wang Daifu said, 'But I can't do it.'

Wang Daifu said, 'My parents gave me life, so I can't.'

Wang Daifu said, 'We have a face.'

Wang Daifu said, 'We care about our face.'

Wang Daifu said, 'We love our face.'

Wang Daifu said, 'Otherwise, how would we continue to live?'

Wang Daifu said, 'I have to treat myself like a human.'

Wang Daifu said, 'Treat myself like a human. Do you understand that?'

Wang Daifu said, 'No you don't.'

Wang Daifu said, 'I can't give you the twenty-five thousand yuan.'

Wang Daifu said, 'If I did, I'd have to become a beggar.'

Wang Daifu said, 'Do you know where I get my money?'

Wang Daifu said, 'From massaging your feet.'

Wang Daifu said, 'Do you know how many feet I need to massage to get that much money?'

Wang Daifu said, 'Fifteen yuan a pair, or seven-fifty per foot.'

Wang Daifu said, 'For twenty-five thousand, I have to massage three thousand three hundred and thirty-three feet.'

Wang Daifu said, 'I'm not giving you the money.'

Wang Daifu said, 'But the debt must be paid.'

Wang Daifu said, 'So I'm giving you my blood.'

The blood had now reached the tops of his feet. It didn't seem bold enough, too tame. He wanted to hear it roar. He sliced his chest a second time. Much better, it really started to gush. It sounded great and must have looked great too.

Wang Daifu said, 'This is all I have.'

Wang Daifu said, 'You can have it all.'

Wang Daifu said, 'No need to be embarrassed. Take it.'

Wang Daifu said, 'Take as much as you can.'

Wang Daifu said, 'There's also my life.'

He laid the blade against his neck. Wang Daifu said, 'Is this enough?'

Wang Daifu said, 'Answer me. Is this enough?'

The blood gathering on the living room floor was turning into a scary sight. The pleasant voice could not make its pleasant sound. The knife remained in Wang's hand, the eyes on the knife's tip open wide. The pleasant voice reached out and grabbed his wrist. Wang Daifu said, 'Don't touch me! Is this enough?'

The pleasant voice said, 'It is.'

Wang Daifu said, 'Enough?'

Wang Daifu said, 'It's enough – is that right?'

Wang Daifu said, 'Are we all square?'

Wang Daifu said, 'You can go now.'

Wang Daifu said, 'Please leave.'

Laying the knife in his palm, Wang offered it to the pleasant voice. 'If that bastard goes to your place again, cut him up with this knife, in as many pieces as you like.'

The room was quiet, now that the pleasant voice had left without a response. Wang could tell they'd left together, all three of them, with six feet, not a chaotic sound, but somewhat ragged. He listened to the sound of six feet growing fainter, still noisy but clearly on their way out; he put down the knife and turned around.

The room was submerged in total silence, quiet as the stench of blood. Wang suddenly realised that his parents were home and knew they must be looking at him. He *looked* at his parents, first his father and then his mother; they stared at each other for about twenty seconds, before Wang sensed something rolling out of his eyes. Tears. His parents had seen everything, they had to have seen everything.

How could that have happened? How? Wang Daifu had originally planned to pay off his brother's debt, but he hadn't – a momentary change of heart. What had he done? Was it Wang Daifu who had made such a ridiculous move? How could he have done it? How was he any different from a common scoundrel? He wasn't. Shameful. On this day he became a typical ruffian, the dregs of society. He was soiled, no longer a man of dignity. His tongue had finally uttered 'blind' talk.

He was not like that, not at all. Since childhood, he had been a good kid and a good student, the teachers told him so. He had never been close to his parents, who had had little influence on him as he was growing up. The teachers at the school for the blind were the ones who had truly made a difference in his life. But there's a problem with that statement. Wang Daifu knew, and only he knew, that the people who had had the greatest impact on his life were, in fact, his parents, not his teachers. What he meant by parents was not father and mother; the parents he meant were abstractions, something for which he was eternally apologetic. Any time he did something wrong, a tiny mistake or a small error, the teachers would say to him, 'How can you face your parents?' He couldn't. His parents were always beside him, right there on the crown of his head.

But that was not enough. As an adult, he was a fanatic about the notion of dignity; deep down, he insisted that he be a man with dignity. He had to be a man of dignity to be worthy of his parents' nurturing and to be able to face them.

But what had he done today? Because of money he had made a scene, and uttered 'blind talk' in front of his parents; he had shredded his dignity. He had lost every ounce of self-respect in front of his parents.

'Pa, Ma.' He lowered his head and said with heart-rending self-reproach, 'I'm sorry I've let you down.'

His mother was still in shock, but she was happy. Her face was awash in hot tears of elation. She grabbed his hand and said, 'If your brother had half what you have he'd be fine.'

'Ma, I've let you down.'

She could not figure out why he was saying that. But his father picked up on what he had said. 'Son,' he said, 'it's I who have let you down. I should never have let your mother give birth to that bastard.'

Wang Daifu sucked in his belly and threw out his chest. He was still bleeding; there were bloody bubbles on his chest. 'I'm not like that, Pa. Ask anyone, I'm not like that.'

His parents exchanged a look, puzzled by what their son was saying. The only possible explanation was that he was out of his head with pain.

'Your son has let you down.' Wang Daifu was unrelenting.

'It's your father who has let *you* down.'

Wang's hands were groping at something, but his father didn't know what it was. He reached out; Wang Daifu grabbed the hand and would not let go. It was a strange feeling that went right to his heart, and he had trouble adjusting to that. Twenty-nine years. In twenty-nine years this was the first time his skin had come into contact with his father. In his memory, his parents' skin was a blank. Wang gripped the hand, feeling its fingers and its skin; tears gushed from his eyes without warning, like spurting blood. He was shaking uncontrollably. His face awash in tears, he managed a soft plea, 'Pa, I want you to slap your son!'

'Pa,' he raised his voice and said hoarsely, nearly sobbing, 'Pa, give your son a hard slap.'

Wang's parents, already in a state of shock, were dumbstruck by the request. What were they to do? What could they say? What was going on with their son? Wang's father was weeping; he turned to look at his wife through his tears and saw her standing there slack-jawed. Then, without a thought for the blood, he pulled his son into an embrace. 'Later. Let's talk about that later, after we go to the hospital. Son, we have to go to the hospital.'

The wounds were shallow, but the slits long, requiring a hundred and sixteen stitches, making his chest look like a pile of rags after the semi-circular needle had dug in at one end and come out the other.

Wang Daifu ached even after he'd had a shot for the pain. He was holding on to his father with his left hand, his mother with his right. But it was his heart that ached. He ached for his parents, who were burdened with two useless sons, one the dregs of society, the other a no-account bastard. What else did life hold for them? Nothing. A life of total blindness.

When the stitching was done, he was detained in the emergency room by the police. The doctor had called the police for him. Those were obvious knife wounds, and if it had been anyone else, they would probably not have bothered. But Wang was disabled, and they had to intervene when someone viciously abused a disabled person.

'Who did this to you?' the policeman asked.

Wang Daifu said, 'I did it myself.'

'Don't lie to me.'

Wang Daifu said, 'I'm telling the truth.'

'You are obligated to tell us exactly what happened.'

Wang Daifu said, 'I am telling you exactly what happened.'

'Let me repeat myself. Even though you're disabled, you are obligated all the same to tell us exactly what happened.'

Wang pursed his lips twice and raised his brows. 'And you are obligated to believe someone who is disabled, even if you are not.'

'Then tell me, why did you do it?'

Wang Daifu said, 'My blood wanted to cry.'

The policeman was tongue-tied. He didn't know what to do with this unreasonable disabled man. 'I'm asking for the last time. What happened? Telling me the truth is for your own good.'

'I did it myself,' Wang insisted. 'How's this for a harsh vow? If I'm lying, the minute I walk out this door, I will have perfect vision.'

Instead of returning to the tuina centre right away, he had to go home to get the twenty-five thousand in the freezer, not to mention change out of his clothes. When he walked in, he was surprised to note that his brother was back. He was lying on the sofa, eating an apple, a good one, crisp and juicy enough for Wang to hear. Wang's heart skipped a beat. His brother hadn't opened the freezer, had he? He went straight to the kitchen, where he fearfully opened the freezer door; whew, the money was still there, just where he'd left it. Taking out the bundle, he stuffed it back inside his waistband. It felt heart-stopping cold against his belly. It pricked his skin. Money is so cold.

Without a word, he left the apartment and walked down the stairs, very slowly, because of the money and also because of the pain from the cuts. An argument erupted inside the apartment. He could not tell what exactly his parents were saying, but he heard his younger brother's voice, so loud he could hear it two stories above him. He was shouting about how unfairly life had treated him.

'Why couldn't you have made me blind? If I couldn't see, I'd be able to support myself.'

CHAPTER SEVENTEEN

SHA FUMING AND ZHANG ZONGQI

UNDER NORMAL CIRCUMSTANCES, Sha Fuming and Zhang Zongqi should have already found the time to sit down and discuss how best to deal with Jin da-jie. But Sha didn't raise the issue, so Zhang decided to keep quiet, initiating a cold war between them.

The tuina centre had not had a meeting for quite some time, which did not bode well. It was clear that Sha planned to fire Jin da-jie, while Zhang wanted to let Gao Wei go. The delay in calling a meeting could mean only one thing, that neither boss was ready or was sure of the outcome, creating a stalemate. But no meeting could also signal that privately neither boss was willing to concede.

Sha Fuming was determined to let Jin da-jie go, but he knew that the only way to get rid of her was through an equal-opportunity firing, letting Gao Wei go at the same time. But Gao Wei mustn't leave. She was Du Hong's eyes, and even her legs. What would happen to Du Hong if Gao left? How would he face her? So that was their dilemma – neither was able to play the cards in his hand. It was a contest of patience.

Time passed as the contest dragged on. Seen on the surface, the delay was fair to both sides, but in fact that was not the case. The matter had to be settled. Sha thought about it long and hard before coming up with a new idea – a split.

After prolonged and careful planning, he asked Zhang out for a talk one night at around one o'clock. They went to the Sifang Tea House, where Sha ordered black tea and Zhang green. Sha came straight to the point with a clear-cut, sound proposal. He would give Zhang one hundred thousand yuan, take down the Sha Zongqi tuina centre sign and put up a new one for the Sha Fuming tuina centre. He had his reason for offering Zhang a hundred thousand: when they'd started out, they'd each put in eighty thousand to pay for the licence, rent, interior alterations and furnishing, and required equipment. They split profits at the end of each quarter, which was why Sha believed it was acceptable for him to offer a hundred thousand now.

Zhang did not hem and haw either, giving Sha a straightforward answer that he agreed to the split. But he had a minor amendment; his price was one hundred and twenty thousand. Direct and frank, he said he would leave as soon as he received the money, an answer Sha had anticipated, all but the amount. Instead of telling Zhang he thought the price was a bit high, Sha changed tactics.

'A hundred and twenty thousand is fine. Why don't we do it this way? You give me that amount and I'll leave.'

If the negotiation had ended there, Sha would consider himself the winner. With a hundred and twenty thousand yuan, plus what he'd saved up, he'd be able to open a new centre. Given the time needed to find a new site, apply for a licence and remodel the place, he'd be a boss again in two or three months. Sha figured he'd planned everything just right: their former friendship dictated that he open his new centre as far away as possible, at least five kilometres, and he'd bring over Gao Wei and Du Hong. Wang Daifu and Xiao Kong could come along if they wanted. In no more than two years, his business would prosper, and when that happened, it was anyone's guess whether Zhang would survive the competition. After all, Sha Fuming had been handling daily management of the Sha Zongqi tuina centre.

Sha Fuming was in a hurry to split up the business, and the dispute between him and Zhang Zongqi was one reason. The critical factor, however, was his relationship with Du Hong. Opening a new business was important, but so was a personal life. Sha was not a young man, and he had to get busy settling down. Du Hong, in her own words, was still young. So he'd set up a new business and wait patiently for and with her. Time only runs one way – it cannot go backwards. When the new centre opened, he'd buy a piano for her; if she didn't object, she could play the piano daily and draw a salary. That would have a two-pronged advantage. With ear-pleasing music in the air every day, the new centre would be different from others, and that would advertise the unique services he offered. Moreover, he'd be able to keep her around, which was the whole point of a new centre. Wherever Du Hong was, there was hope and happiness for him. He could not let himself keep having that dream; he had to stop dreaming about a pair of hands and stop dreaming about two cubes of ice. The ice was too cold, the hands were too hard.

Hence, the split was inevitable; the sticking point was how. Sha Fuming could have started out by asking for a hundred and twenty thousand, but he could not bring himself to do that, and Zhang would have had the right to refuse. Zhang making the demand simplified matters. Sha would even settle for a hundred thousand if that was all Zhang was willing to offer. Put simply, Sha's only concern had been the possibility that Zhang would not agree to the split. He would come out ahead on the deal as long as Zhang made an offer, be it a hundred thousand or a hundred and twenty thousand.

Taking a sip of tea, Sha sensed that the negotiations were nearing the end. He was amazed at how smoothly the issue was being solved; they would split without a row. What better outcome could he have expected? No, nothing else. His happiness reminded him of the early days of Sha Zongqi tuina centre. Business had been slow, but they never disagreed and always opened their hearts to one another. They would have crowded onto the same bed if they could. Those were wonderful days. A honeymoon for friends. A honeymoon for men. Who could have anticipated all the problems in the ensuing years? Luckily the split would go well and they'd continue as good friends in the future.

But Sha Fuming was wrong; he had miscalculated. Zhang Zongqi's experience had manifested itself just as Sha was indulging in feelings of exhilaration.

'Sure I can give a hundred and twenty thousand yuan,' Zhang said. 'We're old friends, so I must be frank with you. I don't have the cash right now, so you'll have to wait a few years, if you're willing. I'll never short-change you. You can trust me. Whenever you want to go, just tell me, and we can sign an agreement.'

Sha could not have anticipated that move in a million years; he was speechless. At that moment, he recalled how embarrassed he'd been when making the plan, unsure of how to broach the subject with Zhang. When he finally mustered the courage to speak up, he realised that Zhang had not been idle. In fact, Zhang had been making his preparations, and he'd thought things out more carefully and planned more strategically. Zhang had formed a superior design. Sha could kick himself for being so rash; he should not have shown his hand first. Now see what happened? No longer having the edge, he didn't know what to say in response to Zhang's offer. What could he say? Lifting the corners of his mouth into a smile, he pressed the talking clock clipped to his belt. It was getting late. No time like the present to leave. He took out his wallet to pay. Zhang followed suit and said, 'Split down the middle?'

'What are you doing?' Sha blurted out. 'It's only a cup of tea.'

'It's better to split down the middle,' Zhang said.

Sha nodded and relented, but felt a surge of sadness, bitterness even. This was not the same split down the middle as when they started out. It marked the end of their friendship.

It was Sha who'd come up with the idea of splitting down the middle when they first talked about opening the Sha Zongqi tuina centre. Back then they'd been working on the Bund in Shanghai, and the split meant a great deal to Sha; it was not just an investment tactic, promising equal profits for equal capital, but an unspoken agreement that they would both be a boss and neither would be the boss of the other. Truth be told, that went against Sha's wishes, for he valued the status of a boss too much to share that with someone else. It may appear odd that blind individuals who work for a living and support themselves are more ambitious than the sighted when it comes to being the boss, but virtually all of them are interested in that special status. When Sha was chatting with his co-workers, a basic truth was revealed. Nearly every one of them shared a thought, or an aspiration; that is, one day, when they had enough money, they'd go back home to open their own business. That may have sounded entrepreneurial, but was in fact motivated by the wish to be a boss.

His friendship with Zhang was the reason why Sha was willing to split down the middle, for they had been very close back in Shanghai. And there was a story behind it.

Like all tuina therapists, Sha and Zhang lived in Shanghai as migrant workers, which meant being cut off from the dazzling city, with all its splendour. To them, Shanghai was nothing but two beds; one was in a massage room, their livelihood, and the other in a dormitory, their daily life. The massage bed was easy to deal with, even if it wore them out. What Sha truly dreaded was the one in the dormitory, where his bed was placed in a thirteen-square-metre room, along with seven others. Eight beds meant eight grown men, who, when they were all in there, strangely did not emit a purely male smell, not even a human odour. Instead, it was a motley smell of low-quality liquor, cigarettes, toothpaste and soap, and high-quality foot and underarm sweat and waste. The mixture was dizzying, a unique smell, the smell of migrant workers.

Sha and Zhang shared the same dorm room, on opposite upper

bunks. They did not talk much at first, something that changed only when they shared the same fate – the men on their lower bunks found girlfriends at almost the same time.

Finding girlfriends was, of course, a good thing, but none of their business. At least not until the men shocked them by having their girlfriends stay overnight. The men tacked up pieces of cloth around their beds, covering all three sides to create a private space. To be fair, the couples practised restraint and self-control inside the closed space, not making any improper or unseemly noise at night. It was hard, to be sure, but they managed. What the couples overlooked was that they could only control the sounds they made, but not the movements of their bodies; the bed rocked as they moved. When their beds rocked, so did Sha's and Zhang's, more, in fact, than the lower bunks. Sha Fuming and Zhang Zongqi rocked rhythmically, soundlessly, evenly and pointlessly, but with significant consequences. They could only lie there, pretending to sleep while they were consumed by flames of desire.

And that was how Sha Fuming and Zhang Zongqi became friends, through commiseration and private curses. They were fellow sufferers, not of an illness, but of maleness. This punishment was not something everyone could endure. Others might not understand, but they did. They shared the same feeling, the same pain, the same resentment, the same torment, the same dejection and the same self-mockery. They could only comfort one another, and from that they found they embraced the same aspiration – to have one's own room. How would they do that? The one and only answer was: be their own boss.

By all accounts, they were comrades in suffering. Had they not braved countless dangers by surviving a sea of fire together? This was no exaggeration. They hated the life of a migrant worker with all their being; put differently, they were dying to be a boss. With that shared and eager wish, they decided to pool their money and became bosses ahead of schedule. 'We'll split down the middle,' Sha had said. 'I have a name ready. We'll call it the Sha Zongqi tuina centre.' The rent for a storefront in Shanghai was beyond their means. What to do? Go back to Nanjing – no matter where you are you can open a business.

Sha was decisive about taking Zhang to Nanjing. Why? The explanation was simple: Nanjing, Sha's stomping ground, was more or less his hometown, while Zhang had no prior connection to the city, since he had come from a small town in central China. They could not possibly open a tuina centre in a remote town.

The opening of the Sha Zongqi tuina centre was a landmark event, not because they had finally become bosses, not that. It was a landmark because it transformed two unrelated migrant workers into good friends who had shared peaks and valleys. The beginning of their friendship was also its high point. Deep down, however, neither of them was happy with the arrangement. Sha, of course, had wanted to open a Sha Fuming tuina centre and Zhang would have preferred a Zhang Zongqi tuina centre. But they were friends who had been through hardships, friends till death, so how could Sha Fuming or Zhang Zongqi be better than Sha Zongqi? Sha Fuming was Sha Fuming, with his own parents; Zhang Zongqi was Zhang Zongqi and had his own parents. But Sha Zongqi was different; Sha Zongqi had no parents. He had Sha Fuming and Zhang Zongqi as his fathers. They did not merely become a boss; in fact they became one person – enterprising, hardworking and courteous, who would do anything to sustain their friendship. They were touched by their friendship and by their magnanimity; having one true lifelong friend was enough, so they treated each other like a brother.

Strictly speaking, there was never any discord between Sha and Zhang. Of course, that was not really the case, since disagreements did crop up once they became bosses, but they were minor, trivial, not serious enough to be called discord. One principle they held in common was to never bring up something that bothered them, no matter what happened; the person who did that would appear petty.

They were like brothers, and troubles would blow over as long as they were willing to compromise. Discord was inevitable, since it was two men running a business with employees. If discord was on the horizon, everything was fine so long as they each kept quiet and acted in a broad-minded, magnanimous manner.

And yet, not voicing displeasure did not mean it wasn't felt. Sha was unhappy with Zhang because he played no role in running the business; he never offended anyone and brought in more money. And he was sharp as a tack. Zhang was unhappy for the opposite reason; he had also put up eighty thousand yuan and, being one of the bosses, was busy day in and day out, but in the end, the centre appeared to be Sha Fuming's; he seemed to be sole owner of the place, barking orders all day long. And he was as vain as a peacock.

Sha Fuming was a vain man who placed a great deal of emphasis on the status of a boss, though money was important to him too. Money meant a lot to Zhang, but deep down he also took the role of a boss seriously. The partnership meant that each only got half of what he wanted, which was cause for dissatisfaction. Time really cannot take care of everything. As time went on, resentment began to accumulate. By itself resentment is no big deal; accumulation is the problem. Accumulated resentment is a wing, and a wing can do only one thing – spread out and flap its way into the darkness.

However, friendship still mattered, so the two bosses bore their resentment privately when they were together, striving to appear unconcerned, that there was nothing wrong. It was a sort of diligence, prolonged and difficult, also useless and laughable. In retrospect, the worst thing they could have done to their friendship was to be diligent, for it was like slow-acting poison. Everything went well each and every day; nothing was out of kilter. What could be detrimental was the unexpected. With the advent of the unexpected, the slow poison would be given its opportunity to take effect; the resultant animosity towards one another would shock not only the others, but themselves as well. How much better it would have been if they'd quarrelled from time to time.

Yet this was not the fatal blow; the critical factor was that they were both blind, and as bosses they had daily dealings with both the sighted and unsighted at the centre. The blind have their own approach to interpersonal relationships, a unique and reliable method that works for them; trouble crops up when the sighted enter the mix. No matter how one looks at it, the blind are vulnerable; they lack confidence in how they interact with others. When dealing with the sighted, they adopt their ways, for the simple reason that they cannot see. 'Truth' and 'facts' are not on their side, so they must judge and act by relying on the eyes of the sighted. In the end, without knowing it, the blind follow the sighted in their social interactions. They are unaware that their judgements are the judgements of others, and yet they have their doubts. That in turn makes it necessary for them to face two different worlds, which leads to a serious predicament. What do they do? They know what to do. Armed with self-esteem and resolve, they divide their inner world into two, one half believing and the other half doubting.

This was precisely the scientific attitude, half believing and half doubting, that Sha and Zhang adopted to deal with the centre. In the strictest sense, there has never been an independent world for the blind that is completely separate from that of the sighted, as the pervasive gaze of the sighted forever sparkles in the world of the blind. The gaze is sharp, hard, omnipresent, eerie and demonic, so when the blind enter mainstream society, they are constantly tripped up by two stumbling blocks – their experience and the eyes of the sighted. They trudge along with great difficulty, like groping rocks to cross a river.

Hence, in a way, Sha Fuming was trustworthy and so was Zhang Zongqi; the only suspicious one was Sha Zongqi.

It was past two in the morning when Sha came back to the dorm from the teahouse. He was the second to return. They had left together but had come back separately: to employees lying awake, the two sets of footsteps implied a problem, a big problem. Zhang was already online, his fingers banging on the keyboard. He sometimes went overboard, staying online till after three in the morning. Computers for the blind incorporate special software that, simply put, transforms data into sounds, which means they act as sound systems. *You there, Zhang Zongqi, by keeping the sound on, you disturb all the other workers, who don't want to hurt your feelings by saying so.*

As soon as Sha Fuming was back in the dorm, he went into the toilet, where he heard someone cough. It was Wang Daifu. The silence, followed by rapid breathing, sounded suspicious. He wasn't masturbating, was he? Sha thought he ought to turn and go back out, but that might seem odd. No, he couldn't be. Sha turned his head in Wang's direction and said softly, 'Is there something wrong, Old Wang?'

'It's nothing,' Wang replied unconvincingly.

So Sha decided to wait, which he did for a while before asking, 'Is there a problem?'

'No.'

'Then what are you doing in there?'

'I'm almost done,' Wang Daifu replied. 'I'm all right, there's nothing wrong.'

That only intensified Sha's suspicion. *What exactly is he doing in there?* He frowned. 'What do you mean, you're almost done?'

'It's nothing,' Wang replied with a laugh.

CHAPTER EIGHTEEN
XIAO MA

SEX CAN BE addictive, particularly in one's youth. It took only one visit for Xiao Ma to crave more, though he could not recall the details of his first time, as if he hadn't done it. The only thing he remembered of the experience was the hurry-scurry, but the outcome was mind-blowing. When he returned to the tuina centre, he felt he had been emptied out, with total relaxation washing over his body and mind. He was so comfortable and calm he wanted nothing, desired nothing. Nothing that wonderful had ever happened to him before. The beauty of sex was in more than the act itself; it lingered long after. Xiao Ma enjoyed a soothing sensation from head to toe; what he had ejaculated was not merely selfish and pitiable semen, but all his agitation and worries.

Totally ignorant of sex, Ma treated his hurry-scurry movements as successful surgery that cured his illness and brought him peace. But the day was barely over before the severity of his situation reared its ugly head; he was dejected to discover that everything he had done the day before was in vain. All his problems returned, with double the intensity. A blind, saturating and evil force that had nothing to do with bones or muscles reappeared inside him, one capable of attacking at random and sweeping over him. It was secretive, violent and impossible to defend against. He fended it off with self-restraint, but evil forces always seem to prevail, and some things are harder than others to endure. When he realised that he could no longer hold it off, his only course of action was compromise; he groped his way back to the hair salon.

His body was not a body but an alarm clock whose inside was equipped with an enormous, taut winding mechanism; time was a vicious hand that, little by little, wound his body after it was completely relaxed, and only the hurry-scurry movements could loosen up his body with a tick-tock tick-tock.

Maybe it wasn't a winding mechanism, but a living object. It was a python, a snake with a coiled body. When it constricted, it stuck out its forked tongue to lick him here and there, creating both a fatal temptation and lively energy, while secreting an eerie force. His body was bewitched, stirring up howling winds and surging waves.

In a semi-dazed state, Xiao Ma entered the hair salon again and again. No longer engaged only in a hurry-scurry, he became increasingly sure of himself, slowly turning his attention from himself to Xiaoman. Through his palms and his fingers, an amazing secret revealed itself to Ma, who finally understood what people meant when they said a girl had all she should have and nothing she should not, a comment used to express admiration for a woman. Sao-zi was one of the women who enjoyed this great honour. With concentration in his hands, his fingers opened up, like seeing eyes, to focus their gaze on 'Sao-zi's' arms, her hands, her hair, her neck, her waist, her chest, her hips, her buttocks, her legs. He could even see her scent, an embracing, encompassing smell; he could also see her breath, uniquely special breath that seemed not to exist at times and was all powerful at others. She was 'Sao-zi'.

Put at ease by 'Sao-zi', Xiao Ma no longer had to hurry-scurry. He wanted no one but her.

The girls at the hair salon quickly noticed something interesting: the handsome young blind man had his 'eyes' on Xiaoman. They began to tease him; when he came in, they'd tell him she was busy with a client. *How about a different girl? We're all the same.* With a stern look, Xiao Ma would sit down and say earnestly, 'I'll wait.'

Noticing his single-minded focus on her, Xiaoman was enormously pleased. She was a plain-looking girl, not pretty at all, and that was a fatal flaw for a working girl. Proud and ambitious, she had started out big, venturing into a large establishment with a good working environment and higher pay, a preferred location for everyone. But she did not do as well as other girls, which is highly embarrassing for people in their line of work. Not making enough money was a minor issue compared to the awkwardness she felt, which got so bad she came to work at the hair salon. The salon was a boring place whose clients, unlike the larger establishment, were mostly working-class men with no romantic appeal or stories, nothing but good bodies. Xiaoman was fond of romantic stories, whether the men were sincere or not, whether they really liked her or didn't, even if they were simply pretending. She liked it all. She was, after all, a woman, and women like hearing stories, no matter what the men actually say or do. Making money while listening to the men's stories was an attraction that kept this line of work in existence.

There were no stories to hear in the hair salon, but she couldn't quit; it was the only kind of work she could do. *So, just keep on doing it. Keep at it.*

While she didn't expect stories, she did get plenty of face from Xiao Ma by his asking only for her each time, something all the other girls noticed. But then she got her stories, after all, from his gaze, in the way he *looked* at her. She was all too familiar with men's gazes, which were bright and spirited before they climbed on. Their eyes were filled with an invincible power, energy and strength, but their talk could be nauseating. Of course this was all before the event. What she feared most was the gaze when it was over. The man would close his eyes, and when he opened them again, he would have been replaced by another man with a clouded gaze, deflated, forlorn and dejected. It was like a used condom, wrinkled, displaying a sloppy, disconsolate air. So she avoided their eyes afterwards, disgusted by every single deflated man, who looked lost, scattered like the yolk of a broken egg.

But not Xiao Ma, who proceeded with caution at first, but was attentive afterwards. He stared at her with his lustreless eyes. He watched her, observed her, studied her, gazed at her, looked down on her. He groped her with his fingers, and wherever his fingers touched, he stared, watched, observed, studied, gazed and looked down on her. A surprising situation developed the first time he touched her eye sockets, for she was looking back at him; his non-existent gaze was penetrating, moist, bright and clear, like that of an innocent child, unguarded, guileless, giving everything away. He stared like that for a long time; his pupils trembled nearly imperceptibly, but he was trying very hard to keep them from moving.

She was frightened the first time she looked back at him, gripped by an unspeakable terror. Was that non-existent, penetrating and bright gaze really a gaze? She wasn't sure. If it was, she wished it was not; but if it was not, then she wished it were. Were they looking into each other's eyes? How and with what? And what did they see in each other's eyes? Flustered by an unknown anxiety, she avoided his gaze, but when she looked back, it was still there, taking her in with earnestness and sincerity.

She did not know what to do about his gaze. Xiaoman, the working girl, loved stories. She loved them because they were made up, but interesting and fun, like playing house. But she was frightened by a story to which devotion and sincerity are added. Everyone in the world knows that a whore is 'a heartless woman', which is the way it should be. How could a whore have a heart, when the men are heartless, no matter how sincere she is? No, a professional whore must be heartless, and nothing else.

Women like Xiaoman sell their bodies, or as they say in Nanjing, earn *bitter money*. People in Nanjing never say 'make money', for to them this profession requires tough, bitter effort; hence, earning bitter money. But not working girls, who have a more graphic, more vivid description for their kind of work: 'screw money'. Xiaoman had no idea which of her sisters invented the term, but it made her laugh whenever she thought about it. *It's true, isn't it? Aren't we screwing for money? If so, then it doesn't concern the eyes, since we don't need to aim; we can do a much better job with our eyes shut.*

But Xiao Ma liked to use his eyes, which she noticed were good-looking, nicely outlined, with a pleasant gaze. *How can a man have such a clean, pure gaze?* She'd never seen that before. *What does he 'see' anyway?*

He did not just look; he also sniffed. Finally utilising his nose, he began to search her body. It was a peculiar kind of sniffing, more like taking deep breaths, as if trying to suck secrets from her body into his internal organs. What secret did her body harbour? None. So his look of concentration turned greedy, as he devoted all his effort and focused all his attention on her. And when he did that, he seemed like an orphan boy, slightly naughty, somewhat ill-treated, but innocent. One time she reached out to touch his cheek, totally unaware that she, not he, was the one who was staring hard, her gaze seemingly boring into his pupils. Xiaoman should not have stared at him like that. But she was a woman who shared the common feminine problem of having a soft spot. A woman's gaze lacks stamina and becomes weak after a while, which in Xiaoman's case, softened something in her heart and lifted her chest slightly. *Oh, no. What's happening?*

'Go on home,' she said.

And he did. After he left, the other girls teased Xiaoman as usual.

'Get lost,' she said, looking somewhat weary.

But he returned the following day at noon. This time he was more violent than before; pressing her shoulders with his hands, he threatened, 'You can only do it with me.'

'What did you say?' She wasn't sure she'd heard him right.

Suddenly deflated, his hands slid down her arms to find her hands.

'I want you to be nice to me only,' he said softly, holding her hands.

Xiaoman froze. She'd had a two-year relationship that had torn her insides to shreds, after which she'd taken up the profession. The relationship had ended when she said, 'I want you to be nice to me only.'

'Sure,' her boyfriend had said, curling his lip, a smirk that stuck on his face and revealed to her how unrealistic her wish was. How could her playboy of a boyfriend be nice to her only? She had never expected, not in her lifetime, to hear that same phrase from someone, a client, no less. A client wanted her to be nice to him only.

'No problem,' she was panting. 'You'll have to support me, though.'

She arched her pelvis as she said this, a superfluous move that got him to respond with his own violent thrusts, creating the extraordinary situation of two bodies moving in precise synchronisation, as if by command. Rhythmically, they formed a perfect match, the remarkable rhythm seeming to be probing the internal potential of both bodies, an irresistible force. Xiaoman began to sense pleasure, an intoxicating feeling that promised an orgasm, an incredible and enchanting yet terrifying sign. Her job was to give men orgasms; she didn't want one for herself. That hadn't happened for a very long time. Now she wanted one. That was it. She wanted one. Matching his movements, her body began to rock; she wanted an orgasm. She wanted one. Moving faster and faster, she pushed upwards until she was close, a millimetre away. She was about to hit that damned wall. She knew what would happen if she did – she would disintegrate. 'Let me die!' she said to herself savagely. 'Let me die now.' She hit the wall, and her body was waiting, waiting to disintegrate. Once a solid crystal object, her body blew apart in a flash of light, shattering not into pieces, but thousands upon thousands of threads, innumerable threads spreading out in her body. All of a sudden, she stretched out her fingers and toes, which had become twenty mysterious channels to which the silken threads swarmed and were pulled out, determined not to return. They vanished as fast as they appeared, forever out of reach. Wrapping her arms around her client, she hugged him tightly. *My God. My God. My God. What were you doing, you harlot? Damn it, you made love.*

She could hear herself breathing hard; him too. Their heavy breathing shared the awesome quality of a mare and a stallion snorting loudly as they rested after galloping through mountains and crossing rivers, overcoming hardships and challenges. They were breathing hot, burning air into each other's face, scented with a smell of green grass and entrails. 'You really are Xiao Ma, a horse.'

He grabbed her hair and called out, 'Sao-zi.'

In fact the words were caught at his lips before he blurted them out, but the sudden thought made him feel hollow inside. She was not Sao-zi. What about him? Who was he? He was nothing but what was left after the ejaculation. Unaware that tears were filling his eye sockets, he focused his non-existent gaze, through the tears, on the woman in his arms; he was looking at her, eyes glued to her.

She saw his tears; she did. Lifting a drop with her fingertip, she stretched out her arm to look at it under the light. Like a crystal object, the teardrop gave off brilliant, prism-like refractions. One angled beam was especially long. This was the first time she'd seen something like that on a client's face; its radiant light lit up her bed. She smiled, pressing her lips into a thin line; she could not see the expression on her face, but her smile was sweet and yet mocking.

Then something ill-fated occurred. His tear fell upon her breast, near her nipple, on the areola, to be precise. She never knew that a woman's breast could have such an unusual capability as she heard a sizzle rising from it; like a parched desert it absorbed his tear straight into her heart.

It can't be, she said to herself. It just can't be.

Before she knew it, she took aim at his lips and, raising her head, she pressed hers squarely onto his, stuck her tongue into his mouth. His surprised tongue didn't move, for he was at a loss as to what to do next.

'I should head back,' he said.

A chilling sensation overtook him as soon as he returned to the tuina centre, as if he were wearing nothing but a thin condom. Xiao Ma was cold.

At the door to the lounge, he nearly bumped into Du Hong, who grabbed his hands and smiled without saying a word. He stood still, his ears pricked up and extending their detecting power through several turns to listen into every room, looking for Sao-zi. She was working, speaking nicely to her client, though he could not make out what she was saying. An unidentifiable scent, mixed with her body warmth, wafted in his direction; he looked around blankly, feeling empty inside, though the emptiness imbued him with a false sense of grandeur. Certain kinds of emptiness can be unforgettable.

Du Hong expected him to say something but he didn't. Instead, he stood there, like a lost soul.

'Did I just bump into you, Xiao Ma?' Du Hong asked.

Still nothing from him. Embarrassed, she let go of his hands and walked into the lounge alone.

He could hear that Sao-zi was finished with her client, who was about to leave. Groping his way over, he brushed shoulders with the departing client before reaching her doorway. Without an overture, he called out, 'Sao-zi.' Then, in a pained voice, he said, 'I'm very sorry.'

Getting to her feet, Xiao Kong was baffled by his comment, before concluding that it must have been about 'that matter'. *It has to be. It was so long ago, what's the point of bringing it up again? Xiao Ma, you're taking it too seriously.* Then she realised that he was afraid, worried that she would tell someone. He was suffering from the fear of discovery. But why in the world would she tell Wang Daifu? He hadn't really done anything to her but act somewhat impulsively. He just liked her a little too much. Xiao Kong bore him no grudge.

Walking up to him, she placed her left hand on his shoulder and whispered, 'Don't worry, Xiao Ma. Hey, it's all in the past, long forgotten.' Patting him a couple of times, she said, 'I didn't say a word to anyone.' Then she added, 'Not even to him.'

To her great surprise, he wordlessly brushed her hand off his shoulder, then grabbed it and slapped himself with it as hard as he could. Then he walked off. He had put everything he had into that slap, which was incredibly loud, louder than the slaps of foot massage.

Left behind in the massage room, Xiao Kong was stunned and dazed. *What are you doing, Xiao Ma? Was that really necessary?* Now she was upset, not just that, but sad, disappointed, and distressed. She felt like crying, but had no time to probe her own reactions; his slap was so loud that everyone at the centre must have heard it. What would she say if someone asked about it? How would she explain it? With no time to spare for her own sorrow, she slapped her palms together and said in a feigned cheerful tone, 'One slap from you, one slap from me, a kid sits on a plane happily.' Two more slaps followed, and she continued with her delighted shouts. 'Two slaps from you, two slaps from me, we fear no wind or rain.' She walked cheerfully back to the lounge, where Wang Daifu turned to her in surprise and asked with a big smile, 'What have you been eating? Why are you so happy?'

Xiao Kong was sizing up Xiao Ma with her ears, but heard nothing from him. *Is he gone? He should still be around.* She wished she could take him outside, find a secluded spot, and reassure him, 'Everything's fine, Xiao Ma. I didn't say a word to anyone. It's okay. I was never angry with you. I'm just spoken for, understand?' *He ought to get the picture.*

'Three slaps from you, three slaps from me, tonight we'll both eat congee,' she shouted out her response to Wang.

A week later Xiao Ma showed up at the hair salon again. Having just finished with a client, Xiaoman was tired, depressed and lethargic. She was somewhat distant as she took him to a back room, acting quite cold. They sat down on the edge of a bed, neither saying a word, giving the room a formal feel.

Tugging at her hair, finally Xiaoman spoke up. 'You went somewhere else, didn't you?'

He didn't understand what she meant.

'I'm not jealous,' she added. 'There's no need.'

This time he understood, which helped him with her first question.

'I didn't,' he said.

'It's no concern of mine.'

'I didn't.'

That was followed by complete silence, a prolonged silence. She ran out of patience. 'Well, let's do it.'

Still seated, he didn't look ready for anything. He raised his head, faced her and said, 'I've let you down. I've deceived you.'

Now *that's* an amusing statement, fascinating. She crossed her arms under her breasts. *What's he saying? What's this all about? How can anyone let anyone down with what we do? No way! Who could deceive someone at a place like this? Everything is done with a clearly marked price.* This was the first time she'd ever heard a client say something so odd, downright incongruous, like attaching a mule's head to a horse. Irrelevant, incoherent, inappropriate.

'I've really let you down,' he repeated.

'What do you mean?'

'You don't understand?'

He lost his cool even before she could respond. Pressing his hands down on the edge of the bed, the veins on his hands popping, he said, 'You don't understand!'

'I don't care,' she said, 'whether I understand or not, as long as you pay me.'

He began pulling the fingers on his left hand with his right hand, once, twice, three times.

'I'm not going to give you any more money,' he said, deadly earnest.

Xiaoman knew exactly what he was saying, but it had come too abruptly and was too extreme for someone who was used to flirtatious, lewd and teasing language that did not usually represent genuine feelings. The weighty, serious tone had caught her completely off guard. His absence over the past few days, honestly speaking, had worried her a bit, though that was more like a fleeting thought. He came, he left, he came back, he left again, and then he didn't show. That was what her life was like, wasn't it? So she didn't give it much thought. It didn't matter. Just a minor transaction. The world might be lacking many things, but men are not one of them.

Yet Xiaoman remained vigilant, conscious of the changes in herself, for she knew that she was at risk, feeling a sense of regret. *Fuck, the bastard actually stole my heart. And he got off easy. The old man up there is wrong; he should never have given this line of work to women. Men are the ones who should be doing it, it's their kind of job. Not women, no way.*

After he finished playing with his fingers, he reached out to find her. She quietly evaded his groping hands, neither playing hard to get nor flirting with him; she simply did not want him to touch her. Self-awareness told her that she would lose everything if he grabbed hold of her, and there would be no end to her troubles.

She evaded his groping hands, again and again, but he was undaunted, he kept at it. He stood up, looking ridiculously clumsy and cautious. She felt like laughing, but didn't. He showed such fortitude in his clumsy caution, but it did him no good, since she was the one with eyes. All he could do was stare blankly into meaningless space as he carefully got on with what he had in mind. His hands were right in front of her. She saw everything; his forehead was soon beaded with sweat, as, finally exhausted, he found a wall. Resting his arms on the wall for support, he looked like a giant, blind gecko. But, unwilling to give up, he turned his head from side to side. Wearing a stiff look, he searched with useless eyes. At one moment, their eyes actually met; they were staring right at each other, but he was unaware of it. His gaze passed across her pupils; she slowly closed her eyes, and when she did, a warmth filled the sockets. She walked over quietly, stood behind him and weakly put her arms around him.

'My karmic enemy!' She tightened her arms and cried out, 'You're my karmic enemy.'

Xiao Ma cocked his head, an endearing smile on his face. He was panting softly. 'I knew you were still here,' he said with a little laugh.

They kissed. *This damned karmic enemy is a lousy kisser. But he works hard at it, like gobbling up food.* He put everything into it. Xiaoman did not want to make love with him here, not in this room. Yet her body betrayed an astonishing hunger in his arms; she had been hungry for longer than she could remember. Tossing the bedsheets and mattress off to reveal the bare bed boards, she took his wrist and urged, 'Come in, and make it quick.'

She was selfish this time; with only self-interest in mind, she focused all her attention and every sensation on herself. There was no thought of caring about the man, nor did she cry out as she moved, not even a simple moan. She pressed her lips together and held her breath. She was spoiling herself, and she found that touching. *You have to be nice to me, you son of a bitch.*

They were so focused on their enjoyment that they had turned a deaf ear to the tiny movements in the shop; they were oblivious of the policemen standing by the bed.

'Still going at it? Really? Enough already.'

CHAPTER NINETEEN
DU HONG

WHEN RETICENT PEOPLE decide to be cool, they are usually cooler than anyone. That describes Xiao Ma. Without even packing up his things, he simply left, cool and carefree. In private, the centre therapists said he must have been disappointed in the place; otherwise, he wouldn't have left without saying goodbye. Sha Fuming tried phoning a few times, but there was no answer; he must have turned off his phone. He was impossibly cool.

During a critical period, everything at a place is often so interconnected that one occurrence will lead to another. Shortly after Xiao Ma left, Ji Tinging said she'd be leaving soon, which seemed sudden, but not really when they thought about it. Blind therapists at tuina centres are old hands at moving around, each carefully watching out for their own interest. With the changed situation at the centre, everyone knew that something bad would happen, and it was perfectly normal that someone would want to leave at a moment like that. The only surprise was that the person who led the parade was Ji da-jie.

She was one of the most senior therapists at the Sha Zongqi tuina centre. Among the first group hired after the centre opened for business, she had been the mainstay of the place ever since. Salary is the criterion for judging whether someone is a mainstay; high pay indicates that a therapist has more clients, and the more clients you have, the greater the benefits you reap. Not surprisingly, the bosses treat those with higher pay differently for two reasons: one, no matter how much a therapist earns, the bosses are still the ones who benefit most, and they suffer the greatest loss if such a therapist leaves. Second, clients can be irrational; they usually ask for the same therapist, and will not return once a familiar therapist leaves.

Ji da-jie was not the most skilful therapist, though she was at the top among the women. This line of work is highly unpredictable; a therapist's skill is most important to some clients, but others place greater importance on the person. Ji da-jie was thick-set and unattractive, with a slightly hoarse voice, and yet she was well liked by every client she worked on. Before Wang Daifu came along, she had more return clients than anyone else. Obviously, her personality was the main attraction; she was kind, with an endearing roughness, making her less feminine, and yet this very unfeminine woman was the one the clients preferred. Many clients frequented Sha Zongqing tuina centre specifically because of Ji Tingting.

Ji da-jie announced her planned departure after lunch. When she finished eating, she placed her spoon in her lunch box, pushed it away, cleared her throat and said loudly, 'Comrades, friends, ladies and gentlemen, I want to call a meeting. Let us welcome Comrade Ji Tingting, who will give an important speech.'

The mood during lunch had been glum up to that point; her action, coming as a surprise, seemed like a joke but portended something serious. Not knowing what she was about to say, everyone stopped chewing and turned their heads towards her.

She began: 'Comrades, friends. As the saying goes, after reaching a certain age, a man must find a wife and a woman needs a husband. Yours truly is not young any more, and I am going back home to get married. Life is beautiful. Why is that? Because it's not every day that I find someone who wants to marry a woman like me.

The young man is a real treasure, and that is wonderful. We have been communicating by phone for over a month, and through our frank but nauseatingly sappy talks we have come to the conclusion that we love each other and can establish a long and amicable partnership. We will eat together and sleep together. In two days we will be paid, and yours truly will leave after that. I hope you will all stay on here, striving diligently to construct a moderately affluent society on a large scale. Let's have a round of applause, after which the meeting will be adjourned.'

No one applauded, as they were all caught off guard. She had expected them to clap and to wish her well. Instead, the lounge was plunged into an unexpected silence, unnervingly quiet. Now everyone knew that Ji Tingting was following in Xiao Ma's footsteps.

'How about a little applause – didn't you hear me?'

Finally they clapped, but reluctantly. With neither any rhythm nor sufficient ardour, it was sparse, like the sesame seeds left around the mouth after eating a fried cake.

That kind of applause could mean only one thing: they believed that Ji Tingting was leaving, but suspected that her wedding was an excuse to keep the bosses from talking her into staying. How could a boss try to talk her around when she was going home to get married?

The mood at the tuina centre was no longer subdued; no, it was demoralised, almost mutinous. Yes, mutinous. It was time to find a way out now that the smart ones were leaving. How could Ji Tingting be going home to get married? Who ever heard of marrying someone after a month of phone talk?

She was not lying; she really was getting married. Bold women tend to be like that. People think that these women are adept at romance, but they are not; they do not know how to love, so romance and marriage often come out of the blue. It was even more the case with Ji da-jie, a blind woman. In her case, it didn't matter if she didn't know how to love; she was resigned to her fate and not picky, waiting for others to make arrangements. When they found a man for her, that was who she would have. People like her share an attitude towards love and marriage: simple, almost careless, and cavalier. Yet, strangely, no matter how careless and cavalier they are, they often end up in marriages that are happier than those who spend excessive energy and thought on the matter. Does this make sense? No, it does not.

Though she knew little about romance, she cared a great deal about the relationship with her co-workers and friends, and was happy and willing to give. So she was sad when she was reminded that she would be leaving them soon. It was partly for fun and partly as entertainment for her to announce her resignation in such a special way, but deep down it was because she was truly saddened. She had expected applause but had not got it, at least not initially, and that meant they did not want her to leave. An emotional bond had formed after being together so long. She blinked several times, feeling more emotional than she would have with prolonged applause.

Zhang Zongqi remained motionless. He may have been the one with the strongest reaction, but only on the inside. For a boss, it was both a loss and a shame to lose a money tree like Ji Tingting. To be sure, it was not the end of the world; what hurt was her timing. She picked a critical moment to leave, and the domino effect of her departure could be inestimable. The blind tend to follow other people; when one moves, others follow. When one leaves, two might go, and when two depart, three more may quit. Major trouble results from a mass resignation; in business the effects are often immediate.

No matter how he looked at it, Jin da-jie had been the direct cause for how things had developed, and he was the root source; he was responsible. He was not convinced that marriage was the reason Ji Tingting was leaving; how could anyone get married after knowing someone for less than two months? He had to get her to stay, even if for two or three months; things might improve by then and her departure would take on a completely different significance.

'Congratulations,' Zhang said. As boss, he was the first to break the ice and offer his best wishes, as representative of the 'organisation'. Turning his head in Sha Fuming's direction, he said, 'Fuming, we ought to get something for the bride.'

'Of course,' Sha said.

'Why don't you see to it, Gao Wei?' Zhang said, before changing the subject and saying earnestly to Ji, 'Marriage is important, but so is work. Why don't you go home and get that taken care of, and we'll talk about other matters later.'

Sitting off in a corner, Sha Fuming, like Zhang, was doubtful of Tingting's reason for leaving, but his disbelief differed from Zhang's. Zhang had never been the talkative type, but today he'd been first to express his reaction. That was unusual, and that meant trouble. The two bosses had just talked about splitting, but before Zhang could leave, Xiao Ma had left and now Ji da-jie was quitting. If all the centre mainstays left, the business would hit the skids, and when that happened, Zhang would leave with a hundred thousand yuan and Sha would be stuck with a big mess. That's how things go in business; it's hard to get the business up and running, but it takes little for it to go downhill, which can happen fast, and with an effect that is as sharp as a knife. The chances of coming back after that? Hard to say. That was why business people believed in feng shui. When the feng shui is ruined, it doesn't matter how hard you work; your fingers can touch sweat, but not money.

While Ji Tingting was giving her *important speech*, Du Hong and Gao Wei were trying to get the other person to take a piece of tofu, which unfortunately wound up on the floor. Such a shame. They were going a bit overboard in their intimacy; even Gao herself once referred to them as *tongzhi*, a gay couple, adding that she was the lustful type. She was, of course, joking, but it was nevertheless flattery that made Du Hong happy. Sha Fuming was pleased, too, as he stood to one side, grinning from ear to ear, nearly blurting out a thank you to

Gao. He had lavished special treatment on Gao Wei in recent days, and she knew it. She was amused by what happened between people and by how her relationship with Boss Sha had taken a detour and manifested itself in her bond with Du Hong.

Du Hong was the one who was most surprised to hear Tingting's news. But what surprised her most was her impending wedding, not her departure. It was a hugely important private matter, and yet she hadn't breathed a word of it. What did that say? It said that Tingting had stopped treating her as a confidante. But Du Hong knew she had no right to complain, for what chance had she given Tingting to talk to her? None, none at all. Now Du Hong was convinced that she was responsible for the departure, at least partially; she'd been the inconsiderate one, a common ingrate, one who destroys the bridge after crossing the river. Rice bowl in hand, she was overcome by unspeakable guilt and resolved to be nice to Ji da-jie, if only for a day, or an hour. She had to let her know that although she might have been a fair-weather friend, deep down she still considered Ji her da-jie, a friend for whom she felt genuine gratitude and fondness.

Du Hong waited all afternoon, waiting for when they got off work. She would not ride Gao Wei's three-wheeler today, no matter what; instead, she'd take Tingting by the hand so they could grope their way home, walking, talking and laughing together all the way back to the dorm. They would resume their intimate connection and sweet sisterly past, and Tingting would know that, no matter where she went, there would always be a little sister in Nanjing thinking about her. *Tingting is a good person. A good friend.* Du Hong was saddened as she recalled all the nice things Ji had done for her; it was her incredible luck to have met someone like Ji. She made up her mind to tell Tingting some of her secrets, since she was leaving. She'd tell her how Sha Fuming was pursuing her in his silly, clumsy, pitiful and disgusting, yet comical, way. She'd never marry Sha, a lustful man who was always staring at her and asking, 'How pretty are you anyway?' *Who does that?* It tickled her to think about it. She would squeeze into Ji da-jie's bed that night and touch her 'little secrets'. She would tease Ji da-jie: *They're too far apart, like separate entities, not a pair*.

And of course there was that really important thing that she wanted to bring up with Ji da-jie and ask for her advice. It had to do with Xiao Ma. After working for some time, Du Hong had begun, quietly and secretly, to pay attention to men. In her view, Wang Daifu was the best man at the tuina centre; he was quite a bit older, but that was no problem. The problem was, he had a girlfriend. If she wanted to break them up and steal him, Du Hong knew she'd have no difficulty removing him from Xiao Kong's side and installing him on hers. She was confident of her abilities, but she wouldn't need to do that; it was just a thought. What interested her most was Xiao Ma. The clients all said he was good-looking and that they made a striking couple when they stood side by side.

Strictly speaking, Du Hong had secretly come on to Xiao Ma once already. Of course, she had employed a special trick, instead of speaking her mind. One day they were both with clients who were associate professors at the Nanjing Institute of Fine Arts, one an oil painter, the other an art theorist, both well known. With nothing else to do, the professors began to comment on Du Hong's beauty in a professorial manner, like putting together a creative work, as they took apart her body and face to admire part by part. She got the amusing idea of pressing the button on the digital clock with each round of praise, with the clear intention of drawing Xiao Ma's attention. 'Did you hear that, Xiao Ma? Did you hear what the professors are saying?' She had gone a bit wild in her mind as she engaged in the wilful, somewhat flirtatious act. She knew she was provoking and seducing him, being a coquette. But he remained unmoved. Afterwards, he even commented to her, 'Du Hong, how come you have such a terrible sense of time?' She was greatly disappointed, naturally; he would never be an associate professor at the Nanjing Institute of Fine Arts.

Du Hong was not sure how much she really liked Xiao Ma, but it was clear that she was interested in him. If he had actively pursued her, she might have thought about it and could have fallen for him, but she would never have gone after him. She didn't like him that much. He was a handsome guy, but not without his flaws; too quiet, too reticent, too solitary and too gloomy. He hardly said a word from dawn to dusk. Would she be able to live with someone like that? She wasn't sure, which was what she wanted to talk to Ji da-jie about. She could never bring this up with Gao Wei; they were good friends but could never be close enough to talk about stuff like that.

On that night Gao Wei was not cooperating; unable to understand what was going on in Du Hong's mind, she would not leave her alone. When it was finally time to return to the dorm, Gao Wei began to close the centre by piling up used blankets and towels. Du Hong wanted Gao to leave without her, but could not say so to her face, so she took Ji da-jie's hand at the door to the lounge and snuggled up to her. Gao did not understand what she was doing, but Ji did, and patted her on the head to signal for her to wait while she went into the lounge to get her purse. Du Hong had no choice but to lean against the wall.

Ji's hands were so big, she fumbled with small objects, making more noise than anyone, even when she was putting things in her purse. Du Hong heard her every move. 'Don't rush, Tingting, I can wait.'

'Hold on,' Ji said. 'I'll be done in a minute.' Her elation was palpable, she was overjoyed, and that was contagious. Du Hong was happy too. But her happiness was short-lived. She had no time to treasure it.

As she waited, Du Hong thought back to when they first met. With her hand on the door, she rubbed the frame and reminisced, as if it were no longer a door frame she was caressing, but Ji da-jie. She wished she wasn't leaving.

At that moment, Gao Wei walked by on her way to load her towels and sheets onto the three-wheeler, so Du thought she might as well explain the situation to Gao Wei. She would understand, since Ji da-jie would be leaving soon and Du Hong wanted to spend some time with her.

A breeze blew in, a natural breeze that felt good. Du Hong's chest expanded as she took a deep breath. Then she heard Xiao Tang yell her name. It was so sudden it startled her into backing up and grabbing hold of the door. She immediately realised that was the wrong thing to do, but she did not have time to let go. *Bang!* The door slammed shut.

It was clear from Du Hong's scream that it was too late. When Ji heard Xiao Tang yell, she knew exactly what was happening. Tossing aside her purse, she ran to the door and found Du Hong's shoulder; Du Hong was doubled up by then and her limp, inert body began to slide from Ji's hands. She had obviously passed out. With one hand under Du Hong's arm, Ji reached out to touch her right hand, finger by finger. They were all fine, all but her thumb, which was badly split. 'Oh my God. Oh no!' Ji stomped her foot and blurted out.

The cab tore down the street. Sha Fuming held Du Hong in his arms, her back tight against him. Holding her was something he'd dreamed about countless times, a long-cherished hope. Today he finally was given the chance to do it, but not the way he wanted. He was cupping her injured hand in both of his. It broke his heart, which slowly turned to ice and appeared in the form of a hand. Sha was baffled by how hands and ice always occurred in pairs in his life, eternally inseparable. He believed that hands were once water that branched out in all directions and were extremely fragile. A hand turned to ice once fate raised its head. This thought turned him half to ice, and spread to Du Hong lying in his arms.

Du Hong woke up in agony. Struggling to bear the pain, she twisted miserably in Sha's arms. Now that he had full knowledge of what pain felt like, he wanted to suffer in her stead, wishing he could drag the pain out of her body, put it in his mouth and chew it into pieces before swallowing it down. He didn't mind pain; he could take it. As long as she was free of it, he could stuff any kind of pain into his own stomach.

Sha held Du Hong's injured hand in the palms of his own and was careful not to stroke it. Then he did, and his heart sank. 'Oh my God!' No wonder Ji had screamed. Du Hong's thumb was broken.

To a tuina therapist, the importance of the right thumb is abundantly clear. A person has but two hands and, except for left-handed people, the left hand plays a secondary role. The strength of the right hand comes from the thumb, no matter what activity is involved – splitting, pinching, pushing, kneading, pressing and rubbing. Once the thumb is broken, a tuina therapist's hand is ruined, even if a surgeon can repair the digit with a steel plate and pins. Being blind, Du Hong was already disabled, and now she became handicapped within her disability. Her hand was no longer just ice alone. To that was added iron and steel.

A term leaped into his head: crippled. The term disabled had first appeared in China a few years earlier; before that the handicapped were called cripples. It was a term the disabled abhorred; it was taboo. Later, society made an admirable concession in agreeing to change the term from crippled (*canfei*) to disabled (*canji*), a major gift by society to China's disabled. This gift of a single word had cheered the blind. *But Du Hong, my dear Du Hong, you are no longer disabled, now you are crippled.* Sha raised his head to look at the sky from inside the taxi. He saw a starry sky made of steel plate that gave off an unpleasant metallic odour.

Du Hong wasn't old enough. She was too young. What would she do in the future, now that she could no longer support herself? All she had left was time. She was faced with huge chunks of future time, vast and abundant time. Time is like that; when there's too much of it, it takes on a sinister mien, fiendish as fangs, surging and rushing from all directions towards this beautiful young woman. You're damaged. That's what you are now, and nothing more.

You have to go on living, Du Hong. How will you do that?

Something warm stirring inside made Sha blurt out, 'Marry me, Du Hong.'

With a shudder she slowly struggled out of his arms.

'How could you say that at a time like this, Boss Sha?'

Now it was his turn to shudder. *Yes, how could you say that at a moment like this*?

Putting his arms around her again, Sha held her tight. 'I swear, Du Hong, I'll never say that again.'

His body was dead, all but his stomach, which was as lively as a leaping dragon and a roaring tiger. That is how his stomach ached.

Du Hong was dreaming. It was a recurring dream as she lay in her hospital bed. It revolved around a piano, but the music was unfamiliar, peculiar, like a tragic past. But it had a surprisingly wide range, which required complex finger movements. She was playing, making the peculiar music flow from her soft, supple fingertips, each of which expressed an emotion. She could feel the flexibility in her fingers, so pliable they did exactly what she wanted them to do, virtually without limit.

She raised her hands at this point, for now she was conducting, not playing. She was the conductor of a chorus with four voice parts, soprano, mezzo-soprano, tenor and bass, the last of which was her favourite, for its penetrating power, the foundation of all voices. It stayed low and began to spread and extend, opening up matchless depth.

Her dream approached its end, when a terrifying scene would play out before her. Though her hands continued to lead the chorus, the soaring music played on; she was shocked when she touched the keys, for her fingers were not playing the notes; the keys were moving on their own, up and down, as if manipulated by demonic fingers.

She woke up, drenched in cold sweat, yet the piano music continued to surge.

Ji Tingting stuck around. She refused to leave. Why? She would not say, so the others did not ask. Twice Du Hong urged her to go. *Go on, please. I beg you.* But Ji quietly tended to Du Hong, with a single logic in mind: if she had not wanted to be married, she would not have planned to leave; if she had been staying on, Du Hong would not have been waiting for her; and if not for that, Du Hong would not have suffered such a disaster. She could not live with herself if she left after what had happened. All she could do was reproach herself; she even thought of suicide.

Ji surely knew that Du Hong would not want her to blame herself. Du Hong wanted her to go home and get married as soon as possible. Viewed differently, sticking around this way was also a torment to Du Hong, and the longer Ji remained, the worse Du Hong's agony. So should she go or should she stay? Unable to make up her mind, Ji thought she might go crazy. But she sat quietly at the girl's bedside, clutching her hand sometimes and occasionally touching it lightly. Most of the time, though, they simply held hands, each finger a display of their distress. Only the old man in the sky knew how intimate the two women were at that moment, wishing the best for one another, though neither could find the proper means, or the method. There was nothing they could say to each other, for anything would sound wrong. In order to force Ji to leave, Du Hong decided to ignore her after three days of the quiet bedside vigil. She would not even let Ji touch her fingers, driving the two intimate friends into a surreal dead-end, each wishing she could pluck out her bloody heart to show the other.

It was a decision made by Jin Yan that finally sent Ji on her way. When Jin Yan arrived at the hospital one day, she found, to her surprise, that Du Hong was not speaking to Tingting, who was fawning on her, but getting no response. Tingting's breath had an unpleasant smell. Jin Yan's heart sank, but she could do or say nothing, except to take each by the hand. Ji Tingting held tightly to her left hand and

Du Hong clasped her right, the two despairing hands extinguishing hope in Jin Yan.

They had been together long enough for Jin Yan to know what was on Tingting's mind and what Du Hong was thinking; she was aware that the two women were at an impasse and that they could not go on like that. She decided to take matters into her own hands, an ideal opportunity to show what she could do. Without a word, she returned to the centre, where she took care of Ji's pay with Sha Fuming and asked Gao Wei to buy a train ticket while having Tailai pack up Ji's things. The next evening, she ordered a taxi and left with Tailai for the hospital, where they tricked Ji out of Du Hong's room and dragged her into the taxi to put her on the train. Just like that, one, two, three, and Ji was on her way home. When Jin Yan returned to the hospital, she called Ji on her mobile phone, and when Ji answered she handed the phone to Du Hong, who did not know what it was all about. She hesitantly held the phone to her ear and heard Tingting say to her, 'Little Sister.' That was followed by the rumbling sound of a moving train, which told Du Hong everything she needed to know. She understood. 'Ji da-jie,' she said into the mouthpiece. The utterance had a powerful effect on the two women, who said nothing more. Now the only sound in the phone was the rhythmic rumble of train wheels. Clank-clang, clank-clang. The train was racing towards an unknown destination, farther and farther away, emptying Du Hong's heart bit by bit as it moved away. Unable to take it any longer, she flipped the phone shut and collapsed into Jin Yan's arms.

'Hold me, Jin Yan, hold me.'

CHAPTER TWENTY
SHA FUMING

THE TUINA CENTRE was palpably emptier, with three people gone – Xiao Ma and Ji Tingting had left for good and Du Hong was hospitalised. Emptiness can be so physical that everyone senses its presence.

After things calmed down a bit, Sha Fuming hired a repairman to install a stopper on the lounge door; now the therapists would hear a loud, reassuring click when the door was pushed all the way open. Though reassuring, it was also malicious, for it was a constant reminder of Du Hong's thumb, each click creating a moment of unease.

There was a thumb on everyone's mind, and it was Du Hong's thumb. It had been broken, and it now supplanted everything in their hearts, in which it stubbornly took up residence. They became exceptionally cautious, afraid to make a noise, further stripping the centre of signs of life.

Abandoning his usual habit, Sha kept walking over to the lounge entrance, where he stood and played with the door for a long, long time. He pulled it off the magnetic stopper, and then pushed it back, over and over, animating the deathly quiet centre with an endless string of *click, click, click*.

People were increasingly annoyed by Sha Fuming's clicking sounds, but no one dared say a word. They felt sorry for him. His crush on

Du Hong was no longer a secret. He must have been consumed by remorse. They had asked him to install a stopper on the lounge door long before, yet while he had agreed to do so, he hadn't taken the request seriously. Viewed from one angle, he was responsible for what had happened. No one would blame him, but that didn't mean that he would not blame himself. All he could do was obsessively open and shut the door, over and over, *click, click, click*.

He was racked by remorse, to the extent that he felt the pain in his gut. His regret ate at him, not because of the doorstopper, but something greater than that. He should have signed a contract with his employees, but he hadn't, not a single one.

Strictly speaking, blind people do not count as persons, not in the full sense anyway, as even when they join society and work to support themselves, they do not have an organisation or a club, no insurance and no contract. In a word, they never form real and effective communal relations with society; they end up with another blind person when they get married, and that amounts to an accumulation of quantity, not a change in quality. Do they really lack all bonds with the rest of society? Not quite. For instance, every month they receive a one hundred yuan subsidy from a civil administrative office. One hundred yuan, a symbolic act by society intended to help themselves sleep better, is calculated not to aid the blind but to provide society with the justification to forget them altogether. In the end, the blind, or all disabled, for that matter, can be ignored and neglected. But life is not a symbol; it is real, constructed of years, months and days, of hours, minutes and seconds, and not a single second can be ignored. A person lives in a collective every second of the day, and no one can get by solely on the fruit of one's own labours.

The blind constitute an undocumented population, all of them, including Sha Fuming himself; and they have lives that are like those on the Internet. When a sighted person needs one of them, a metaphorical click will make them appear, while a second click relegates them to virtual space. In any case, the blind exist and yet they are never fully real, they live in a sort of limbo. When dealing with the blind, society itself is virtually blind. The blind are forever confined to their blind realm, which makes their life a gamble; it can be nothing but that, and a blind individual can lose everything as a result of a minor accident.

Sha Fuming left the lounge and stood at the entrance to the centre, where he blinked desperately. He looked up towards the sky and looked down towards the ground, but saw nothing. The blind have neither heaven nor earth, so they cannot ask for help from either.

As a boss, Sha Fuming could have created a small community in the tuina centre; he had the ability, maybe even the obligation, to do that. He could have signed hiring contracts that would have made it possible for the employees to buy insurance and thus remove them from the legions of the undocumented; they would have been connected to society. They would have become 'real people'.

He had given thought to contracts, starting back when he was in Shanghai, where he'd longed to have a contract with his boss. He and the other therapists had talked about it back in the dorm, but no one had been willing to bring it up with the boss, and so nothing had been done. Chinese people typically are reluctant to act on behalf of a collective, and that characteristic is even more pronounced among the blind. The tendency leads to their golden rule: why me? There is another Chinese characteristic, and that is a heavy reliance on chance, which is also more noticeable among the blind, and which gives rise to yet another golden rule: no disaster will ever befall me. No way. Why would it be me?

Sha had not been unaware of the importance of a contract; it would be his safety net. Put crudely, without one he would be a mutt, someone who had no control over his own life. He did not know what fate was. The only thing he knew about it was that it was lethal, that it had frightening magical powers. In the end he had got angry over the contract issue. His anger was directed at his co-workers, who got together to say how smart and competent he was, but in fact treated him as a fool. He did not want to be the fool; why should he be the sucker who talked to the boss if no one else would? So they never got a contract. Being blind, Sha Fuming trusted to luck as much as the next man: the others got along fine without a contract, so why couldn't he? He had even quietly asked around and learned that no contract was offered at any tuina centre; now he knew it was more or less an unspoken rule at all tuina centres not to sign contracts with the therapists.

During the planning stage of the opening of the Sha Zongqi tuina centre, Sha Fuming ambitiously decided to break the vile hidden rule; no matter what, he would dutifully sign a contract with each employee. The centre might be small, but he would make it a modern business whose humanistic character would be manifested in him. While strict management was essential, the basic interests of the employees must be guaranteed.

Yet something strange occurred after Sha became the boss; it just happened naturally, not on any particular day. Not one of the prospective employees raised the issue of a contract during the interview; they didn't ask and he didn't offer, the logic being that it was already a huge favour for the boss to give them a job, so why talk about a contract? After giving the lack of inquiry some thought, Sha came up with three reasons: the blind are naturally timid, they are too proud and they feel gratitude too easily. They thanked the heavens for being given a job by the boss, so how could they ask him for a contract? It takes little for the blind to be grateful. They get so little in life that, once sight is lost, a person quickly learns how to be grateful. While lustre is absent from their eyes, tears are not.

So, no contract. None of the therapists brought up the matter of a contract, and none was ever signed. By contrast, Sha was exhaustive in formulating rules and regulations for the centre in order to simplify matters. These rules and regulations became the sole binding relationship between the employees and the centre. In accordance with these rules and regulations, the employees had only obligations and responsibilities, which were all perfectly justified; they had no rights, which was all right with them. The blind are truly special people, who, no matter how much the times have changed, remain, at bottom, ancient, primitive, primal and eternally changeless. Society does not provide them with an organisation or mechanism to protect or assist them, so they turn around to embrace one thing with unwavering conviction – fate. Fate is invisible and only the invisible exists for them, an enormous, encompassing, manipulative, determining, even omnipresent existence. It is like the *lovely* danger they will bump into if they are not careful. How should they deal with fate? The most positive, true and tried approach is acceptance. *Hey! – accept it, just accept it.*

But acceptance has a prerequisite – a valiant and steadfast faith in luck. You must learn how to use luck in dealing with everything in life, going so far as to liquefy the heart and infuse it into the marrow of your bones. *Dong – dong, dong – dong,* sonorous and powerful. A person who cannot see clouds will never have to worry about which one carries rain. If it rains, fine; if not, that's fine too. Accept. I accept that.

What happened later followed a logical course. Back when Sha Fuming and Zhang Zongqi were best friends, they could sit on a bed cross-legged and talk about everything. The two young bosses enjoyed their conversations, cheerful and pleasant as if bathed in a spring breeze, but the topic of contracts with their employees never arose. On several occasions, Sha was about to bring it up, but something unexpected always made him swallow the words. As for Zhang, a shrewd businessman, he could not possibly have been unaware of the importance of a contract, which could only mean that he too swallowed the words. That is a natural gift of the blind. A boss can swallow a lot, and so can his employees. No one can better them in this, for they have an unmatched tolerance for everything.

Subsequent developments in the situation were both intriguing and strange. No one mentioned the contract, yet it became a well facing everyone, employees and employers alike, who consciously skirted the issue as if by command. Sha Fuming was neither happy nor disappointed, for, at the end of the day, no boss would care to sign a contract with his staff. Its absence simplified everything; the boss solved all problems with a simple yes or no. He had the power, and that was that. How easy this made the boss's life, which can be described only as *sweet*.

Then fate struck, revealing its barbed figure, spreading terror the moment it appeared. It touched everyone at the centre like an invisible hand, and then, with a sneer, settled on Du Hong, laying both hands on her back and pressing her down into the well.

Du Hong was in the well, which was just big enough to contain her body. Sha heard no sound from the well, no sign of any struggle. In fact, no one chosen by fate can struggle out of its control. Sha felt that he was suffocating, feeling far worse than if he could hear splashing from below. The well water concealed everything, its depth determining the degree of gloom. *Poor Du Hong. Baby. My little sister.* He would be happy to dig up the well if that would save her, but how would he do that? How?

One-sided love is a torment, persistent and excruciating, but in fact, not always. Before she was injured, it was simply persistent, not tormenting, every time Sha Fuming thought about her. He could sense his own softness and unforeseen gentleness, which made him feel good. So who could say it wasn't love? His heart felt as if it had been sunning itself, warm and languid in the sun's rays. Once he even took her name apart and considered the meaning of each character: Du could be read as *dou*, which is all inclusive, and *hong*, red, is the colour of the sun, he was told. Taken together, Du Hong's name referred to an all-encompassing red. She was the sun, distant and yet nearby. Sha had never seen the sun, but was sensitive to it, and in the winter, he loved nothing better than sunning himself. The half of him under the sun was warm and languid.

But the sun had set and fallen into a well. He did not know if his sun would rise again. He knew he was now in shadows, in the path of wind coming off a high rise, mussing his hair and presenting a dishevelled sight to anyone who could see.

If not for the mutton incident, if he and Zhang had not discussed splitting up, Sha might have been able to put the Du Hong issue on the table and retroactively given her a contract and compensation. It might have worked.

Even with the mutton incident and the split, Sha could have done that if not for his one-sided love for Du Hong.

But not now. With the deterioration of the relationship between Sha and Zhang, and the ambiguous relationship between him and Du Hong, to try that would be seen by all as favouritism. He could not allow himself to propose it. Nor would it work if he did.

Sha asked himself why he loved her. *Why have you got into this one-sided affair? Why are you so infatuated with the accursed notion of beauty? Why couldn't your heart let go of that hand?* In a certain context, love can be immoral.

Sha felt that he had let Du Hong down, for, as a man and a boss, he could do nothing for her, not even this one last thing. He had wanted only one thing – to be a boss, and he had succeeded. But so what? He descended into a state of untold agony.

What if the injured person had not been Du Hong? What if she had not been a beauty? What if she had not been blessed with pretty hands? Would Sha be spared the agony? With this thought, he felt the threads of his soul threatening to exit through holes in his scalp.

His thoughts reached an impasse, so he began chain smoking. He inhaled and he exhaled, but somehow it felt as if the smoke he had inhaled never emerged. He could not blow it out. The smoke from all those cigarettes seemed to stick in his chest and gut, where it swirled itself into a blockage the size of a large stone. His stomach ached. All the pain in his body was concentrated firmly there. For the first time ever, he felt too weak to stand. He sat down. He needed to go to the hospital. No matter what, he'd go as soon as things quieted down.

A hospital was another sore spot for Sha Fuming. How could it trigger such anxiety? Then again, who could be immune to that apprehension? It was expensive, with a visit over a sneeze starting at three or four hundred yuan. But money was only secondary. What he feared most was the trouble he had to go through, particularly at big hospitals, where, appointments for exams aside, he had to queue up to register, queue to see a doctor, queue to pay for the visit, queue for the examination, queue to see the doctor a second time, queue to pay again and, finally, queue to pick up his medicine. You need to plan on spending the better part of a day there. Every time Sha Fuming went to the hospital he was reminded of the idiom about *a blind man feeling an elephant*. That's what a hospital was, an elephant, its body a virtual labyrinth. Find your way around it if you can. To Sha, a hospital was more than an elephant or a labyrinth; it was solid geometry. He never could get his head around the points, lines, surfaces or angles of the geometric figure. They were complex and intricate, appropriate for exploration but not medical treatments.

Sha vowed to go to the hospital one day soon. He curled his lip into what looked like a smile. Where seeing a doctor was concerned, he had mastered the art of vowing. And yet not one of his vows had led to action. He made his vows not because he was strong-willed, but because he was in pain. Whenever pain surfaced, out came the vows. If he was not in pain, then taking a vow would be like farting. What can a person expect from that? Absolutely nothing.

With a cough, Wang Daifu pushed the door open and walked outside. Obviously sensing Sha's presence, Wang stood next to him and wordlessly cracked his knuckles. From the meaningful sounds,

Sha knew that Wang had something to say, but could not get it out.

Sha also coughed. What did he want to convey? Even he wasn't sure; he just wanted to make a sound, as a beginning or as an end to their encounter. Either would work.

Wang detected an unpleasant odour on Sha, which could only mean that he had not showered for days. He guessed right, and the substandard bathroom situation at the dorm was to blame. With only one water heater, the dozen or more therapists had to line up and take turns to shower. A stomach ache drained a person's energy, and Sha was fatigued all day long. He went straight to bed the minute he returned to the dorm, and once he was lying down, he did not feel like getting up again. He knew he smelled bad, but he was simply too tired to take a shower.

'Fuming,' Wang said. 'Is everything all right?' It was such a meaningless question he might as well have not asked it. But Sha noticed that for the first time since Wang began working at the tuina centre he did not call him Boss. Wang had called him by his name.

'I'm fine,' Sha said. 'And you?' An equally meaningless reply, like an echo.

Wang Daifu clammed up after he too said 'I'm fine.' He thrust his hand under his shirt to rub his chest. The wounds had healed, but itched badly. He didn't dare scratch them with his nails, so he lightly brushed the scars with his fingertips. Sha also held his tongue, but he still felt that Wang had something important to say, though it remained on the tip of his tongue.

'Fuming,' Wang finally worked up the courage to say, 'take my advice and stop brooding. It's pointless, so don't think about it.'

That too was a meaningless statement. *Don't brood over what? Stop thinking about what? What is pointless*? Sha wondered. But a second later it was clear to him that Wang was referring to Du Hong. He hadn't anticipated that Wang would be so direct; only close friends can be that direct. Needless to say, Sha knew it was pointless, but knowing it was one thing and hearing it from someone else was another. He wordlessly stewed in the anger caused by the embarrassment, feeling that his heart had been ripped open. After a prolonged silence, he calmed down and, unwilling to feign ignorance with an old friend, he asked, 'I assume everyone knows about it?'

'We're all blind,' Wang said, 'so who couldn't see it?'

'And what do you think?'

Wang hesitated before replying. 'She doesn't love you.' He turned his head before adding, 'Listen to me, old friend. Give it up. I can see that she's all you think about, but you are not on her mind. It's not her fault, is it?'

After this, anything he said would be cruel. Wang had spoken as gently as he could because he felt sorry for Sha, whose stomach began to ache and churn. The truth can be brutal, and this time it emerged from the mouth of his friend.

'It would be better to think of a way to help her,' Wang said.

'I've been doing just that.'

'No, you haven't.'

'What do you mean by that?'

'You've only been suffering.'

'Can't I suffer?'

'Of course you can. But only the selfish indulge in suffering.'

'How dare you!'

Wang shut up and lowered his head; he began pawing the ground with his right foot, rapidly at first and then more slowly. He switched feet and did the same thing with his left foot. He eventually stopped and turned around to walk back inside. Sha reached out to grab hold of him, and even though he was holding on to only a trouser leg, Wang could sense that his arm was trembling, it was weeping.

'Come have a drink with me, my friend,' Sha said, ignoring the pain in his gut.

Wang crouched down. 'We haven't knocked off for the day yet.'

Sha let go of the trouser leg and stood up. 'Come have a drink with me, my friend.' He managed to drag Wang along with him.

Wang had barely stepped out of the door when Xiao Kong found an empty room and sneaked in. She'd wanted to phone Xiao Ma, but had never found the opportunity. Now here it was. He had left without saying goodbye. *Why did he do that?* Unlike everyone else, she knew the story, the whole story. It was because of her. As his 'saozi', she had a responsibility to phone him, if nothing else so that she could say goodbye.

She could not pretend that Xiao Ma hadn't fallen for her. There had been times when she'd wished she could have been nicer to him, but she could not. In fact, she had been intentionally cold, not just for Wang Daifu's sake, but for Xiao Ma's sake as well. She'd been unfair to him. Strictly speaking, she had to take the blame for making the relationship with him so awkward. She'd been selfish, thinking only of herself, with no thought for his feelings. His falling in love with her was her doing. If she hadn't flirted and carried on, this never would have happened. About that there was no doubt. Her behaviour had been improper and inappropriate. Ah! Why is life so full of dead ends, places you walk into out of carelessness?

Xiao Kong could call forever but never get through. His number was no longer in service. Apparently he had made up his mind to sever all relations with the Sha Zongqi tuina centre, but in fact he wanted to cut off ties to her. *I hurt you, Xiao Ma, so go ahead, have a safe journey. I wish you the best. You should not have just up and left without saying goodbye to me. I owe you a hug. There are different kinds of farewells and those accomplished with an embrace are unique; we would part on solid ground and you would be on solid ground in the future. Take care, Xiao Ma. Take good care of yourself, you hear? Don't get into trouble. You had feelings for me and I thank you for that.*

Xiao Kong put away her phone and took out her Shenzhen phone. So much had been happening in recent days that she'd neglected to call home. She ought to give them a call. As she was taking out her Shenzhen mobile, it occurred to her that her parents had not contacted her for quite some time. Could something have happened at home? Her apprehension grew as she punched in the home number but there was no sound. Yet another problem – the battery was dead. She cleverly snapped off the back cover to take out the SIM card, which she would put in her Nanjing phone and hopefully continue to deceive her parents.

But the Shenzhen SIM card was gone. She checked again and again – it was gone. It was a lethal discovery, since no card meant no Shenzhen number, and her lie would soon be exposed. She broke out in a cold sweat. How could she keep the lie alive? She couldn't. How could the card be missing?

Impossible. She still had the phone, and the card should be in it. Someone must have messed with her phone. Then she figured it out. Jin Yan. It had to be Jin Yan. It could be no one else. Wang Daifu had never touched her phone. Xiao Kong was outraged by the thought. *We had our problems, Jin Yan, but since we made up, I've always treated you like a sister, as heaven is my witness. How could you do something so insidious, so mean?* Slamming the phone down on the bed, she spun around, ready to confront Jin Yan. She'd ask her to her face: What do you want anyway? What do have in mind?

She paused at the door, as if she'd received some sort of mysterious hint. Turning back, she walked to the bed and took out her Nanjing phone. As soon as she dialled from this phone, her secret would be exposed, now that she'd lost the Shenzhen SIM card and could never get it back. In other words, sooner or later she would be found out; yet the exposure could be positive and might even be significant. She could lie, she could live a lie, but no one can lie all her life. No one.

So she punched in the number and the call went through. The word 'Hello' had barely got out, when a shrill cry from her mother erupted from the other end. Obviously they'd been waiting by the phone for days.

'So you're still alive, you crazy girl! Why has your phone been off? Crazy girl, your father and I have been worried sick. Tell us, where are you? Are you all right?'

'I'm in Nanjing and I'm fine.'

'Why are you in Nanjing?'

'I'm in love, Ma.'

Being 'in love' is a peculiar term. So common and mundane, at a moment like this it turns lively, imbued with profound emotive power. She was just telling the truth, blurting it out, not realising that saying 'I'm in love' could be conducive to weeping. Two streams of hot tears ran down her face.

'Ma,' she repeated calmly, 'I'm in love.'

'Is it a boy or a girl?' her mother blurted out after a momentary pause.

After not hearing from her daughter for so long, her mother, shocked and upset, asked the question without thinking. Apparently, they'd guessed that she was in a relationship and thought she'd had a baby. Ah! How parents dote over their inconsiderate children. Xiao Kong giggled.

'A boy,' she said like a proud new mother in a maternity ward, 'and completely blind.'

It went quiet on the other end; a long time passed before she heard a voice again. This time it was her father, not her mother. 'Little girl,' he sounded exasperated as he shouted into the phone, 'why won't you listen to us?'

'Pa, my love for him is one eye, his love for me is the other, so now we have two eyes. Your daughter is no princess, Pa, so what do you expect she'd get?' She surprised herself with her own words. Since she began lying to her parents, she'd had to prepare over and over each time she called them, and the more she lied the harder it became. On this day she'd prepared no lies and had just said what was on her mind.

She never thought she could be so open, honest and transparent. It sparkled, beams radiating everywhere.

Flipping her phone shut, Xiao Kong found it hard to believe that things could be so easy. Since falling in love with Wang Daifu, she had agonised over how to tell her parents. Now she'd finally told the truth, and her problems were solved, just like that, a simple fact untying all the knots. It was completely unexpected.

Jin Yan groped her way in at that moment with the important news that Du Hong was raising hell at the hospital, crying and demanding to leave. But she was barely inside the room before Xiao Kong wrapped her arms around her, not giving her a chance to share the news. Since Jin Yan was so much taller, Xiao Kong had to bury her face in Jin's neck, where Jin Yan felt Xiao Kong's tears. Xiao Kong patted her friend's back with the hand in which she held the phone, which told Jin Yan everything she needed to know; she breathed a sigh of relief and then reached out to rub the small of Xiao Kong's back.

'Little tramp,' Xiao Kong whispered. 'I'll have to watch out for you all my life.'

'What does that mean?'

'You're a thief,' she whispered, 'you steal.'

'Stop it,' Jin Yan said listlessly, pushing her away. 'Du Hong refuses to stay in the hospital. So what do we do about her?'

CHAPTER TWENTY-ONE

WANG DAIFU

IN THE END, Du Hong left the hospital early, helped by Sha Fuming, who was in turn led by Gao Wei. She returned to the centre at noon, a time that Sha Fuming had chosen, since everyone was free then and available for a small welcome back ceremony. A ceremony was called for, not so much a means to express their sentiment as a display of the depth of their feelings. Sometimes, a ceremony can explain a matter better than the matter itself – Du Hong, welcome back to the Sha Zongqi tuina centre.

'We're back!' Gao Wei made a point of announcing their arrival with a shout, bringing everyone running and creating a festive air. Crowded into the lounge, they clapped for Du Hong, a jumble of loud, warm applause mixed with a chorus of chatter. Sha Fuming was pleased, Zhang Zongqi was too, and so was everyone else, even more than the bosses, it seemed. Ever since the mutton incident, so many things had happened at the centre that the lounge had lost its carefree atmosphere. The pressure was constant; everyone was on edge, plagued by a sense of crisis. Now everything was fine. Their elation was not simply joy over her recovery, but it also had the effect of letting off steam. There was an exaggerated mood of excitement. The gloom that had loomed over them was swept away, refreshing and energising them all.

Sha Fuming was genuinely happy, and he had Wang Daifu to thank for that. Wang was not the boss, but he had been born with the natural traits of a leader, a man who was never flustered. When Sha was at the end of his tether where Du Hong's future was concerned, Wang stepped up with two bits of advice. First, keeping Du Hong's secret was the best thing he could do for her. If word got out that she had broken her thumb, no clients would come to her. If it was kept a secret, even if she left, she could find a decent job somewhere else. Wang reassured Sha that he would see to that. Second, Wang Daifu had closely examined Du Hong's injury. Her thumb was indeed broken, but the other four fingers were undamaged. What did that mean? It meant that she was still able to do foot massage, which, though also requiring the thumb, relies primarily on the middle and index fingers. The only clients who would ever be able to tell were themselves tuina therapists. And no therapist would spend the money to get a foot massage. This would solve their problem. Du Hong would no longer be involved in tuina therapy, and all the foot massage business would go to her. She would work on five or six clients a day. Everything stayed the same. Nothing had happened.

Yes, things were back to normal. *Nothing had happened. Du Hong's thumb was never broken.* It's the same old Du Hong. Could anyone ask for a better outcome? No. An ecstatic Sha Fuming clapped his hands and announced, 'Tonight I'm treating everyone to a late-night snack.'

His invitation was greeted by happy shouts as they gathered round Du Hong, all talking at the same time, quickly turning the centre into a small ocean of joy. Sha stepped outside, where he was overcome by his emotions. The lively atmosphere was wonderful. A sense of human energy surfaced. *What exactly is human energy?* In Sha's mind, the lounge was alive with arms and hands that had risen out of the ground to swirl in the wind, carefree, light and cheerful. Without doubt, the most affecting, the happiest hands, belonged to Du Hong; he could see that they smiled in the midst of the crowd. The smile rippled and split into two, three, four. Yes, four altogether, wriggling off in different directions, all-encompassing, blanketing every space in a formidable array. Sha breathed a secret sigh of relief, as an indescribable calmness and sense of ease settled over him; he was like a feather drifting on the wind; even his bones felt lighter. Spring waters flow to the east.

He hadn't felt this way for a long time. Too long. Blinking repeatedly, he tried his best to pretend that none of this had anything to do with him; that made him feel very good. He was the happiest of all, yet this had nothing to do with him, so he stood to the side to let the others cheer and celebrate. And for that, he must thank Du Hong, whose accident restored life to the centre. Except, of course, she had paid too high a price; it would have been better if it had happened to him instead.

If he had broken his thumb – if it had been him, would Zhang Zongqi have been the one who brought him back from the hospital? Yes. For sure. He'd have done the same for Zhang. With a full understanding of their relationship, Sha knew that the two of them might not be able to share in wealth and glory but they would definitely weather storms together. Maybe it was time they had a talk. Yes, they needed to talk. Sha's lips moved as a new problem caught him by surprise.

For the blind, a mouth is not just a mouth, not only a combination of two lips; it is, in a way, upper and lower eyelids, between which the pupil resides on the tip of the tongue. Sha suddenly saw a light on the tip of the tongue; it was feeble, flickering and shifting, but a light nevertheless. It was illuminating. Raising his head, he opened his mouth and sighed, a sigh that became a straight, non-reversible light. Like a nail, it possessed unyielding power of penetration, it was invincible.

Sha quietly tugged on Wang's sleeve and led him outside, where the two of them lit up and paced aimlessly. Wang said nothing, though Sha had hoped he would. But since he didn't, Sha had to let him be. Finally, unable to endure the silence, Sha spoke up. 'Old friend, I'm worried. There's one thing I've yet to bring up with everyone. I'd like us all to leave foot massage to Du Hong. But what if they disagree? I can't possibly order them to do so. I couldn't do that.'

Wang smiled faintly as he recalled a cliché – people in love turn foolish. Sha was not in love; he had a one-sided infatuation, which made him an idiot, not a fool.

'You,' Wang said gravely, 'you're acting more and more like a sighted person. And I don't like that. You don't have to say anything. With how things are, it can only end one way.'

While they stayed outside doing nothing, Jin Yan and Xiao Kong were bringing the atmosphere in the lounge to an impossible high. Pushing her way through to Du Hong, Jin Yan raised her arms and said loudly, 'Quiet, everyone. Be quiet.' Knowing what was coming, everyone went silent, creating a cheerful, heightened sense of anticipation.

The sound of a zipper opening was endearing and tender, circumspect and gentle, short and brief, like an emotional chant. Jin Yan opened the purse strapped across her body and with one hand took out a thick packet of money in different denominations, and felt for Du Hong's arm with the other. She laid the packet of money in Du Hong's hand.

'Du Hong,' she said, 'this is a small token from all of us. Just a little something, you know.'

Betrayed by her emotions, Jin Yan's voice trembled, and everyone heard it, that and her laboured, emotional breathing. Holding the thick packet of notes, Du Hong stroked it with her injured hand.

'Thank you, everyone,' she said.

Jin Yan waited, so did Xiao Kong and everyone else, waiting for a climactic moment. They did not need Du's gratitude, really, they did not. And yet it was, after all, a warm and touching scene that required intense emotion and plenty of hugs, as well as heated tears, flowing thick and fast. That's how it's written in novels and shown in movies and on TV, so it must be the same in real life.

After saying thank you, Du Hong repeated her thanks before adding, 'I really, truly am grateful to all of you.' She spoke in an even tone, calm and noticeably polite. So instead of the anticipated high point, the scene concluded in a matter-of-fact manner, which no one had expected. Reality is different from fiction, from film and TV, and from news reports. They did not know what would happen next, changing the mood of tranquillity into a sense of loss, not knowing what to do.

Luckily they had clients, three of them, anyway, spurring Du Li into making assignments. Loudly calling out names of therapists, she paired them with the clients in high spirits. Given the circumstances, this was the best diversion anyone could have asked for. Wang Daifu was outside and could not hear what was happening, so Du Hong went to the doorway and shouted, 'A client for you, Wang Daifu!'

Wang Daifu, Zhang Yiguang and Jin Yan went to work. The atmosphere returned to normal. Du Hong walked over to the lounge, where she opened and shut the door, and listened to the pleasing sound of the stopper, over and over.

Before her discharge from the hospital, she had learned about the stopper via her Gao Wei hotline. It was funny how she actually knew more and in greater detail about what was happening at the centre when she was lying in a hospital bed. Gao had told her everything, until it was little different than if Du Hong had witnessed it with her own eyes. Gao was her personal news broadcast – comprehensive, detailed and all-inclusive, not just covering news but also including 'editorials' and 'station recaps'. Little by little, Du Hong comprehended what Gao Wei was getting at, for the broadcasts carried her central idea, or mental orientation, which was for Du Hong to know how nice Sha Fuming had been to her. The purpose of her editorials and station recaps also became clear, which was for Du Hong to return the favour and be nice to Sha Fuming.

Du Hong had not needed those broadcasts. She was agitated and troubled, but she couldn't block out Gao's eyes or mouth. She had to admit that Sha had turned out to be different than she had pictured him; he was a good man, not just one with a burning desire for her. His feelings for her were sincere and genuine, but she did not love him. She just didn't. She was grateful for all he'd done for her, but that was not love. The two things were not the same.

A major shift had occurred one day in Gao's hospital news report: it was now a live broadcast, a large-scale, lengthy live performance. Du Hong heard Gao whisper, 'Boss Sha and Wang Daifu have gone outside. Jin Yan walked into the lounge with Xiao Kong after shouting in the hallway, "We're having a meeting, everyone. Did you all hear me? I'm calling a meeting." I don't know what they plan to do.'

Through Gao Wei's open phone, Du Hong heard Jin Yan say, 'We thought we weren't indifferent, but we are, and that has to stop.'

Jin Yan was really the only speaker at the meeting, and she spoke for five or six minutes, until Du Hong realised that the so-called meeting was in fact a collection campaign to encourage everyone to do something for her. Jin Yan spoke in a quivering voice, and it was hard to tell whether she was mad at herself or at others. She shed tears of emotion, making her speech both touching and tough; she was, in a word, issuing a threat. Everyone must make a gesture. No longer speechifying or trying to persuade, she was giving an order – 'Now that poor Du Hong is in such a state, what can she do? She can do nothing any more, and we cannot stand back and watch without doing a thing.' It came as a surprise to Du Hong that Jin Yan could be so warm, so eager to help; and she was impressed by how articulate she was. 'We have the same kind of eyes,' Jin Yan concluded, 'the same kind of pupils, but in the end what do our eyes see? Think about what you can do.' She was not all talk; without checking with Tailai first, she generously made a donation for both of them. Then there was Xiao Kong, who was a famous miser; she treasured every penny, round and black like her own pupils. But in the face of such raging passion, she did not hedge. Wang Daifu was not in the room, so she offered both their shares on his behalf, rousing everyone in the lounge, which was taken over by an emotional high that brought everyone to the brink of tears.

The mobile phone reproduced every sound in the lounge. With her eyes tightly shut, Du Hong began to quake; she clamped her hand over her mouth to stop herself from crying out. She didn't want them to hear her. They were wonderful sisters and brothers; she felt herself breaking up inside as an indescribable current of warmth coursed through her body. The live broadcast was not over yet; Jin Yan and Xiao Kong were counting the money as they talked, or more accurately, were having a discussion: no one was to breathe a word of this. There was no need to tell Wang Daifu, since 'you already made the donation for him.' There was 'even less need to tell Sha Fuming . . . let's not worry about what's going on between him and Du Hong.'

She lay back down after flipping her phone shut and stuffing it under her pillow. Du Hong was both moved and grateful, but her strongest feelings were sadness and despair, as cruel reality proved that she was finished. Deep down she knew she would have to depend on others for the rest of her life; she had no choice but to live in a world of gratitude from now on. She would forever be inferior to everyone else, to both the sighted and the blind. What did she have left? Nothing but her beauty. And what was that? Nothing but the breath in her nostrils, seemingly belonging to her, but not really. It entered and left, coming and going like a shadow.

Du Hong pulled the blanket up over her head, expecting to wail. But all she did was shed silent tears, unusual tears that spilled in great, speedy streams, unlike in the past, when her tears had always fallen drop by drop. Her pillow soaked up the tears, including the sound, leaving a large wet patch. She turned the pillow over and immediately wetted the other side.

Recalling the painful experience, she descended into a state of self-pity. Her pride hit rock bottom, her dignity was gone. It had been affixed to a door and smashed into unrecognisable pieces when a wind blew the door shut. She lost it in the lounge of the Sha Zongqi tuina centre.

No, she said to herself, no. I won't. I'd rather die first.

Tossing the blanket aside, she sat up and found a towel, and groped her way over to the bathroom. She was about to wash her face when a nurse came in to help her. She turned towards the nurse, smiled, and gently but firmly pushed the arm away. 'Thank you,' she said.

No, she said to herself, no. Until she breathed her last, she would not allow herself to become an object of pity in people's eyes. She wanted to live without having to always be grateful.

She would not owe anyone anything; she refused to be indebted to someone else, not even her closest brothers and sisters. If she did, she'd have to pay them back. If she couldn't pay them back, that was all the more reason not to owe anyone. All debts need to be repaid, and she had always harboured a deep-rooted fear over repayment. She had come into this world with nothing and wanted to leave the same way.

After washing her face, she made up her mind to leave, to leave the Sha Zongqi tuina centre. She would first go home, where she'd ask her parents to pay back Sha Fuming for the medical expenses, and she'd repay them later. How would she do that? She did not know, and that nearly brought her to tears again, but she forced them back. A phrase leaped into her mind – heaven never seals off all exits. Heaven – Never – Seals – Off – All – Exits.

With her mind made up, she rang for the nurse and asked her to book a train ticket. Naturally she had to ask Gao Wei to bring her a writing board, something she always needed to write on. There was so much she wanted to say to her brothers and sisters, and she wanted to thank them. No matter what, she must show her gratitude. *Goodbye, my friends. So long, my brothers and sisters.* Heaven never seals off all exits. She would proudly get on the road with dignity and self-respect. She'd leave without owing anything.

Some of the therapists were working; others were resting. The tuina centre had returned to normal. Du Hong placed the thick stack of bills in her locker, shut the door, put on the lock – without locking it – and then hung the key behind it. She went up to Gao Wei and handed her a sheet of paper. That done, she headed out the door. Gao wanted to go with her, but she said no.

'Where are you going?'

'Where could I be going, silly girl?' Du Hong said. 'Can't I be alone for a moment?'

Sha Fuming happened to be standing just outside the door, so Du Hong wound up leaving the centre by walking away from him. Holding the sheet of paper in her hand, Gao Wei had looked out the window and, to her surprise, seen Du Hong and Sha Fuming in an embrace. His back was to Gao, but that did not stop her from seeing how happy he was. His shoulders seemed to have swelled high into the heavens. With a smile, she turned and cast a glance at Du Li before walking off. It was all she could do to keep from calling everyone over to see what she'd witnessed.

Naturally, Gao Wei was the first to sense that something was wrong. Still holding Du Hong's paper, she remained in the lounge, not feeling like going outside or walking the hallway. She fidgeted with the paper, which was filled with tiny holes, mere pinpricks. Not knowing what it was, she decided to ignore it. Nearly half an hour later, when she got to her feet, she realised that no one was outside any more. So she pushed the glass door open, only to see Sha Fuming pacing the area just beyond the entrance. He circled the four- or five-foot area, rubbing his hands the whole time. Not seeing Du Hong, Gao closed the door and went back inside. Then she opened every therapy room door, but there was no sign of her. *Where did that damn little girl go? Where could she have gone? Could she be secretly crying somewhere?*

Two hours later she began to panic. 'Hey,' she muttered, 'where's Du Hong?'

'Isn't she with you?' Jin Yan asked.

'No, she isn't,' Gao replied.

Two hours may not be a long time, but it is for a blind person to be absent. That was when everyone realised that something was wrong. They crowded into the lounge, where they sat quietly, looking around.

'Did she say anything to you?' Sha Fuming asked Gao Wei.

'Nothing,' Gao said, 'she just gave me a sheet of paper and said she wanted to be alone for a while.'

'What did it say?' Jin Yan asked.

'Nothing.' Gao held the paper up before her and said innocently, 'There's nothing.'

'Are there tiny pinpricks on it?' Sha asked.

'Yes.'

Being the closest to Gao, Wang Daifu reached out and took the paper. He crossed his leg to lay it on his thigh so he could read it with his index finger. After two lines, he raised his head, and Gao saw an awful look on his face; his brows were raised up high. Without a word, he handed the paper to Xiao Kong.

The lounge went quiet again, a different kind of quiet. Du Hong's note was passed from one hand to the next until it reached Sha Fuming. As she watched the scene of passing the note unfold before her, Gao Wei felt a sense of foreboding, but she was completely in the dark. She turned and caught the eye of Du Li, who was standing by the door. Du looked puzzled. They both looked away. The mystery was solved; it had to have been, but neither of them knew for sure. Their eyes shone, but they saw only darkness. They saw nothing; they were the sighted blind. They could never have imagined that something could have been so real, right in front of their noses, clearly in sight, and yet invisible. The silence in the lounge was getting scary.

Sha's index finger trembled, his mouth was open, his jaw hung slack. Gao noticed how his finger kept passing over the last line. Finally, he took a deep breath and exhaled before tossing the note to the sofa and standing up. He walked over to Du Hong's locker, located the lock and key, and opened it. He reached in, felt around, but did not bring anything out. The look on his face showed that he was convinced, that he had verified something, that he was utterly heartbroken. Wordlessly he walked into a therapy room across the way.

Everyone, except Gao Wei and Du Li, knew that the last line of Du Hong's note was meant for Sha Fuming. She had called him 'Ge', elder brother.

'Fuming Ge, I don't know how to thank you. I can only wish you happiness,' she had written.

Something was bound to happen in the lounge that afternoon, not to Du Hong, but to Wang Daifu.

'Xiao Kong,' Wang Daifu said out of the blue, 'was that your idea?'

'Yes.'

Overtaken by rage, he roared, 'Who told you to do that?'

As if the question alone were not clear enough, Wang demanded more. 'Who told you to do that?' He sounded and looked scary, spittle flying. 'You're blind and should know better. You don't deserve to be blind.'

Everyone was shocked that Wang Daifu, a gentle man, would yell like that at Xiao Kong, costing her a great loss of face.

'There's no need to shout, Lao Wang.' Jin Yan pushed the others away and came up to Wang. 'It was my idea. Xiao Kong had nothing to do with it, so you can deal with me.'

Wang was enraged. 'Who the hell do you think you are?' He turned around. 'You think you deserve to be blind, don't you?'

Jin Yan obviously had too high an opinion of herself, and had not expected that Wang Daifu would treat her like that. His voice was loud and deep, stunning her so much that she froze.

What surprised her even more was that Xu Tailai, a normally spineless man, reached out and pulled her behind him. His voice was not as powerful as Wang's, but he was not going to hold back.

'What are you shouting for? Who are you to yell at my wife? You think you're the only one who deserves to be blind, don't you? You may be better than me in other respects, but we can have a good contest when it comes to blindness.'

Tailai was the last person Wang ever thought would come forward to challenge him. Caught off guard, he was speechless; his bravado quickly lost its force. Fixing his gaze on Tailai, he knew that Tailai was *staring* back at him; two sightless men glaring at each other, breathing into each other's face, neither willing to back off as they panted like overworked beasts of burden.

Laying one hand on Wang's shoulder and another on Tailai, Zhang Zongqi spoke up. 'No pissing contest, brothers, please.'

Tailai was about to raise his arm, but Zhang held it down.

'Not over this,' he said sternly.

EPILOGUE
DINNER PARTY

NO. 109–4, GENERAL Boulevard was the address of a restaurant, or more appropriately, a roadside diner; calling it a restaurant was too formal. Roadside diners, whose primary characteristic and greatest attraction is the absence of cleanliness, seldom serve large groups. The floors, neither carpeted nor tiled, are made of concrete, for the convenience of the diners, who can toss whatever they like – bones, fish bones, cigarette butts, bottle caps – wherever they feel like it. A diner might be dirty, but its food is usually good, due mainly to the heavy sauce and smokiness – so-called family-style cooking. Most of the customers are manual labourers, blue-collar workers who couldn't care less about an elegant setting, fresh air or a clean floor. They don't mind the absence of these; all they want is for the food to be to their liking, plentiful and cheap. And if they feel like it, they can bare their chests, put one foot up on their seat, and cradle their knee as they eat, drink and talk. A different kind of enjoyment.

Not all roadside diners are alike. Some do most of their business during the day, others rely on night-time customers. This second type has the feel of 'ghost' trade, since business doesn't really get started until after midnight, catering to night workers such as subletting cabbies, employees at bathhouses or dance halls, customers leaving bars or tea houses, mah-jong players, drug users, and idlers with indeterminate professions, including hookers and pimps. Sometimes local artists visit these places; being the arty and romantic type, they look for something different when they tire of fancy restaurants, but only occasionally.

Those who follow a normal schedule more often than not don't know how lively and exciting life can be after midnight. Urban management personnel usually slack off at night, while policemen on the night shift prefer not to take on too much, which gives owners of roadside diners free rein to run their business on the kerbs and take over the sidewalks. They drape electric wires over plane tree branches, add lights and put out a few makeshift tables and chairs. Firing up a stove on the kerb, they can handle all the cooking methods: stir-fry, pan-fry, deep-fry, braise and roast, filling the bustling, disordered streets with dense cooking smoke and enticing aromas. A country feel right in the city. They are favoured and frequented by those who are down and out, or, put differently, marginal urbanites.

It was not yet midnight when everyone from the tuina centre walked over to No. 109–4, General Boulevard: Sha Fuming, Zhang Zongqi, Wang Daifu, Xiao Kong, Jin Yan, Xu Tailai, Zhang Yiguang, Gao Wei, Du Li and Xiao Tang. Even Jin da-jie made a point of joining them. It was late and the street seemed deserted as they stood in a group at the diner entrance. The owner and employees had seen them before, but only in twos or threes; this was the first time all the familiar faces had shown up together. The friendly owner came out to welcome them.

'Why, you're all here. Is this a celebration?'

No one replied until Sha Fuming smiled and said, 'Nothing to celebrate. We've all been working hard, so it's time to get together and enjoy ourselves.'

'I'll get it started for you.'

Sha was utterly worn out; his smile might have seemed pleasant, but it was forced. Since reading the last line in Du Hong's note, his strength had left him completely and suddenly; his energy and his soul seemed to have been snatched away by something mysterious. Fortunately, his stomach ache persisted. If not for that, he would have felt completely empty, so empty he could have heard a hollow echo inside when he walked.

He had invited everyone out for a late-night snack to celebrate Du Hong's discharge from the hospital, but everything had changed in a matter of a few hours. Life can be so unpredictable. Something uncanny can crop up during the most ordinary times. Life is fragile and chimerical, incapable of sustaining minor disruptions. People tend to think that the blind live a monotonous life, but that depends on how you look at it and on whether they are willing to bare what is in their hearts. Even if the life of a blind person is in disarray, everything seems fine, for each day appears to be calm and uneventful, a copy of the previous day, with the same length, width and height. But once they open up, it can be startling, as their lives can turn out to be unusual and bizarre.

Wang Daifu, who was keenly aware of Sha Fuming's dilemma, had suggested that he postpone the outing to another day. 'Why not?' he said. But Sha Fuming wasn't about to do that. 'Du Hong getting out of the hospital calls for a celebration,' he said.

Yes, Du Hong was discharged from the hospital, and that did call for a celebration. But what would the celebration feel like? Only Sha Fuming would know. Wang Daifu had been sincere when he made the suggestion, but he also had an ulterior motive. At lunchtime he'd had a falling-out first with Xiao Kong, then with Jin Yan, and then with Tailai, making a late-night snack an uncomfortable occasion for him. None of the others felt comfortable saying anything to Sha, but they too wished he would cancel the outing. But he wouldn't. What could they do? Besides, they felt sorry for him – *You're being stubborn. How can you be so stubborn?* No one talked along the way, as they sensed his sorrow and dejection. He was devastated.

Zhang Zongqi's feeling was, by comparison, more complex. He had great sympathy for Du Hong and Sha Fuming, but deep down he was filled with a peculiar elation, which came suddenly out of nowhere and for no obvious reason. After reading Du Hong's letter, he felt his heart lurch and, with careful examination, discovered to his surprise that he experienced more jubilation than sympathy. He was startled by this realisation, which brought on a sense of self-loathing. How could he feel that way? But the joy was real, coursing and lingering in his veins, unstoppable. A close and prolonged rumination reminded him that he had longed for her departure, but safely, of course. She had not left in the best shape, and that was the reason for his sympathy.

This was not a meal he felt like eating, but skipping it was not an option. He was forced to join the others.

It was a formidable array of people standing outside the diner, but scattered in twos and threes. No one said a word, and the silence was one of desolation and latent violence.

After the waiters prepared two tables, the owner, who had taken a headcount, walked up to Sha and invited everyone to take a seat. Sha hesitated, for the arrangement of the tables meant that he and Zhang would each sit at one. With his hand on the back of a chair, he considered the situation as an odd expression appeared on his face. Du Hong had not been the cause of the rift between him and Zhang; in all fairness, she'd had nothing to do with it. And yet she had been the root of the problem. The question was, where was she now? Du Hong was gone, without a trace.

Sha managed to pull himself together.

'We'll eat as a group, so would you please put the tables together?'

The waiters quickly went back to work, arranging three square tables into one large, rectangular one, on which beer, soft drinks, glasses, bowls and chopsticks appeared, creating the feel of a grand feast, a rare scene for a roadside diner. The sky was above their heads, the ground under their feet, and to their left stretched a broad, empty street named General Boulevard. This was more than a typical night out for a group of blind therapists; it was a splendid dinner party.

'Let's take a seat,' Sha Fuming said.

Zhang, who was standing nearby, could not pretend he hadn't heard Sha's invitation, directed at no one in particular and therefore not specifically targeted at him. So he hesitated to say anything. But a moment later: 'Let's take a seat.'

There was no logical connection between the tones of their utterances, but there was meaning. They both sat down at the head of the table and instantly rued their choice, suddenly as uncomfortable as if they were sitting on pincushions, holding their elbows in so as not to touch one another.

The others also hesitated. Wang Daifu had the most difficulty deciding where to sit. He thought long and hard: Xiao Kong was mad at him, so were Jin Yan and Xu Tailai, which left him few if any choices. He wasn't too concerned about Xiao Kong, since they were a couple – she'd be easy to deal with. But not Jin Yan and Tailai. After a bit of thought, he decided to get Xiao Kong to sit with him. He easily sniffed her out, walked up to her and tugged at her sleeve. But she was still angry and flung his hand away, a rapid, violent motion. She did not want him to touch her. *You made me lose face. I don't want to ever see you again!*

Staring straight ahead, Wang grabbed her wrist, this time so forcefully she could not resist, but she turned stubborn and struggled to pull away. It was quickly getting out of hand.

'How many are we?' he whispered.

No one paid any attention to his abrupt question, since they all thought he was counting heads. Not Xiao Kong, of course, who remembered that it had been a question she'd once asked him while they were making love. 'One,' he had said shortly before he had an orgasm, followed by her, and she'd never forgot that riveting lovemaking experience. Her arm went limp, as did her legs. Love can be strange, like an on and off switch. Only a moment before she'd been gnashing her teeth, furious with him, and a second later her lips parted and the anger lost its power. She turned her hand around to hold his, tightly, and dug down with her nails. Tuina therapists cannot keep long nails, and hers were naturally ineffective, so instead she went for the spaces between his fingers. On his part, Wang held her hand and observed closely what was going on around him; in the end, he and Xiao Kong sat across from Jin Yan and Tailai, a perfect spatial relationship filled with endlessly rich and positive meaning.

Everyone took a seat, but no one said a word. As an awkward silence crept into their dinner party, Zhang Yiguang, who was sitting at the far end of the table alone, picked up a bottle and began to drink, like an outsider. It was out of character for him, someone who got garrulous at the first whiff of alcohol. Everyone at the centre knew he was like a bottle that spewed beer the moment it was opened. He was all foam.

Wang Daifu was lost in thought, trying to come up with something to say to Jin Yan and Tailai. The party turned spooky, as, except for the sounds of restrained chewing and clanking chinaware, it was deadly quiet. Wang Daifu hoped that Zhang Yiguang would liven up, which would get more people to talk, and then Wang could find an opportunity to say something to Jin Yan and Xu Tailai. But he had to find the right moment for it to come out naturally, to avoid further worsening their relationship.

But Zhang remained stubbornly quiet. He had always been a marginal figure in the group, not someone the others paid much attention to. He had barely spoken in days, as he harboured a huge secret, one about Xiao Ma. He'd gone back to the hair salon – why had the young man left and where was he now? Zhang was the only one in the centre who knew what happened to Xiao Ma. He was wretched. If not for him, Ma would not have left. He was to blame for what happened to that poor man. He should never have taken him to the hair salon. Some people just don't belong in such a place. *Xiao Ma, your brother took you whoring, why did you go and fall in love? Didn't you have any self-awareness? I guess you were fated to fall in love once and suffer the consequences.*

No one spoke at either end of the table. Sha Fuming and Zhang Zongqi were strangely quiet; their silence was restrained, reserved, though with hidden good will. At that moment, they each were feeling a myriad of complex emotions, profound and substantial accumulated energy that was looking for an outlet. It might find a broad opening that would lead them down a smooth path. But a slight disagreement can make a bad situation worse. Which was why they were particularly cautious, trying their best to catch signals from the other person while at the same time trying to withhold their own intentions. Luckily for them, they were patient. *What's the hurry? Let's wait and see.* They both looked grave.

Picking up his mug, Sha took a sip and Zhang did the same. Zhang thought that Sha wanted to say something. He didn't. Instead, he jumped to his feet, a little too fast and a little too forcefully. He apologised before walking off. Zhang didn't turn to follow his departure; he used his ears for that. Sha appeared to be on his way to the toilet.

His sudden departure was caused by an uncontrollable need to throw up, but he managed to hold back until he groped his way to the toilet. Leaning over, he threw up and immediately felt better. Opening his mouth wide, he sighed.

'What's happening to me?' he asked himself. 'I didn't have that much to drink.'

He had no idea that this was just a beginning. Before he could wipe the tears from his eyes, another wave of nausea hit him, stronger than the first, quickly getting so bad he had to bend over and vomit again. He was mystified. Except for a couple of stuffed buns on the way to the hospital, he hadn't had much to eat, so where had all the stuff come from? He wasn't just vomiting any more, he was spewing everywhere.

A diner, a total stranger, was on his way to the toilet. He and his friends had waged a bet to see who could drink the most without going to the toilet, and he had lost. With a bladder nearly bursting, he rushed inside, only to be stunned by what he saw before he had a chance to take his tool out. Someone was in there, bending over and throwing up, splattering the place with blood, bright red blood everywhere, including the walls.

'Hey you, what's wrong?'

Sha turned his head and smiled pleasantly. 'Me? I'm fine.'

The stranger grabbed him and turned to shout at the others outside. 'Hey, you out there! Something's wrong with one of your people.'

'I'm okay,' Sha said unhappily.

'Hey, you out there! Something's wrong with one of your people.'

Wang Daifu was the first to grope his way to the toilet door, where he took Sha's arm from the diner, who walked off quickly. He couldn't wait to get away from there and find a clean spot somewhere to relieve himself.

'I didn't have that much to drink,' Sha said, 'I really didn't.'

Wang could not see what had happened in the toilet, but Sha's arm and his hand gave him a terrifying foreboding. Both were icy cold, but before he could ask what was wrong, Sha crumpled and slid to the floor. 'Fuming,' Wang shouted. 'Fuming!' Sha ignored him. He couldn't hear a thing.

The feast ended before it began. Everyone from the centre left, piling into four taxis that raced towards the Jiangsu First People's Hospital. Wang Daifu and Zhang Zongqi were in one cab with Sha Fuming, the others shared the remaining three taxis in various groupings. It was after midnight and the streets were deserted, so they made it to the hospital in under twenty minutes. By then Sha was unconscious, so Wang Daifu carried him on his back into the emergency room. 'We need a doctor!' Wang was panting. 'Hurry, please!'

The others, also out of breath, arrived in groups and crowded into the emergency room entrance, anxiously hoping to hear what was going on inside. A nurse wiped the blood from Sha's mouth. He was covered with it.

A doctor walked up to Wang. 'What caused this? Did you see anything wrong?'

'What do you mean what caused this?' Wang asked.

The doctor could tell that he was blind. 'Your friend is haemorrhaging. What caused it?'

'I don't know,' Wang replied.

'Do you know if he has had any prior medical problems?'

How would he know if Sha had any prior medical problems? He could only *stare* blankly at the doctor. Then he was reminded of what the policeman had said. *You have an obligation to tell the truth.*

Wang Daifu had an obligation. He wanted to tell the doctor the truth. But he didn't know what that was. That despite the fact that they were schoolmates and friends, and that Sha was his boss. Did Sha Fuming have a medical history? All he could do was stand there nervously in front of the doctor. They *stared* at each other.

'Hurry, tell us. This is really important.'

Wang knew it was really important, and he was anxious. He instinctively turned to his fellow therapists in the doorway, but none of them said a word. They didn't know anything. A chill ran through Wang Daifu's heart, as cold as well water. He and Sha Fuming, he and the others, the others and Sha Fuming, they were together every single day, and yet they were so distant from one another. In the end, none of them knew any of the others.

The only thing any of them could do was *look* around. While they were *looking* around, their ears were doing the same thing. They all heard each other's heavy breathing.

A flurry of activity occurred in the emergency room, with medical staff coming and going. Wang backed out, and the other therapists instinctively parted to let him pass, some standing to the left of the hallway and others to the right. Silence reigned; no one wanted to be the first to speak. They neither moved nor made a sound. The footsteps of the medical staff were sounding more and more urgent. They were rushing in and out of the emergency room. Wang Daifu and the other therapists were swallowing hard because the frantic footsteps told them how serious the situation was.

The only thing Wang heard all that time was the emergency physician's shout: 'Take him into surgery! We need to open him up to see what's wrong.'

The emergency room door opened for two nurses to push Sha into surgery on a gurney, followed by the therapists, who were stopped by the nurses at the lift door. After asking where the operating room was, Gao Wei took Wang by the hand. Wang grabbed the hand of Zhang Zongqi, who took Jin Yan's hand. Jin Yan took Xiao Kong's hand, Xiao Kong took Xu Tailai's hand. Xu took the hand of Zhang Yiguang, who took Du Li's hand. She took Xiao Tang's hand, and she took Jin da-jie's hand. They arrived as a group at the operating room door, where they stopped, let go of their hands, and formed two lines, leaving space between them.

'Who's in charge here?' A nurse walked up to them. 'I need someone to sign.'

Wang Daifu stepped forwards, but Zhang Zongqi pushed him aside. The nurse handed him a ballpoint pen. He put it in his mouth, broke it with his teeth, took out the ink filler, pulled out the nib with his teeth and blew onto the filler to send ink flowing. He dabbed his right index finger with the ink and smoothed it over his thumb. Then he showed the nurse his thumb.

The hallway outside the operating room was deathly quiet. In all his years, Wang Daifu had never experienced such total silence. It was as if an enormous weight had pressed down from above and was squeezed into a desolate space. Wang Daifu, Zhang Zongqi and all the others were pressed down for an hour and fifty-three minutes, until their eyes were nearly popping out of their heads. No one dared asked questions. That would have been a bad thing to do. In all situations, the blind staunchly believe that good news arrives only through others, that news brought by other people brings them pleasant surprises.

After an hour and fifty-three minutes, a doctor came out of surgery. They crowded around him.

'The operation was successful. We've done what we can. But it's too soon to tell. We'll know better in seventy-two hours.'

We'll know better in seventy-two hours. That was not the best news, but definitely good enough. At least Sha Fuming remained unchanged. Yet Wang Daifu could not keep from wondering exactly who the man lying in there now – and who had been with them all this time – really was. He could not have suddenly come down with that ailment; he must have been suffering from it for a long time, but no one had an inkling of it. None of them knew a thing about him. Sha Fuming turned out to be a void around them, one that could talk and breathe, a hole he had dug himself, a hole that served only to drag himself down. Maybe every one of them was a hole, all madly hurtling down a bottomless, murky pit; the thought made Wang feel that he was falling. He suddenly felt ill, a discomfort tinged with a deadly panic. He lurched; his body shook. He felt like crying, but told himself he mustn't; he could not let himself become a void. His heel bumped into who he thought was Xiao Kong. He grabbed hold of her, like grasping at a straw, and at that moment he felt unbearably frail. Holding her in his arms and resting his chin on her shoulder, he began to feel the tears well up, followed by a snivel that smeared snot all over her.

'Married. Let's get married.' He was incoherent. 'We'll be married.' It was a choking plea. 'We'll have a fine wedding.'

The woman in his arms was not Xiao Kong, but Jin Yan, who knew that he was holding the wrong person, but was reluctant to let go. She too was crying.

'Tailai,' she said, 'everyone heard that, so you have to keep your word.'

Witnessing the touching scene from behind the surgeon, the operating room nurse was moved by the blind therapists. Next to her stood Gao Wei, whose eyes the nurse saw when she turned her head. Her eyes were unusual, small and not at all like the others. The nurse stared at Gao's eyes for a while, and, still unsure, reached out and waved her index finger in front of Gao's eyes. Gao returned the nurse's gaze; not knowing what she had in mind, she cocked her head, reached out, and took hold of the nurse's finger, moving it aside. Then she blinked at the nurse, once and then twice.

It was clear to the nurse when she saw it – a gaze that was most ordinary, most pervasive, most common. She froze at the realisation as her soul, frightened and pierced by something, nearly left her body.

CHINA LIBRARY

MO YAN

LIFE AND DEATH ARE WEARING ME OUT

In this multifaceted tour de force, Mo Yan flexes his skills both as an astute observer of society and history and as a leading practitioner of experimental and imaginative fiction.

Ximen Nao, a wealthy landowner, loses his farm and his life as angry villagers redistribute the land after the establishment of the People's Republic of China. In Lord Yama's underworld, Ximen refuses to admit any wrongdoing even under torture. Exasperated, Yama returns him to his farm as a donkey, the first of many reincarnations. Over the next five decades, Ximen lives through the absurdities and excesses of Chinese history as a donkey, ox, pig, dog, monkey and finally an infant with an unusually large head.

'*Life and Death* remains a wildly visionary and creative novel, constantly mocking and rearranging itself and jolting the reader with its own internal commentary.'
Jonathan Spence, *New York Times Book Review*

CHINA LIBRARY

MO YAN

THE REPUBLIC OF WINE

When Special Investigator Ding Gou'er arrives in the fictional province of Liquorland, the air reeks of coal and liquor. Tasked with investigating rumours that local officials are practising cannibalism, he transforms from observer to participant in the bacchanalian rounds of lavish banquets and intemperate drinking. Unable to keep up with Diamond Jin, an official with a notorious capacity for holding his drink, Ding falls into an intoxicated haze until the arrival of a new dish at the banquet table: a 'golden, incredibly fragrant little boy' which leads to an explosive and surreal series of events that test the limits of his sanity.

A true example of Mo Yan's 'hallucinatory realism,' *The Republic of Wine* is a tale of modern China's indulgence and corruption.

'In turns satirical, grotesque, hypnotic, hallucinatory, fantastic and wild.'

Asian Review of Books

www.penguin.com.cn

CHINA LIBRARY

THE KITCHEN

And Other Stories

Five stories from China's foremost writers, including Jia Pingwa, Liu Zhenyun and Chi Zhijian, capture the domestic bonds and dramas of its people living in modern China today, exploring the challenges and strange graces of life in this vast and complex land.

Chi-Tzu daydreams of home-cooked meals surrounded by family and more while diligently navigating Sun-Tze's bachelor kitchen; a young ex-soldier attempts to escape his prescribed rural life by sitting the national college entrance exam; Qin Shan and his wife grapple with illness, love and loss amidst their precious potato plants; two estranged sisters reflect on memories of a long-lost bond; Liben and Shunshun's fortunes ebb and flow on the shores of Backflow River, where everyone crosses to make it big somewhere else.

www.penguin.com.cn